Praise for *Wake Up, Nat & Darcy*

"A fun and flirty enemies to lovers romance, *Wake Up, Nat & Darcy* is perfection on ice. A stunning, sporty sapphic debut you won't soon forget."

—Jennifer Dugan, author of *Love at First Set*

"This book will have you on the edge of your seat until the final buzzer! Nat and Darcy will be your new favorite team."

—Camille Kellogg, author of *Just as You Are*

"*Wake Up, Nat and Darcy* had me kicking my feet from the start. Everything about it is delicious: the banter, the Winter Olympics hijinks, and most importantly of all, the genuine chemistry and history between Darcy and Natalie. I was rooting so hard for both of them, and for their lovers-to-enemies storyline to finally loop back to lovers. The sapphic hockey romance of my dreams!"

—Anita Kelly, author of *How You Get the Girl*

WAKE UP
NAT & DARCY

KATE COCHRANE

carina
press®

ISBN-13: 978-1-335-95374-2

Wake Up, Nat & Darcy

Carina Press
22 Adelaide St. West, 41st Floor
Toronto, Ontario M5H 4E3, Canada
www.Harlequin.com

Printed in U.S.A.

For Jennifer. Even if I write a thousand love stories,
I will never come close to capturing how I feel about you.

For Augusta and Beatrix, being your mom is the coolest.

And for Bear, the world's most perfect dog.

Chapter One

Darcy LaCroix always got nervous before a big game. Nerves were a good sign. It had been three years since she played her last hockey game but the jittery, excited feeling was familiar. It meant she was ready.

"Five minutes," a PA called into the room.

Darcy's stomach swan-dived for the floor and her hands trembled, making the script flutter like a hummingbird's wings. Darcy sat as still as possible, terrified to mess up her hair or makeup while reading over her script for the tenth time.

It took her three years of working at *Wake Up, USA* to get this chance to be on camera. Three years of fetching coffee, pitching stories that got swatted away, and staying late to learn as much as she could about every aspect of the show. It all came down to this.

She knew how to deal with pressure. High stakes were her happy place. You don't win three gold medals if you can't handle the stress.

Tell that to her racing heart.

She glanced at the script. It wasn't much, but it was what she'd been begging for. A chance to get out from behind her desk.

At four o'clock that morning when Raquel, her boss, had

stopped by her cubicle to talk to her, she assumed there was a script that needed rewriting. Instead, Raquel told her to change into a suit and get her ass to hair and makeup.

"Here's the script," Raquel said, shoving paper at Darcy. "Don't let me down."

That's how she ended up flush with adrenaline and covered in more makeup than she'd worn in her life.

A different PA rushed in to escort her to the set. "Stand there, look at that camera, and read the prompter."

Darcy nodded, her eyes trained on the taped X on the floor. One last deep breath.

Don't blow it, LaCroix.

She took her place and waited for her cue.

The news anchor, a generically handsome man with shiny black hair, and an unbelievable tan for the middle of winter, smiled into the camera. "Welcome back to *Wake Up, USA*. We're all excited for the upcoming Olympics, which you can watch right here and on our sister stations. As part of our coverage, we have some news to share with you. The United States has named the members of its women's ice hockey team."

On the monitor, Darcy could see the list of names for the team and waited for her turn to speak.

"To help us give context, we have four-time Olympian, three-time gold medalist, and former captain for Team Canada, Darcy LaCroix."

Darcy smiled into the camera and hoped no one could tell that it felt like every one of her organs was trying to rearrange itself inside her.

"Darcy, is anything about this roster a surprise to you?"

Darcy nodded to the anchor. "Yes, Dave. As you just saw, the team is without its former captain. Fans of women's hockey will likely be shocked to see that three-time Olympian Natalie Carpenter has been left off the roster."

Darcy swallowed and stared into the camera.

Steady. You can do this. Slow down.

"Carpenter's hockey résumé is impeccable. She was the captain of the team that won gold in the last Olympics. She won the national championship as a college freshman. She's been a star for years. But she had a nagging quad injury for much of training camp. Combine that with the fact that she's thirty-five and I think the coaching staff felt like they had to go with a younger, healthier squad.

"Looking at the roster, it looks like JT Cox is the player they think can fill Carpenter's skates. Filling in for an all-time great is never easy and the team's asking a lot of such a young player."

Darcy turned to the host. "Even if this isn't the way she hoped her career would end, Carpenter can retire with her head held high."

The anchors took over reading the news and the camera operator told Darcy she could leave.

She walked out of the studio, her heart beating so hard she thought she might burst. She felt awful for Natalie, for the way her career ended and having to be the one to announce it. But she did it. It took three years, but she finally got herself on TV. And not just any TV, on the number one morning show in the country. She didn't even try to keep the smile off her face.

She heard someone call out that they were in a commercial break as she walked past the control room.

A PA, Sadie, stuck their head out of the door. "Raquel says you should come to her office after the show's over."

Darcy swallowed. "Shit. Did she say why?"

Sadie gave her a warm smile. "She liked it. Don't be nervous. I think it's a good thing." They gave Darcy a quick pat on the arm before hurrying back into the control room.

Darcy looked down at the now crinkled script in her hands. Damp spots appeared at the edges where she'd been clutching it. She wiped her hands on her pants and tried to smooth the paper as she walked to her desk.

Her mind served up possible reasons Raquel might want to see her. The most tantalizing was that she was going to get to be part of the on-screen team for the Olympics. She took a deep breath and allowed the possibility to wash over her. Maybe her day had finally arrived.

Chapter Two

Natalie Carpenter woke up to the sound of the *Wake Up, USA* theme song. It brought back memories of elementary school sick days spent watching daytime TV with her grandma. She wiped a hand across her face and squinted at the screen. She hadn't turned it on. She scanned the room, her eyes bouncing over the beer bottles on the coffee table, and realized she'd fallen asleep on the couch. Pathetic.

She sat up at the word "Olympics." She turned up the volume, regretting it immediately when the throbbing in her head intensified. She needed to hear the news again. Maybe if she heard it on TV, it would feel real. Real was all she could hope for because she wasn't going to feel better anytime soon.

Her phone vibrated with a new text. Her best friend, Grace.

Turn off the TV. If you are watching right now, turn it off. Seriously, Nat. Don't torture yourself.

Natalie flipped her phone over. Grace meant well, but Natalie needed to watch the anchor read off the names and tell the viewers, most of whom didn't follow women's hockey, who the next star was going to be for Team USA. She needed to hear the anchor say that she'd been cut, that she'd gone from being the captain of the gold-medal-winning team four years ago to a has-been sitting on her shitty couch in her shitty apartment.

Hungover and running on a few hours of sleep didn't help but it was fitting that her physical and mental states matched. Natalie Carpenter never did anything halfway. Why would feeling like a dumpster fire be any different?

She saw the roster flash on the screen next to the anchor. She expected not to see her name—she *knew* it wouldn't be there—but she didn't anticipate the cold, prickling sensation flooding her body. The shame mixed with sadness overwhelmed her. She watched, not hearing the words coming from his mouth until he said "Darcy LaCroix."

She blinked, forcing her sluggish brain to make sense of seeing Darcy for the first time in four years. What the hell was she doing on TV? Then Darcy was talking about Natalie's career as a player, and why she got cut.

Natalie sat up, her head pounding. Damn, she looked good on that screen. Deep inside her, teenage Natalie's heart stuttered at the sight of her former teammate. It only lasted a second. As soon as Darcy explained why Natalie lost her spot on the team and mentioned her replacement, Natalie's heart hardened. Hurt-infused anger consumed her.

"Even if this isn't the way she hoped her career would end, Carpenter can retire with her head held high."

Natalie punched the remote and muttered, "Fuck you, LaCroix."

She looked across the room at her Team USA bag. She should have been getting ready to fly with her team one more time, not lying on her couch listening to her former teammate, a woman she once loved, talk about her retirement.

Retirement was for old people, not thirty-five-year-olds. Unless you were one of those douchebag hedge fund manager guys, no one retired at thirty-five. Natalie's parents weren't even retired yet.

But they weren't professional athletes.

Now, neither was she.

Her phone buzzed on the table. She ignored it until it vibrated off the table and onto the floor with a crash. Fuck, her head hurt.

She smacked the phone and put it on speaker. Holding it to her ear was more than she could manage in her pathetic state.

"You watched it, didn't you?"

"Hi, Grace."

"I told you to turn that shit off. Your life would be so much easier if you would listen to me."

Natalie groaned. "Unless you can go back in time and tell me not to drink that fourth beer last night, I'm not sure how listening to you would change anything."

"I know this sucks, especially because of Darcy."

Natalie sighed. Grace had been her best friend since they were randomly assigned to be roommates her first year of college. Grace had an irritating ability to be right most of the time, even if Natalie didn't want to acknowledge that now.

"I can hear a 'but' coming."

"It sucks, but you have to think about what you're going to do next. You're thirty-five, you have to have known you weren't going to be playing hockey forever. What's your plan?"

"You sound like my parents. I don't know what's next. I thought I had a couple more months to figure it out. I thought we'd win gold and then I'd see what kind of offers came my way."

Grace snorted into the phone.

"Yes, I know that I sound like a gigantic asshole. Instead, it turns out I'm a washed-up hockey player with no job."

"You're not a washed-up anything. You knew this was coming eventually. Stop moping around, take a couple Advil, drink some water, and figure out what you want to do with the rest of your life. I'll call you tomorrow when you're not hungover and whiny."

"I'm not whiny!"

"Talk to you tomorrow! Love you, Nat."

After she hung up, Natalie collected the beer bottles from the table and tried not to bang them together as she rinsed them and put them in the recycling bin. Every time they clinked together, it sent a shock wave through her brain. Fuck, why on earth did she drink that last beer?

The beer didn't fix anything, but at least it helped her forget the look in her coaches' eyes when they told her she was done.

Getting cut sucked but having them look at her like she should have seen it coming made her feel worse than anything. It made her feel ashamed in a place where she was used to being proud. And now she had to see that same look in Darcy's eyes. Fuck this day.

Her phone buzzed again. Her parents. Dammit. They'd been sad and supportive when she broke the news that she wasn't going to her fourth Olympics. They said all the right things, but it didn't take away how awful she felt being cut from a team that in the past felt more like a family. Being told you were no longer good enough hurt more than she could explain to anyone who hadn't been through it.

"Hi, Mom."

"How did you know I wasn't your father?" She could hear her mom's smile through the phone.

"Dad never calls. If I talk to him, it's because I've called and he hasn't found you to hand over the phone yet."

She laughed. "How are you doing, sweetheart?"

"Fine."

"It's not nice to lie to your mother, Natalie." The silence stretched between them. "I know you're devastated. I'm sure you've cried and had too many beers." She paused. "I thought it might be time for you to come home for a bit."

No way. "I'm not twelve."

"And I'm not stupid. You can't wallow in that apartment forever. The sooner you come home, eat some decent food, and get your feet back under you the better."

Natalie rolled her eyes. "I'm fine. I can handle myself without you and Dad hovering over me. I'm a grown-up."

Her mom laughed. "You're nothing close to a grown-up."

"I'm thirty-five!"

"I know, sweetie, but the only job you've ever had is playing hockey. No matter what you do next, it's going to be a big transition. If you come home we can support you until you figure out whatever the next thing is."

Natalie took a deep breath; her mom was just being kind. She was trying to make sure Natalie was all right. But having to move back home with her parents would really be the cherry on top of her failure sundae.

Unemployed, former hockey player sounded bad enough without having to tell people she was sleeping in her childhood bedroom.

"You could help your father. He always needs someone to help out around the shop."

Natalie sighed. "I'm not a plumber." Her headache had stopped being a persistent throb and turned instead into a blinding pulse she couldn't ignore. "I appreciate the offer, but I'll find something to do with myself. I'm a big girl. I can handle finding a job here."

Her mom sighed into the phone. "I know you can, but we think it would be easier, better for you to come home. Your brother's right up the road. If you don't want to work with your father, I'm sure Brian would be happy to pay you to watch the boys."

From three-time Olympian to charity case babysitter in less than ten days. *Fuck. My. Life.*

"I gotta go. There's someone at the door." She hung up before her mom had a chance to point out how absurd that lie sounded. Natalie slumped onto her couch and ran a hand through her shoulder-length, dirty-blonde hair before cradling her forehead. She needed water, Advil, and a nap.

Instead, she opened her banking app. Natalie's bank account showed exactly how poorly she and her teammates were compensated for their world-class skills.

She needed a job. Soon. Otherwise, she was going to be spending the next few weeks packing everything she owned into her beat-up Honda and driving back to her parents' house.

But what could an unemployed, former hockey star find for work on short notice? A hockey player who hadn't had a "real job" in years thanks to the rigors of training with the national team.

She let her head fall back against the soft cushions on her couch. She was utterly and completely fucked.

Chapter Three

Inside Raquel's office, the shades were pulled against the afternoon sun. She gestured to the chair in front of her desk and Darcy walked in and took a seat.

"Did Chip find you?" Darcy asked, half curious, half anxious.

Raquel nodded but even in the dim light, she couldn't hide the eye roll from Darcy. "He wants to change the coverage team for the Olympics."

Darcy's heart sped up. "Really?"

Raquel leaned her chair back. "He wants to ditch one of the segments he's been doing for a while. Thinks it's beneath him and undignified." Raquel shook her head slowly. "That's where you come in."

"Because I'm unimportant and undignified?" Darcy couldn't stop a laugh from bubbling up and escaping her mouth.

Raquel allowed the tiniest hint of a smile to twitch across her lips before squashing it. "You want to be on TV, right?"

Darcy nodded.

"Then you won't mind starting from the bottom."

Darcy forced herself to rein in the locker room quips running through her head. She was *not* going to joke with her boss about being a bottom, not when she was so close to finally getting her chance on TV.

"You know the segment where Chip learns how to play the Olympic sports?"

Darcy nodded. "I've seen the segments. The one where he gets a water polo ball to the face is a classic." She laughed and made a mental note to pull up the GIFs of it when she got back to her desk. Watching Chip look like an asshole was always a good time.

Raquel's mouth twitched again at the corner. She covered it with a beleaguered sigh. "He doesn't want to be the subject of any more sports-related viral videos. So, would you like to learn how to do some curling? Cross-country skiing? Ski jumping?"

Darcy paused for a second at the mention of ski jumping. She wasn't a fan of heights. But it didn't take her long to recover. "You're offering me an on-camera job?"

Raquel nodded.

"Then, yes! I'm up for learning whatever sports you can throw my way." She grinned, any pretense of remaining professional melted away in her enthusiasm.

Raquel leaned forward so her elbows rested on the desk. "I know this isn't the opportunity you were hoping for, but it gets you on-camera experience and a chance to make America fall in love with you."

Darcy smiled. "How stupid do I have to look for America to forget I'm Canadian?"

Raquel clicked her pen half a dozen times. "Here's the thing. We don't want America to forget you're Canadian. In fact, we found someone to do the segments with you who should help everyone remember you played for Team Canada."

A chill slipped down Darcy's back. "Raquel, who do I have to work with on this?" Her brain spun wildly, trying to figure out who on earth could be worse than working with Chip.

Raquel cocked her head to the side. "Is it going to be a problem for you to work with a partner?"

"Who, Raquel?" Darcy couldn't keep the edge out of her question. She didn't like surprises and she didn't like being fucked with.

"Don't worry, you two go way back."

"Raquel."

Raquel grinned, enjoying Darcy's anger a little more than she should. "Natalie Carpenter." Her eyes sparkled with mischief. "At least that's the plan if Natalie can read a teleprompter."

Darcy was speechless, but it didn't stop her mind and stomach from going on a wild roller-coaster ride. The last time they were together, they had gotten into a fight and were sent off the ice for two minutes. Darcy spent the time staring at the game passing her by while Nat spent most of it screaming at her from the other penalty box. Chirping was one of Natalie's skills. It's what started the fight in the first place.

Darcy stared at Raquel across the desk. "You think you can put her on TV? She can't make it through a sentence without swearing, and she's got to be the most inappropriate person I've ever met."

Raquel clicked the pen a few more times before speaking. "You done?" Darcy crossed her arms over her chest. "The network wants to play up the rivalry the two of you had on the ice. She just got cut from the Olympic team, she's bound to be a little pissed off about it and frankly I think the two of you duking it out on camera—" she paused "—appropriately, of course, could be exactly what we need to stand out in the ratings." She cocked her head to one side and let her appraising eyes travel over Darcy's face. "But if you can't manage that, let me know now. I'm sure we can find someone else."

Darcy let out a long breath. "That would be great. It's just that Nat and I have this history and—"

Raquel stopped her by putting one hand in the air. "Oh

no. I meant that if you can't handle working with her we can find another Canadian to do it. The network likes her and as long as she can read, they want her to be the one opposite you. You're not going to make me tell them that you'd rather work at your desk than play a couple goofy games against a former rival, are you?"

Darcy shook her head. How the fuck did this happen? How did she go from asking to work the Games to being put in some dopey puff spots with Natalie fucking Carpenter?

Getting an on-screen job was her dream. If her chance to do that required her to get along with Natalie Carpenter, the biggest pain in the ass she'd ever met, she'd find a way. There was no way she was letting that mouthy American get in the way of her dream.

"Nope. I can handle Carpenter." Darcy stood up. "But you might want to see if she can handle me." She paused at the door. "I won't let you down, Raquel."

"I know," she said, eyes already back on her computer. "I know you won't."

Chapter Four

If there was a limit to the number of times Natalie could hear no in a day, she hadn't reached it yet. She called every single person she could think of who might have a job for her only to hear "Wow, I wish I had something for you, but good luck" over and over.

All that rejection was exhausting, but not like the exhaustion she was used to from training. This didn't leave her muscles sore and her skin bruised. It left her angry, depressed, and nursing a battered ego.

After one final "We'll keep you in mind if anything opens up," she needed to get out. Out of her house and out of her head. She put her sneakers on and headed out for a run.

The fact was, she hated running. It was a means to an end when it came to training. She didn't enjoy the sprints, the beep test, or any of the dry land training she had to do for the team. But she loved how it felt to be strong and powerful on the ice. She loved being *good*.

Today, she ran to clear her head of all the noise in there. Every no was like another shot at her already bruised sense of self-worth. Not good enough for the team, not good enough for a job. Not good enough. Not good enough. The words echoed in her head as her feet punished the sidewalk.

Running this hard hurt but if it hurt she couldn't think about what might happen a week from now, or tomorrow, or even ten seconds in the future. The pain of her lungs, the burning, metallic taste in her mouth, and her legs screaming at her to stop drowned all of that out.

By the time she got home, everything hurt except for her mind. That was finally as clear as the late afternoon sky. She filled a water bottle and took it into her living room to stretch. She flicked on the TV and caught the end of the show before *SportsCenter*. The hosts were arguing about who was going to take home gold this year in hockey.

There's no way Canada wins this one. Not as long as I have something to do about it.

It hit her all over again. She had nothing to do about it. She had nothing to do with the team or the Olympics. She was on her own.

She turned the TV off and chucked the remote onto her couch, disgusted with everything in her life. She stalked into her kitchen and yanked the refrigerator door open. While she contemplated whether eating cereal for dinner was too pathetic even for her, her phone rang. She grabbed it and answered without taking her eyes off the twelve bottles of condiments populating the fridge door.

"Mom, I'm not moving home."

"Natalie?"

Oh shit. Not her mom. Her agent. "Keena? Sorry. My mom's been calling…never mind. What's up?"

"How do you feel about television?"

Natalie closed the refrigerator door and moved to forage in the pantry. "Love it. It's how I spend most of my days now that I'm a has-been," Natalie said, hoping she sounded less bitter than she felt.

"You're not a has-been, Natalie. You accomplished more in your playing career than most people will in their lifetime. It just happens that you picked a job where getting older isn't a benefit." She paused. "I'm sorry. This sucks. Nothing I can say is going to change the fact that this is completely shitty. But I might have an opportunity for your next career."

Natalie hopped onto her counter and let her legs dangle above the floor. "Keena, I should tell you right now that I can't act."

A throaty laugh blasted through the phone, forcing Nat to put the phone away from her ear. "Nat, don't worry, this doesn't require anything but acting like yourself and not swearing on live TV."

Nat leaned forward in anticipation. "I can work on the swearing, I promise."

"I got a call from a friend who works for *Wake Up, USA*."

"The morning show?"

"Yes. They're thinking of changing things up a little bit for their Olympic coverage and wondered if you'd be interested in giving it a shot."

Natalie's heart leaped. After all the disappointments, this felt like a lifeline. But as her head caught up with her heart, she realized Keena wasn't giving her a lot of specifics.

"What do they want me to do? Do they know I don't have any experience on TV?"

Keena laughed. "They remember you from the last Olympics when they interviewed the whole team. You made a bit of an impression on the producer who called me. She liked your energy."

Nat winced. She had been sleep-deprived and hungover when they were interviewed. She hadn't dropped an f-bomb but she had been way freer with her comments than she would have been normally. In her defense, they had just won the gold medal. Who could blame her or her teammates for having a hell of a lot of fun the night before? If they hadn't exactly made it to bed before the interview, no one needed to know.

"You still haven't said what they want me to do," Nat said, dread creeping into her chest. What if this wasn't the lifeline she thought it was?

Keena was silent for a second.

"Keena, come on, what's the catch?" Panic tinged with annoyance crept into Natalie's voice.

Keena took a deep breath. "It's nothing bad. They want you to come in to see how your chemistry is with one of their people who they have in mind for the segment."

"Who is it?"

"Darcy LaCroix."

Natalie's mind served up a montage of her greatest battles with Darcy. Most of them included shoving, trash-talking, and, though she would never admit it, the nightmare of Darcy raising her arms over her head in triumph each time Canada beat the U.S. Natalie closed her eyes and shoved aside the memories before they could slip back any further to when she and Darcy first met. She didn't need to think about college, or how they left things when Darcy graduated and moved on to the national team. Nope.

"I know you two have a history on the ice."

And off.

Keena paused before speaking. "My contact tells me Darcy's trying to get out from behind a desk and in front of the camera. Sounds like she thinks the Winter Olympics are her best shot."

"Makes sense," Natalie mumbled to herself. "If they already have a hockey player, why do they want me?"

"They think having the two of you do the segment will be more entertaining." She said the last word carefully, like she was trying to weigh how Natalie would react and soften the impact even as she said it.

Natalie heard the words Keena wasn't saying. "Entertaining? Like they're going to put us in a boxing ring? That kind of entertaining?"

"Not exactly. Boxing is a Summer Olympics sport."

Natalie was willing to give anything a chance if it kept her from having to move back home, but that didn't erase her skepticism about teaming up with Darcy again.

"Just get on the plane. I'll see you there," Keena said before hanging up.

Natalie stood in her kitchen stunned by the combination of her agent hanging up on her and the idea of working with Darcy.

Natalie opened the refrigerator again. The contents hadn't miraculously changed but she hardly saw them. She was too busy thinking about Darcy. She hadn't seen her in a couple years but the memory of her sea-glass green eyes still made Natalie's stomach flip over. *Shit.* No. She would not allow those memories in. She reminded herself of the last time they saw each other. It was the last Olympics and Natalie scored the winning goal to put Team USA on the gold medal podium. Yes, that was better. It was so much easier to think of them that way. Rivals. Bitter, screaming, trash-talking rivals. Not the stuff that came before. No. Not the way a nineteen-year-old Natalie had fallen hard for her captain. That girl was gone.

Add to that having to listen to Darcy tell the world that she'd been the last person cut from the team. *I bet she fucking loved that*, Natalie thought.

She slammed the refrigerator door, disgusted with the way her heart still fluttered at the thought of Darcy. She cast her eyes over her apartment. No way she was moving back home. And nothing, not even Darcy fucking LaCroix, would get in her way of landing this job if it meant keeping her apartment.

Chapter Five

At home, with a glass of wine next to her, Darcy settled into doing research for her real passion, becoming a commentator. After she retired from competition, she'd taken the first job she found in television. *Wake Up, USA* wasn't going to give her a chance to do hockey commentary but it got her in the door at the network that owned the rights to broadcast the women's team.

When she was a kid, she would watch the games with the sound on low and practice what she would say. In college, when she'd have video sessions with the coaches, she had to keep herself from commenting about each player as they rolled through footage of games, their opponents, and watched endless loops of their power play and penalty kill units. Occasionally, when the coaches stepped out of the room, or let her finish the session, she'd amuse her teammates with her commentary.

"Oh look, there's Hinch floating out by the red line. That's unsurprising to me, Bob, since she's never back-checked a day in her life." That time Hinch had thrown a towel at her head but it was worth all the laughs from her teammates.

The Olympics segments Raquel offered her, no matter how goofy she looked doing them, were the next step in getting to that commentator role. If she could get her ass to the Games, get in front of the camera, she could prove that she belonged on-screen and not stuck behind a desk.

She took a sip of her wine and opened her laptop. Her ex, Sabrina, used to be so pissed at her for coming home and immediately jumping into more work. Whatever, she was going to be on-screen, halfway to her dream. All that time working instead of going out with Sabrina was about to pay off. She could almost taste it.

Darcy scanned the rosters for all the women's teams. Her eyes skimmed the U.S. team, unable to believe that Natalie's name wasn't on the list.

Darcy blew out a long breath. Any time she saw Natalie's name, her brain served up a montage of every memory of the two of them together. In college, in the Olympics, on the ice. Every single second flew by as she considered just how much it sucked to end your career by getting cut. There were other memories, too—the feel of Natalie's hand in hers, the way her skin smelled behind her ear—but she shoved them aside. Those only made her heart ache.

After watching her dad have his career end with a trade to a shitty team and a stint on the fourth line, Darcy was never going to play until she got cut. She had way too much pride for that, but Natalie never met a challenge—whether it was beer pong, a set of stadiums, or a race on the ice—that she wasn't willing to try and fail at.

When she started to lose out to younger, faster players, Darcy made a plan for retirement. She decided when she was done rather than risk getting told by a bunch of coaches that it was time to hang up her skates. Her plan meant deciding to retire after the last Olympics, win or lose.

Darcy took a sip of wine and grabbed her phone. She opened her group chat filled with former teammates.

Anyone talked to Natalie?

It took less than a minute for several sets of dots to appear.

The first message to pop up was a link. When Darcy clicked on it, she found herself on Natalie's Instagram page where she'd posted a picture of her still-packed hockey bag with a caption that read "time to hang this up. Not sure how to do it. Can anyone help?"

Yiiiikes! came the first message from the group.

You looking to rub it in her face, LaCroix?

Or looking for a booty call?

Darcy winced. No! Just worried...

Sammy, shut up. It's not like Darcy can call Nat to check in.

Darcy closed her eyes. She shouldn't have asked. Now everyone thought she was an asshole, again. God, what was it about Natalie that made her so stupid?

While the chat bubbled in the background, she scrolled through Natalie's feed to happier times. Darcy's favorite was one where Natalie met a Labrador named Pancake who licked Natalie's face so much that she fell over backward laughing. She missed that laugh.

Enough.

It was too easy to get sucked into a Natalie Carpenter-shaped rabbit hole.

Back in the group chat, she asked her friends if any of them knew the players on the Olympic squads. The TV audience loved to know as much as they could about the stars, but even more than that they loved to know about any player with an interesting backstory. If the players had overcome some kind of hardship, a sick parent, not enough money, the audiences would eat it up.

Her former teammates were retired from competition; some had kids and boring jobs. Whenever they got together, they laughed about the surprised looks they got when people found out that they were Olympians. One of her teammates told her about volunteering to go to her kid's school to talk about the Olympics and the teacher didn't realize she was going to show up with a couple of medals. If they were men's players, everyone would know who they were, but women could fly under the radar, even if they would have preferred a little more fame. And a lot more money.

Instead, Darcy and her teammates found regular jobs. Some went to graduate school, a few even became doctors. More than a few became coaches, but the rest found regular jobs like everyone else. They just got to put it off a decade or so after graduating from college.

After an hour of compiling interesting information from her friends and the internet, Darcy's eyeballs felt dry as potato chips. She finished her wine in one gulp. Tomorrow she'd see Natalie for the first time in years. The thought unleashed a kaleidoscope of butterflies in her stomach. She tried to dismiss them as nervousness about her new job. But like every other time she thought of Natalie, her brain fed her a montage of their time together, including the time after the national championship game when everything had felt so good before it went horribly, horribly wrong.

Chapter Six

Natalie couldn't shake the sense that Keena planned to meet her at the studio to keep tabs on her. All the same, she was happy to see a friendly face waiting for her when she stepped out of the long black car the network sent to pick her up.

"How was your trip?" Keena asked on their way to the elevator.

"Fine," Natalie said, automatically. Her nerves were getting to her. The trip from Boston wasn't long but it still gave her too much time to overthink everything that was about to happen.

For starters, how had the producers convinced Darcy to go along with having Natalie try out for the show? Had she gotten over their history? It was easier to set aside their on-ice rivalry than the other stuff. The pain carved into her heart in college never left her. Not that she'd ever admit that to anyone. The only person who knew about that part of their history was Grace.

Natalie would deal with her questions and judgment when she got the job. Until then, she told herself to focus on nailing this interview or tryout or whatever this thing was.

Inside the elevator, Keena reached out and fixed the lapels of Natalie's suit. Natalie let her, too nervous to object. If this involved skating, she'd be fine, but this was entirely new. Yes, she'd been on TV before but not like this.

"Remember, they already liked you on their show. That's why they called me." Keena gave her a warm smile. "Be yourself. Just with fewer f-bombs, okay?"

Natalie nodded and fussed with the cuff of her jacket until the elevator opened to reveal a small woman with a round face and an easy smile waiting for them at security.

"We are so happy to have you here," the woman said, her smile growing with every word. "My name is Amy and I'm in charge of getting you to Raquel. Do you need anything? Water? Coffee? Bathroom stop?"

Natalie shook her head, trying to keep her focus on Amy instead of the pictures covering the walls. Photos of the hosts posing with politicians, athletes, and actors lined the walls. As she followed Amy around a corner, they passed one of Natalie with her team after they won gold. Joy bloomed in her chest along with a sadness that she wouldn't be with them this time. She squared her shoulders and forced herself to focus on today.

But it wasn't easy to think about the interview while literally walking past her former self. Nat tried to focus on Amy's back and nothing else as they walked quickly through the warren of offices. Every door looked the same and none of the names on the placards meant anything to her. The last time she felt this nervous, she was trying out for the national team for the first time.

At least then she'd been playing hockey for more than a decade. She was a complete amateur when it came to TV. She'd been interviewed along with her teammates in the past, but that allowed her to fade into the background if she wanted to. Not that she'd ever chosen that option.

The way her parents told the story of her birth, Natalie had burst into the world with a scream that startled the nurses and made the doctor laugh. When the OB handed her to her mom, she said, "You might have a handful here." She heard this story throughout her childhood. She never did anything halfway, whether it was competing against the boys on her street in any sport they could play or busting her ass to land a college scholarship and earn a spot on the Olympic team. Usually, her spirit made her stand out in a good way. But not always.

Not in the last Olympics when she and Darcy got as close to a fistfight on the ice as you can without being suspended for a couple games. And not when Natalie showed up to this very show with her gold medal around her neck, a hangover, and shit-eating grin. She didn't fade into the background. Ever.

When they reached Raquel's office, Keena stepped to the side and flicked through her phone. Natalie resisted the urge to fiddle with hers. She could stand here for a minute without needing to look busy. She could do that. As she was reconsidering her decision, the door behind her opened and a woman with long dark hair and thick, black-frame glasses smiled at them. "Miss Carpenter, I'm Raquel Garcia. I don't know if you remember me from the last time you were here."

Natalie held out her hand. "Of course. It's nice to see you again. Thanks for inviting me down for the day. Please call me Natalie."

Raquel held the door open and gestured for them toward the chairs in her office. "Can I get you both anything? Water? Tea?"

Keena shook her head and took one of the chairs.

Raquel, satisfied that no one needed anything, took the seat behind her desk. "Like I said, thanks for coming down on such short notice."

Not like I had anything else to do.

"My assistant, Jamal, who you'll meet later, was able to pull together clips of your appearances on the show over the years to show the executives. They were impressed with the way you handled yourself and the way you made an impression with the audience."

Natalie laughed. "Hopefully, a good impression. The last time we were here it was after quite a bit of celebrating, if I remember correctly."

Raquel smiled. "I think the joy you showed was part of why the audience loved you so much."

"Joy" was an interesting word for a hangover. But Natalie was smart enough not to argue about whatever impression Raquel seemed to think worked in her favor. Either she landed this job or she had to get her stuff back to her parents' house. But it was more than that. Without this job, she'd be watching the Games from the couch with nothing to distract her from the misery of not being there with her team and nothing to give her hope that maybe her best days weren't behind her.

"Today, we would like you to do a couple of reads on camera to make sure you can handle this job and then we're going to want to see you on-screen with Darcy to make sure the two of you make as good a pair as we think you will."

Natalie laughed. "Did your assistant happen to pull up footage of the two of us?"

Raquel nodded slowly. "If you're asking if we are aware that the two of you have a colorful history on the ice, we're aware."

"Colorful" is one way to put it. She tried to keep her face as neutral as she could. Apparently, these folks knew that she and Darcy spent much of their time on the ice at each other's throats and didn't care. So why should she? Maybe they were going for that kind of dynamic.

"Are you hoping that our 'colorful' history comes through in these segments?" Natalie asked.

Keena reached out her hand to touch Natalie's arm. A warning not to get ahead of herself or stir the pot too much.

Raquel laughed. "As far as I'm concerned, chemistry is chemistry. As long as you two don't get into a fistfight on the air, I don't care if you're a little competitive with each other. Your rivalry is part of what we wanted to try on camera." She leaned forward. "This is a family show, though. We are on the air when people are having breakfast and getting ready for work with their kids. Keep it PG and you'll be fine."

Natalie smiled. "When do we start?"

Chapter Seven

Whatever apprehensions she had about working with Natalie, Darcy needed her to do well enough for Raquel to say yes to the segment. Without her, Darcy would be stuck in New York while the rest of the team flew to Switzerland for the Games. Three years of working her ass off for an opportunity and it all came down to how a woman who hated her guts did in her screen test.

Darcy felt sick.

If Natalie got the job, it would mean Darcy would be stuck working with Carpenter for weeks. They hadn't been on the same team for more than a decade and the last time they were… she didn't want to think about it. Not that it had been bad, mostly. But the ending was a different story.

Darcy shook her head at the thought. Making it onto the show was all that mattered. She could deal with Carpenter's mouth if it meant being on camera.

Darcy hurried through the hallway, snagged an apple from the break room, and slipped into the back of the room where Carpenter was doing her test. Natalie stood in front of the camera while a couple of hair and makeup folks fussed with her appearance. Natalie looked relaxed and confident as she spoke to them. She laughed, sending the sound across the room to where Darcy was trying to stay out of sight.

Darcy hadn't heard Nat laugh like that in a long time. There wasn't much joking around when they were on the ice screaming at each other. The happy sound reminded her of college. It reminded her of before everything went to shit. She liked the reminder of how she used to feel. Not that she'd ever tell Natalie that.

Once the flock of stylists disappeared, Raquel gave Natalie a short pep talk before stepping out of the frame.

For a moment after the camera went on, Natalie looked like she was going to choke. She stared at the camera, eyes unblinking, body stiff as a corpse.

Oh my god, she's going to pass out.

Darcy took half a step forward in case Natalie needed help.

Natalie blinked once more before finally reading the teleprompter. "Good morning and welcome to *Wake Up, USA*! I'm your host, Natalie Carpenter, coming to you from St. Moritz where today I'm getting a lesson in curling from members of Team USA. I can't wait to get back onto the ice. Even if it's not the way I'm used to." Her gaze shifted to Raquel. "So, how'd I do?"

Darcy stepped into the light where Natalie could see her.

Unable to resist, Darcy called from the back of the studio. "You were great after you finished doing your statue impression." She took a giant, loud bite of her apple and grinned.

Even from across the studio, Darcy could see the way Nat's jaw bulged as she gritted her teeth.

"Nice to see you too, LaCroix. I certainly didn't expect a warmer welcome than that." Natalie gave her a grin. The exact kind of grin Darcy had been trying to wipe off her cocky face every time they stepped on the ice together for the last decade.

God, she was an arrogant little shit. Not even getting cut

from Team USA dimmed her confidence. *Must be nice*, Darcy's subconscious whispered at her.

Raquel stood next to Darcy. "I'm glad you're here. I was hoping you would give Natalie a tour before the two of you do your test segment together."

Darcy tried to decide if Raquel was seriously fine with the performance Natalie gave or if she was trying to provoke Darcy to see what she would do around Natalie. Darcy wasn't going to take the bait. "I'd be happy to. Let me know when you are done here and I'll come pick her up for the tour."

"Aw, stick around, LaCroix. I know you're dying to see the show. Don't you want to see what I can do?" Natalie asked with another infuriating grin.

Darcy was going to wipe that thing off her face one way or another. But not with her boss watching, and not before she got the chance to be on-screen at the Olympics. She swallowed the words she wanted to say and stepped back to watch the rest of Natalie's rehearsal.

Darcy wouldn't have admitted it to anyone, but Natalie improved a lot each time she ran through the sample script. Her manner relaxed and she was charming on camera. The fact that she was a complete natural pissed Darcy off more than anything.

People saw the LaCroix last name and assumed she'd gotten everything she had because of her dad. But the truth was, for all her inherited talent, she worked her ass off. Once, when she was a kid, she'd been cut from a team and was so hurt, so humiliated that she vowed that no one would ever work harder than she did. That way, if she ever failed to make a team or achieve a goal, it wouldn't be because of a lack of effort.

The idea of someone, especially Natalie, being a fucking natural at something she'd spent hours working at pissed her off almost as much as Natalie's smug expression.

After the fourth time through, Raquel stopped the rehearsal. "I think we've seen enough to know you can handle reading."

"Yes, Nat can read," Natalie said in a mock caveman voice.

Raquel smiled. "We like funny people around here. We'll keep that in mind for your pieces. You two should be able to play off each other. Natalie, you may be the comedian and Darcy here can be the straight man, so to speak."

Something like a cloud passed over Natalie's eyes but she didn't say anything. Relief flooded Darcy's chest. She wasn't in the closet, but at work she wasn't the type to make jokes about how not straight she was. Those were the kinds of jokes she would have shared with her friends and her teammates. Including Natalie.

But that was a long time ago.

"You going to show me around or what, Princess?" Natalie asked, her hands shoved deep in her pockets. She lowered her voice. "Or did you just come to gloat about me getting cut?"

"What are you talking about?"

Natalie's eyes blazed, her anger barely contained. "I saw you the other day. You looked pretty fucking pleased to tell the world about how I was the last one cut from the team."

"Un-fucking-believable," Darcy said before heading for the door, not slowing her pace for Natalie in spite of their four-inch height difference. If she wanted to be an asshole, fine, but Darcy didn't have to wait for her slow ass.

Natalie's shoes clacked against the tile floor. She caught up to Darcy only when she had to wait for a group of people blocking the way. Darcy took another bored bite of her apple.

"You can't be seriously pissed right now." She followed until they got to the end of the hallway. "Still eating ten apples a day?"

Darcy cocked one eyebrow but didn't respond, as she walked to the end of the hallway. "This is the break room. If you need coffee or a snack, you can usually find it here. Careful you don't spill on your clothes, the costume folks hate that and if you do it too often they will give you ugly shit to wear."

Natalie nodded. "Do they keep the apples stocked for you?"

Darcy made a face but Natalie nodded at the core dangling from her hand. She rolled her eyes and chucked the core in the trash. She forced herself not to remember their first meeting.

Natalie grinned. "Nice to see some things never change."

Darcy strode down the hallway until they got to Raquel's office and the space outside it where Jamal and Darcy had their desks. "I sit over here. I assume they're going to give you a desk, although I can't imagine they're going to expect you to do much."

"Why not?" Natalie asked, scowling.

"They brought you in to see if we would work well together doing a bunch of goofy shit. They didn't bring you in because you have a ton of TV experience. Why, were you hoping to write stories? Book guests? Chase down sources?" Darcy crossed her arms over her chest. "What hidden talents do you have to share with us?"

Natalie rolled her eyes. "I'm not stupid, even if you're treating me like an overexcited Labrador. We graduated from the same college, remember?"

Darcy rolled her eyes and walked Natalie over to Jamal. After she introduced them, she continued the tour for fifteen more minutes before giving up. The bickering was giving her a headache. She had to be sharp for their paired demonstration if she had any hope of this stupid experiment working well enough to get her on a plane to Switzerland with the rest of the *Wake Up, USA* team.

Chapter Eight

College

The longer they bumped along the dirt road, the more convinced Natalie became that she was about to get hazed. She expected it but hoped she wouldn't have to eat or drink anything gross. The last thing she wanted to do was barf in front of her new teammates. Not on the first day.

She was squished in the back seat of a beat-up Honda between two other freshmen, Callie Sullivan and Bridget Wolfowitz. Sully and Wolverine. It didn't matter that the three of them had met only twenty minutes earlier, those were going to be their nicknames.

Driving the clunky Honda was a senior named Hinch. If Hinch had told them her first name, Natalie must have missed it.

"If you're taking us to the woods to murder us, my parents are going to be really pissed."

Hinch looked at Natalie in the rearview. "Quit your whining, Carpenter."

Three minutes and one massive bump that felt like the back axle was going to fall off the car later, the road curved and the trees gave way to a field and a big, red sign shaped like an apple that read "Pick Ur Own."

"Apple picking?" Natalie asked, turning to Sully. "What the hell?"

Hinch put the car in Park with a lurch and turned to face them. "Come on, freshies. I'm hungry."

The three freshmen piled out of the back seat and wandered over to a cluster of picnic tables. Natalie had met most of the team on her recruiting trip but sitting on one of the tables was the one player she hadn't.

Darcy LaCroix had her elbows resting on her thighs and an apple between her teeth. She took a bite, a huge chunk of apple breaking off the core, and smiled at one of the other players who was telling her a story.

Darcy's eyes flicked to where Natalie stood near the back of the group. She smiled wider, like she'd been waiting for Natalie. Natalie's stomach did a swan dive for her toes. Darcy said something to the other girl and jumped off the table. Two steps later, she stood in front of Natalie.

"Carpenter, right?"

Natalie nodded, trying to find some way to keep cool with Darcy so close to her. Darcy was a legit hockey superstar. Natalie's lack of cool had nothing to do with the way Darcy's short sleeve rested on her arm, revealing killer shoulder muscles. And it definitely had nothing to do with Darcy's sea-glass green eyes looking down at her. No, it was because Darcy was already on the Canadian National Team. It was her hockey skill, nothing more, that made Natalie nervous.

It had nothing to do with the way Darcy's mouth twisted up at the corner that made Natalie's heart jump out of her chest.

Stop being such a loser, Natalie.

"I'm Darcy. Sorry I missed your trip. Hinch told me you had a lot of fun with the team."

Natalie looked over at Hinch, who was busy explaining something to one of the other seniors.

"Uh, yeah. It was good. Nice to meet you, finally." Natalie stuck out her hand like a massive dork.

Darcy's mouth broke into a grin. She shook Natalie's hand before throwing an arm around her. "How do you feel about moving to the wing?"

Natalie shrugged.

Darcy took another bite of her apple and Natalie's eyes focused on her lips. Fuck. Two minutes together and Natalie was already staring at her captain's lips and eyes and imagining what she could do with her long fingers.

Natalie couldn't believe how ridiculous she felt. She told herself to get a fucking grip and stop being such a disaster lesbian.

"I've seen you play, Carpenter, and I think you and I would be very good together." Darcy, four inches taller, looked down at Natalie and maybe she could see the gay panic on Natalie's face because she quickly added, "On a line together. I think we could score a whole lotta goals. You up for it?"

"What makes you think that of the two of us, I should be the one to change positions?" Natalie asked.

A laugh burst from Darcy's mouth. "Oh shit. The coaches told me you were confident, but I see they really meant you're cocky." She paused, her eyes boring into Nat's. "Okay, freshie. You're on. If the coaches think I should be the one to move to the wing, I'll do it. But I've been on this team for three years and no one's made me change positions."

She walked over to Hinch, who had taken a spot standing on a picnic table. The way the owners eyed her from the farm stand gave the impression they weren't too pleased about it.

"All right, listen up!" Hinch clapped her hands together. "Cap has something to say before we get down to business."

LaCroix stood on the grass, still gripping her apple core.

"We're here to have some fun, get to know each other, and pick some apples."

"Wait, we're here to pick apples? This is shocking information," a girl with bright red hair yelled sarcastically from the back.

"Newbies. That's McD. Ignore her, we all do. Tonight, Coach is having us over for dinner and freshmen and seniors are in charge of making dessert. We need to pick enough apples for a couple pies and crisps. But mostly we want to have a little time away from the rink to get to know each other. Every group needs to grab a bag and head out to fill it. Any questions from anyone other than McD?"

Her eyes scanned the team and landed on Natalie. "Carpenter, you're with me," she said, lifting her chin in Natalie's direction.

The other seniors walked around rounding up their groups but Darcy walked toward Natalie, a bag in one hand, her apple in the other. She took a final bite and tossed the core into the woods with one fluid flick of her wrist. Natalie's mouth went dry at the sight of the muscles on her forearm and she had to lick her lips before she could say hi to the other players in their group. The whole time, Natalie had to remind herself to take her eyes off Darcy.

Get a grip, Natalie.

Darcy handed Natalie the bag, their fingers brushing on the handle. "Come on, kid. The best ones are this way." She grinned and nodded her head toward a grove of gnarled apple trees.

Anyone else calling Natalie "kid" would have made her ready to drop her gloves right there, but Darcy said it with a sweet smile and those fucking eyes. That was it. Natalie would have followed her anywhere.

Chapter Nine

Natalie didn't expect LaCroix to welcome her with a hug or anything, but she had expected her not to be an asshole in front of her boss. Clearly, she'd been wrong. But Natalie wasn't a freshman anymore. She wasn't intimidated in the presence of the hockey princess the way she had been when she'd walked into their locker room in college. Back then, she'd been more than happy to be anywhere near Darcy.

Now, she was older, wiser, and still a little pissed off that her best option right now was talking about the Olympics instead of playing in them.

After the tour, if you could even call it that, Natalie and Darcy ended up in another studio. This one had a Ping-Pong table set up in the middle. Natalie walked over to it and picked up one of the paddles and started bouncing the ball on it.

"Wanna play?" she asked, knowing there was no way that Darcy would pass up a chance to compete.

Darcy grabbed a paddle from the other end of the table. "Is this all a game for you?"

"Ping-Pong? Yes. It is literally a game."

Darcy glared. "You know that's not what I meant. Are you

here because you actually want to be on TV or is this a joke to you?"

Natalie sent the ball to Darcy, catching her momentarily off guard. Darcy returned the ball but it caromed off the table. Natalie picked it up and served again. This time Darcy returned it easily and they fell into the rhythm of a rally.

"I'm here, aren't I?"

Darcy frowned. "That's not what I was asking. This is my job and I want to know if you're going to swoop in here and fuck around because it doesn't matter to you."

Natalie snagged the ball out of the air with one hand. "Jesus, it's always about you, isn't it?" She shook her head. "Whether I'm here because I think this is a hilarious joke or because I want to be the next Rachel Maddow doesn't matter."

"It matters to me."

Natalie rolled her eyes. "Oh, in that case. God forbid someone upset the princess. I'm not going to ruin your job, LaCroix. From the looks of it you need me for this just as much as I need you."

"What?" Darcy asked, clearly sending the ball whizzing back at Natalie a little harder than she meant to.

"This whole thing only works if they get us to be rivals on the screen. They want the whole Canada-USA thing. So, if you're trying to run me off, you might want to think twice. Because I don't think they're going to put you on that screen without me."

Natalie smashed the ball across the net and past Darcy. The ball smacked against the wall behind Darcy and skittered across the floor.

Darcy dropped her paddle on the table and walked out. Natalie put her paddle down and found a chair off to the side of the room. *Fuck.* How did she let Darcy get under her skin so quickly? They'd been friends once. They'd been something else, too. Something more. That was a long time ago, so long it felt like a whole other life. But they'd been in the same room for less than two hours and they were already at each other's throats and smacking Ping-Pong balls at each other.

Maybe this wasn't going to work so well after all.

Natalie forced herself not to run her hand through her hair. She'd had people fixing it all morning for the screen test and she did not want to have to sit through that again because Darcy bleeping LaCroix—she was trying to cut down on the swearing—was the most frustrating woman on the planet. No, she could keep her shit together, even if Darcy couldn't.

Raquel walked in as Natalie was picking up the Ping-Pong balls they'd scattered around the room. She had Darcy with her. Darcy had the fierce look of a teenager told to behave by a parent. Natalie suppressed a smile. It was petty as hell, but she loved knowing she'd gotten under Darcy's skin. Served her right for being such an arrogant asshole.

Raquel pointed to the cameras. "We want the two of you to watch this clip of the segment we did during the last Olympics. Chip learned how to play from one of the Team USA players. Then I want to see you improv a segment around what you've learned about playing table tennis." Natalie gave her a confused look. "I know this isn't exactly what you'll be doing if we go forward with the segment, but we don't happen to have a bob-sled track in the building. This is the best we can do."

Natalie looked at Darcy, who was standing at the other end of the table. "Ready?"

"I'm always ready to kick your ass, Carpenter."

Chapter Ten

Darcy couldn't believe that Raquel hadn't shared this stupid-ass plan with her. She'd been at the show for three years and Raquel didn't feel it necessary to mention that they were going to test her chemistry or whatever with Natalie by having them play fucking Ping-Pong?

Raquel didn't do things half-assed. She didn't test people to be on her show by having them watch a video like they were going to learn how to frost a cake or crochet from YouTube. This was the Olympics, so why was Raquel being so weird about this whole process?

"You ready, Princess?"

Darcy glared but wasn't going to yell at Natalie in front of her boss. She'd find another way to get back at her.

"Princess?" Raquel said with a chuckle. "Don't tell me you're secretly royalty. I might feel bad about making you get me coffee."

Darcy shook her head. "Nope. Just a regular person."

Natalie bounced the ball on the table. "Aw, come on, La-Croix, don't be shy. Her dad is in the Hall of Fame. He won the Stanley Cup three times. She's certifiable hockey royalty." She smirked and Darcy wanted to wipe it off her face. "I can't believe they didn't know that here. I assumed it was how you got the job."

Darcy was going to kill her. It would be the shortest screen test ever because she was going to launch herself across the room and murder Natalie Carpenter right there.

Raquel gave Darcy an appraising look. "Royalty?"

Darcy hurried to contradict Nat. "She's exaggerating. It's a long-running joke. One I thought we had all outgrown." She threw Carpenter a glare she hoped made it clear that Natalie should shut her stupid mouth for five minutes. Nothing about the way Raquel looked at her gave the impression she was buying Darcy's explanation, but she didn't say anything.

Raquel turned on a screen behind the cameras and played the clip of Chip learning how to play table tennis. Darcy got a horrible case of secondhand embarrassment as Chip dropped the paddle, whiffed on his attempts to serve the ball, and got increasingly red in the face the longer the segment went on. At the very least, she and Natalie had more athletic ability in their little fingers than Chip could ever dream of.

A couple of times during the video Darcy caught Natalie's eye and had to cover her mouth with one hand because they were both on the verge of laughing at him out loud. In those few seconds, she remembered what it had been like to be Natalie's friend and teammate. There was a time when they'd shared inside jokes, goofy team traditions, and even a few moments alone. She remembered bus rides where their legs touched and neither of them wanted to move away, late nights watching stupid movies and sharing Natalie's favorite M&M's and popcorn concoction. "Sweet and salty, like me!" she'd said with a proud smile, like she'd discovered it herself.

But that evaporated the second the video ended. Darcy walked to her side of the table and picked up her paddle. As soon as she did, Natalie started yapping at her.

"You weren't paying attention. You don't hold it like that.

Come on, Captain Canada, I expect more out of you." She held up her own paddle to demonstrate the funky way real table tennis players held it.

Darcy glared at her. "Wow, thank you so much for helping me with that, Carpenter. There's no way I would have been able to figure it out on my own. Thank god you're here to help me."

Raquel clapped. "Glad to see you getting along so well. I can only imagine how great you two bickering will look on camera." The look she gave both women rivaled any they'd received from coaches over their playing careers. "So, if you're done posturing, would you care to give this a shot?"

Darcy nodded and stuffed down the feeling of wanting to kill Natalie for being such a complete jackass and making her look bad. This was Darcy's shot at making it onto the Olympics broadcast and Natalie was going to screw it up if she didn't start taking this seriously.

After flipping her paddle around to match what Chip had done in the video, Darcy grabbed a couple of the balls from a bin beside the table. Raquel disappeared behind one of the cameras to watch via the monitor.

Natalie did a couple of deep knee bends like she was preparing to go for a long run, not play a gentle game of Ping-Pong.

"We're going to start with you first, Darcy, then pan over to Natalie. Introduce yourselves and then go from there. We just want to get a sense of what you two are like on camera together."

Darcy's posture changed when the camera swung her way. She stopped thinking about what Natalie would say about her "princess" posture and faced the camera. "Good morning, I'm Darcy LaCroix coming to you live from inside the studios where we are going to be giving you a taste of the Olympics."

The camera turned to capture Natalie. She smiled but seemed shaken for a second. "And I'm Natalie Carpenter, happy to be showing you, uh, a little bit about a sport neither of has played professionally."

The camera paused. Natalie adjusted her grip on the paddle. "But that won't stop us from doing our best, even if our best isn't very good."

Darcy served the ball toward Natalie, who took a swing toward the ball but instead of hitting it back to Darcy, sent it right into the ceiling. "As you can see, we were both better hockey players than we are at table tennis."

Natalie smiled. "Yeah, there's no way we're winning any medals in this sport." She tried serving this time and they managed a short rally before Darcy accidentally sent the ball right toward Natalie's face. As she ducked, Natalie was able to slap the ball back toward Darcy and it smacked right into her stomach.

Both women cracked up before Darcy remembered what they were supposed to be doing. "I want a rematch," Darcy said, pointing her paddle at Natalie. "In the meantime, we hope you will all tune in to see the *real* table tennis pros take on their opponents today."

Raquel stepped away from the monitor. "Not bad for a first attempt. Natalie, how do you feel being on camera?"

Natalie shrugged. "Feels fine. How did it look? If I sucked, just tell me."

Darcy laughed and Natalie gave her a withering look.

"Good to know you won't melt if I give you feedback." Raquel walked over to her. "Be sure when you're saying things to the camera you're actually looking into it. Otherwise it looks like you're distracted. I know it's weird but you have to look right into it, because when you don't you look like you're talking to someone other than the viewers."

Nat nodded.

Raquel turned to Darcy. "You did well, but you're both going to have to practice moving the segments forward. You'll have one of us in your ear when we do this for real but it takes practice to keep going back to the guest to make sure they remain a focus of the piece. We want to make sure that the athletes don't feel like they're an afterthought for these segments. We expect it to be goofy, but make sure they're the stars, got it?"

Being judged based on a set of unknown, and impossible-to-meet, criteria pissed Darcy off. But she wouldn't let that show. Instead, she tried to make her point more subtly. "Got it. Maybe next time we practice we can have a third person with us? That way we can practice engaging them and not just flinging Ping-Pong balls at each other."

"Yes. I think we can make that happen." Raquel looked at Natalie. "How do you feel about bobsledding?"

"Bring it on."

Chapter Eleven

The van arrived at Natalie's hotel when it was still pitch-black outside. She'd set three alarms in her room to ensure she got up, but that didn't mean she was fully awake, even standing in the cheery light of the hotel lobby. The cup of coffee in her hand was nowhere near enough to keep her going but it was a start. Hopefully they'd stop somewhere for more before they put her on camera.

Sliding into one of the seats, Natalie couldn't believe this was where her life had taken her. Instead of getting sleep to recover from hard workouts and exhausting practices, she was up in the middle of the night to try out for a job she'd never considered. Then again, she thought she was going to be flying to the opening ceremonies with her teammates, not with a camera crew.

She hated being on the sidelines. The few times she'd been injured in her career, it had been torture to watch her teammates play without her. Being part of a team was essential, like it was part of her DNA. Some people reveled in being solo, being the only one, but Natalie came alive in a locker room or on the bench, looking around at her teammates and knowing they were all pulling for the same goal.

Hockey took that kind of trust. It wasn't like soccer where you played the entire game. In hockey you played for a minute at a time before turning the ice over to your teammates. You had to trust that when you hopped over the boards your teammates would pick up where you left off. She loved that sense of trust, that sense of team.

But that was gone now.

Now she was sitting in a van winding its way out of New York City before the sun even considered coming up. She sipped her coffee and stared out the window.

The van stopped at the studio and one of the crew members hopped out. "I have to grab a couple things from inside. Be right back."

Natalie let her eyes close, and her head fell forward for a few blissful seconds before she heard the sliding door open.

"Good morning," Darcy's voice filled the van. She dropped a bag on the floor behind Natalie's seat.

Natalie looked up. "Were you in the studio already?"

Darcy shook her head and climbed into the front seat. "I've been here all night."

"Why?" Natalie asked, horrified at the prospect of spending the night at work.

Darcy turned in the seat while they waited for the crew member to finish loading supplies into the back of the van. "I had work to do to prepare for today." She faced the front. "I can sleep on the way up."

"Lucky you," Natalie grumbled. "How come you get to ride in the front?"

"Because I'm a goddamned princess."

Natalie laughed but tried to cover for it by pretending she was coughing.

Darcy turned around. "I get really bad motion sickness. Usually, I take Dramamine but if I take it this morning, I'll sleep through our segment. But if you would rather have me puke in the van, we can trade seats."

In the dim light of the streetlights, Natalie could tell Darcy wasn't lying. A flicker of memory, long-ago bus rides, a reminder that Darcy always had to sit in the front with the coaches, even when all the fun was happening farther back. Even that tiny reminder sent Natalie's mind rocketing back to those road trips, back when Natalie would have done anything to be nearer her captain, would have done anything to make Darcy feel better. But that was a long time ago.

Darcy added, seemingly oblivious to Natalie's college memories, "I'll take the medicine on the way home so you can have the front seat then if you want. I'll be asleep before we hit the highway so it won't matter what seat I have.'"

Natalie shrugged. "It's fine. I can sleep anywhere."

Darcy turned around and settled into her seat. A crew member slid into the driver's seat and the other took the seat next to Natalie.

"Manny, what are you doing letting Josh drive?" Darcy asked, looking back at the guy next to Natalie.

Manny smiled. "I'm fine with him driving if it means I get to sleep."

Josh turned the ignition. "You don't even have cars in Canada, do you?"

Darcy cracked up. "You're right. Only dogsleds and the occasional snowmobile. Sometimes we just ride our moose to Tim Hortons."

The guys laughed. Natalie smiled. This felt good. The banter—talking shit—felt like being on a team again. It didn't matter that she was on the outside of the jokes right now, it was the best she'd felt in a while.

Josh steered the van into the road and they made it out of the city before Natalie finished her coffee. There was no hint that the sun existed, let alone planned to rise anytime soon. Outside the city, everything was darker, the sky blacker, the flickering lights of the few passing cars on the road the only sources of light on the highway. Between the dark and the steady rhythm of the van zipping along the road, Natalie started to lose the battle to stay awake. Manny and Darcy had already given up trying to stay awake when her eyes got harder to open.

"You okay if I fall asleep, Josh?"

He caught her eye in the rearview mirror for a second. "No problem. But thanks for asking."

She turned to try to find a comfortable position, but it didn't matter. A decade of riding buses and planes to and from games had made her a champion sleeper.

A little over five hours later, they pulled into the parking lot for the bobsledding experience at Lake Placid. The van rolling to a stop woke everyone. She immediately wiped at her face, hoping she didn't drool during the trip. She didn't need to give Darcy any more reasons to be insufferable. The Canadian princess would never drool.

Darcy was out of the van before Natalie had her seat belt unbuckled. "Jesus, what's the rush?" she muttered but laughed when she saw Darcy practically sprinting to the bathrooms. The sliding door rumbled in its track as Natalie hopped out into the chilly, but blissfully fresh, air. A few breaths and the gross feeling of being in a car for too long evaporated. She stretched her arms over her head, hoping it would undo the damage of six hours in a van. It didn't fix everything but between the cold air and being able to move, she felt more human than she had since she got up in the middle of the night.

A middle-aged woman with a tight ponytail and a severe expression strode toward the van. "Morning. You're the folks here to learn how to sled?"

Natalie nodded, unsure she was the best person to talk to

out of the group, but not willing to risk a stern glare from this woman.

"Liz Burton-Wu. Nice to meet you." Her voice didn't give the impression she was asking a question, but Natalie hurried to say something anyway.

"Natalie Carpenter. Thank you for meeting us."

Liz smiled, changing her entire demeanor. "My pleasure. I'm a huge hockey fan. My wife gives me shit for it, but I've watched the gold medal game like three times."

Natalie laughed. "Tell your wife to give you a break. It's a hell of a game." She looked over Liz's head to where Darcy was marching back to the van. "Unless you're Canadian, of course."

Darcy heard her and narrowed her eyes. "That's a lot of yapping from someone who only has a single gold."

Liz cracked up. "Oh shit. I didn't realize I was teaching rivals to sled. This should be fun."

"Single gold."

Fuck you, LaCroix. But the thought needled at her. She had hoped to add a second this time around. Instead, she'd be spending the day shoved into a tiny sled next to Darcy. What a terrible fucking consolation prize.

Chapter Twelve

College

As much as Darcy hated bus rides, she loved road trips. The entire team together, watching movies, talking, spending time together. It's where the team solidified. During her senior year, it was her job as the captain to make sure that happened quickly. She was already a front-runner to win the player of the year award, but what she really wanted was a national championship. And she would do anything she could to make it happen.

While the rest of the team bonded in the rows behind her, Darcy sat in front with the coaches and stared out the windshield to keep from throwing up.

Darcy stood so she could see over the rows of seats all the way to the back of the bus. Half the players were sitting in their seats, while the others were lingering in the aisle or leaning over the back of their seats to talk to the person behind them.

No one sat behind Darcy. No one else wanted to be that close to the coaches.

Carpenter climbed the steps and paused next to her seat. "Hey, Cap. What exciting thing do you have planned for the ride?"

"Mostly my plan is not to get sick."

She shoved her hands into the pockets of her sweats. "Solid plan. Sorry you can't sit back with the rest of us."

Darcy shrugged. "Yeah. It sucks but if I moved back, I'd have to take so much Dramamine I'd pass out and miss all the fun, anyway."

Natalie stood there like she was weighing whether to say something else.

"Move, Carpenter." Hinch stood behind her on the steps.

Carpenter gave Darcy an unreadable look before shuffling down the aisle toward the back of the bus.

Later, when the movie played on tiny screens throughout the bus, Carpenter appeared next to Darcy's seat.

"Do you mind?" she asked, pointing to the empty seat, looking more nervous than on her first day with the team.

Panic flickered in Darcy's chest. Did something happen? Was she hurt? Was she pissed? Darcy pulled her books onto her lap and gestured for her to sit.

Nat opened her messenger bag and pulled out a sleeve of saltines, some hard candy, and wristbands. Her eyes stared into her bag and her cheeks turned pink. "I thought these might help you with, you know, not feeling great on the bus. My mom used to keep saltines in the car just in case and my roommate swears these band things work." She shoved them toward Darcy, keeping her eyes focused on the crackers.

The stuff spilled onto Darcy's lap when she tried to hold it all. "You brought all of this for me?"

Natalie nodded, her cheeks turning a deeper red. "It sucks that you feel like shit on our trips and I... Anyway." She swallowed. "I wanted to see if there was anything you needed help with? Like do you need any help reading stuff or anything on the bus? It doesn't bother me, and it must be hard to get all your homework done if you can't do it on the bus..." She looked at Darcy, her deep blue eyes meeting Darcy's for a second before skittering away. "I can help. That's all I wanted to offer." She leaned forward like she was preparing to stand up.

Darcy grabbed her arm. "Thank you." Darcy lifted all the things Natalie gave her, and the sleeve of crackers fell onto her lap. "This is so nice." Nat's eyes softened, and her cheeks were deep crimson. "You want to hang out a little bit?"

She nodded and rubbed her palms down the front of her sweatpants.

Darcy bumped their shoulders. "Do I freak you out or something?"

She dipped her head. "No. I didn't want you to think I was weird or whatever because I brought you..." She gestured to the bundle in Darcy's lap.

"I don't think you're weird for this. I think you're weird for like a thousand other reasons but not because you're nice." *Not because you're surprisingly soft.*

She looked at the screen to the left and then back at Darcy. "Does watching make you sick?"

Darcy nodded. "It's fine. I've seen *Youngblood* like a thousand times. Hinch brings it every time we travel."

Natalie laughed. "It's a classic in that not very good but enjoyable kind of way." She studied Darcy's face. "You okay? You got kinda gray all of a sudden."

Darcy closed her eyes and let her head rest against the seat. "Yep," she said, taking a slow breath. "I'll be fine in a second."

"Give me your hand," she said.

Darcy felt something soft but tight going over her hand. Natalie adjusted it until a hard bead pressed into the soft skin of Darcy's wrist. "It might take a minute but it's supposed to help."

Darcy heard crinkling and opened one eye. "Eat one of these, too." She handed Darcy a saltine carefully, like it was priceless.

"Thank you," Darcy said in a low voice. She hated being the center of attention when she was sick. Natalie sat next to her, silent, but Darcy could feel herself being watched. Every so often she handed Darcy another cracker, tucking it gently into Darcy's outstretched hand.

After a few minutes, Darcy felt human again. She took several gulps of ice water and breathed more easily.

Natalie handed her the sleeve of crackers. "If these don't help, try one of the candies. Sometimes sugar helps me."

Darcy couldn't believe how gentle the concerned look on Natalie's face was. Her heart tugged, like Natalie had wrapped a string around it and given a little pull, like she was testing the connection. Darcy couldn't remember the last time she had felt so safe and cared for.

Natalie stood, one hand gripping the seat in front of her for balance. "I'll leave you to rest. But let me know if you need anything." She pointed to the seats. "I'm only two rows back." She blushed, but it was hard to see in the dim light of the bus.

"Thanks, Carpenter." Darcy smiled weakly and returned to staring straight ahead. Her stomach flipped over, but not from the bus ride.

Shit. I'm in so much trouble.

This couldn't be happening. Darcy had vowed she'd never date another teammate. Not after it nearly tore her team apart. And now she was getting all fluttery about a freshman. No. She would not be the creepy senior crushing on the new kid. She let her head fall back against the seat.

Too late. She was definitely into Natalie. Goddammit.

Chapter Thirteen

A flicker of anger ignited in Darcy's chest when she heard Natalie talking shit about her. But never one to represent herself or Canada poorly, she pasted on a smile and stuck out her hand. "Darcy LaCroix, nice to meet you. You must be Liz?"

Liz shook her hand. "I know who you are. I was just telling Natalie that I'm a bit of a hockey junkie. I can't believe I'm meeting both of you! Your penalty shot in the gold medal game was a thing of beauty."

We still lost.

Darcy's smile faltered for an instant, but she recovered. "Thank you. I wish it could have won the gold for us, but complaining about not having four golds seems a bit obnoxious, don't you think?" If Natalie was going to talk shit about her *one* gold medal, Darcy sure as hell would remind her that she had three times as many.

"Oh man, you all are going to be fun, I can feel it." Liz leaned closer to them. "It'll be nice to have some athletes around the place instead of the tourists we usually get."

Darcy smiled. "I've been retired for a few years, but Carpenter here is still in top shape."

Natalie glowered. "Yeah, that's the perk of being the last one cut."

Darcy's eyes widened. "That's not—"

"Save it, LaCroix." She snatched her backpack out of the van and slammed the door. "Lead the way, Liz."

Darcy was stunned. She hadn't meant it as a dig, she'd meant it to be self-deprecating about her own less-than-world-class fitness. She was still in shape, but since she'd retired from the national team she didn't have to worry about trying to increase her strength or passing the fucking beep test anymore. She worked out because it made her feel good. She lifted because she liked being strong, but she didn't have to run sprints or stadiums anymore. And she didn't miss any of that shit for a second.

When she looked at Natalie, she saw how fit she used to be and for a moment there was a twinge of sadness. She'd worked for decades for the strength and speed she had on the ice. She'd earned every bit of it, and she'd also let it go, along with the ice baths, trips to the training room, and long road trips. There were trade-offs, and one of them was a certain lack of definition to her muscles she had always taken for granted when she was playing.

Natalie hadn't lost that yet.

Darcy frowned. She really hadn't meant to piss Natalie off but understood how her remark had felt like a dig. Not that she'd admit it.

Josh and Manny had already set up their equipment inside the little room off the track. Josh had the camera on his shoulder and a vest of equipment attached to his torso, while Manny was clipping mics on Natalie and Liz.

Darcy stripped off her winter coat and put on the one with the show logo on it. It wasn't as warm, but the instructions said not to wear puffy coats, presumably so they fit in the sled. Manny clipped a mic to her lapel, next to her zipper, and handed her the mic pack to go around her waist.

"I don't know what you did, but Natalie seems real pissed off," Manny said as he adjusted the mic.

Darcy shook her head. "I complimented her for being in good shape." She rolled her eyes. "So, I'm definitely an asshole."

Manny chuckled. "You guys always at each other's throats?"

Darcy shrugged. "Have you seen any video of us on the ice together?"

Manny shook his head.

"Google it sometime. I think there are compilations of us on YouTube. People loved to watch us mix it up on the ice."

"So, why the hell put you two on a show together?" Manny asked.

Darcy shrugged. "They liked the idea of the conflict. I don't think they'll like it if we actually drop the gloves, though."

Manny laughed. "I'll warn Josh if you think we're going to have to jump between you two."

Darcy shook her head. "I'm a journalist now. I've given up getting into scuffles with yappy Americans."

Manny didn't look convinced, but he moved on to testing the mic levels and helping Josh set up the shots.

They had to do the setup twice before they got it to work right, but then the intro segment went smoothly. Liz was a former bobsled driver who missed out on the Olympics, twice, by virtue of terribly timed injuries. Darcy couldn't imagine the heartache of missing out on the once-every-four-years opportunity due to an injury one time, but to have both chances ruined seemed exceptionally cruel.

Darcy felt greedy for the disappointment she'd felt when her last Olympics ended with a silver medal. How fucking selfish of her to be anything less than grateful for every chance she had to fight for gold. She didn't say any of that, of course, but she felt it like a slap shot off her shin.

Off camera, Liz walked them through all the safety stuff. They had to sign waivers and promise to follow all the rules.

"How many times do we get to race?" Natalie asked, her voice tinged with giddiness.

Liz shrugged. "I assumed you two would want to go together and be done with it."

Natalie shook her head. "No way. I want a shot at winning. What do you say, LaCroix? You up for a challenge?"

"Whoa. No way. We're supposed to shoot the two of you going down the track together. Raquel wants video of the two of you, smashed together in that thing, preferably scared out of your minds. That's what she wants," said Manny.

Darcy caught Natalie's eye. "Okay, so we give her what she wants."

"Suck-up," Natalie growled.

"Would you shut up for five seconds? Liz, any chance we can each do a second run? Slowest one buys lunch."

Nat's eyes sparkled. "You're so fucking on."

Liz laughed. "How can I deny you two? Hell, I'll even drive the sled for both of you to make it fair."

Josh followed them with the camera out to the track, where they awkwardly shuffled toward the sled behind Liz.

"How does this work?" Natalie asked, trying to figure out how she was going to run after the sled and throw herself onto it without dying.

Darcy raised one eyebrow. "You see, we get in the sled and then it zooms down the mountain."

Natalie rolled her eyes. "I mean, in the Olympics they do the whole running start and hop in one after another. Are we going to do that?"

Liz laughed. "Uh, no. There's not enough liability insurance to cover that. I'll be in the front and then you two will wedge in behind me." She pointed to two men the size of football linemen. "They'll push the sled and then we get our asses down the hill as fast as possible."

"Bummer, I was hoping for those shoes with the spikes on them."

Darcy gave her a look. "Oh yeah, so you could nail me in the ass with them. No thanks."

Liz got into the sled and coached Darcy on how to sit behind her with Natalie in the back. "Natalie, wrap your arms around Darcy's middle. I don't want you flying off when we take turn two."

Natalie leaned forward. "You okay with this?"

Darcy nodded and pulled Natalie's arms forward until they hooked around her waist.

Darcy's heart grave a traitorous jolt. Whatever, this was work. She could smash herself against Natalie without it being weird. This was part of the job, nothing more.

They gave Josh a wave and a thumbs-up before being shoved down the track. They hurtled faster and faster down the track, g-forces slamming them from side to side. Natalie was in the rear of the sled and her arms squeezed Darcy in each turn.

Thank god Darcy wasn't the only one feeling alarmed by how fast they were going. At the bottom, the track leveled off and they glided to a stop, Darcy's heart hammering in her chest.

When they reached the bottom, Darcy turned but couldn't see into Natalie's helmet, it was so fogged up from her breath. "You okay?" she yelled, hoping Nat could hear her.

After a pause, Nat unhooked her arms from around Darcy and scooted out of the sled. "Yeah. Fine. That was great."

"For someone who doesn't get motion sick, you don't look so good," Darcy said when Natalie flipped up the visor on her helmet, revealing her sickly green-gray skin. "You're not going to puke are you?"

Natalie shook her head and forced herself to swallow. Her face betrayed panic before she ripped the helmet off her head and took huge gulping breaths. For an instant she looked better. But when she turned to give Darcy a look, her face betrayed the wave of nausea overtaking her. Natalie lurched toward the side of the track and leaned over half a second before barfing.

Liz looked over at Darcy. "First round goes to Team Canada, I think."

Darcy took off her helmet, being careful not to hit the GoPro Josh had mounted on it. "With any luck, we got every second of it for the show."

Natalie stood up. "You wouldn't dare."

Darcy laughed. "We can talk about this after you're done tossing your breakfast all over the ground." She walked away from the track, singing at the top of her lungs "O, Canada, our home and native land." It wasn't a gold medal but seeing Natalie puking her guts out after talking so much shit felt pretty fucking great.

Chapter Fourteen

There was no way Natalie could wipe that stupid grin off Darcy's face while she was throwing up, but she could plot her revenge. If they were going to be working together, and based on the way everyone was giddily talking about their first test segment, they were, she would find a way to beat Darcy at every single stupid sport they tried.

Natalie hated losing. You didn't get to be an Olympian by not caring about wins and losses, but she *really* hated losing to Canada. Neither of them was wearing their team uniform anymore but that didn't change her desire to crush Darcy every second of every day.

The sound of Darcy singing the stupid national anthem echoed in her ears as she trudged back up to the top of the hill. The cold air was helping her stomach, but not fast enough.

"You sure you want to do this again?" Liz asked, looking warily at the side of Natalie's still-green face.

"I'm not giving her the satisfaction of winning," Natalie said, her teeth clenched.

Darcy stopped a few feet ahead of them and turned around. "Carpenter, there's no shame in calling it a day." Darcy couldn't keep the hint of a smirk from her mouth.

"I said I'd do it. I'm not backing out because my stomach's upset." Natalie gave Darcy the fiercest look she could while her stomach roiled.

Liz laughed. "Upset? I think throwing up all over the side of a mountain qualifies as more than 'upset.'"

"I can handle it," Natalie said, not entirely sure that was true. Darcy's singing and that stupid smirk were enough fuel to keep her trudging to the top of the hill. She'd make it down the track faster than Darcy even if it meant feeling like her insides were trying to escape her body. Backing down wasn't an option.

Liz stopped at the top of the track. "You're not going to barf on me, are you?"

Natalie shook her head. "I'll wait until we get to the bottom. Be sure to get us down the hill as fast as possible, though. I can't hold it forever, and I want to win."

Darcy rolled her eyes and put her helmet on. "Jesus, you're stubborn."

Natalie put her own helmet on but left the visor up. "It was my idea and I'm not giving you the satisfaction of backing out."

Darcy shrugged, her whole body looking like a sigh. "Just don't use puking as an excuse when I kick your ass." She crossed her arms over her chest and waited for Natalie to climb in behind Liz.

Liz waited for Natalie to get settled, her arms tucked into the sled and her shoulders against the sides. "Ready?"

"Let's fucking go," Natalie said, stuffing down the feeling that this was a terrible idea and sending up a silent prayer to the universe to help her not throw up all over Liz and the sled. If she lost her lunch a second time, she was sure Darcy would never let her forget it. Not to mention all their mutual acquaintances. Women's hockey was a small community—there was absolutely no way she'd escape getting shit from all her friends by the end of the week.

Knowing what to expect from the ride made it easier for

Natalie. She was prepared for the rapid shifts from side to side, the bouncing from the bumps in the ice, and the feeling of having zero control as her body hurtled down to the bottom of the hill.

"How fast were we?" she asked as soon as they crossed the finish line and came to a stop.

Liz flipped her visor up and waited for Natalie to get out. "Do I look like I'm carrying a stopwatch?"

Natalie laughed and extricated herself from the sled while searching for the time display. She had no idea what a good time was, so she had to ask Liz. "Good enough to win?"

Liz shrugged. "How should I know? We'll see who the better rider is in a minute." She paused. "No, I will not consider throwing the race your way."

Natalie feigned shock. "I would never ask such a thing of a fellow competitor." She paused. "But I thought that Team USA sticks together. Maybe you don't feel the same way."

Liz laughed and extended her hand to take Natalie's helmet. "Nice try. See you back down here in a few minutes."

"Take your time!" Natalie called after Liz headed up the hill.

She took a seat on a bench next to the track to watch the end of Darcy's ride. It didn't take long for her to see the sled coming around the bend and then down the final straightaway. Natalie looked at the clock. The numbers were moving way too slowly. "Come on, come on," she muttered under her breath.

The sled crossed the line and came to a juddering stop at the end of the track. The clock went blank for a second before revealing the final time. Darcy had won by less than half a second.

"Fuck," Natalie said, louder than she intended.

Darcy ripped her helmet off her head and bounced out of the sled like she'd been doing it all her life. *How is she so good at everything?* Natalie wondered, bitterly.

"What was your time, again?" Darcy asked, her smile brighter than the sun in the clear blue sky.

"Whatever," Natalie said and walked toward the van. She wasn't being a sore loser but she didn't have to pretend to be happy about Darcy beating her. She turned around. "It's basic physics. You're bigger so you slide down the hill faster."

Darcy laughed. "Did you just call me fat?"

"No. Maybe you didn't take physics in school. You're bigger, therefore you create more speed coming down the hill."

Darcy shook her head. "Whatever you have to tell yourself to sleep at night." She handed her helmet to one of the folks who worked there. "O, Canada, our home and native land..." she started singing again at the top of her lungs.

Natalie groaned. At the van, the strains of the Canadian national anthem echoed in her head as she stuffed her gear back into her bag. She shoved it into the car before walking over to find Liz.

"Thanks for the ride, Coach. Sorry I puked out there."

Liz laughed. "Don't worry about it. Happens all the time. I'm surprised Darcy didn't join you. She looked a little green around the gills."

Natalie shrugged. "She probably held it in just to spite me."

Liz laughed again. "I'll be watching you two when the Games start. I hope you have time to have some fun while you're there. Seems like a shame to get to go all that way with your girlfriend if you can't have a little fun on the way."

"Girlfriend? LaCroix? No. No way." Natalie couldn't believe Liz thought she and Darcy were together.

"Really?" Liz shrugged. "My mistake. I figured you were one of the Canada–USA couples you hear about on social media."

Natalie raised an eyebrow.

"What, you think I'm too old for Instagram?" She smacked Natalie gently on the shoulder. "Please. I'm not a thousand."

Natalie let the idea of her with Darcy sink in. Were people going to think they were together if they were on TV together? She doubted it. Not in a world of straight ladies who watched morning shows. They were much more apt to ship a couple of guys together than to realize that lesbians exist. Besides, Darcy hated her guts, and that was fine with Natalie. Growing up she never wanted to play princesses and she'd never wanted to date one either.

Liar.

She swallowed the memory of the night she learned what Darcy tasted like. Like cheap beer and laughter. She shouldn't know what her cohost tasted like. She shouldn't wonder if Darcy still drank cheap beer or if she still laughed like she did back then. She wondered a lot of things, but not how Darcy tasted. That memory was seared in her brain.

Chapter Fifteen

College

"Carpenter, LaCroix!" Sammy yelled their names before handing them each a room key. "Can't believe they're making you room with a freshie, Darce. That sucks."

"Hey!" Natalie said, snatching the key from Sammy's hand.

Darcy took her key with a smile. "Better than rooming with you. At least Carpenter doesn't spend half her life in the bathroom." She shot a glance at Natalie. "I mean, if you need to spend time in there or whatever, it's fine."

Natalie laughed. "I pee a normal amount, thanks for asking." Joking helped keep her mind off rooming with Darcy. It wasn't a big deal. They would go to the room, dump their bags on the floor, and go to sleep.

Easy.

Nothing to it.

If she could have rolled her eyes at herself without anyone noticing, she would. Crushing on the team captain had felt like such a stupid cliché. But every time they had a team meeting or practice, her eyes drifted to Darcy. She couldn't help it. Even when she told herself to stop staring, stop being a creepy, stupid freshman, her eyes still found her, like they couldn't bear to rest anywhere else.

And now the coaches had assigned them to share a room for their first road trip. Natalie's heart sped up as her imagination ran wild. In the elevator, she pushed the button too hard, causing Hinch to shout at her.

"It doesn't go faster if you beat it up, Carpenter."

Natalie clenched her teeth together and hoped she wasn't blushing. The team would never let her live that down. She wasn't going to try to explain why she wanted to get to her room or why her stomach was doing somersaults the closer they got to reaching their floor. Being alone with Darcy was a dream and a nightmare rolled into one.

She was a stupid freshman with a crush on her captain. There was no way she could possibly like her back, right? Darcy was way too cool for her. But sometimes when they sat in meetings, or on the bus, or at team meals, Darcy's eyes would find hers and she'd offer Natalie the sweetest smile. So maybe.

Oh god, that maybe was enough to send her stomach crashing for the floor.

"What would it take to make you move faster, Hinch?" Darcy asked, before smiling at Natalie.

Hinch's response was swallowed up by the doors opening and the players spilling into the hallway to find their rooms. Natalie followed Darcy to their room.

"Do you have a bed preference?" Darcy asked while Natalie reached for the light switch.

"What?" Natalie asked, her brain glitching at Darcy asking her about beds.

Darcy gestured at the two double beds. "Do you prefer to be near the door or the window?"

"Oh," Natalie said, dropping her bag and ducking her head to hide her cheeks, which felt like they were on fire. "I don't care. You pick." Natalie didn't think it would matter which bed she was in. As long as she was in the same room with Darcy she didn't think she'd be able to sleep much.

Darcy took the bed closest to the door and they spent a couple of quiet minutes getting ready for bed. Years later, if you'd asked her how it happened, Natalie wouldn't have been able to say for sure. One minute they were lounging in their beds, *SportsCenter* on in the background, talking about everything and nothing, and the next, Darcy was sitting on the edge of her bed.

Natalie watched Darcy's hands as she fiddled with them in her lap.

"What's wrong, LaCroix?"

Darcy clenched her hands into fists and shook her head. "Nothing. Except... Okay, I..." She looked up, her eyes searching Natalie's, and it was only a second, maybe two; time is weird when you feel like your entire life hangs in the balance of a single possibility.

Natalie leaned forward, taking a chance and hoping like hell she was right. It was a risk, but Natalie felt like her entire body would explode if she didn't find out how Darcy's lips felt against hers. For one heart-stopping second, she thought Darcy was going to push her away but when she moved her hand, it was to grip the back of Natalie's neck.

After a minute or an hour, Darcy pulled back. The smile on her face was so fragile, Natalie thought she would die. Darcy looked so unsure of herself, so full of worry. She never wanted to see Darcy like this, ever.

"What's wrong?"

Darcy shook her head. "Nothing. Except I really like you and I want to keep kissing you but we're teammates and..."

Natalie smiled. "You have a policy of not dating teammates?"

Darcy sighed.

"Oh shit, I was kidding."

Darcy grabbed her hand. "There was someone a few years

ago, and we dated for a while and it was great until the rest of the team found out."

Natalie scowled. "Were they mean? I'll kill them."

Darcy shook her head. "The team was fine until we weren't. We broke up and half the team sided with me and the other half with her and everything just kind of broke. The team was never the same. I don't want that to happen again."

Natalie scooted back. "Okay, so you don't want this?"

Darcy reached for her, took her hand again. "No, I *really* want this. But we have a team that could be great. And I don't want to be the reason that falls apart. Not again." She ran a hand through the hair falling into her face. "I think we can win a lot of games. I think you and I are magic together."

"On or off the ice?" Natalie asked, only half kidding.

"Both." Darcy blushed. "I like you a lot. But I'm the captain and I feel like it's my responsibility not to fuck everything up again."

Natalie leaned forward, resting her head on Darcy's shoulder. "So don't fuck it up. Kiss me again. No one needs to know except for the two of us."

Darcy searched Natalie's face. For a moment, Natalie thought she was going to say something but she leaned forward and kissed Natalie, and kissed her, and kissed her until it was way too late and the two of them finally agreed to give it a rest.

Darcy fell asleep in Natalie's bed, one hand resting on Natalie's stomach.

They lost so much sleep that night, and were such zombies the next day, the coaches never put them in the same room again.

But it was worth it. The lost sleep, the not getting to room together, all of it. Even when Darcy told her that they had to keep their relationship a secret from the rest of the team, Natalie didn't care. She didn't need Darcy to hold her hand in public or kiss her in the middle of the quad. She had shared looks, stolen moments, and the hottest girlfriend on campus.

Chapter Sixteen

Adrenaline was enough to get Darcy through the bobsledding but once the van hit the highway and her Dramamine kicked in, she was out. The only reason she woke up when they reached the studio was that Natalie shook her by the shoulder.

She wiped her face, mortified to find she'd drooled like she'd worried about, especially since Natalie was close enough to see it. Natalie didn't say anything but she'd probably tuck it away to use later when she got pissed off that Darcy beat her at something else, like curling or whatever the network people wanted them to do.

"What time is it?"

Natalie checked her watch. "Almost seven. Come on, you're too tall to sleep in that seat without doing serious harm to your body."

Darcy sat up and turned her head, earning several satisfying pops from her neck. "I can't believe I slept the whole way."

Natalie pulled her coat and bag out of the front seat and slid the door open for Darcy to hop out. "Didn't you say you were at the studio all night? You're going to need a whole lot more sleep if you're going to be able to function in our meeting with Raquel tomorrow."

Darcy clambered out of the van with less finesse than she managed earlier with the bobsled. Sleeping in the van for that long had been a mistake. She was going to be sore in weird places tomorrow. "Did Josh and Manny leave us behind?"

"No, they took some of the gear inside. Both of them were too chicken to wake you up. Do you have a reputation for being an asshole or something?"

Darcy laughed and stretched her arms over her head. "I think the only one around here who thinks I'm an asshole is you. I feel so lucky knowing my future cohost has the lowest opinion of me in the entire company."

"That's not true," Natalie protested. She crossed her arms over her chest. "I'm sure plenty of people here know you suck."

Darcy smiled, in spite of herself. "Fair enough. You are certainly the most vocal about it." She paused to put her coat on. "If you hate me so much, why are you here?"

Natalie shrugged. "If you hate me so much, why did they call me to come work with you?"

Darcy scowled. "I don't hate you."

"It's a good thing you play hockey better than you lie, because you suck at it." Natalie walked toward the exit of the parking garage. "See you tomorrow, LaCroix."

Darcy hadn't been lying, so why did Natalie assume she hated her? They'd had plenty of fights in the rink over the last decade, but that wasn't personal, that was geography. Would all of this have been different if they'd both been born in the same country? It would have made some things easier and their breakup less inevitable. Maybe Darcy wouldn't have sabotaged the whole thing because she worried there was no future for them. If they played for the same country, they would've had a fighting chance of staying together after college. But maybe Darcy would have still found a way to screw everything up. She sighed.

She should go to the office to check in, but no one from the show would be there. Even Raquel didn't spend that much time in the office. Instead, she slid the van door closed and headed for the subway.

She made it home without falling asleep and shoved the door to her apartment open with her foot while sifting through the day's mail. She dropped it, along with her keys, in a bowl by the door and jammed her coat into the closet on her way to the kitchen. Living in New York after growing up in Canada had taken some getting used to. The house they lived in when she was a kid wasn't palatial but it had space and a yard. They had dogs and a backyard rink where she and her friends and cousins beat the shit out of each other until her mom told them to come inside to eat. After dinner, they'd play until their hands got too cold to hold their sticks or they stopped being able to see the puck in the dark.

Her apartment felt smaller than their backyard rink. But being away from home and doing a job she loved, most of the time, felt as freeing as those nights they played forever. It was hers, only hers, in a way that hockey never was. It let her try to be the best at something again but without all the baggage and expectation that came with her last name.

America truly cared so little about hockey that no one here blinked at the sound of her last name. It was just another name in the seemingly endless array of names in New York City. She loved it. She loved the freedom to be herself and chase her dream. Even if chasing it meant being lonely sometimes.

Her drive to get on TV had been the reason she and her last girlfriend broke up. Darcy hadn't seen the breakup coming even when her friends had.

How does someone with an uncanny ability to anticipate plays and see the future on the ice get blindsided by the person they love? They'd been living together and she hadn't seen the signs that Sabrina didn't have any patience left for Darcy's late nights and constant striving. She wanted time with Darcy, brunches and vacations together, and Darcy wanted to make it on camera.

Reaching into her fridge, Darcy took out the second half of the two-person meal kit she'd made earlier in the week. She and Sabrina used to cook them together but Darcy never canceled her standing order.

Pathetic.

While the food was warming, she reached for a beer. Her phone rang. She checked the name and took a sip of beer. If her sister was calling instead of texting it was probably something annoying.

"Hey, Kit, how's it going?"

"You a famous TV reporter yet?"

Darcy laughed. "If doing a goofy segment on bobsledding is what it takes, I'm a step closer." She explained what she'd been doing all day.

"Natalie Carpenter? Like, *the* Natalie Carpenter, who you…"

Darcy slid the food onto a plate. "The one from Team USA, yes, that's the one," she said before her sister could say anything else. She had no interest in discussing Natalie.

"Okay," Kit said, stretching the word until it sounded more like four syllables. "So, are the two of you going to be on my TV soon? And if so, how long before you end up dropping the gloves and killing each other."

"Kit, I am perfectly capable of being civil to Natalie. We're not fighting over gold anymore."

Kit made a sound. "Fine. Clearly you don't want to talk about her. Mom wants to know when you're coming home."

"Never."

Kit laughed. "Try again, kiddo. Mom and Dad are having an anniversary party and they expect all of us to be there."

Darcy groaned dramatically. "Dad already gave me the pitch. I'm not inclined to rush home after he tried to get me to meet with his buddy at Canada Broadcasting."

Kit was silent for a moment. "He misses you, Darce."

Darcy took a swig from her beer. "Don't you dare take his side. He knows I don't want him meddling but he won't stop!" It was bad enough for people to assume her last name paved the way for all of her successes without her father meddling on her behalf. She wanted to be able to tell people she'd done it all on her own, and if he tried calling in favors she couldn't do that.

Kit sighed into the phone. "Are you coming to the party? Please don't leave me to hold down the fort."

"Please tell me it's scheduled during the Olympics so I have an excuse."

"Definitely not. They're not stupid enough to give you an easy out. It's after the Games are over." She chuckled. "Who knows, maybe by then you and Natalie will be back..."

"Don't even think it, Kit. There is nothing between us."

"That's so not true and you know it. It may have been a long time ago but—"

"Goodbye, Kit." Darcy hung up the phone and went back to devouring her dinner. Why had she ever told her big sister anything about Natalie? All of this would be so much easier if no one knew what happened in college.

At the time, she had to tell someone and Kit was the only one she could trust. Her teammates wouldn't have understood, and then she graduated. Fuck. Why on earth did Nat have to be the one the network found to do this stupid show with her?

Not stupid. It was her dream, or at least a step toward her dream. If working with Natalie was the price to pay to get where she wanted to go, she would handle it. She would handle the snarky digs, the eye rolls. She'd handle Natalie calling her princess. She'd even handle the memories that floated into her head whenever they were together and had more than five seconds of downtime.

She could handle it. She just needed everyone else to pretend whatever history they had didn't exist. If they could, she could.

She collapsed on the couch, turned on *SportsCenter*, and listened to the commentators talk about how Team USA was shaping up for the Olympics. First up, their take on women's ice hockey.

Fuck, this was going to be impossible.

Chapter Seventeen

It defied the laws of nature, but somehow sitting at a giant table in a conference room was more nerve-wracking than playing in the gold medal game. Natalie's right leg bounced up and down underneath the table while she waited for Raquel and the other producers to come in to watch the edited segment they shot the day before.

It wasn't a championship game, but her immediate future depended on what those producers thought of their mock segment. If they didn't like it, she was going to have to find a regular job. The boring kind that didn't involve a trip to the Olympics and the chance to be made instantly famous. Women's hockey players aren't generally household names. Maybe during the Games every four years, fans might learn a few names, but that wasn't the kind of fame that might help her pay her bills.

Once the Games ended, most of the fans in the U.S. went back to watching men's sports. Being on TV, even doing something silly like learning how to play other sports for entertainment, would make her more famous than winning gold ever could.

The door swung open and Raquel walked in, trailed by a group of white men in matching suits. She plugged a flash drive into the computer at the front of the room. "Okay, are you ready to see this?"

"Where's LaCroix?" Natalie looked toward the door in time to see her question answered.

"Aw, did you miss me?" Darcy said, taking a seat across the table.

Natalie sighed. "No, just wondering if royalty had to be here or not."

Darcy rolled her eyes and leaned her chair back. "This would be a lot more annoying if it wasn't so obvious how jealous you are. Get over it, Carpenter."

Raquel flicked the lights off and on. "If you two are done shit-talking, we can get started." She looked at them with the air of an incredibly disappointed teacher. "We pulled together what we think is a good intro for your new segment and then we cut together some of the footage from yesterday so you two can see what we're looking for from this. Any questions?" She made it clear that she didn't actually care if anyone had a question.

The intro began with still photos of Natalie and Darcy along with highlights of their careers. Natalie squashed the jealousy rising in her at the sight of "three-time Olympic gold medal winner" next to Darcy's name and only "gold medalist" next to her own. She should have been on the team this year to win that second gold. That was the plan, not sitting here watching a list of all the ways she was second-best scroll across the screen.

The intro quickly morphed from photos to footage of Darcy and Natalie playing against each other. The montage seemed to contain every time the two of them had collided on the ice. The final shots, of each of them receiving their gold medals, were the proudest and hardest to take. Each time one of them received gold the other had gotten silver. It sucked to know that one of them winning meant the other had lost in the biggest game of her life.

The final clip was of the two of them, looking like kids, from their college days. Together, they hoisted the NCAA championship trophy and skated around the ice. It ended with two pictures, side by side. One from college with their arms around each other's shoulders and one of them shoving each other in the Olympics.

"The tagline is 'Friends or Foes?'" Darcy asked, her voice full of skepticism. "Come on, Raquel, why trot all this out?"

Raquel clicked on the lights. "We're here to sell a story and you two have a good one. Teammates turned bitter rivals now joining together on our show to try out a bunch of sports you know nothing about. It's going to be great TV."

Natalie scowled. It had been a long time since she and Darcy hoisted that trophy together, but it still brought back memories of what happened after. She didn't want to share any of that with America. They didn't need to know.

"Do you want us to pretend to like each other or hate each other?"

Raquel shrugged. "Whatever the public likes better, honestly. Like I said, we're here to tell a story and if that means you two have to play up the fact that you took a second run on a bobsled that made you throw up the first time because you refuse to back down, that's fine with me. If it means you want to show America that you're besties, I don't care. All I care about is that people are invested in the two of you as friends or enemies. Just as long as they're invested enough to tune in."

"Jesus Christ," Natalie muttered under her breath. She wasn't an actor. She could play to the crowd but she couldn't fake how she felt about Darcy. No matter what Raquel decided, it would be complicated between the two of them.

Darcy cocked her head to the side. "Can we see the rest of the segment before we decide whether we're BFFs or blood enemies?"

Raquel smiled and rolled the rest of the video. First, it was them introducing Liz to the audience and getting tips on how to ride the bobsled along with Liz explaining her history with Team USA and how she ended up at the training center. Then it showed footage from the GoPros attached to their helmets as they hurtled down the track. Someone had added a graphic that showed how fast they'd been going.

"No wonder I got sick," Natalie said when the screen showed them going over forty miles an hour.

They cut to the two of them agreeing to another race, complete with a short intro from Liz about how she didn't think it was the best idea for Natalie to do it.

"I don't think I've ever seen someone get sick and still want to do it again," Liz told the camera with a shake of her head. "She's some kind of competitor."

Finally, it ended with their second runs and final times. Even though she knew the outcome, Natalie still hated seeing the confirmation that Darcy beat her down the mountain.

"I'll get her next time," Natalie told the camera.

"We hope you'll tune in to all of our coverage," Darcy said to end the segment.

Raquel paused the footage. "It's rough and far from perfect, but whatever competitiveness you two have going on, friendly or not, we think it's going to make people want to tune in. We're going to run with it. First of all, it should be obvious that we want you two to do this job. Congratulations."

Natalie let out a breath. Thank god she could put off being a real adult for at least a few more weeks.

Darcy smiled, big and dazzling. "You're going to put us on the broadcast?"

Raquel smiled back. "Yes, we all agree that the two of you will be an excellent change from our usual coverage."

One of the other producers, Gerry, chuckled. "Yes, it will be nice to have athletes learning how to play these sports instead of Chip." The other producers all laughed; some looked nervous about doing so, though.

Natalie raised her hand. "Okay, so the angle is that we're athletic but still making an ass out of ourselves trying these other sports? And you want us to be cutthroat with each other? Am I getting all of this right?"

Darcy shot her a warning look. Natalie didn't care. She wasn't planning on fucking this up but she wanted to know what she was getting herself into before she agreed. Making a complete ass of herself on television wasn't exactly what she had in mind. If she was going to do it, she wanted to make sure it was worth her while.

Raquel adjusted her glasses. "We aren't asking you to do anything that will damage your brands but we're hoping that the audience will love watching the two of you compete against each other, and if you look silly trying sports you've never played before that will be good TV, too. But I promise, we're not trying to make anyone look stupid."

Darcy looked across the table. "You know how hard it is to play at a high level. Of course, we're going to look silly doing stuff we've never done before but think of how much more respect the other athletes will get if people can watch world-class athletes sucking at sports that look easy on TV."

Natalie nodded slowly. "That's fine. But I draw the line at goofy outfits. I will not wear a tutu. Understood?"

Chapter Eighteen

The idea of Natalie Carpenter, a woman who spent most of her life in team sweats, in a tutu nearly killed Darcy. She laughed so hard the sip of coffee in her mouth threatened to exit via her nose.

Raquel and the other producers seemed to be considering the idea for way too long.

"I swear to god, if you try to put me in one of those ice-dancing outfits, I will walk out." Natalie's voice had a hard edge beneath the joking.

Raquel held up her hands. "Fine. We agree that we will not ask you to wear any figure skating outfits." She looked at the other producers. "Much as it kills me."

Natalie nodded and caught Darcy's gaze. "Anything you want to add, LaCroix? Do you need only green M&M's or your tiara polished every day?"

Darcy swallowed the urge to tell Nat to fuck off. This was her job, after all, even if Natalie seemed to think it was all a joke. "Yeah, one question. When do we leave?"

Raquel grinned and slid packets of information to each of the newly hired hosts. "Details are in the packets. We, of course, have to negotiate with both of your agents over terms and whatever else, but I promise, Darcy, you're getting a raise for being on camera and Natalie, I'm sure our terms are better than whatever you made on the Olympic team."

Darcy caught the briefest of shadows pass over Natalie's face at the mention of the team she was no longer on.

"Dog walkers get paid more than the national team, so I sure hope you are giving me a raise," Natalie said, her eyes skimming the pages of the packet in front of her.

Everyone around the table chuckled. Everyone except the two players who knew just how crappy the pay was. While the men raked in millions, they sometimes had to work second jobs to be able to pay for food and rent.

Darcy stood up. "Did you send a copy of this to Angie?"

Raquel nodded. "And a copy to Keena. They got it first thing so they could get back to us with any issues ASAP. We want you both to be ready to shoot some more segments before we put you on a plane. That way, we have some stuff to show if we have any technical issues. And you both need the practice."

Darcy laughed. "How dare you imply we weren't perfect."

Natalie paused at the door. "Come on, that footage of me puking had to be Emmy-worthy."

Raquel ushered the other producers out and then returned to the room. "Look, I had to push to get you this opportunity. The bigwigs are nervous that neither of you has much on-camera experience and they're worried that the two of you…"

"Are gonna suck?" Darcy finished the thought.

Raquel nodded. "I watched the footage you shot. You two have room for improvement, obviously, but don't lose that sense of fun. I love the way you two play off each other and bicker like an old married couple. Don't lose that. Keep the trash talk PG but don't stop doing it. I think our viewers are going to eat it up."

Darcy looked over at Natalie, who was chewing on the side of her thumbnail. "You up for this, rookie?"

"Bring it the fuck on, LaCroix."

Raquel grinned. "Get your butts down to wardrobe. They need to fit you both with all the Olympic gear before you head out."

After she left, Darcy and Natalie stood in the conference room staring at each other until Darcy shut the door and let out a whoop. "Holy shit, we're going to the Olympics!"

Natalie laughed and gave Darcy a high five. "This isn't how I planned it this year, but I guess this is as good as it's going to get."

Darcy's smile slid off her face. "I know you wanted to be there playing but this has to make up for it a little, right? You get to be there, at least, and you're going to get an all-expenses-paid trip without having to risk getting in a fistfight with any Canadians." Darcy smiled, hoping Natalie would join her.

"Those Canadians *are* a bunch of assholes." She sighed. "I'm glad I don't have to move in with my parents. That was feeling like a slap shot to the gut."

Darcy pulled the door open. "Come on, let's go load up on swag while our agents bicker over how much these people are going to pay us to learn a bunch of new sports."

Chapter Nineteen

An hour later both Natalie and Darcy were fully stocked with *Wake Up, USA*-emblazoned gear. There were enough shirts, jackets, sweaters, hats, mittens, and anything else you could dream of to keep them outfitted for months.

"They're going to send all that stuff over for us, right?" Natalie asked. "I don't own a suitcase big enough to hold it all."

Darcy smiled. "Yeah. They'll take care of all that stuff. We have to pack anything we might want that doesn't have the logo all over it."

Natalie pressed her lips together, fighting a giggle. "I was honestly surprised they didn't have *Wake Up, USA* logo underwear for us."

Darcy laughed. "I think they would have tattooed the logo on us if they could."

Natalie made a face. "I don't think it would go with the ones I already have."

Darcy stopped and stared at Natalie, trying to imagine Natalie's tattoos. She hadn't had any when they met, something she knew from getting changed in the same locker room for a year. *And all the times you saw her naked.*

After they won the NCAAs, a bunch of players got matching

ink, and she imagined Natalie was the type of person to have the Olympic rings somewhere on her body. She forced herself not to imagine where. She swallowed her curiosity along with a healthy dose of unwelcome interest in what Natalie had under her clothes.

Stop thinking about her naked.

Natalie cocked her head. The smirk on her face told Darcy that she knew exactly what was happening in Darcy's head. Darcy hurried past her toward Raquel's office.

She knocked on the open door before taking a seat in front of Raquel's desk. Natalie joined her, her leg jiggling up and down like she thought it was game day, not a meeting.

Raquel leaned back, her chair bouncing slightly under her weight. "I know I told you both that we'd be shooting a few more segments before you left, but that's off the table. We're sending you to St. Moritz tomorrow morning. The producers and I think your time is better spent shooting as many of these segments as we can on-site, not in the training centers or whatever."

Natalie leaned forward. "Why the rush? Don't you all have to hash out what you're going to pay us?"

Raquel sighed. "Yes, and if your agents would be quick about telling us what you want, that would be great. But it's a long flight and we don't want the two of you to be zombies when we film, so we're sending you now so you can see the venues, figure out who you need to talk to for each segment, and get ready to make us all smile first thing in the morning."

"What changed?"

Raquel looked at Darcy, her face unreadable.

"An hour ago you wanted us to stick around here for a few days and now we have to go tomorrow? What happened to make you change your mind?"

Raquel looked at Natalie and back to Darcy. "Chip asked me to make sure you were both over there when he arrives in a few days. Apparently, one of the producers showed him your segment. He liked it." Raquel's voice was even but her eyes flitted away from Darcy's.

"Chip? The lead anchor?"

Darcy cut Natalie off. "Yes, that's the guy."

Natalie made a face. It must be nice to be brand-new and feel free to make faces about the longest-running anchor in morning TV. Darcy had learned to keep her feelings about Chip to herself. It wasn't worth having anything she said filter back to him. He was mostly harmless. Mostly.

Natalie sighed. "You want me to get home to Boston, pack everything I need to go to Switzerland, and get on a plane tomorrow morning? I don't know if you noticed but I'm not Superman."

"Carpenter," Darcy said, her tone a warning. She wanted this job badly enough that she would personally pack Natalie's suitcases if it meant they got the job.

Raquel waved a hand. "You're right. It's an absurd request. How much time do you need?"

Natalie took a deep breath. "I've been in a hotel for three days. I have to get home, wash my clothes, and pack everything I need for, what, three weeks?"

"A month," Raquel said.

"A month." Natalie wiped her hands on her thighs. "This is nuts, you know that, right?"

Raquel held eye contact, unfazed by Natalie's mini-meltdown. "What do you need?"

"Teleporter," Natalie said under her breath. "Look, am I at least flying out of Boston? Because there's no way I can get home and back to NYC by tomorrow."

Raquel picked up her phone. "Jamal, make sure you schedule Natalie's flight home and to Switzerland out of Logan, okay?" She dropped the receiver before he had a chance to respond. "Anything else?"

Darcy had never seen Natalie so flustered.

Yes, you have.

The last time she was this flustered was when Darcy's lips were wrapped around her nipple. Darcy mentally shook herself. She didn't want to think about that night, especially not in her boss's office.

Natalie stood up. "I'm going to tell my agent to ask you for a ton of money."

Raquel shrugged. "Fine by me. Now, if that's all, you have a flight to catch back to Boston. If you need anything to make your trip to St. Moritz possible, you can call me or Jamal, and I'll be following shortly to the satellite office. It is very important that you make it there as soon as possible. Otherwise, we might not get to shoot at some of the venues, okay?"

Natalie gave a salute. She was a massive pain in the ass, but Darcy had to admire her spunk. She was diving right into a wild situation and not falling apart. It was as good a quality as any in a partner. Maybe working together wouldn't be a total disaster. Assuming they could keep their competitive nature to acceptable levels.

And so long as she could keep the memory of the feel of Nat's nipples hardening in her mouth safely locked away.

Chapter Twenty

She must have been out of her mind to agree to this. Natalie had taken a car to the hotel, thrown everything in a bag, raced to the airport in time to catch her flight home, and now was standing in her living room staring at the mess of clothes she'd spread on literally every available surface. What the fuck do you take to the Olympics if you're not playing?

In the midst of shoving all of her clothes into the washer, her Mom called her.

"Hi, Mom, you're on speaker."

"You are, too. I have your father here with me."

Natalie picked up an escaping sock and threw it in before starting the load. "Hi, Dad, what's up?"

"Well, we hadn't heard from you in a few days and we were worried."

Natalie rolled her eyes. "I had an interview, I'm fine."

"For a job?"

Natalie trudged down the hallway. "No, it was an interview series about failed athletes." Her parents didn't deserve her biting sarcasm but she was tired and stressed out and she did not need this shit right now.

"You aren't a failed anything, Natalie," her mom said with a mixture of pity and anger in her voice.

Natalie slumped onto the floor next to her bed to pick through the clothes spilling out of her bag. "Thanks, Mom. But I do have some news. I'm going to the Olympics."

Her parents started cheering before she could explain. "We thought they chose someone else, what happened?"

Natalie kicked herself for not choosing her words more carefully. "Not like that. I'm not going to play. I'm going to work." She explained about the job. "I'll be working with Darcy La-Croix."

Silence.

"Hello?"

Her father's voice came through the phone. "Darcy? The one you always fight with?"

Natalie sighed. "I don't always fight with her. We were teammates once." When her parents didn't respond, she could picture them looking at each other with raised eyebrows. "Guys, it's fine. The network likes the fact that we played against each other. They're using it in the segments. We're going to be learning how to do all this stuff and then competing with each other. I think they might be keeping score or something."

Her parents didn't speak for long enough that she was worried the call dropped and she'd just spent five minutes talking to no one. "Hello?

"It sounds like a good opportunity." Her mom couldn't keep the skepticism out of her voice.

"When do you leave?" her dad asked.

Natalie crawled across the floor to fetch her water bottle that had somehow rolled under her dresser. "Tomorrow morning. I'm home long enough to pack and then they're sending us to the Games. The timing is bananas but they want us to start filming segments right away so we can have access to all the venues."

"Tomorrow? But that's so soon! We haven't even seen you since you got back from Colorado."

Natalie flopped onto her bed. "Do you guys want to try to have dinner tonight? I don't have a single thing in my fridge but we could get pizza or something."

Her parents were silent for a minute. "We actually have plans tonight." Her mom sounded sheepish.

Natalie laughed. "Of course you do. I'll see you when I get back from Switzerland. Until then we can FaceTime if the time difference isn't too brutal."

"Are you sure you're going to be okay with this? Didn't you and Darcy have a huge falling-out?" Nat's mom really wasn't going to let this go.

"Mom, college was forever ago. I don't have to be her best friend to work with her. We'll be fine." She said it without knowing if it was true. She had to believe it, though. She had to believe that she and Darcy could work together and not flame out on national TV or kill each other over a curling match or whatever else the network planned for them. Of course, it could all go sideways, but Natalie had no choice but to hope for the best and fight like hell to make it happen.

Her parents didn't know the story of what happened with Darcy. They didn't know anything other than they had a falling-out and spent the next ten years beating the shit out of each other in every international tournament they played in. Her parents assumed it was just a USA-Canada thing. And it was, but there was so much more. There was also the kind of hurt that festers the longer you let it sit undiscussed. And she and Darcy had *never* talked about it.

Finally, her dad cut in. "We're proud of you. A little surprised that all this happened so quickly but really proud."

"Thanks, Dad. I have to finish packing if I'm going to be getting on a plane tomorrow. I love you and I'll let you know when I arrive, okay?"

"Love you, honey. We'll be watching!"

"Try not to swear on live TV!"

Natalie laughed. "It was one time!" Her parents hung up.

She stared at her suitcase. How had she only come home from camp a week and a half ago? One second, she was getting dumped from the team and now she was packing to go to the Games to be on TV. None of it made any sense. But that was part of the adventure.

She made sure she packed all her favorite things, comfortable pajamas, sweats, and workout gear. If they were going to have her learn to play a bunch of random sports, she sure as hell was going to do it wearing a sports bra that fit, and her favorite leggings.

Her phone dinged.

Pack your skates.

A second later it dinged again. It's Darcy. Unless you want to have to borrow when we're over there, bring your own.

Natalie walked into her living room, where her Team USA bag was still taking up most of the floor space. She couldn't bring herself to unpack it when she got home. What was she going to do, sell her stuff? Put it in storage? All of that felt too final. So, she'd left it sitting in the middle of her floor.

She unzipped the bag, revealing red, white, and blue equipment that reminded her that she wasn't going to be there with her team this time. She pushed everything aside until she found her skates and grabbed her gloves, too.

They were going to take up half her suitcase, but Darcy was right, if she had to go on the ice on national TV it was going to be in her own skates, not some shitty rentals.

She finished her laundry and shoved more clothes into the suitcase than she probably needed but she had no idea what the next month was going to bring; at least she would have her favorite clothes.

It was after nine that night that she remembered to eat dinner and almost 1 AM by the time she crawled into bed, clutching her phone to keep from missing the alarm she set.

Natalie wandered through Logan Airport feeling like someone had dropped a bag of gravel in her eyes. What was it about this airport and feeling terrible? It felt like yesterday that she was here with her equipment bag slung over one shoulder and nursing a broken heart. When she reached the counter to check her bag, the attendant's demeanor changed as soon as he saw her ticket.

"Ms. Carpenter, welcome. For your comfort, our lounge for our first-class passengers is located not far from your gate."

"I'm sorry, what?"

The guy smiled. "Show your ticket at the door and they'll let you in."

"Did you say first class?"

He chuckled and pointed to the number on her ticket. "Did you not know you were in first class?"

She blushed, feeling sheepish. "Someone booked it for me."

"Nice person," the guy said, before turning to the next customer.

Natalie hitched her backpack over her shoulder and found the lounge as soon as she got through the security checkpoint. She could get used to this kind of treatment. Maybe this would be the only time she'd get a chance to enjoy it, and she was going to make the most of it. She grabbed a cup of coffee and a stack of pastries from a continental breakfast buffet. The coffee tasted amazing. She didn't know if it was because it was an ungodly early hour or because the coffee was actually good.

When they called her row to the gate, she dumped her trash, grabbed a banana, and got onto the plane. The seat next to her stayed open even after the plane filled up around her. This had to be her lucky day.

When they landed in New York, the empty seat made much

more sense. Darcy stopped next to their row. "Good morning." She stared at Natalie's backpack, currently taking up the space on her seat.

Natalie moved it and shoved it under the seat in front of her. "Good morning. You sitting here?"

Darcy nodded and slid into the seat. "Have you ever traveled like this?"

Natalie shook her head. "I didn't know we had these seats until the guy at the gate told me I could go hang out in the fancy lounge. I thought he was fucking with me, honestly. What about you?"

Darcy chuckled. "Princesses travel in style, didn't you know?"

"I expected you would take your private plane, honestly," Natalie quipped. "But here you are slumming it in commercial with the rest of the riffraff."

"I wanted a private plane. I got you instead." Darcy shook her head. "Worst consolation prize ever." She gave an exaggerated eye roll.

Natalie let her head rest against her seat and studied Darcy's face. There was a hint of kindness under the words. "Seriously, are you happy I'm here?"

Darcy smiled. "And why would I be happy to have you here?" she teased. "All you do is give me shit. You're a giant pain in my ass and have been since you arrived on campus." Her laugh ended with a long sigh. "Jesus, was there ever a cockier freshman?"

Natalie tried to scowl but couldn't fight the laugh bubbling inside her. "Good to know you bought my act."

"What?"

Natalie paused, unsure if she really wanted to reveal this, or anything, to Darcy. "I was nervous about joining the team. You and the other seniors were players I'd watched and looked up to and I wasn't sure whether you were going to like me or hate me."

Darcy's smile disappeared. Her face softened. "You were nervous about meeting me?"

Natalie laughed. "That's what you took from my story? Such a princess." Natalie looked at the seat in front of her. Her heart pinched at the memory of how nervous and scared she'd been when she first joined the team. It was so much easier to give Darcy shit for having a famous father than it was to tell the truth.

She was scared out of her mind that they'd find out she couldn't keep up. She had been the best player on every team she'd been on since she was in elementary school, but this was a team full of players who had also been the best on their teams. What if they made her look like a fool on the ice? What if the coaches decided they'd made a terrible mistake?

It was easy to remember how that day felt because she felt it all over again in this job. She was a complete imposter. This wasn't a case of imposter syndrome, not this time. She had zero experience being on TV. She had zero experience doing any of this and she kept waiting for the network to figure it out and send her packing. Instead, she was sitting on a plane on her way to the Olympics.

Chapter Twenty-One

Once they had been in the air for an hour, Darcy took out a book and her neck pillow. She didn't expect to sleep, she was far too excited. Three years of working diligently behind the scenes finally paid off. She was going to be on TV. She was in first class, on her way to the Olympics. She felt like a shaken bottle of seltzer. She rested her head against the seat and stared out the window.

She couldn't help feeling a sense of déjà vu. Natalie waltzing in—fresh-faced and full of energy—and Darcy the more experienced one left feeling all the pressure of success. She looked at Natalie, asleep with her head against the wall. Clearly the pressure wasn't getting to her. No, that was wrong. Darcy was still trying to understand how Natalie had fooled her all those years ago. She'd been so sure that Natalie walked onto campus genuinely feeling like she owned the place. Finding out it was all an act threw Darcy more than she wanted to admit. What else had she gotten wrong about Natalie?

Rather than think about it, she pulled out a notebook and pen. Preparation always helped calm her down. She couldn't do a thing about the people who thought she got where she was on the power of her last name, but she could outwork them.

She could train harder, study more, and outwork every single person on the ice or in the office. She could control that. If she worked her hardest and people still thought she didn't deserve her success, screw them. The work was what mattered.

Kit's voice floated into her head. "When anything gets hard you retreat into your work. That's why you're single."

Darcy's jaw clenched. She shoved the thought aside and went back to work.

She started with a list of all the sports in the Winter Olympics. She'd tried skiing when she was a kid, before hockey took over her life and it became stupid to risk an injury. Her mom loved skiing but her dad never joined them on the slopes because if he got hurt he was in trouble with his team.

Once Darcy got serious about hockey they would hang out in the lodge. It had been their own time to sit and talk. Sometimes they talked about hockey but as much as she and her dad loved the sport, they didn't want to spend all their time together talking about it. Not when they could relax together. Sometimes the lodges had a puzzle set out for guests and they'd hover around that, racing each other to see who could put in the most pieces. They might not be talking about hockey but they never shut off their competitiveness. Once they played Sorry and she got so mad that her dad had sent her pieces back to the start she flipped the game board. At first, her dad was angry but then he busted out laughing and couldn't stop.

When she asked why he was laughing, he wiped his face. "Because when I was your age we had to stop playing checkers because your aunt beat me and I threw the board across the room. Your grandparents tried to discipline me but they couldn't stop laughing long enough to yell."

Darcy hadn't thought of that trip in a long time. It had been ages since she'd played a game for fun. She looked over at Natalie and hoped this trip, this job, would be fun like that.

Looking at the list of sports, she didn't see anything that

they could do where they wouldn't end up looking like fools. Yes, they could both skate but figure skating was a whole other thing. The skates alone were weird enough to make her fall on her face. That's probably what Raquel was hoping for. What's funnier than a couple of gold medalists looking like mortals on the morning show?

Next, she moved on to compiling the sorts of questions she might want to ask all of the athletes, regardless of the sport. How did they get into it? Who in their lives helped them master the sport—coaches, parents, friends? What tips do they have for people wanting to try it? And most of all she wanted to know if any of them had tips to keep them from making fools of themselves on TV.

When she'd asked for a chance to cover the Olympics, this wasn't what she had in mind. Maybe if she wanted to be a sports reporter she should have gone to ESPN or one of the other networks that were dedicated to sports. But if she'd called up *Hockey Night in Canada* she wouldn't have known if they were giving her the job because they thought she'd be good at it or because they felt like they owed it to her dad.

She wanted to do it all on her own, which was why she was working in the U.S. for a show that had nothing to do with sports except for once every two years when it became Olympics central.

Three years she'd been working for this chance and the fizzing in her chest reminded her of the way she felt on game day. She hadn't realized until that moment how much she missed this part of her. She looked over at Natalie. She wasn't going to admit it, but Natalie made her feel fizzy like that, too.

Chapter Twenty-Two

Jet lag was kicking Natalie's ass. Hard. To make matters worse, Darcy looked obnoxiously put together and awake. Natalie rubbed her face for the third time, hoping it might help her wake up. It did nothing other than capture Darcy's attention.

"Are you all right? Do you need more coffee or something?"

Natalie grumbled. "No. I'll be fine. How are you so freaking chipper this morning?"

Darcy shrugged. "I'm excited."

Natalie sat down on a folding chair and watched Darcy flick through her notebook. She was like a kid on Christmas morning. Despite her exhaustion, Natalie felt a nagging sense of anxiety. She'd come a very long way without much training and now they were really going to put her on TV. They had no idea if she would be any good or if she'd fall flat on her face.

No. There was no way she was going to fail in front of Darcy. She wouldn't give her the satisfaction of screwing up.

A production assistant led them to a truck where they had a bunch of equipment waiting. "We didn't know what you would want to wear for this, so we kind of brought everything."

The truck was filled with rows and rows of skis, boots, and

outerwear. "What do they normally wear for this?" Natalie asked.

Darcy giggled.

Since when did Darcy giggle? Natalie gave her a look.

"Cross-country skiers wear those spandex suits when they race." Darcy reached in and tugged at the leg of something that looked like it came from Spider-Man's closet.

Oh hell no.

"You want us to wear tights? On national TV?" Natalie touched the fabric and gave it a tug. Like compression leggings but for her entire body. No one needed to see that.

Darcy laughed again, this time sounding slightly hysterical. "*International* TV. Don't you want to wear this for millions of people to see?"

It was too early for this. "I'm not sure America can handle my hockey ass in those things. Do they even make sizes that would fit us?"

Darcy rolled her eyes. "It's spandex, Carpenter. The whole point is that it stretches."

"Fine, then you go first." She sounded like a petulant child. But whether it was jet lag or the thought of cramming herself into full-body spandex, Natalie couldn't stop whining.

Darcy smiled. "If it will make you feel less scared about the big bad spandex, I'll go first." She took the suit the PA handed her. "Come on, you big chicken."

Natalie took her suit and followed Darcy to the makeshift changing area to the side of the van. On the hanger, the suit looked too small to fit a tween, let alone over her ample thigh and shoulder muscles.

The athletes' changing area was in a building a few hundred yards away. The sight of it reminded Natalie that she wasn't one of them anymore. She was a TV person now. Not belonging in those places she used to feel at home made her wince more than putting the spandex on.

She stepped into the suit and the only word that came to mind was *wrong*. It was all wrong. She was used to the way her hockey gear felt, the way it sat on her shoulders and against her shins. She was at home in her skates. Here she felt like she was back to being an awkward little kid again, feeling like nothing fit right, scrambling along, pushing a chair to keep from falling over.

The suit was too tight. There was no way she was going to be able to fit into it without ripping it or horrifying America. She pulled it up over her shoulders and it felt like it was squeezing her toward the ground. She missed the comfort of her hockey gear. She missed her identity even more.

"Are you done yet?" Darcy's voice cut through her self-pity.

She looked up. "Hoping to catch me mid-change? Come on, LaCroix, have some class."

Darcy laughed. "Nothing I haven't seen before, kid."

Natalie blushed at the memory.

Darcy rolled her eyes. "We were teammates, or have you blocked that out?"

Natalie turned around and pointed at her back. She hadn't blocked any of it out. Darcy didn't need to know how many times she'd replayed it in her head over the years.

She remembered every second of it, from the euphoric beginning to the terrible end. That memory of Darcy blowing her off, pretending Natalie was nothing more than a teammate, was seared into her brain. "I think something's twisted back there. Do you see anything wrong?"

Darcy stepped closer. Natalie could hear the snow crunching under her feet and the whisper of her breath on the back of her neck. Fuck, this was going to be harder than she thought. No, she would remember that look on Darcy's face when she left Natalie behind. Fuck her.

The feel of Darcy's breath on Natalie's neck sent a shiver down her spine. Natalie chastised her traitorous heart for thumping faster. "It's something in the suit. Do you want me to look and see?"

No, Natalie didn't want her to see. Why on earth would she want Darcy unzipping the suit and running her fingers underneath it and along her skin? That was a terrible idea. But there *was* something wrong in there and it wasn't like she could see what was going on back there.

"Fine," she huffed.

Darcy snorted. "Wow, Your Highness. How kind of you to let me have the honor of doing you a favor."

Natalie stiffened at the first touch of Darcy's cold fingers. "Jesus, did you dunk them in the snow or something?"

Darcy spun Nat around by her shoulders. "Do you think you could stop giving me shit for five seconds so I can fix whatever it is that's pissing you off so much? God, you're a pain in the ass." She waited for Natalie to say something.

Instead, Natalie turned back around and gritted her teeth while Darcy used her icicle fingers to unzip the suit low enough to see inside it. If she weren't so grumpy she might have noticed the way Darcy's fingers trailed along her skin between her shoulder blades, or the way her heart sped up when Darcy pulled the suit back and let her fingers trail down her back below her sports bra. She might have noticed the way her body remembered the last time Darcy had been this close. She might have noticed the way her body reacted to Darcy's breath ghosting across her skin as she reached into the suit and plucked out the offending object.

She might have noticed all of that. But there was no way she'd admit any of it to Darcy.

Chapter Twenty-Three

"Here's your problem," Darcy said, showing Natalie the tiny bit of plastic that had scratched at her back and kept the suit from sitting right. She pulled her hands out of Natalie's suit, ignoring the way her hands wanted to keep touching Natalie's skin. It was only because her hands were cold.

That was definitely it.

Natalie turned around and took the piece of plastic. "That's it?"

"What were you expecting, a kraken?"

Natalie narrowed her eyes. "Thank you for saving me from the tag thingy. How can I ever repay you?"

"You could stop being such a gigantic smart-ass."

Natalie shook her head. "Never going to happen."

Darcy laughed and rotated her finger to indicate that Natalie should turn around. She zipped the suit all the way up. "You ready to learn how to ski?"

Natalie shrugged. "I know how to ski. I'm originally from New Hampshire, remember? I used to cross-country ski in gym class. The more important question is, are you ready to get your ass kicked?"

Darcy shook her head. "Carpenter, if you played half as

well as you talk shit you would've had more than that one gold medal."

Natalie's face flushed a vibrant red. "Fuck you, Darcy. Not all of us got where we are thanks to our famous last name. Some of us had to work for it."

She was going to kill her. Darcy LaCroix was going to ruin her chance at doing this job that she'd worked years to get by doing murder right there on the cross-country ski track. She walked after her, her eyes boring into the spot between Nat's shoulder blades. Who the fuck did she think she was? This was *her* gig. She worked her ass off to get here. Her dad had nothing to do with it.

Fucking Natalie Carpenter.

When they got to the tent at the front of the building, their equipment person handed them boots to try on. "You'll put them on when we're shooting but we need to make sure you have the right size."

Darcy slipped the boots on only to realize halfway through lacing them up that they were too big. "Do you have a half size smaller? These are way too loose."

The guy grabbed another pair out of a box and handed them to her. "What about yours?"

Natalie pulled the laces tight. "They feel fine to me. I'm not as picky as Cinderella over there."

It took every ounce of Darcy's restraint not to scream at Natalie. Instead, she ground her teeth together hard enough she was afraid she might break a molar and finished tying her boots. It took another ten minutes to get them the right skis and poles and finish outfitting them with hats and gloves.

"We have one with a Canada flag for you, and USA for you." He looked unreasonably proud of himself as he handed them the pom-pom hats. On the front they had the *Wake Up, USA* logo and on the back their country flags and their last names.

"Nice touch," Natalie said. She popped the hat on and fiddled with her gloves. "Wait, does this mean we're not going to have to get our hair done before we shoot, or did I just screw this all up?"

The guy shook his head. "Nah, I think you can have the hats on. It's freezing out here. I'm sure they're going to want to give you both makeup touch-ups before we shoot but you can wear the hats."

Another half an hour later, they were shaking hands with the Team USA skiers who had agreed to give them a tutorial. One was a white woman, shorter than both Natalie and Darcy and skinny as a marathoner. Even in her parka it was clear she was tiny in comparison. The white guy who came with her was tall, but also built like a greyhound.

He seemed really enthusiastic to meet them. "Oh gosh, I'm a huge hockey fan. My little sister loved watching you both play and got me hooked, too."

Darcy smiled. "Nolan, that's so nice of you to say. How old's your sister?"

He pulled out his phone to show her a picture. "She's seventeen." The picture showed him with his arm around a girl with his same deep brown eyes.

Natalie looked over his shoulder. "We can send her a message or sign something for her if you think she'd like that from a couple of has-beens."

"Really? I didn't want to bother you but she would love that." He stepped next to Darcy and waved for Natalie to get into the picture, too. He handed the phone to the other skier and she took a series of pictures.

"One of those has to be halfway decent." Karin handed the phone back to Nolan. He flicked through the pictures.

The camera operator walked over to the group, her camera balanced on her shoulder. "Are you all ready?"

Darcy and Natalie moved to the side so Karin and Nolan

would both be in the shot. The camerawoman gave them a thumbs-up.

"Good morning. We are coming to you from the home of the cross-country ski competition. We're lucky to have with us this morning two members of Team USA who are going to help a couple of hockey players learn how to ski." Darcy turned to Nolan and Karin to tell a little about themselves and how they got into the sport.

"You two are obviously pros at this, but how can beginners like us get started?" Natalie asked, transitioning the conversation to the part of the segment where she and Darcy made asses out of themselves.

Nolan handed them each a set of poles and walked them through how they would use their arms to help propel them forward as well as use them for balance. Then, Karin helped them put on their skis.

"Okay, now that you're all ready," Karin said, "I want you to practice moving your feet back and forth, just to feel the way the skis slide on the snow."

Darcy and Natalie moved their feet and looked more like penguins on dry land than graceful skiers. Darcy planted one pole in the snow to save her from toppling over.

Nolan chuckled. "Okay, some of this shouldn't be too hard for you. The other way we move through the snow is by using a skating technique. You're going to turn your skis out and push like you would on the ice."

Both Darcy and Natalie gave that a try and made it about three steps before Natalie's ski ran over the back of Darcy's and they both took a tumble into the snow.

Nolan and Karin glided over and helped both Darcy and Natalie to their feet.

Darcy looked into the camera. "You can see it's not as easy as it looks when these two do it."

Karin laughed. "Maybe it would be better if you went one at a time?"

"I'll go first," Natalie and Darcy said at the same time.

Nolan and Karin smiled. "Okay, why don't you go that way, Natalie, and then, Darcy, you can start a few seconds after her."

The camera operator took a few steps closer and gave them the thumbs-up to start. Natalie dug her poles into the snow before looking over her shoulder at Darcy. "Eat my dust, Canada!"

She took off, her arms and legs flailing as she found a rhythm. For all the motion, she wasn't moving forward very quickly. Darcy caught the eye of Nolan, who covered his mouth with his gloved hand.

Karin waved to Darcy. "I think you can start now. Try not to run her over."

Darcy jabbed her poles into the snow and surged forward, nearly toppling over. But being a world-class athlete, even a retired one, had excellent side effects. She recovered quickly and surged forward. "You ski about as well as you skate, Carpenter!" she yelled into the wind.

Natalie dug her skis into the snow faster and pushed as hard as she could with her poles. Darcy smiled as she gained ground. She came up behind Natalie and had to cut to the outside to try to pass. Natalie dug in harder, her strides improving as she got the hang of the movements. Sweat beaded up on Darcy's forehead, she could almost hear the producers freaking out about their makeup being ruined, but she didn't care. She was going to crush that cocky smile off Natalie's face, no matter how she looked doing it.

Chapter Twenty-Four

Back in the studio, Raquel had some thoughts about their performance. "Look, I love your enthusiasm and we got plenty of
footage for the segment…"

"But?" Natalie could hear it coming a mile away.

Raquel sighed. "But maybe you two could have given up
on that ridiculous race before we hit twenty minutes?" Natalie
heard the hint of a laugh bubbling beneath Raquel's stern words.

"You wanted us to be competitive, right?" Natalie looked
over at Darcy. "Besides, I would have stopped if she did."

Darcy shot Natalie a look. "We hear you. We can tone down
the competition."

"Can you though?" Raquel raised a single, perfectly arched
eyebrow, a smile tugging at the corner of her mouth.

Natalie laughed. "No. You saw us out there. We can't turn it
off. But we can use it." Natalie said it without thinking through
how. Raquel waited for her to continue. "You hired us, at least
in part, because we're Olympians, right? Why not use that instead of making us behave like every other boring TV host?"

"Carpenter, shut up." Darcy glared at her. "Raquel, we can
be whatever kind of hosts you want us to be. You hired us to
do the job and we'll do it however you like. You're the boss."
She shot Natalie another look.

Natalie rolled her eyes. "Fine. You want us to be just like every other show you've ever done, we'll do it. But you'd be missing out on the exact thing that makes this show better and more interesting than every other morning news show. And you'd be making a huge mistake to try to take something amazing and make it just like everyone else."

"Jesus Christ, Carpenter. You've been here five minutes and you're trying to tell everyone how to do their jobs." Darcy rolled her eyes. "You haven't changed a bit.

"Maybe not," Natalie said. "But you have."

"What?"

"You heard me," Natalie said, leaning back in her chair. "I don't know what happened to you over the last three years but you're nothing like the player you used to be."

Smack. Raquel's palm slapped against the desk. "Enough. Are you two done bickering like a couple of little kids?"

Natalie shrugged, not looking at Darcy. Darcy seethed. Not only had Natalie pissed her off but she'd been cut off before she could defend herself because she wasn't about to yell over Raquel. She liked her job too much to risk losing it now. Maybe she had changed, but not so much that she couldn't hold on to a grudge for later.

"Darcy, what do you think of Natalie's suggestion?" Raquel asked.

Darcy sat up, her elbows resting on her thighs. "I don't know what exactly Carpenter is proposing."

Natalie sat up, her posture matching Darcy's. "I think you hired us because we're a couple of former professional athletes who have competed in the Games. We played against each other for gold. I don't think it would be smart to put that aside and ask us to do whatever your hosts usually do, like bake cookies with snowboarders or talk knitting with biathlon competitors. I think you should let us loose out there. Of course we want to compete. We've been doing it all our lives." She gave Darcy an unimpressed look. "Or at least I have. Why not let us learn how to do whatever the sport is and then let us see how well we can master it. Tell me that's not good TV." She sneered at Darcy. "You may think I'm a stupid rookie but reality competitions are a big deal on TV. This could tap into that while also giving the athletes a platform to introduce themselves and their sports."

Raquel looked at Darcy. "What do you think?"

"I'm willing to mop the floor with her any time you want."

Raquel covered her mouth, but too late to disguise the smile. "What do you suggest?"

Natalie looked at Darcy, unsure for the first time. Darcy sighed. "Why don't you let us film it both ways. We can do the first segment where we learn how to do whatever the thing is and then do it a few times. Then we can film extra where we have some kind of competition. You can try it out by putting those videos on your YouTube channel. Give it a test run. It's not going to cost you much to do it and you get your regular segment either way. If the viewers like it, you can move the competition segments to the main show. You can come up with some kind of scoring system."

Raquel drummed her fingers on the desk. "You'd do all of that? And if people like it, will you do extra?"

Natalie shrugged. "What are the odds we get another gig like this if we do well here?"

Raquel thought for a second. "We cover the Summer Olympics, too. We could consider extending it. But no promises."

Natalie looked at Darcy. "I'm game but there has to be some kind of incentive. If our ratings are great, we have to get some of that benefit." She gestured to Darcy. "She's wanted this gig forever, right? If we crush it, she has to get something in return. We're going to be the ones busting our asses and looking like fools out there."

Darcy blinked. Was Natalie sticking up for her? After giving her shit a minute ago? She looked across the desk at Raquel. "She's not wrong. If we nail this, I want an on-air spot permanently."

Raquel wiped a hand over her eyes. "We haven't aired a single segment and you two are already trying to negotiate your next thing?" She stared at them but neither Darcy nor Natalie blinked.

"That's right. We know that the players never have the same power or security as the bosses so we're making sure we get some promises up front. If we perform, we want our due. That's all." Natalie crossed her arms over her chest.

If Darcy hadn't known her since she was a teenager she might have bought the bravado. But Natalie's smile was too tight, her fingers gripped a little too hard. She was just as nervous as Darcy, but Raquel didn't know that.

Raquel looked at Darcy, who nodded in what she hoped was a convincing approximation of confidence. "Okay. If this works out the way you two seem to think it will, you'll reap the reward. But if it blows up, don't come crawling back to me."

Darcy and Natalie stood up.

Natalie gestured between them. "Nothing to worry about. Together, we're absolute gold."

Darcy grinned. "I believe the count is three to one when it comes to golds."

Natalie shoved Darcy on the shoulder. "Why are you such an asshole?" She looked at Raquel. "Don't worry, the last time we were on the same team, we won it all. We're good together."

Darcy's mind flew back to the night they won that championship. She could taste the shitty beer, hear the sounds of her teammates laughing and shushing each other in the hotel room. But mostly, she remembered the way Natalie's body felt pressed against hers, the taste of her lips, the delicious feel of Natalie's hands snaking under her shirt.

"LaCroix!"

Darcy blinked.

"Are you coming, or do you need a minute with Raquel to tell her what an annoying shit I am?"

Darcy swallowed. "Please, like I need privacy to tell her you're a pain in the ass." She turned her back to Natalie. "You know she's an annoying little shit, right?"

Raquel gave a weary sigh and picked up the phone. "You assured me you could work with her if it meant getting on camera. So, if she's annoying you, you only have yourself to blame. I'll email you all the details for tomorrow's event. Try to get some sleep. The makeup people can only do so much."

Darcy followed Natalie out of the office.

"She just called us ugly, didn't she?" Natalie said with a giddy laugh.

Darcy closed the door and caught Natalie partway down the hall. "Not ugly so much as not as gorgeous as the people they usually have on camera. Everyone else looks like a model with a journalism degree. We're just a couple of has-been hockey players."

Natalie laughed. "With all the scars to prove it."

Chapter Twenty-Five

After they finished their work, they made their way back to the hotel.

"Look, I think we should talk about..." Darcy wasn't sure how to finish that sentence.

Natalie walked past her into the hotel lobby. "If you want to talk, that's fine, but I have to eat or I am going to lose my mind."

Darcy jerked a thumb toward the hotel restaurant. "This good?"

Natalie nodded and led the way. After the waiter took their drink orders, Darcy set her menu flat on the table in front of her.

Natalie stared at her menu like she was trying to memorize it. "Say whatever it is you're thinking." She glanced up. "You know you're going to say it eventually, just get on with it."

Darcy closed her menu and took a deep breath. "You can't go off on Raquel like that."

"I didn't go off. I was honest." Natalie looked up. "It's not like you were going to stick up for yourself or your value." She flipped her own menu closed and slid it to the side. "You're welcome, by the way."

Darcy ran one hand through her hair. Heat filled her cheeks and she tried to tamp down the anger and annoyance threatening to overtake her. "You are the most insufferable person I've ever met."

"Bullshit."

Darcy paused. The waiter arrived to take their orders and left their beers on the table. If she heard Natalie swear, she didn't show it.

Natalie leaned forward. "We both know we've been teammates with way worse people than me. But go ahead, tell me why it was wrong for me to get Raquel to promise you a permanent gig when this is over." Natalie tipped her beer toward Darcy before taking a triumphant sip.

Darcy's fingers curled tighter around her glass. "This isn't the same as college. You can't pitch a fit about playing time and get what you want. You have to be able to back it up. I've been working here for three years."

"Yeah, and it wasn't until I showed up that they let you on camera."

Darcy looked like she might commit murder right there in the restaurant. Natalie grinned. This was too easy. On the ice she usually needed half a game to get under Darcy's skin, but off the ice it was much easier. And much less likely to end with a stick in the gut.

Darcy took a long sip from her beer. "Did you just take credit for getting me on-screen when I have been working at it for three years?"

"Wouldn't be the first time I put you over the top, would it?"

Darcy set her drink down and glowered at Natalie. She put her hands on the table and Natalie thought she was going to leave. Instead, she let her head fall forward. Her shoulders started shaking.

"Oh shit," she whispered. "LaCroix. Darcy. Darce, I'm sorry."

Darcy looked up and when she saw the terrified look on Natalie's face she couldn't contain her laughter any longer. "Carpenter, you are hands down the biggest pain in my ass to ever walk the planet. But no, you do not have the ability to make me cry."

That makes one of us.

Natalie refused to allow herself to be dragged back into those memories. Not now. Not ever. Instead, she glowered. Whatever kindness she'd felt when she thought Darcy was upset evaporated.

"Any chance you can stop being a smart-ass for five minutes so I can say what I want to say? Then you can go back to be an annoying little shit, okay?" Darcy asked.

Natalie shrugged but didn't say anything.

Darcy waited another second. Once it became clear Natalie wasn't winding up for another onslaught, she took a breath and looked up. She held eye contact so fiercely Natalie squirmed internally. "You may think it's pathetic that it took me three years to get on-screen when all it took for you was to waltz through the door." Natalie started to interrupt but Darcy held up a finger. "Maybe it was that easy for you because I've *been* here, laying the foundation, doing the unglamorous work of showing up every single day so that when the timing was right I could take advantage of the moment.

"You didn't think that you showing up was the only reason we won in college, did you? That would be stupid. It was all of us. Working every single day to get better. Just because you showed up when all the pieces fell into place doesn't mean you won the title by yourself any more than you showing up here and getting on camera means this was all your doing either."

Darcy lifted her beer. "I'm not trying to take away the credit you deserve. I think we have the potential to do something great together, but not if you're going to act like you have nothing to learn. And while you're here, I'd appreciate it if you don't screw things up for me with my boss. Because you may not want a career doing this, it might only be a fun thing to try before you move on to whatever is next. But this is what I do. This is where I have been working for a break for the past three years and I will be pissed if you fuck that up for me. Got it?"

Natalie tried her best not to look like a teenager who knew her parent had made a valid point.

The waiter arrived with their plates. "Is there anything else I can get for you? Another beer? Some water?"

"No, thank you. This looks great," Darcy said with a bright smile. Zero trace of the fierce tone she'd used with Natalie two seconds before.

Unfailingly polite. With fans, reporters, random people who asked her about her dad. Darcy was always polite. Natalie had never seen her lose her temper or be anything but the nicest person to everyone she met. Everyone except Natalie.

Natalie waited until Darcy bit into her grilled veggie sandwich to speak. Darcy wasn't the only one who hated to be interrupted. "I'm not here to ruin your life, you know? I got cut."

Darcy looked up as Natalie worked hard to swallow her emotions.

"When this job became a possibility, I figured it was worth a shot. And so far, it seems fun. I like it but I don't want to be part of something that sucks just because you're so busy trying to hold on to your job that you won't go after doing something great." She took another sip of her beer. "I might be a giant pain in your ass but maybe you've forgotten that we were great together once, too. We won, together. And I think if you stop thinking small and safe, we might be able to be great here, too. Tell me you don't think a competition will be ratings gold. Tell me that and I'll go back to doing whatever boring-ass thing they do every morning to sell paper towels and fabric softener."

Darcy sighed. "Are you done?"

Natalie gestured for Darcy to have the floor.

"I don't know where you got the impression that I'm some kind of risk–averse ninny."

Natalie looked over the top of her glass at Darcy, whose gaze faltered for a barely perceptible moment. But neither of them was going to bring up what they were both thinking. That night, everything that happened after, was a big mistake. But it was also a long time ago. They were both over it, weren't they?

Darcy continued. "There are a lot of easier jobs than this one. Closer to home, cushier. But this is what I want to do. And I'm happy to take a big swing and try to make this segment memorable with you, but I'm not willing to have you come in here full of your usual bullshit swagger and fuck it all up for me. You got it?"

Natalie smiled, a little stunned. "Got it. Now how do we make sure we're unforgettable?"

Chapter Twenty-Six

College

The locker room after winning the NCAA championship was the happiest place Natalie had ever been. Her teammates were terrible dancers, especially with their skates on, but it only made the room and its thumping music more joyful.

Natalie was exhausted but she couldn't stop smiling. Her shoulder pads were halfway across the room but she was too tired to pick them up. Instead, she leaned back into her locker stall and took in the scene.

Someone shouted her name over all the laughter and terrible singing. She scanned the room and found Persky grinning at her.

"Carpenter, what are you doing sitting there like an old lady? We won!"

Natalie threw a tape ball at her. "What are you doing trying to dance? You look like a drunk penguin."

Persky flipped her off and continued her ridiculous dancing in the middle of the room.

Natalie should have been untying her skates and peeling off the rest of her gear but she didn't want the moment to end.

They'd won the NCAAs. They were the fucking champions. Every early-morning lift, every one of the awful dry-land training sessions, every practice that got them to that point was worth it and she was going to soak it in for as long as possible.

She finally gave in and let her eyes travel to the person she'd been trying not to stare at for most of the year. Darcy had the stall across from her. Natalie let herself look at her, her view intermittently blocked by the groups dancing in the middle of the room.

Darcy sat with the trophy next to her. She looked up and caught Nat looking. She smiled. It was the first time Darcy had smiled like that in months. There was nothing wary in it. It was uncomplicated, like she finally set down all the things that had been worrying her and allowed herself to feel this joy.

Natalie had to look away. She told herself that it was because it was too much to look directly at Darcy. But that wasn't true. It was because they were hiding this thing between them. They were hiding for the good of the team, hiding so they could win that trophy sitting next to Darcy. And now that they had...maybe things would change. Maybe she wouldn't have to look away.

Darcy's smile reached into her chest and tugged. Seeing it made Natalie want all the things she'd been avoiding the entire season. Natalie had been pushing aside that particular want for months. If Darcy spent months worrying about winning, Natalie spent the time worrying about how to avoid wanting things she couldn't have.

But with this final win the season was over. No more practices, no more games, and no more reasons not to reach for Darcy in public, no more reasons not to smile at her across the locker room. No more reasons to stay apart.

Natalie bent to untie her skates, her heart pounding at the realization. She snuck a glance across the room again. Darcy looked so happy leaning against the wall between the cubbies.

And hot.

Fuck, she was hot.

Natalie went back to focusing intently on her skate laces. They were soaked from the game and stubbornly refused to come undone. By the time she got them untied, Darcy was walking around the locker room, stopping at each stall to say something to her teammates. She hugged her fellow seniors and jubilantly thumped them on their shoulder pads. Natalie couldn't take her eyes off Darcy, her heart kicking into high gear as Darcy got closer to where she sat.

Was she going to hug Nat, give her a high five? If she hugged her would she whisper into Nat's ear, her breath tickling Natalie's neck? Would she acknowledge what was between them in front of the whole team?

Darcy stopped in front of Natalie and smiled.

"What's up, Cap?" Natalie asked, hoping to cover her nerves.

Darcy smiled but her eyes betrayed something else. Natalie hoped it was everything they had been pushing away since they met in the fall. But with the music blasting and the fluorescent lights, Natalie couldn't be sure it wasn't just a shadow.

Darcy dropped her hands to her sides, letting them swing. She looked nervous, maybe. But maybe that was wishful thinking.

She put one hand on Natalie's shoulder. "Nice work out there, freshie. Glad you figured out how to keep up with me."

Natalie laughed. "More like you figured out how to keep up with me, old-timer." Darcy shoved Nat playfully. "You would have half as many goals without me out there feeding you perfect passes every shift."

Darcy shook her head. "Maybe winning NCAAs as a freshman wasn't good for your ego. We're going to have to buy it a seat on the plane."

"It's not bragging if you can back it up," Natalie said, automatically. This argument was a well-choreographed dance between them. Next, Darcy would make a crack about Natalie being American and Natalie would respond with a dig about Darcy being a princess. It was comfortable, familiar, and the easiest way to move around the electricity between them without risking the kinds of sparks that could start a fire. Like waving sparklers in the air. It was a pretty sight without too much danger.

Maybe now, they could stop pretending they didn't know the kind of heat there was between them.

Darcy rocked back onto her heels. "We're going out later. And you're coming." She reached over and let her hand rest on Natalie's arm. Not on her shoulder, not on her wrist, but a spot in between. Like their dance. In between.

They had been doing this all year. What was another couple of hours? She could at least wait until they were out of the locker room to tell everyone they'd been dating all season.

"You got it, Cap," Natalie said, risking a smile that might give away the thoughts swirling in her head—thoughts she hadn't shared with her teammates, not even with her best friend.

But tonight, the season was over. They'd kept the secret. They hadn't torn the team apart, or screwed up the delicate balance of chemistry and magic required to take home the national championship trophy. There was nothing left to keep them from telling everyone, to keep them from kissing in celebration, and holding hands on the plane ride home.

Natalie was filled with a warm, fizzy calm. No more hiding. She smiled to herself before realizing she was the last person still in all her gear.

Crap.

Their assistant coach walked in as she pulled off the last of her equipment. "Carpenter, you plan on getting clean sometime this century? Some of us would like to go home."

Nat took a towel from the stack in the middle of the room before walking to the showers, carefully avoiding looking at

Darcy. "Coach, Cap over here is still making the rounds like the goddamned mayor and you choose me to yell at?"

"Darcy's the captain and a senior. She's earned a little respect. You are a pain-in-the-ass freshman."

It took every bit of willpower for Natalie not to flip off the coach. Across the room, Darcy looked up and met her gaze. Her eyes destroyed Natalie.

"Carpenter, are you trying to throw me under the bus?" She stood on the far side of the room, her skates and lower half of her equipment still on, her gray T-shirt clinging to her shoulders and, as if designed to kill Natalie, her chest. Darcy cocked a hip out and rested her arms over her chest, accentuating the lines of her well-muscled forearms.

Natalie turned away, entirely incapable of keeping her shit together anymore. She didn't know how to exist in this new world where she didn't have to keep them a secret. It was like her brain had gone from "no one can know during the season" to "we won, season's over, let's make out in the locker room" in the last ten minutes.

At least in the shower no one could see Natalie blush. When she stepped out of the shower, she found Darcy walking in. It took every ounce of restraint Natalie had not to stare. The arena towels barely covered Natalie, and Darcy was four inches taller. It was practically obscene.

Not that Natalie was complaining.

Natalie hurried to get dressed before Darcy got out of the shower. It was a stupid dance. They got changed and showered together every day and it was never a big deal. But today, once people knew, they would think back to every look, every second they were alone, and they would wonder. Natalie wasn't afraid of being teased by her teammates. She was happy.

She'd never been so happy. Tonight, finally, she was going to tell Darcy she loved her. Nat couldn't wait to be alone with her so she could say the things she'd been holding back for weeks.

But that didn't mean she wanted her teammates to know she was lingering, waiting for Darcy to drop that entirely too small towel. Darcy was more than a hookup; she might be the love of Natalie's life.

On the bus, Natalie was sitting in her normal seat by the window when Darcy appeared.

"Do you mind if I join you for a minute?" Darcy asked.

Natalie shook her head and moved her backpack off the seat. "What's up, Cap? Come to thank me for those assists out there?"

"You wish," Darcy said, folding her legs up to rest her knees on the seat in front of her. She stared at the ugly multicolor stripes on the fabric. "I thought maybe we could…" She trailed off and whatever she planned to say was cut off by their coach walking down the aisle, tapping each player on the head as she counted out loud.

"Anyone missing?" she yelled. "If you're not on the bus, call out." It was a stupid, corny joke, one she made on every road trip. But the team didn't groan this time. The season was over. They only had a few more trips on the bus together. Corny or not, the stupid humor felt comforting.

Coach waded through the aisle back to her seat at the front of the bus. "Okay, the national champions are ready to eat!" she shouted and the bus erupted into cheers.

Natalie screamed and banged her palms against the seat. She locked eyes with Darcy, who had her mouth open, her lips spread into a grin and her eyes sparkling with joy and something else, desire maybe. Natalie's stomach swan-dived at the thought of those curled lips against her.

Shit. I'm such a goner.

The bus stayed loud until halfway to the restaurant when exhaustion hit all of them in a long wave that crested through each row.

"What were you going to say?" Natalie asked, bumping her shoulder against Darcy's.

Darcy shrugged. "Nothing. It was stupid."

Natalie wanted to push. Normally, she would never let Darcy off that easily. But this wasn't their usual thing. That electricity, sparking around them for months, crackled in the air. They'd fallen into the mode of hiding the heat between them, but knowing they didn't have to now brought them back stronger and brighter than ever. One wrong move, one wrong word, and it might have exploded and devoured them both. Natalie kept her mouth shut and let her hand rest on her thigh. If her finger drifted to touch the outside of Darcy's leg, that could have been an accident. If it needed to be.

Chapter Twenty-Seven

After their segment on curling, Raquel called them into her office. Natalie and Darcy had a whispered freak-out in the hallway.

"Do people hate us?" Natalie asked.

Darcy shrugged. "I don't think so. I mean, the ratings have been fine." Natalie's eyebrows went up. "I've been checking," Darcy said, blushing slightly.

Natalie looked at Raquel's office door. "Great. If the ratings are fine, why is she calling us in like a couple of delinquent high schoolers?"

Darcy shook her head. "Let's go find out."

Inside the office, Natalie and Darcy sat next to each other waiting for Raquel to finish whatever she was working on. Darcy had a sneaking suspicion Raquel was making them wait simply because she could. Finally, Raquel shut her laptop and stared at them, her eyes unreadable behind her glasses.

She turned toward a TV set up against one wall. "Now that you two have done a few of these, I wanted to take the time to watch through today's with you."

Darcy swallowed. This couldn't be good.

Raquel's face gave no hint of how angry she was. Darcy

frantically thought back to every minute of the morning. She and Natalie hadn't done anything that outrageous. They'd both fallen a couple times on the ice but neither of them had dropped an f-bomb on live TV or anything. What the hell was Raquel mad about?

She turned on the segment. Darcy's eyes flicked to Raquel every five seconds in hopes of understanding why they'd been called in like a couple of teenagers being sent to the principal.

They reached the moment when Darcy, attempting to slide gracefully across the ice with the stone, ended up wiping out sideways and sending the stone careening almost into the next sheet. The camera caught Natalie doubled over laughing as Darcy slowly got to her feet, one hand rubbing her very sore ass. She moved in her chair, trying not to sit on the bruise rapidly forming on her butt.

Another minute into the segment, Natalie took a turn using the brooms to sweep for one of the real curlers. Instead of keeping herself moving up the ice, her broom ahead of the rock, she ended up slipping and smacking the rock like it was a puck instead of a forty-pound chunk of granite.

Darcy giggled but covered her face when Natalie shot her a look.

On-screen, the rock hardly deviated from its course but Natalie stumbled and when she tried to recover by using the broom like a cane, it snapped, sending her sprawling across the ice.

Raquel let the scene play out to the end, including a series of outtakes in which both Natalie and Darcy got second chances to land their rock in the house and failed slightly less spectacularly. She paused on a frame of the two of them having a sword fight with their brooms.

Darcy's heart sank. They had so much fun play-fighting and teasing each other that they forgot to act professional and now Raquel was so mad she was definitely going to fire them.

"Raquel, I'm so sorry. We got carried away. The segment was over and we got caught up in having fun. It won't happen again."

She turned in her chair, wincing as her bruise smashed against the chair. "Right, Carpenter?"

Natalie kept her eyes on Raquel.

Raquel cut in. "No. You're not going to change anything."

"What?" Darcy turned back, surprised.

Raquel rewound to the start of what Darcy thought was going to be their downfall. She paused on a moment when Darcy leaned toward Natalie and said something the camera didn't catch. She paused on the two of them leaning closer, Natalie's tongue caught between her teeth, her smile wide.

Raquel walked to the screen. "I don't know what this is. I don't know what's going on between you, or not, but whatever it is you have to keep doing it."

Natalie and Darcy looked at each other. "You want us to keep falling on the ice and breaking shit?"

"No. I mean, people like you two falling and looking stupid. But this…" She gestured to the screen again. "This has gotten people talking." She returned to her desk, hit a few keys, and then spun the monitor to face them. "You have a hashtag."

"#PuckingHotties?" Darcy's cheeks flushed crimson. "That's us?"

Natalie flicked through a few more tweets. "A portmanteau?" Natalie asked. Both Darcy and Raquel stared at her. "I know what a portmanteau is. Jesus, how stupid do you two think I am?" Darcy made a face. "We went to the same college!" Natalie rolled her eyes.

Darcy stared at the screen and scrolled through a page of tweets. "These people are shipping us?"

Raquel giggled. "Yup. Obviously we'd prefer they use the show's actual tags but we're happy to have so many people tweeting about the two of you." She sat down. "You have quite a vocal fan club."

Natalie stared over Darcy's shoulder, her face uncomfortably close to Darcy. Darcy told herself to ignore the way Natalie's body curved around hers. "It's not that many people, though."

Raquel shrugged. "Maybe. But they're dedicated. They made GIFs from the show today." Raquel played several GIFs that made it clear that Darcy's eyes had wandered to Natalie's mouth several times during the segment.

Natalie took a step to the side, Darcy's traitorous body noting the loss of pressure with disappointment. "Oh, come on." She pointed at the screen. "They've gone overboard."

Raquel pulled up a GIF set where they'd cut together a series of Natalie biting her lip. "Don't think you got left out of this."

Darcy sank into her seat, *not* looking at Natalie biting her lip over and over. "Why are you showing this to us?"

Raquel swung the monitor out of the way. Natalie remained standing, her weight shifting between her feet every few seconds.

Raquel gestured to the TV. "I think we can use this. But only if you're comfortable with it."

Natalie crossed her arms over her chest.

Darcy noticed the swell of her biceps and then chastised herself. *This is exactly the kind of thing that got people making GIF sets. Stop being so damn thirsty.*

Raquel placed her hands on the desk as if to show she was unarmed. "You are under no obligation but we thought if you were game, we let people run with this."

"This?" Darcy asked, afraid she already knew the answer.

Natalie slumped into the seat next to her. "Come on, La-Croix. You know what she's asking."

"I want her to spell it out," Darcy said, her eyes meeting Natalie's for an instant before she looked back at Raquel. She didn't trust herself to hold Natalie's gaze for longer.

Raquel leaned forward, her elbows on the desk, her face betraying her excitement. "We aren't asking you to do anything other than not shoot down whatever rumors appear online. You don't have to pretend to be anything other than..."

"Two retired hockey players who used to beat the shit out of each other on the ice?"

Raquel laughed. "Sure. Frankly, they seem to love the idea that you were these brutal rivals and now you're..."

Darcy cocked her head, waiting for Raquel to finish the sentence.

"Something more."

Natalie laughed. "We're barely friends at this point."

Darcy sighed. "She's not wrong. Before this..." She looked around the room.

"We hadn't had a conversation in, what, a decade?"

Darcy nodded, trying not to wince at how many years they'd been out of touch. "And now you want us to pretend we're dating?"

Raquel shook her head. "No. You don't have to do anything except continue to be your usual *friendly* selves. Keep up the banter and whatever you're already doing."

"We are not friends," Darcy said, a little too forcefully.

Raquel shrugged. "That's not what the viewers saw. Whatever it is, your chemistry is off the charts. I never dreamed you'd have this kind of following so fast. Keep doing what you're doing and if someone asks about you dating, just play coy. That's it. You don't have to hold hands or anything like that. Just let the internet do its thing."

Natalie gestured at Darcy. "Did you consider the possibility that we aren't single?"

For the first time in the meeting, Raquel looked taken aback. She looked at Darcy and then back to Natalie. "Oh shit."

Darcy sighed. "Raquel, she's messing with you. I'm single." She looked at Natalie. "And I bet she is, too."

Natalie shrugged. "The point is, you shouldn't assume that

the two incredible women you hired don't already have girl-friends."

Raquel's face changed from relief to annoyance. "So, you're just messing with me? This hashtag thing isn't going to be destroying your marriages or anything?"

Darcy laughed. "The job destroys relationships all on its own." As soon as she said it, she wished she hadn't. "I mean. Never mind."

She felt Natalie's eyes on her but didn't want to see whatever pity she might find there. Natalie didn't need to know that Sabrina had broken up with her because whenever they had a fight Darcy would retreat into her work. Sabrina had been right. But when it came to work, Darcy knew how to measure success. In her relationships, Darcy wasn't sure what success looked like. Maybe that's why she kept fucking them up.

Raquel clapped her hands. "Now that we've established that the two of you are single."

"And gay," Natalie said with a chuckle. "What if you'd hired a couple of straight women? Would you have asked them to play along with this?"

Raquel paused to consider the possibility. "I'm not asking the two of you to do anything that you aren't already doing. If you were both straight but so flirty that the internet was going wild with speculation? Yeah, I'd ask you to keep it up. It's not about whether you're gay or not, it's about the fact that the internet can't get enough of the two of you together and my job is to make sure our viewers are getting what they want."

Darcy looked at Natalie. "Can we get back to you about this? I want us to talk this over before we commit."

"Still allergic to commitment?" Natalie asked. "Or just to me?"

Darcy struggled to keep her face neutral. She didn't need a reminder of the way she'd screwed up with Natalie. That mistake lived rent-free in her head. Disappointing people, not living up to the hype of who they thought she was because of her last name or her own hockey stardom, was her biggest fear. Natalie was a walking reminder of her biggest failure.

She took a deep breath. "I'd like a chance to discuss this with you before we say yes to becoming the talk of the lesbian internet."

Natalie nodded. "We already *are* the talk of the lesbian internet, LaCroix. In the meantime, Raquel, have you considered what this might do to your straight audience? Are you going to be supportive when the right-wingers flip the fuck out over the idea that your cohosts are dating?"

Raquel nodded. "Yes, they might lose their shit but I don't really care. Besides, you're not going to be making out on camera or anything. If this goes the way I think it will, you'll develop a cult following that will boost our numbers and the right-wing conservatives won't even notice."

Darcy laughed. "True. They'll think we're just good friends."

"Gal pals," Natalie said with a giggle.

Raquel nodded. "Why don't you two take some time to think about it and let me know your answer by the end of the day. That way we can prepare for how to shoot the segment tomorrow."

Chapter Twenty-Eight

Natalie's stomach grumbled. "If we're going to talk about this, can we do it while we eat? I'm starving."

Darcy slung her bag over one shoulder. "When are you not hungry?"

"I know it was a long time ago but try to remember how hungry you were during your playing days."

Darcy shoved Natalie on the shoulder and then froze. "Oh my god. I'm sorry. That was super unprofessional."

Natalie laughed. "Are you kidding me right now? Come on."

They filed out of the office and found their way to the makeshift cafeteria the network set up for the duration of the Olympics. They gathered their lunches and found a table in the back corner where they could hopefully talk without interruption.

Natalie looked over her glass at Darcy. "First of all, since when do you apologize for shoving me?"

"Since we started working together in an office instead of on the ice." Darcy stabbed at a pepper in her salad and made a face when it flew out of the bowl. "Dropping the gloves isn't appropriate in a conference room."

"Maybe it should be," Natalie said under her breath. She had no idea how to talk to Darcy about Raquel's proposal. They should have said yes in the office and figured out the rest later but instead they had to sit here and talk about it. Ugh. Natalie did not want to talk about thirsty internet lesbians shipping them. Not while their chemistry was still off the charts.

Darcy rescued the wayward pepper and popped it into her mouth. To Natalie, she seemed in no hurry to talk about the weird speculation percolating on the internet and Raquel's request that they do absolutely nothing to make it go away.

Dammit, Natalie was going to have to be the one to suck it up. "LaCroix, what do you think about..."

Darcy looked up. "Climate change?"

"Oh my god, why are you the worst?" Natalie said, resisting the urge to throw an ice cube at Darcy.

Darcy laughed. "Come on. Stop being such a chicken."

Natalie's face heated. "Me? Since when am I the chicken? You're the one—" Natalie stopped, shook her head. "Never mind. We both know what happened. This is about now. Are you okay letting gossip run wild?"

Darcy shrugged. "People are going to speculate no matter what. Who cares?" She jabbed at her salad before abandoning it for a sandwich.

Such a Darcy answer. Don't rock the boat, go along with whatever as long as it doesn't cost her anything. God, she hadn't changed since college. "Seriously? I'm surprised you aren't more protective of your image. I thought you didn't want people knowing you're gay."

Darcy's head snapped up, her eyes fierce. "Fuck you, Carpenter. You know that's not true."

"Why would I know that? Because you've done such a good job of coming out during your career?"

"Is this still about college? I said I was sorry. I screwed up. But that was forever ago. Let it go."

Natalie gave a harsh laugh. "I'm not still hung up on college but it's interesting that you bring it up. You were so scared that anyone might find out that you weren't the straight girl poster child, so scared of being vulnerable. You didn't care who you hurt."

Darcy couldn't hide the surprise on her face. "If you really think that I'm that shitty of a person what are you even doing here?" Her hand gripped her fork so tightly her skin turned white at the knuckles.

"I'm here for a job. And my feeling is we can do whatever they want us to do to get the job done. If that means playing coy if someone asks if we're dating, I don't care. But it sounds like you might want to pull up Twitter and kill the rumors right now." Natalie opened her phone and slid it across the table. "Go on. One word from you and no one will think you would ever date me in a million years. Go ahead. I know you know how to say that." Natalie hadn't meant for the hurt in her voice to be there. She was over what happened. She didn't care that Darcy had called Sammy out for thinking she'd ever have anything to do with Natalie.

That was ages ago.

"Carpenter." Darcy's voice was low and gentle. "I'm so sorry."

Natalie waved her hand. "It's fine. Like you said, it was a long time ago. What are we going to do now?"

Darcy stared at the screen. "I'm not in the closet. People know I'm gay."

"Do they, though?"

Darcy huffed. "Do you want me to come out right now because you're daring me to? That seems pretty stupid especially given that there's a hashtag for people who think we're sleeping together."

Natalie leaned back in her chair. "You don't have to make any kind of big statement if you don't want to. I don't care." She kept saying she didn't care but it sounded like a lie even in her own ears. "All we have to do now is decide if we are going to go along with this silly little stunt or not. It's your call."

Darcy sat there, staring at Natalie, every thought playing across her face. "If you can handle it, I'm in."

Natalie laughed. "If I can handle it? What is that supposed to mean?"

Darcy shrugged, a smile playing at the corners of her mouth. "I don't want you to get confused or overwhelmed by my hotness, that's all."

Natalie shook her head and threw a balled-up napkin across the table. "Believe me, I can handle whatever you throw at me." Natalie had long since shut down whatever part of her had been in love with Darcy. She'd replaced it with a thick wall that never let anyone get close enough to hurt her like that ever again. Sometimes it was hard to remember that other people weren't Darcy and might not crush her the same way. But not this time. This time she was not going to have any problem avoiding being hurt. She wasn't a nineteen-year-old anymore. She knew how to protect herself.

Darcy smirked. "Challenge accepted, Carpenter."

Chapter Twenty-Nine

College

When the team reached the hotel, the coaches stood at the front of the bus to tell the players to stay in their seats for an announcement.

"Darcy, I'm counting on you and Sammy to make sure no one gets out of hand. If you are worried at all, you call me. You can call any of us. Got it?" Coach held eye contact with Darcy and then Sammy for what felt like an eternity. Natalie's finger rested on Darcy's leg. She didn't move away.

"Ladies, let me remind you that you are representatives of your university. If you wish to remain students at the school and members of this team, you will do well to remember that and keep your shit under control. Am I understood?"

"Yes, Coach," the players said in unison.

As the team shuffled off the bus, Coach stared at each player as she passed. Darcy walked in behind the rest of the team, hovering near Natalie. Natalie was keenly aware of her presence as she had been all year and knew where she was all the time. On the ice, it made their chemistry unbeatable. She could find Darcy with passes other people wouldn't even attempt. But off the ice, it was absolute torture. Torture for Natalie to know where Darcy was and having to remember not to stare, not to find herself "accidentally" wandering over to her at every event, every party, only to realize she had no other reason to be there.

"Star" was the right word. From the moment they met in the orchard, Natalie orbited Darcy. A lone planet circling without getting any closer until the coaches made them roommates and the force of their attraction was too much to resist. But after that, in public, Natalie kept away, the force of their status as teammates keeping them from letting anyone know they were more than friends. Natalie would circle but find herself unable to cross that threshold, that barrier between them. In private, tucked away from their teammates and roommates and anyone else, they could be together. Stolen kisses, study sessions in the library where they found an abandoned corner in the stacks to make out, trips to the movie theater two towns over, they could be themselves only when they were alone. It had been hard to pretend she wasn't deeply in love with Darcy.

After they'd kissed that first time, Darcy had told Natalie they had to be a secret. She explained, her eyes wet with tears, how breaking up with one of her former teammates had torn the team apart. Darcy had vowed never to date another teammate, especially not in her final season, not with a national championship on the line.

But that was ending. The season was over. They'd won. And now they could stop pretending that they weren't pulled together like a pair of magnets, like every bit of their personal gravity wasn't forcing them closer and closer.

That night, with the NCAA trophy secured, that orbit changed. No longer was she forced into large circles, she could crash into the star that was Darcy LaCroix with the entire world watching and it wouldn't destroy anything because the season was over.

They weren't teammates anymore and the accident of having

been born in two different countries, two intense rival countries, meant they would never be teammates again. Goodbye orbit, hello collision course for two women who spent the better part of seven months trying not to appear too close.

That was over. Forever.

What they would decide to start that night was entirely up to them. They were in charge of what came next. For Natalie that meant saying the words she'd been holding back for weeks. She knew she loved Darcy but she didn't want to admit it until she could hold her hand and kiss her in public. She was giddy with anticipation. She had to remind herself to stop smiling.

They walked into the hotel and milled around by the elevators, waiting for their teammates to shuffle in ahead of them.

"Where are you?" Darcy asked, her voice low.

"Right here."

"What room?"

"Oh. 1224."

"1230."

Four digits never felt so loaded. Natalie forced herself to breathe. Passing out in the lobby was a bad idea given the night she planned to have with Darcy.

Darcy nodded and jabbed the elevator button again. All the other players squeezed into the last car, leaving Darcy standing with Natalie, the air between them thick. When the elevator opened, they waited for a family to step out before getting in. Natalie selected the twelfth floor and punched the close door button, not wanting to share any more time with prying eyes.

Of course, there was a camera in the elevator. Natalie wasn't stupid, but it wasn't the same as looking around the lobby and wondering if parents or fans or their coaches were watching them.

Not that either of them was a stranger to being watched. They'd just finished playing a game in front of a couple thousand people. They had both suited up for their junior national teams and Darcy had worn the sweater for Team Canada, too. Scrutiny wasn't new. But it was mostly reserved for how they performed on the ice. As long as they didn't embarrass their teams or countries, few people cared about a couple of women's hockey players.

They didn't get recognized on the street but that didn't matter now. It felt like the entire world could see the way Natalie's body tilted toward Darcy. Like a flower turning toward the sun, Natalie could feel her shoulders turn, even slightly, to give her a better look at Darcy.

Now, finally, they were alone and Natalie felt like a shaken can of seltzer, or one of the beers Sammy snuck into the hotel in her hockey bag. Natalie had waited months and if she didn't get to kiss Darcy soon she was going to lose her mind.

Darcy looked at her phone. "Everyone's meeting up in Sammy's room. 1214. See you there?"

Natalie couldn't keep the disappointment off her face. She didn't even try.

Darcy smiled the warmest, sweetest smile. "I don't want to go either, but everyone will wonder where we are if we don't."

"It would make telling everyone a lot easier," Natalie said with a shy smile.

Fear flickered across Darcy's face, but was gone in an instant, replaced with Darcy's eyes roving over every inch of Natalie. "I wasn't planning to tell everyone while they're drunk and celebrating. Were you?"

Natalie swallowed and shook her head, disappointed.

Darcy checked the hallway before leaning forward and pressing a kiss to Natalie's cheek. "Hey, we'll tell them, I promise. I just don't want to tell Sammy and those dumbasses when they're five beers in, you know?" She reached for Natalie's hand and gave it a squeeze.

Natalie nodded, delighting in the way her skin burned everywhere Darcy touched her. "Okay. Meet you in 1214 in a few minutes. I gotta ditch my coat and shit," Natalie said, her hands busy fidgeting with the zipper on her coat. Their faces drew nearer each other. But not close enough.

The elevator doors opened with a loud ding.

"Dammit," Darcy whispered.

Natalie grinned. That was all the confirmation she needed that she wasn't the only one feeling this way.

She grabbed Darcy's hand for a quick squeeze. "See you soon, Cap."

Darcy bit her lip and nodded, her eyes locked on Natalie's… Fuck. Her eyes looked like sex and fireworks. Natalie was so overwhelmed with the need to taste Darcy she could hardly breathe. Going to the party was the right thing to do, but Natalie *really* didn't want to do the right thing.

Chapter Thirty

Their first chance to set the internet on fire was in the figure skating arena. If anything was going to make the #Pucking-Hotties hashtag blow up, it was the sight of Darcy and Natalie trying out pairs figure skating.

"Good morning and thank you for joining us this morning. I'm Darcy LaCroix and this is my partner, Natalie Carpenter. We're coming to you live from the ice palace where in just a few days the figure skating will be getting underway."

Natalie smiled into the camera. "Today we are lucky to have with us two of the figure skaters from Team USA. Jenny and Jeremy Shankowski have been skating as a pair since they were kids and are here to show a couple of hockey players how it's done."

The couple, whose romance and subsequent wedding was the talk of the last Olympics, smiled their toothpaste-commercial smiles into the camera. Jenny spoke first. "We're happy to be here. We know you both are amazing skaters so this shouldn't be too hard for you."

Natalie laughed. "We've all seen *The Cutting Edge*, we know we're probably going to fall on our faces." She looked at Darcy. "Watch out for that toe pick, right, Darce?"

Darcy picked her foot up so the camera could get a shot of

the figure skates she was wearing. She hated them. The ice was her second home, it wasn't supposed to feel this awkward. She'd been skating since she could walk but never in figure skates. "I'll try to keep from falling on my face. We'd love it if you'd show us how it's done, so then we can show everyone at home just how hard this is."

Jenny and Jeremy pushed off and paused at mid-ice for the preplanned music to start. Natalie scooted closer to Darcy so they'd be out of the way of the camera operator. Jenny and Jeremy skated for about a minute before returning to the side of the rink, cheeks pink from the cold air.

"That was amazing. Can you give me a few tips before we try to recreate any of the standard figure skating moves? I don't know that we can come close to skating together without falling over, but we're going to try," Darcy said with a laugh.

Jeremy flashed a practiced smile, his hair falling over his forehead in a manicured swoop. "You have to be careful about not getting your feet too close together. It's really easy to get tangled up with each other if you're not careful."

Natalie smirked at Darcy. "Wouldn't want to get tangled up with you, that's for sure," she said.

Darcy could almost see the hashtags flying over that comment. Leave it to Carpenter to take things too far. There was a fine line between not killing the rumors and straight-up trolling. Darcy swallowed. She did not need to be picturing them together in bed while they were on camera. Jesus, what was she thinking?

"When we come back from commercial, you'll get to see Darcy and me try to skate like figure skaters. I hope you all bring the popcorn because there's no way this won't be entertaining," Natalie said.

The camera operator let them know when the feed had cut away.

Darcy leaned toward Natalie. "Dude, there's such a thing as going too far."

"Is there, though?" Natalie said, her eyes sparkling with mischief. She licked her lips.

Natalie was being her normal annoying self, but Darcy's body reacting to the sight of Natalie's tongue was unexpected. It was fine. They could do this. Darcy was a professional and she was not going to let Natalie throw her off her game. This was all fine.

She turned to Jenny and Jeremy. "Okay, this is for sure going to be a disaster. Feel free to laugh at us. If there's footage they can use of you two cracking up, that's great."

"You don't think people will think we're jerks if we laugh?"

Natalie pushed off the wall and skated backward toward the center of the ice. "If this is half as bad as I expect, you'll look uptight if you don't laugh." She stood up and nearly toppled backward. "Fuck! These skates are the worst."

Darcy covered her mouth with one hand, but her smile was obvious.

"You think it's funny, LaCroix? Come on, let's see what you've got," Natalie said, coming to a wobbly stop.

Darcy pushed off with the toe of her right skate and glided toward Natalie, feeling like she'd never skated before. The skates felt like aliens strapped to her feet. The only time she felt awkward in her hockey skates was walking in them from the locker room to the ice. Once she got on the ice, she felt free to fly.

These skates were the opposite of that feeling. The edges felt all wrong and she was keenly aware of the toe pick. She wanted to get through the segment without falling, and tripping over the toe pick was the fastest way for her to end up flattened.

She reached Natalie without falling over. "Ready?" she asked.

"One trip around the ice holding hands and then we're supposed to try to spin side by side. There's no way this ends well," Natalie said with a chuckle.

Darcy smiled, a warm feeling blossoming in her chest. It felt like old times. Before she'd made a mess of it all. They were smiling and bantering. This was how their friendship started. Easy, fun, with that hint of sparks just below the surface. It was so easy to fall back into that old habit. If the twelve internet lesbians and their hashtag liked it, that was a bonus. This friendship was a welcome surprise. Friendship. Yeah, her heart didn't get that memo. It fluttered of its own accord at the sight of Natalie's deep blue eyes and cocky smirk.

They got the word that they were ready to start shooting. Darcy took Natalie's hand, trying her best not to focus on how strong it felt. Her memory chose this moment to remind her that she knew what those hands felt like on her skin. She forced the memory away, focusing instead on the feel of the ice under her feet.

Music played and they pushed off, trying to sync their steps but failing miserably. "Oh my god, I forgot that you have no rhythm," Natalie said into Darcy's ear.

"What?"

Darcy pushed Natalie as far away as she could to avoid tangling their feet. This became much harder when they reached the corner of the ice and had to turn together. They bumped hips and nearly lost their balance. Thankfully, Natalie was strong enough to keep them spaced apart and upright.

They made it all the way down the ice without falling. Natalie pushed Darcy away with both hands and the two of them attempted to spin. Later, when they watched it back, they saw the wreck coming before they started the spins. A quarter of the way around, Darcy's foot clipped Natalie's skate and sent them both sprawling. Natalie spun halfway around on her ass and Darcy ended up sliding to the boards on her hip.

Darcy looked over at Natalie, worried for a moment that she'd gotten hurt. Instead, Natalie sat up, laughter rolling off her in waves. The sight sent Darcy into a fresh round of laughter, too.

Claps echoed through the mostly empty building. Darcy

looked over to find Jenny and Jeremy clapping as they glided toward them. "That was good!" Jenny said.

"That was terrible!" Darcy shouted back with a laugh. She found the camera and allowed Jeremy to haul her to her feet. "Tune in later tonight to watch these two professionals show you how it's done. Take our word for it, all those graceful spins and jumps are much harder than they look on the TV."

Natalie skated over to Darcy and Jeremy. "We'll be cheering for you to bring home gold." She grinned at the camera. "I hope you will all come back tomorrow to watch Darcy and me butcher another Olympic sport. Until then, we're going to find a few ice packs."

Once the segment was over, they thanked Jenny and Jeremy and wished them good luck.

"I really am going to find some ice packs," Natalie said, bending down to take off her skates. "These things suck. Have you ever felt so awful on the ice?"

Darcy laughed. "I haven't felt this awkward on the ice since I was a toddler." She kicked her skates off and left them in a pile to the side. "Good riddance."

Natalie reached into a duffel bag beside the bench. "Any chance you want to play a little?" She pulled out two pairs of hockey skates and a puck. "They said the ice is free for another hour. They aren't using it for practice or anything." She talked fast, her sentences ending like questions.

Darcy's chest felt warm at the realization that Natalie was nervous. Darcy *made* her nervous. "Hand me those skates so I can kick your ass."

Natalie grinned. "Whatever you say, old lady."

Chapter Thirty-One

The ice palace, which was designed for figure skating, didn't have any hockey nets. But once she put her skates on, Natalie went in search of something they could use instead. She found a couple of cones and a bucket in the hallway by the dressing rooms. She looked around but there was no one there to stop her from borrowing them for a few minutes.

She walked back to the ice with her bounty and slid one of the cones to Darcy before stepping out onto the ice herself. She retrieved one of the sticks she'd brought from the side of the ice.

She sent a perfect saucer pass to Darcy across the ice. Darcy caught it, her hands still as silky as Natalie remembered.

"When was the last time you played?" Natalie asked.

Darcy shrugged. "We had a pickup game with my family last Christmas, but I don't know if that counts. There's not much in the way of hockey for a has-been in New York. It's mostly dudes. And playing with a bunch of high school heroes isn't that appealing."

Natalie took a lap, enjoying the wind in her face. "I bet once they figured out you were an Olympian they all wanted to take a run at you."

Darcy grimaced and sped up until she was alongside Natalie. "Yeah. What is it with dudes thinking they have to prove themselves?"

Natalie shook her head. "It's only the ones who suck who feel like that. The guys who are actually good aren't jerks about it." She took the puck and fired a shot off the boards before sprinting to grab the ricochet.

Darcy slapped her stick against the ice, waiting for Nat to pass. "That's true. The men's team was always supportive of us."

"Yeah, because they have nothing to prove by trying to make you look bad."

Darcy took the puck and stickhandled, threading the puck between her feet and spinning with it before sending it back to Natalie. "Fuck, I missed this," she said with a sigh. "Don't get me wrong, I don't miss the beep test or lifting until my hamstrings feel like they're going to snap, but I miss the ice, you know?"

Natalie gave her a brittle smile. It had been a month since she learned she wouldn't be on the team for the Olympics. Less than five weeks since she went from national team member to TV host. It felt fine at first. The feeling of having something, anything to do after being told she wasn't good enough anymore to do the one thing she'd been doing her whole life.

"Yeah." She breathed the word more than spoke it. Skating was a part of her. The loss still ached. Being back on the ice reminded her of what she lost but maybe that was okay.

Darcy skated toward her, the puck seemingly glued to her stick. "You know, if you ever want to talk about anything, I'm here." She focused on the puck, not meeting Natalie's eyes at first. "I know how hard it is to go from living hockey to not." She looked up. "I know you hate me but I do know what it's like."

"I don't hate you," Natalie said without thinking.

Darcy made a face and bent at the waist to scoop the puck up with her stick. "Bullshit. You've hated me since… A long time."

Natalie shook her head and stole the puck. She didn't want to have this conversation. She wanted to skate until her legs and lungs screamed for mercy. That was easier than talking to Darcy about this, about anything real. The anger, the snarky banter, all of it was easier than talking about that night.

She took off with the puck, tossing a glance over her shoulder, daring Darcy to chase her. She heard the grinding of skates, the clop of steel against the ice as Darcy's legs churned toward Natalie. Darcy used to be faster, not that Natalie would have admitted it to anyone, but not anymore. Natalie was in top shape, ready to play in these Olympics if not for the decision of her coaches. She would have been walking in the opening ceremonies, pulling on the USA sweater, and doing everything she could to demolish every other team that got in her way.

Darcy was years from having trained like a world-class athlete. She was strong and fit but it was nothing like she once was. And Natalie enjoyed the feeling of taking off down the ice and leaving Darcy in the dust. At least she enjoyed it for a couple of minutes. Once it became obvious that Darcy wasn't going to catch her, she eased up. It was no fun to simply run away if the race wasn't going to be close. She stopped, cradling the puck with her stick, and sending a spray of ice flying before grinning at Darcy.

Darcy took the opportunity to poke the puck away from Natalie and sprinted toward the cone they set up in one end of the ice. She slid the puck across the smooth ice and yelled when the puck knocked the cone over.

"One, nothing, Canada."

"Oh my god. You're a child." Natalie took three strides toward Darcy and then swooped in to steal the puck while Darcy was still crowing about her goal. She took the puck out toward center ice before turning back. She dangled the puck off to one side, daring Darcy to make a play for it. Darcy did and Natalie slid the puck through her feet and caught it on the other side in time to redirect it toward the cone.

"One, one. And a nutmeg." Natalie said it with a laugh. "You better watch your five-hole otherwise this could get embarrassing for you."

Neither player scored on their next two attempts with the puck. They heard the telltale sound of a Zamboni starting and looked toward the end of the ice.

"Shit. We can't end in a tie."

Darcy nodded gravely. "Sudden death, Carpenter. Loser buys lunch."

"Lunch is free, dipshit," Natalie chirped back. She grabbed the puck and drove for the cone. Darcy poked the puck away at the last minute and leaned her shoulder into Natalie as she skated as hard as she could for it.

Darcy beat her to the puck and circled back toward the cone. She tried for a quick shot between Natalie's feet but Natalie was too fast. Natalie took the puck and raced for the cone.

The Zamboni honked at them. Darcy looked up. Natalie took her opportunity and slid the puck toward the cone. Darcy looked on in horror as the puck, seemingly in slow motion, hit the cone and knocked it over.

Natalie thrust her hands toward the sky. "Do you believe in miracles?" she shouted before picking up the puck and taking a victory lap. She waved to the nonexistent crowd. "Did you see that, folks? Carpenter took LaCroix on one-on-one and crushed her."

Darcy's laugh echoed through the building. "Come on, we have to get out of here," she said, scooping up the cone and the bucket and one of the errant pucks.

They hopped off the ice and waved to the Zamboni driver, who looked grumpy and annoyed. Darcy fell onto the bench next to Natalie, a smile breaking across her face.

"I haven't had that much fun in a long time," she said, her words punctuated by heavy breaths.

Natalie bent over to untie her skates. "I'm not a total monster. If you aren't looking for every reason you can to be pissed at me, we might have a little bit of fun while we're here." She cocked her head to the side so she could look up at Darcy.

Darcy's face was partway in shadow, so Natalie couldn't make out exactly what Darcy was thinking. "I don't think you're a monster. A gigantic pain in the ass, but not a monster. You're still the same cocky freshman who showed up on my team like she owned the place."

Natalie laughed, her fingers pulling at her laces. "It seems like I keep showing up places you've staked out as your own, eh?"

Darcy shrugged. "I'm glad you do." They looked at each other for a moment, their eyes softening.

"Hey! Are you two ready to go?"

Natalie and Darcy sat up, startled by the camera operator who popped his head around the corner to find them.

"Truck's loaded and we're starving. Do you want to ride with us or do you want to figure out your own way back?"

Darcy shook her head. "Two minutes and we'll be there. Thanks for waiting."

Natalie kicked her skates off, wondering if the moment between them had been real or imagined. With Darcy hunched over untying her skates, there was no way to tell if what floated between them was something or a mirage.

Natalie sighed and placed her skates in the bag. "Hand me those?" she said, pointing to Darcy's skates.

Darcy handed them over. "Thanks for thinking of this. I had a really good time," she said, a touch of pink creeping up her cheeks.

Whether it was from the cold or something else, Natalie couldn't be sure. Either way, it was nice to have some time with the Darcy she remembered from before everything went wrong.

She'd like to think they could go back to how they were, even if they couldn't go back to who they were.

That Natalie who fell for her captain and was destroyed by a few awful words was gone. But maybe this Natalie could be friends with this version of Darcy. Friends would be all right. Friends don't destroy each other, not like that anyway.

Chapter Thirty-Two

College

Hinch's room was a disaster even without twenty hockey players perching on beds, the desk, and the one rolling chair.

"Beer's in the tub," Hinch called to Natalie before she got three feet into the room.

Natalie stopped at the bathroom and found a tub full of shitty beer and ice. Gross. But she could nurse a single beer, it might even help her chill the fuck out before... She caught her reflection in the bathroom mirror. Was it obvious to everyone else what she was thinking about? Could they tell that her skin felt like it was on fire and the ache below her stomach was distracting her from everything that wasn't Darcy?

Natalie hoped that the face she saw in the bathroom mirror didn't give all of that away. As much as she was ready to stop sneaking around, she didn't need her teammates knowing how horny she was and how she planned to spend the rest of the night with Darcy.

Natalie waded through the players sitting on the floor watching an NHL game. She took a single disgusting sip of beer on her way to the only place she could see to sit. She perched her ass on the windowsill and waited.

It didn't take long for Darcy to walk in looking like the star she was. She walked through the room offering high fives, grabbing a beer from the tub, and flopping onto the bed closest to Natalie. Her long legs dangled off the end of the bed, keeping her shoes off the comforter. She took a long sip of beer and licked her lips.

Fuck.

Natalie took a sip of beer and forced her eyes to the TV. She watched the game without taking in anything that was happening on-screen. She made it thirty seconds, maybe a minute before her eyes found their way back to Darcy's face.

Darcy was talking to Sammy, her roommate for the trip. Sammy said something that made Darcy laugh and she tipped her head back, exposing her neck and the contours of her jaw. Why the fuck did she have to be so hot? This season—everything—would have been so much easier if Darcy was boring or not even ugly, just not hot.

Instead, Darcy was blessed with not only the best hockey genetics ever but also brilliant green eyes and the kind of cheekbones that would make a model weep. And her mouth. Natalie took another sip of her disgusting beer just to have something to do other than stare at Darcy and remember every time she'd felt those perfect lips against her skin. Natalie scowled.

Get a grip.

Natalie was jealous of the beer can because Darcy's lips were touching it and not her.

Natalie swallowed the last quarter of her beer way too fast and waded through her teammates toward the bathroom. She knew someone was already in there but it was a good excuse to leave.

"I'll be back," she said to no one in particular. "Gotta pee."

She caught Darcy's eye before yanking the door open and

disappearing into the hall. Natalie hoped Darcy understood because she was about ten seconds from losing her goddamned mind.

Natalie reached the door to her room and traced the numbers. 1224. How long could she stand there and not look like a complete creep? She didn't have to find out because Darcy's voice carried down the call. Not her words, but the sound found Natalie.

Darcy paused in the doorway and laughed at someone inside. She shut the door and turned down the hall, her face morphing as soon as she caught sight of Natalie.

Natalie slid her key into the reader and pushed into her room, letting the door hang open behind her. The time it took the door to close could have been a minute or a year. She had no idea.

She turned at the sound of the door clicking shut, hoping Darcy would be standing there. When she smiled, her back against the door, her hands tucked deep in the pockets of her jeans, Nat's stomach did an Olympic-caliber dive straight for the floor.

"Hi," Natalie said. *Wow, really smooth, Carpenter.*

"Did you need to go?" She nodded to the open bathroom door.

Natalie shook my head. "I needed an excuse to get out of there." She stepped forward, halving the distance between them. "I hoped you needed one, too."

Darcy shrugged. "I thought you might be trying to get away from me."

Her shy smile destroyed Natalie. "I've spent the entire season trying to keep a little distance between us when we were with our teammates. But I never, *ever*, wanted to get away from you." Natalie's eyes never left hers. "I came up with a dozen reasons to stay away, but none of them apply anymore."

Darcy shoved off the door, bringing her closer to Nat. Her

shampoo, something fruity, covered the rest of the distance. "You had reasons?"

Natalie stared at the way Darcy's collarbones peeked out of the V-neck she was wearing under her flannel. "Some were my reasons, some yours. You're my captain. You're my teammate. We had a championship to win. Team chemistry is important."

She waited while Natalie ticked off all the reasons. Her mouth curved into a crooked smile. "We won the championship. We'll always be teammates but I don't think we have to worry about team chemistry anymore." She stepped forward, her toes nearly touching Natalie's. The nearly was killing Natalie. That inch of carpet between them. Darcy was so precise, so careful.

"Why do you think I wanted you to follow me?" Natalie asked, running her tongue over her lower lip.

"I think some team chemistry still matters," Darcy said, her voice low.

Natalie's eyes flicked to Darcy's lips. It was heaven to be able to look at her without worrying that someone might notice.

Darcy shook her head. "You really are the cockiest freshman I have ever met."

"And you love it," Nat shot back. *And I love you.*

"You *are* impossible to resist." She leaned forward, her hands still in her pockets, like she wasn't sure if she had permission to touch Natalie and didn't want to scare her off. After all these months of stolen moments, she was still nervous around Natalie.

Natalie reached for her, her hand wrapping around Darcy's forearms, Natalie's fingers flexing against her muscles. A single tiny tug was all it took to connect their mouths. Months of staying away from each other on road trips, over. A season of avoiding sitting too close in team meetings so no one would notice the way Natalie's heart sped up when their eyes met, over. Sitting a few seats away from Darcy because the one time Natalie sat next to her their thighs touched and Natalie couldn't breathe for the entire team meal, over. They'd won the championship, and this freedom to be together was the prize Natalie wanted most of all.

Darcy smiled against Natalie's lips and Natalie couldn't help but smile, too. They broke apart for a second before Natalie stepped forward, pinning Darcy to the wall. Natalie stood on her tiptoes and gripped Darcy's hips for balance.

Darcy tasted like that shitty beer , and she probably did too, but after scrupulously avoiding each other in hotel rooms like this one, Natalie didn't care. All the electricity they built up over months shorted Natalie's brain because nothing registered but the feeling of their hips pressed together and Darcy's hands cupping her cheeks.

Natalie pulled back, her chest heaving. "Fuck," she breathed.

"What's the matter?" Darcy reached for Natalie but stopped short of grabbing her arm.

Natalie shook her head. "Nothing. Nothing's wrong. I just need a second, Cap."

She shoved her hands in her pockets, her shoulders curling forward. "No problem. I didn't mean to do anything or not do anything or…"

Natalie looked up. "You didn't do anything wrong." Nat reached for Darcy, her hand grabbing a fistful of her shirt. "I've been wanting to do this since that first road trip when I kissed you. It's just a lot."

Darcy raised her eyebrows. "Only since then? We met in August."

Natalie laughed and whatever tension there was in her head evaporated. "And you say I'm the cocky one." Natalie leaned forward to let her lips brush against Darcy's. Slower, gentler, less urgently this time. But that didn't last because the instant they touched, Natalie's brain broke all over again and the only thought she had was *more*. She wanted more of Darcy. Her hand squeezed Darcy's shirt, balling it into her fist so she could tug her closer. It took every ounce of restraint not to run her hands over Darcy's abs. She didn't want to rush this. She wanted to take her time, savor every single square inch of Darcy's body. Before she told Darcy she loved her, she wanted to show her, starting with running her tongue over Darcy's abs.

Darcy's hands found the hem of Natalie's shirt. "Can I?"

Natalie nodded and she had to stifle a moan when Darcy's hands splayed across her lower back. Darcy's hands were hot and Natalie felt where the calluses on Darcy's fingers traced the ridges of her back muscles.

Natalie stopped holding back. Instead, she shoved Darcy's shirt up and let her mouth find Darcy's stomach. It tightened under her fingers, the ridges of her muscles enough to make Natalie's knees weak. "Fuck, Darce."

Natalie's hands pushed Darcy's shirt higher and raked her fingers over Darcy's hot skin. She was like a furnace. Natalie paused, waiting for Darcy's permission before she let her hands find her chest.

Natalie was falling apart so fast. Her underwear was a mess, her brain hardly worked at this point except to urge her on. She needed more of Darcy and Darcy seemed happy to provide whatever Natalie wanted.

Darcy grabbed Natalie's shoulders gently. "Wait. Wait."

Nat dropped her hands to her sides. "I'm sorry. Did I—"

"No. You're good. I want to check with you. How much did you have to drink?"

Natalie smiled, delighted by Darcy's sweetness. "I had one nasty-ass beer while I waited for you to show up. I'm not drunk. I know what I'm doing." Natalie kissed her cheek, her lips feather-light on Darcy's skin. "You?"

She closed her eyes and let out the softest hum. "Same. I'm good. But this is too important to screw up, you know?"

"I know, Cap. I know." A wave of panic hit Natalie. "Do you want to go back? If you don't want to… We can go back."

Natalie was not a person who prayed. Religion was stupid, as far as she was concerned, and asking someone who doesn't exist for things, like god is a vending machine, seemed like one of the most pointless things Natalie could imagine. But in that moment, she prayed that Darcy would say no, I want to stay with you.

Darcy's smile spread crookedly up one side. "Nat," she breathed. "I've wanted to be here, with you, for months. The only thing I care about is making sure you want this, too."

Natalie crashed their mouths together. Who knew how long they had before one of their teammates came looking for them or—god forbid—their coaches came knocking for curfew. Natalie had waited far too long to take it slow now. She pulled Darcy's flannel off her shoulders and let it fall to the floor before tugging at the hem of her V-neck.

Darcy broke the kiss to pull her shirt over her head, leaving Natalie staring at her boobs.

"Jesus, Darcy." Natalie reached to undo Darcy's bra but, in her excitement, couldn't get the fucking thing unhooked. "Goddammit. Help me get this stupid thing off!" Natalie said, her voice husky. Natalie kissed down Darcy's collarbones to the tops of her breasts peeking out of her bra.

Darcy reached behind her and dropped the bra to the floor. "And to think you're a girl who prides herself on her hands," she said with a wicked smirk.

Natalie grinned up at her before moving her mouth over Darcy's nipple. Natalie paused, hovering over it for long enough that Darcy huffed impatiently. Natalie hummed and flicked her tongue over it, savoring the taste and the way Darcy's breath caught in her throat.

Darcy might have been three years older and the captain of their team but Natalie didn't defer to her then. Natalie had a plan to get her into her bed as fast as possible. Darcy's shoulders fell back against the wall. She felt like a rock star knowing she had this kind of effect on Darcy.

All this time, while they were keeping their relationship a secret, Natalie worried that Darcy thought of her as an annoying freshman with a crush, not someone worth telling the world about, but the way she reacted every time Natalie flicked her tongue across her nipple was unmistakable.

Darcy LaCroix wanted her.

Natalie pulled away, her eyes trained on Darcy's kiss-swollen lips. "Hey, before this goes any further, and I really hope it will, I wanted to tell you something." Natalie took a deep breath. She could do this. She could tell Darcy she loved her, she could say those words. "Darcy, I—"

Before Natalie could finish, someone banged on the door. "LaCroix! You in there?"

Natalie looked at Darcy, her heart racing. "Do you want to open it?" They were going to tell people. Now was as good a time as any.

Darcy stepped into the bathroom. "Fix your shirt, then open the door. We can say we both had to pee." Darcy closed the bathroom door.

Natalie's heart sank. Okay, maybe getting caught half-dressed wasn't the way she pictured telling people, either. Disappointed, Natalie pulled the door open, revealing Sammy standing in the hallway looking like she had enjoyed several of Hinch's tub beers.

"This your room, Carpenter?" Sammy walked in and leaned against the wall like she needed it to stay upright.

Natalie scanned the floor and saw Darcy's flannel. Shit. Natalie stepped in front of it, hoping Sammy was drunk enough not to register what she was looking at.

Darcy opened the bathroom door and stepped out. "Sammy, what the fuck are you doing here? If you had to pee you have your own room."

Natalie ducked into the bathroom and closed the door. She stood in front of the sink, her hands shaking. When she looked in the mirror she was sure Sammy knew that she and Darcy hadn't snuck away to go to the bathroom. Natalie's cheeks were flushed, her shirt bunched on one side.

Through the door, she heard Sammy's loud voice.

"LaCroix, is that your bra on the floor?"

Oh fuck.

"What?" The shake in Darcy's voice was clear even through the door.

"Are you hooking up with the freshie? Oh my god! You fucking cougar!"

Natalie stood on the other side of the door, willing Darcy to say the right thing.

Sammy laughed. "Oh, this is hilarious. After all the shit you gave me for dating Matty, and it turns out you're banging a freshman, too?" Sammy cackled. "Hinch is going to have a fucking field day with this."

Natalie's blood turned to ice. *Come on, Darcy. Tell her the truth. Tell her what I mean to you. Please.*

"Pfff. Come on, Sammy. I would never. You know me better than that." Darcy laughed.

She fucking laughed. And it hit Natalie like a dagger in her heart.

"Dude, she's in love with you, though."

Natalie couldn't breathe.

Darcy laughed again; this time it came out sounding tight. "I can't help it that I'm irresistible. But, come on, Sammy, I would never fall for her."

Natalie slid to the floor, her back against the door, and listened as Darcy swore to Sammy that she would never hook up with Natalie.

I'm such a fool.

The room door opened and closed but Natalie didn't budge.

It had been a roller coaster of the highest highs Natalie had ever felt but now she was stuck at the bottom and couldn't imagine she would ever get up. She clenched her jaw but it was no use. The tears came and she didn't try to fight them.

A year of following the rules, pretending there wasn't anything between them, only to have Darcy treat her like a joke. Natalie had never been so humiliated or heartbroken. And she never wanted to see Darcy fucking LaCroix ever again.

Chapter Thirty-Three

After lunch, Natalie and Darcy got back to the hotel and went their separate ways. They needed to prepare for the next day's show, but first Natalie needed a shower. She'd made it into her room and turned on the shower when her phone rang.

She flipped it over and saw who it was. "Hello?" She walked to the bathroom to turn the water off. She'd never had a short conversation with Grace.

"Don't give me that hello crap. I find out you're dating Darcy fucking LaCroix from goddamned Twitter and all you have to say is hello?"

Natalie laughed. "Most people, when answering the phone, say hello. But, of course, you would think you deserved your own special response." She sat down on her bed but as soon as Grace started talking, she got up and paced the room. They hadn't asked her to lie but telling her best friend that the flirting—and whatever the shippers thought they saw—was fake felt like something Raquel would not be happy about. Especially because Grace had a big mouth.

"Stop stalling, Nat. What the hell is going on with you and the ice princess? Do I have to remind you what happened in college?"

Natalie felt a prickle of anger. "Oh yes, please remind me again how it felt to get my heart broken. I've forgotten."

"Clearly you have if the internet is to be believed. Nat, she treated you like shit!"

"I remember! I was there!" Natalie shouted into the phone before realizing she was in a crowded hotel and should probably keep her voice down. She took a deep breath, then another. "Do you really think I would be stupid enough to give Darcy a second chance to break my heart?"

Grace was silent on the other end of the line for a moment. "I hope you know what you're doing, Nat."

Natalie laughed. "I'm a TV host, of course I have no idea what I'm doing." She sat on the edge of the bed and felt exhaustion creep into her body for the first time all day.

"I've seen the clips, you're good at this."

"Clips? You mean you're not watching the whole segment? You're my best friend. If I can't convince you to watch, we must be really awful," Natalie said with a laugh.

"In case you forgot, some of us have full-time jobs that don't involve flirting with our college girlfriend for all of America to see."

"Stop being dramatic. It's not a big deal. We go out there, do some goofy shit, fall on our asses, and generally look like dorks. It's not the worst job I've ever had."

"So you admit you're flirting with her!" Grace gave a triumphant whoop.

Natalie let herself fall onto her back. "Oh my god, will you let it go? It's nothing. We have good banter but that's it. The network likes how we are together. We've known each other for a really long time, it's not surprising that we'd have a good rapport, right?"

"Hmm." There was silence for a moment before Grace sighed. "This good rapport, does it include you forgiving her?"

Natalie groaned. "Grace, that was a really long time ago."

Over the years, Natalie had tried to get to the place where it didn't hurt so much. But no matter how much she tried to logic her way out of it, the hurt remained. She wouldn't admit it, but that hurt kept her from being able to trust any of the women she'd dated in the time since.

No way. I'm not into Carpenter. It's nothing, really.

She knew it made no sense. She knew none of the other women she'd dated had done anything to deserve her wariness. She'd tried to let them in, but it never worked. She kept waiting for them to laugh and say "This isn't real, it was never real. It was all in your head." So, she'd kept them at an arm's length, or worse, never let them get that close.

"Nat. Whether you want to hear it or not, I'd be a shitty friend if I didn't remind you to protect yourself."

Natalie sighed. "I know. And I love you for looking out for me. But I promise you, I am not going to fall in love with Darcy fucking LaCroix. I'm too smart for that. This is a job. Nothing else."

Grace made a noise that suggested she was not convinced but willing to give it up for now. "Tell me about this job. From what I can tell, you and Darcy do a little interview, flirt a little bit, and then make complete asses out of yourselves doing shit like curling?"

Natalie laughed. "Nailed it. That's exactly the job. But the ratings have been good so far. Apparently, people love to watch us fall on our asses. And the athletes like us because we show the public just how hard sports are that they otherwise think they could do."

Grace giggled. "That part is true. Curling always looked like such a beer league sport but you guys convinced me to leave it to the pros."

Natalie checked the time. "Shit, I'm sorry but I have to get showered so I can go back to work."

"You're trying to get rid of me."

"No, we have to prepare for whatever we're doing tomorrow."

"I hope it's ski jumping," Grace said with a laugh.

Natalie groaned. "God, I hope not. I don't have a death wish."

After they hung up, Natalie collected some clean clothes and made her way to the shower. Grace was wrong. She didn't need to be protected from Darcy because she'd never let her get close enough again. She may have been a teenager when it happened, but the lesson was burned into her. This was all fake. There was no way Darcy could hurt her again when they were just pretending for the cameras.

Chapter Thirty-Four

After her shower, Darcy lay on her bed noting each place where her muscles already hurt. She couldn't believe that skating for less than an hour had left her muscles this tired. She used to skate for hours. She knew that skating muscles were unlike the muscles she used in her Peloton classes or even when she ran, but this was ridiculous. Natalie was going to give her so much shit when she realized Darcy was hobbled by a quick pickup game.

Lying there, waiting for Natalie to be ready to go back to the office, she was overcome by the urge to check out their hashtag. It was stupid but she wanted to see what people were saying. The people commenting on what terrible skaters they were and crowing about how hard figure skating is mostly used the official show hashtag. She was less interested in what they had to say than the folks who posted on the #PuckingHotties feed.

These people were funny and queer. They were her people. She wondered if they knew she was gay. She'd been relatively quiet about it but no one had ever asked her. It wasn't really polite in an interview about a hockey game to be like "and how many of you are lesbians?"

Clearly, it didn't matter to this crowd because they were having a really good time commenting on their chemistry. The GIFs were what had her laughing the hardest, though. Folks had taken clips from the show and turned them into slow-motion GIFs to "prove" that they were secretly dating. Every time their eyes met or one of them leaned infinitesimally toward the other, someone clipped it and turned it into a GIF.

She scrolled through them, realizing that they'd stopped being hilarious and started making her wonder. People had captured Natalie smiling at her, her eyes flicking from Darcy's eyes to her lips and back again like they were in a rom-com. Another caught the moment when Darcy and Natalie bumped hips on the ice. Darcy remembered it because Natalie was being a goof by hip checking her in their ridiculous figure skates and it almost made both of them fall over. But played over and over as a GIF, it looked flirty, like they'd been dating forever and this was the kind of fun they had together.

No matter what any of the tweets said, no matter how many GIFs she looked at, it wasn't real. She'd be lucky if she and Natalie were back to being friends by the end of the job. Everything these people saw on-screen was an illusion. It was their regular, former-teammate-turned-rival chemistry. They weren't pretending to date, they were simply leaving the rumors to percolate online without shutting them down. No big deal. It didn't mean Natalie had feelings for her, no matter how many GIFs she watched where Nat's eyes lit up when they looked at her. Not even the GIF of Natalie's tongue gliding over her bottom lip.

People's lips get dry. It's a thing! She argued with herself, one voice telling her that faking it was way too easy. They fell back into those old habits too easily for it to be fake. But the other voice shouted at her about how any chance she had disappeared a decade and a half earlier. She'd failed at being the kind of person Natalie could want to be with. She was so worried her friends would think she was a hypocrite—the same kind of "cradle-robbing senior" they'd long complained about—that she fumbled a stupid, nothing question from a friend and it hurt Natalie so badly she'd spent a decade trying to bash her face through the boards. In hindsight, a part of her had been so worried about how strong her feelings were and how that could derail all her other goals. Without her singular focus on hockey—and now TV—could she achieve the things she wanted? If she ever wanted to be more than "Marty LaCroix's daughter," she literally had to make a name for herself, and her feelings for Natalie were the only thing that came close to matching her drive for recognition.

She sighed and walked into the bathroom to brush her hair once more before Natalie showed up to go back to work. She only wanted to make sure it dried okay. Nothing weird about re-brushing her hair before she saw Natalie again.

"Oh shut up," she said to the voice pestering her.

There was a knock at the door. When she checked the peephole she saw Natalie waiting outside. She pulled the door open. "Ready?" Darcy asked.

"Uh, yeah. Were you talking to someone? I thought I heard you say 'shut up.'" Natalie raised her eyebrows, waiting for an explanation.

"What? No. I mean, there's no one here…and it would be weird if I were talking to myself…" Oh my god. Five minutes scrolling through Twitter, and she'd become incoherent.

Natalie shrugged. "Okay. I didn't want to interrupt if you were on the phone or something." She stepped back so Darcy could leave the room. "Grace called me before my shower."

Darcy turned and walked backward so she could face Natalie. "Really? Why?" Darcy held up a hand. "No, let me guess. She wanted to call and tell you how terrible I am and that you shouldn't even pretend to like me for a silly TV show because… what did she call me? Oh right, 'the fucking evil bitch who I hate with the power of a thousand suns.'"

Natalie blinked and jabbed at the elevator button. "That's some memory you have."

"It's not every day that you get screamed at in the dining hall by a near stranger. It left an impression."

Natalie tried to hold in her laugh but her shoulders shook. She was practically cackling when the elevator doors opened. A white, middle-aged couple stepped out and gave Natalie a look.

Darcy filed into the elevator and waited for Natalie to follow.

Natalie wiped her eyes. "Oh my god, she is going to *love* that you remembered. Yes, she was concerned that I might fall prey to your feminine wiles."

It was Darcy's turn to crack up. "Tell me she didn't say 'feminine wiles.'"

"No. But she remembers you and her hatred burns to this day. I told her there was no way in hell it was going to be a problem. Right?" Natalie looked up at Darcy.

Darcy was not going to give any hint of the way her heart took a dive at Natalie casting aside the idea so casually. "Obviously. You hate me, so..."

Natalie stared at her for an unnerving amount of time. When she looked ready to respond, the elevator dinged and the doors slid open to the lobby. Whatever the rest of their conversation might have been died when they stepped out of the shiny metal box. Darcy let Natalie walk ahead of her. She *did* hate her, right?

Chapter Thirty-Five

Natalie and Darcy took over a conference room when they got to the office so they could work together while they ate their lunch.

Darcy slid her laptop across the table. "Have you seen this?"

Natalie clicked the link and found an article that was a compilation of the funniest #PuckingHotties tweets. "Oh god, we're a listicle? Good lord."

She scrolled through them. Darcy leaned over her shoulder and pointed to a short video that spliced together their figure skating fall with seemingly every bit of eye contact caught on camera.

"Damn, this makes you look super thirsty, LaCroix. I mean, I get it. I'm super hot, but chill out."

Darcy laughed. "My favorite is the one where they compare you to Pepé Le Pew chasing after me on your skis."

Natalie scowled until she watched the GIF of his eyes turning into hearts right before he chased after a cat. "So I'm an inappropriate skunk who doesn't understand consent? Hard pass."

Darcy shook her head. "If you don't want me, stop staring at me like that." She pointed to another GIF of Natalie's eyes staring very obviously, *not*, at Darcy's face.

Natalie covered her face with her hands. "Do you think everyone thinks we're dating?" Natalie asked as a couple other employees walked past the room.

Darcy looked up. "What?"

Natalie unwrapped her sandwich. "I assume they've all been on Twitter and seen the hashtag. Do you think they believe it?"

Darcy shrugged. "Who knows?" Two people looked into the conference room, their eyes lingering on Nat and Darcy as they walked by. "Okay, those two were weird. Maybe you're right. But who cares?"

Natalie frowned at her sandwich, which was so tall she couldn't figure out how she was going to be able to take a bite. "It means we can't do anything here that would kill that rumor. We have to keep up the illusion in the office, too."

"Oh," Darcy said, her voice betraying her disappointment. "Yeah. I guess. I hope being friendly to me isn't too much of a hardship for you."

Natalie looked up from her sandwich conundrum. "Oh my god, stop being so dramatic." She lifted the sandwich and attempted a bite. It was a disaster. The middle of the sandwich made a speedy escape out of the bread and plopped onto the paper wrapping.

Darcy couldn't hide her smile. "Graceful, ladylike, refined. However can I resist your charms?"

Natalie picked up a pickle and feigned tossing it at Darcy. "It's too big!"

"That's what she said," Darcy quipped, taking a bite of her own, reasonable-size sandwich.

Natalie cackled. "Oh my god, you are such a massive dork. Were you this dorky in college?" She attempted another bite. It ended with more of her sandwich on the desk in front of her.

Darcy nodded. "I've always been a dork, but maybe you didn't notice until now."

Natalie stared at the mess of sandwich innards in front of

her. "I noticed everything about you," she said quietly and then blushed.

Oh my god, get a grip, Carpenter.

She was actually flirting with Darcy when there was no one around who needed to be convinced.

She looked up. "I'm observant, you know, in general."

Darcy nodded along, but there was something in her eyes. Natalie tried to figure it out but that didn't help because the longer she looked at Darcy, the more she remembered—her body remembered—how much she loved those pale green eyes. They'd been her undoing dozens of times in college. They'd be in a team meeting and she'd catch sight of Darcy and her coaches could have been on fire and she wouldn't have noticed. More than once she had to ask one of her teammates, sometimes Darcy, to explain what she missed.

A decade and a half hadn't changed their effect on her. She dropped her gaze to her deconstructed sandwich and tried to find a way to put it back together.

"Tomorrow," Darcy said, clearing her throat. "How on earth are we going to learn how to ski jump? There is no way in hell I'm flying off the end of that giant ramp."

Natalie rolled her eyes. "You think that they'd make us do that? There's not enough liability insurance for that. We're going to have to try doing whatever it is they do to train. We're going to look absurd."

"That'll be a change."

"Are you saying you think we look silly doing these segments? How dare you? I know for a fact that I looked so graceful out there today that I have fielded several calls from skating coaches hoping to reenact *The Cutting Edge*."

Darcy laughed. A real laugh. Natalie loved that sound.

Fuck. Grace was right. She *was* falling for it again. No way. There was no way she was going to fall for Darcy's myriad charms and have her heart demolished again.

"You have a certain Douglas Dorsey quality," Darcy said, cocking her head to one side.

"Yeah, and you're the perfect ice princess counterpart," Natalie snapped. Shit. She didn't mean for it to come out so forceful. She meant for it to be teasing, light, but the look on Darcy's face darkened and she focused on the laptop in front of her.

Natalie should say sorry but she didn't get a chance. Darcy pulled up a series of videos from the Olympic training center that showed the kinds of things the ski jumpers did to practice. "We are going to look so stupid," Darcy said. "Ski jumpers and hockey players do not have the same build."

Natalie looked over her shoulder. "It can't be worse than how we looked next to the figure skaters." She watched the video through to the end. "Oh god, it's definitely worse."

Chapter Thirty-Six

Darcy hated being called an ice princess. The implication, especially coming from Natalie, that she was cold and aloof, that she lacked any feelings, really bothered her.

She wasn't cold. She didn't lack feelings. If anything, she had too many that were too easily hurt. Caring too much about what her friends thought, about their future as a couple, about *Natalie* had led to her making the biggest mistake of her life. It had cost her Natalie and broken both their hearts.

She looked at Natalie and tried not to pick a fight. They were getting along better every day and it made working together significantly more fun. But the way Natalie casually mentioned Grace's concerns coupled with how easily she dismissed the notion that she'd ever have feelings for Darcy burned.

People treated her differently when they found out who her father was or that she'd won a bunch of gold medals. She was proud of those accomplishments but wished it didn't change how people spoke to her, how they treated her. It was too much pressure to live up to that image. Anything she said or did could only ruin that impossibly high opinion. Her anxiety told her there was nothing she could do to improve on people's expectations of her. She could only disappoint them.

If she didn't fall all over herself to be kind and polite, or if she was having a bad day, people might think she was rude or aloof or full of herself. Or, like Natalie, they might claim that everything she had was given to her because of her last name and not because she'd worked her ass off for it.

This had bothered her for years, and she'd mostly realized that there would always be people who thought she'd been handed all her successes on a silver platter. She couldn't change who she was, but she could try to care less about the people who would never look past her last name.

Back in college, she thought that Natalie saw through all that bullshit. They joked with each other, and being a Canadian princess was a big part of that, but it was always light-hearted. She thought Natalie knew that all of that was a joke, not a real thing. It made her relax in Natalie's presence. She could be herself with Nat.

Back then, when they were together, she didn't think about the pressure to be perfect. She didn't worry about disappointing Natalie because Natalie didn't expect her to be superhuman. Darcy didn't worry about disappointing Natalie by failing to live up to some image of her that wasn't real.

Except, she blew it. She ruined all of that. She disappointed Natalie, and herself, and she'd never really recovered. She vowed she'd never disappoint another person like that ever again. Having Natalie bring up Grace brought all the memories flooding back.

A couple days after they got back from the NCAA finals, it felt like everyone on campus stopped her to say congratulations. When Darcy looked up from her meal, she expected another round of congratulations. Instead, Grace started screaming about how Darcy was a "selfish, overrated, asshole who deserved to spend the rest of her life alone and miserable." Darcy tried to shake it off but Grace's words ate away at her, even years later.

She looked over at Natalie, who was making notes on her

legal pad. Was she thinking about what an asshole Darcy was all those years ago? Did she still hold that grudge? Or was it nothing to her now? Was Darcy's biggest regret something Natalie never thought about because Darcy was just some insignificant footnote to her life? Was Natalie taking shots at her for fun, or was there real hurt behind her words?

Darcy couldn't decide which was worse, being someone Natalie never forgave or something Natalie never considered at all.

"What about this?" Natalie shoved her own laptop toward Darcy and hit Play on a YouTube video. Darcy watched as a skier took off over and over again and then demonstrated indoor training where he jumped off a platform and his coach held him aloft.

"Who knew ski jumping had so much in common with *Dirty Dancing*?" Darcy said, her eyes on the screen.

Natalie laughed. "I think if they have us do that we might kill someone. These jumpers are built like whippets and we…"

"Are not," Darcy said with a laugh.

Darcy found another trove of videos and watched ski jumpers flying off the end of massive jumps again and again. There had to be some videos of people training, little kids or beginners, learning how to do this wild sport because there was no way she was going to go to the top of the ramp let alone ski down it and off the edge. No matter how badly she wanted this job, she wasn't going to die for it.

She turned her screen to Natalie. "I'm not keen on killing some poor, unsuspecting skiing coach, but I'm also not excited to fly off the end of that ramp and die in a fiery crash."

Natalie scoffed. "The hill's covered with snow, there's zero chance we'd catch fire."

Darcy shoved Natalie's shoulder without thinking about it. Then realized what she'd done. "Sorry. Unprofessional."

"Remove your hockey stick from your ass, LaCroix. You're allowed to joke around with me. I'm not calling HR because

you stopped pretending we haven't known each other for fifteen years."

Darcy nodded solemnly. "Things with us…" She had no
idea how to finish that sentence. "I didn't know if I was allowed after everything."

Natalie held her gaze. "I'm a grown-ass woman, Darcy. People have said mean words to me before. I'm sure they'll do it
again. I can take it."

Darcy swallowed. Natalie hadn't forgotten what she'd done.
But it wasn't clear she had forgiven her either. It felt worse,
somehow, to be dismissed as one of a group of people who
had been shitty to Natalie. When it came to Natalie, she never
wanted to be one of a crowd, she wanted to be the only one.

She tried to read Natalie's expression, searching for any bit
of hope she could find there. Natalie wasn't giving anything
away but her eyes weren't angry. If anything, Darcy would
have said they were soft and gentle, the blue sparkling with
mischief and something else. Darcy wouldn't let herself hope
that there might be more there. How could she even dare hope
for a second chance after what she'd done? She'd hurt Natalie, the first girl she'd ever really loved. She didn't deserve a
second chance.

But sitting in that stupid conference room, watching videos
of skiers flying into the air, she realized she wanted another
chance with Natalie.

And she had no fucking idea how to get Natalie to give
her one.

Chapter Thirty-Seven

Raquel hadn't made Natalie and Darcy wear the ski jumping suits. It turned out they were both wildly expensive and too customized to make sense for a ten-minute segment. Instead, Natalie and Darcy were decked out in *Wake Up, USA*–branded workout gear and sneakers.

Samira and Jeff, the two ski jumpers who were going to teach them to jump, agreed that it made sense to give the tutorial inside, in one of the training gyms on the Olympic campus.

"The first thing you have to be able to do is get into the tuck position we use to glide down the ramp before takeoff," Samira said as she demonstrated how to get into a low crouch. She squatted down and kept her chest long and over her knees.

Jeff gestured to Samira's position. "In this position she can zoom down the ramp and then explode out of the stance for the takeoff." Samira jumped out of the position as he said this, her feet coming several feet off the ground.

"Wow, you're really quick!" Darcy said when Samira landed.

Samira grinned. "It's all about getting the timing right so you really launch yourself off the end of the ramp."

They gave Darcy and Natalie tips as they crouched, gently adjusting their positions.

"We look ridiculous, don't we?" Natalie asked, shaking her head. "Hockey players are not meant to fly."

"Except on the ice," Samira said with a smile. "I've seen you both play. I know you can fly out there."

Darcy blushed. "You're way too kind. Okay, now that we have tried that, show us what we need to know for the takeoff."

Before they started the show, they'd set up a small box for them to jump off. Jeff demonstrated how he got into position and then jumped into the air where his coach caught him and held him aloft while Jeff held the flying position.

"That looks simple enough," Natalie said. "Which probably means we'll look completely uncoordinated. You're welcome, America," she said into the camera.

Jeff laughed. "Who wants to go first?"

Darcy looked at Natalie, who grinned. "If you're chicken, I'm happy to show you how it's done." She looked at the coach. "Are you sure I'm not going to hurt you?"

He chuckled. "I've been doing this a long time. I think I can manage."

Natalie stepped onto the box. She got into the tuck position and tried not to think about what might happen if she knocked the coach on his ass on live TV. "Ready?" she asked, cocking her head up so she could see the coach. He nodded. She checked her balance and pushed off the box as hard as she could.

Too bad jumping was only half the battle. She got into the air and the coach caught her, but instead of holding the correct position in the air as Jeff had done, her legs dangled, her middle twisted, and the coach nearly lost his balance before setting her down on the gym floor.

"Great job!" Samira said.

Natalie laughed. "Now you're just lying. But let's see how Canada does."

Darcy was already on the box, ready when the coach got back in place. Natalie stepped out of the way and waited. Darcy checked with the coach before launching herself straight up into the air.

Natalie tried to keep her face neutral for the camera but her competitive nature wouldn't let her. Darcy did a much better job. She held the right position and didn't come close to killing the coach.

Natalie clapped slowly. "All right, showoff. Now's the time you admit to having done this before."

Darcy grinned, her cheeks slightly pink. "Nope. Must be a natural," she said with a wink. The viewers were going to have fun with that.

"Folks, I hope you tune in tonight to watch our coverage of these incredible athletes doing what they do best," Natalie said, gesturing to Jeff and Samira.

"And we promise, you'll never have to watch us fail at this ever again," Darcy added with a laugh. "See you back here tomorrow when we prove what amazing athletes these folks are by demonstrating how awful we are when we try to do what they do."

They stood next to Jeff and Samira and waved into the camera until they got the signal that they were done.

After a round of thank-yous, good-lucks, and handshakes, Jeff and Samira left the gym. The crew packed up the equipment while Natalie and Darcy waited. The crew shuttled the equipment out of the gym piece by piece.

"We didn't die," Darcy said with a smile. "Of all the sports, this is the one I was sure we were going to get hurt trying."

Natalie sighed. "Jumping off a box isn't exactly death-defying."

"Maybe not, but when they said ski jumping, I thought they were going to strap us to skis and send us flying."

Natalie laughed. "It seems like one of us might have survived that segment, but it sure as hell wouldn't have been me."

Chapter Thirty-Eight

"You weren't that bad," Darcy said, her lips curling at the corners.

"I looked like an awkward fish."

Darcy cocked her head to one side. "Are you implying that some fish aren't awkward?"

Natalie smacked her on the arm with the back of her hand. "You know what I mean."

Darcy laughed. "You bet I do. I saw you jump." She placed her hand on Natalie's shoulder. "The important thing is that you tried your best." She couldn't help teasing Natalie. Not after yesterday when she'd been so much better on the ice. It was nice to get the upper hand even if it was only jumping off a box.

"Do you want another chance? I can catch you," Darcy said, pointing at the equipment the crew hadn't cleared yet.

Natalie shook her head. "No way. I'd kill you."

Darcy rolled her eyes. "I know you think I've become some kind of delicate flower in the last three years, but I work out enough to catch you. Come on. It'll be fun."

Natalie hesitated, her eyes moving from Darcy to the box she was going to jump off.

"Oh my god, stop being such a baby. It's not like if you

jump off the box and land on the ground you're going to break something from the twelve-inch drop." When Natalie didn't relent immediately, Darcy pointed at a stack of mats in the corner. "We can put those out if you're worried you'll break your ankle."

Natalie got onto the box. "You're so annoying. I bet you drove your sister completely nuts as a kid."

"Stop yapping and jump, you big American chicken."

Natalie tucked into the deep squat position Jeff and Samira had taught them and checked to make sure Darcy was ready. "On the count of three," Natalie said.

Darcy braced herself and put her hands up to catch Natalie. The thought that this was a bad idea flitted through her brain but disappeared as soon as Natalie launched herself from the box. Darcy's hands found Natalie's stomach and held her aloft long enough for Natalie to try to hold the flight position Samira had demonstrated.

It wasn't much better than her first attempt and had the distinct disadvantage of being caught by someone without any experience. As soon as Darcy caught her, Natalie started to twist. In a moment of panic, she let her legs drop, changing her center of gravity and forcing Darcy to hug her around the waist to keep her from crashing to the floor.

Darcy set her down as gently as she could manage. In the process, Darcy found her face pressed against Natalie's chest. She pulled her head back. "Sorry, I didn't mean to..." There was no way to finish that sentence that didn't involve acknowledging that her face had been pressed against Natalie's boobs.

"It's okay," Natalie said.

Darcy's arms were still wrapped around her waist. Her heart pounded, probably from the adrenaline rush of thinking she was about to drop her former teammate on top of herself. Of course that was it. Natalie's face was so close to hers she could see the constellation of freckles across Natalie's nose. They were faint under the TV makeup but from this distance Darcy could still see them. Natalie's eyes were brilliant blue and sparkling with something. Maybe it was the rush of having Darcy catch her so badly, or maybe, Darcy hoped, it was something else.

Natalie looked at Darcy's lips and then back at Darcy's eyes. It happened in a split second but it was enough to convince Darcy. She leaned in, her lips brushing Natalie's. For the second Natalie didn't return the kiss panic flooded Darcy.

She dropped her hands and moved to step back, an apology already on her lips, but Natalie grabbed her hips and pulled her closer. For a minute they forgot where they were and what they were doing and kissed like it hadn't been fifteen years since the last time. Fifteen years of good, but not like this, kisses. Fifteen years of wondering if anything would ever compare to kissing Natalie.

Darcy cupped Natalie's cheek with her right hand before letting her fingers find the back of Natalie's neck. Natalie's hand on her hip squeezed them closer together. Whether it was the sensory overload of feeling Natalie pressed against her or the sound of the door to the gym creaking open, Darcy couldn't be sure, but they sprang apart.

They both took a half step back; Darcy dropped her gaze. Natalie turned around to see who was walking back into the gym.

"You need any help?" Natalie asked the crew, her voice significantly louder than necessary.

Is her blood rushing in her ears, too?

"No. We've got it. Are you two riding back with us?"

"Yep," Darcy said, not meeting their eyes. "We just need to grab our coats. We'll be out in a second." She walked over to the side of the gym, where they'd left their belongings. She dawdled, waiting for Natalie to join her.

She picked up their coats, handing Natalie hers. She kept her eyes lowered.

"You ever going to look at me again?" Natalie asked.

Darcy looked up from the floor and found a cocky smirk on Natalie's face. God, she was annoying and so, so hot. "We should go. And maybe talk about what happened, or something." Dammit, she didn't know what to say and it all came out jumbled and sounding like she was nervous.

Which she was, but Natalie didn't need to know that. Darcy was a grown-ass woman who kissed other women all the time.

Okay, that was a lie. Not all the time. Not really since she and Sabrina broke up. And never a coworker.

Oh shit. She was going to end up at HR or something over this. She took a deep breath and tried to let it out slowly.

"Stop freaking out. It's not a big deal." Natalie took her coat and snatched her hat and gloves from the bench, too. "Of course we can talk about it, you giant lesbian. But I swear to god if you try to U-Haul with me, I'm on the first flight home."

Darcy laughed, her anxiety dissipating like magic. "Settle down, Carpenter, you're not that good a kisser."

Natalie stepped closer. "That's bullshit and we both know it," she said in a low voice. The vibrations traveled through Darcy.

Holy shit. Natalie had always been this way but that was part of what made Darcy want her so much. Nat might brag but she never did it without having the skill to back it up. An ache built low in Darcy's stomach. She'd fucked all this up the first time.

She was not going to make the same mistake twice.

Chapter Thirty-Nine

In the van on the way back to the offices, Natalie replayed their kiss a dozen times. She couldn't figure out how it had happened, how they'd crossed the line from flirting for the cameras and the #PuckingHotties fans to kissing. But it didn't matter how it happened. It mattered that she liked it.

She looked at Darcy, who was staring out the window. Their thighs were deliciously close to each other as they bounced along the roads, occasionally touching when they hit a bump. Darcy turned and saw Natalie looking at her. A wary look passed over her face until Natalie smiled.

"Hey," Natalie said. *Very smooth, Nat. Absolutely legendary.*

Darcy bumped her leg against Natalie's. "Hey yourself. I'm sorry that your dream of being a ski jumper fizzled this morning. It must be devastating." Darcy smiled, her impossibly green eyes sparkling.

Natalie hung her head. "It's a real blow to my dreams, but I'll carry on somehow."

Their kiss sat between them like another passenger in the van. The camera operator and tech sat in the front and she and Darcy were in the middle seats of the van, gear at their feet and stacked behind them. But none of that felt as weighty as knowing they'd gone from flirting for the cameras to kissing. And now they had to deal with it.

Darcy pulled out her phone.

Or maybe they didn't have to deal with it.

Darcy flicked her thumb across the screen. Natalie was not going to stare at Darcy's hands. She was not going to remember how they felt on her skin. Nope. She was going to take out her own damn phone and think about literally anything else.

"They've already made GIFs from this morning," Darcy whispered.

Natalie craned her neck to look at Darcy's phone. The cameras had caught Darcy looking at Natalie while they both worked on their tuck position. The way the shot was framed, it looked like Darcy was staring at Natalie's ass.

Natalie cracked up. "Wow, my eyes are up here. I don't blame you for looking, but that's not even subtle, LaCroix."

"Oh my god, I was not staring at your ass!" Darcy said in a harsh whisper.

Natalie tapped the phone screen. "That's not what the video evidence shows. It's okay, plenty of women have fallen prey to the wonders of my ass." Natalie could hardly finish the sentence without dissolving into giggles.

"Everything all right back there?" the camera operator, Lisa, asked from the passenger seat.

"Yeah. We're just laughing about what people are saying on Twitter."

Lisa looked a bit skeptical but turned back around.

Natalie scrolled through the hashtag. God, these people were hilarious and completely unhinged. "Thank god they didn't get footage of you catching me. They would have been splicing it with *Dirty Dancing*."

Darcy considered the possibility. "I can live with being Johnny in this situation. He was way cooler than Baby. I can call you Frances if you want me to."

Natalie bumped her shoulder against Darcy's. "You're the worst."

"You keep saying shit like that, but I don't think you believe it," Darcy leaned close enough to whisper in Natalie's ear. "And that kiss tells me you don't think I'm the worst at anything."

Natalie flicked her eyes to the front of the van where the driver and Lisa were chatting away, oblivious to the fact that Natalie was so turned on by the feel of Darcy's mouth inches from her skin that she thought she might pass out. *Get a grip, Carpenter.* She wasn't a giddy nineteen-year-old anymore. The feel of Darcy's breath on her ear should not have this effect on her.

It was no use. She resisted every inch of her body screaming at her to turn and let her lips find Darcy's. She swallowed. It didn't help. "Darcy," she breathed. "We are in a van, with our coworkers."

Darcy sat back in her seat, but left her thigh pressed against Natalie's. She had an unmistakably smug expression on her face like she knew exactly what effect she had on Natalie. Natalie shifted uncomfortably in her seat.

She needed to get out of here. She couldn't be this close to Darcy and not lose her mind. Not after that kiss. Not while the memories of college bubbled to the surface.

She replayed the kiss in her head over and over until her brain started serving up fantasies of what could come next. It was excruciating to sit next to Darcy and be required not to let anyone know that in her head they were back in her hotel room, with her hand slowly unbuttoning Darcy's shirt, slipping it off her shoulders and finally getting to run her hands over Darcy's skin. Fuck, she should not be having these thoughts at work. She needed this day to be over.

When they arrived at the offices, Natalie hopped out of the truck and offered to help with some of the equipment. Lisa waved her off. "We can't allow you jokers to carry anything. If you break it, we get in trouble."

Natalie and Darcy walked into the offices and took over the conference room again. This was not a good idea. How had Natalie ended up in another enclosed space with Darcy, this time one with a wall made of glass? There was literally nowhere to hide.

They didn't have long to sit awkwardly, though. Raquel walked into the office and handed them each a sheet of paper. "You two are going to be at the hockey game tonight."

"What?" Darcy said, skimming the paper.

Raquel sighed. "I thought you wanted to do commentary?"

Darcy sat up. "Wait, are you offering me the commentator job?"

Raquel shook her head. "No. We need you two to make us look good at a reception in the box during the game." Natalie made a face. "I know this is asking a lot, especially because you'll still be doing the morning thing tomorrow, but we'd really appreciate it."

Natalie shot Darcy a look. They were going to have to go to this hockey thing and drag their asses out of bed tomorrow regardless of how long they had to spend schmoozing. Natalie pointed to the paper. "These are all the details?"

Raquel nodded. "Dress nicely, but not over the top. This isn't a red-carpet thing. And feel free to leave by eleven so you don't look like zombies on my show tomorrow." She closed the door and kept her hand on the knob. "I want you to stick together. I don't think any of these guys will get out of line, but..."

Darcy looked at Natalie. "Got it. Clearly you don't think they follow lesbian hashtags."

Raquel laughed. It caught them both by surprise. "No, I don't think these guys are probably following #PuckingHotties. Although if it turns out they are, let me know." She shook her head, amused by the idea.

Natalie looked at Darcy, wishing she could read her mind. "Okay, we'll do our best not to embarrass you at the game."

Raquel pulled the door open. "You can get out of here now if you want, might as well take a little break while you can. I can have someone else pull together what you need for tomorrow."

After she left, Darcy turned to Natalie. "Looks like we have a date tonight, Carpenter." She bit the inside of her lip.

Natalie nodded, unable to form words.

Chapter Forty

Natalie and Darcy clutched their wardrobe-department-provided garment bags and got into the car waiting to take them back to the hotel.

Natalie climbed into the back, leaving the front seat open for Darcy. Darcy waited for a snarky remark, but none came.

She turned. "Thanks for letting me sit up here."

Natalie shrugged. "No big deal. I know you get car sick."

There was the Natalie from college. The sweet, thoughtful, kind, pain in the ass Darcy fell in love with. So far, there had been glimmers of the old Natalie, but that version of Natalie had been buried under a deep layer of sarcasm. Her heart melted a little knowing that that big marshmallow center was still in there, even if it was harder to find underneath all the prickly outside.

In the hotel elevator, Natalie pressed the button for their floor and stared at the doors. Darcy tried to read her expression.

"What is this thing going to be like tonight?" Natalie asked, her eyes darting to Darcy and then away.

Darcy shrugged. "I don't know. I don't usually get invited to anything involving important people. We'll have to figure it out together, I guess." She gave Natalie a hopeful smile.

Whatever misgivings she had about Natalie joining her on the show were long gone, replaced by relief that she had someone she could count on.

After they got off the elevator, they paused outside the door to Natalie's room. She should say something about the kiss. She shouldn't pretend like nothing happened.

Darcy gathered her courage. "Do you want me to come get you here or do you want to meet in the lobby?" Darcy asked, losing her nerve as soon as she started speaking.

You absolute chicken.

Natalie's hand paused over the door handle. "I..." She swallowed and smiled a fake-ass smile if Darcy had ever seen one. "It would be great if you'd stop by here when you're ready."

"Are you okay?" Darcy's mind immediately assumed she'd done something to upset Natalie. It was probably the kiss. Why did she do that? Ugh.

Natalie pressed down on the handle and opened her door. "Of course. Why wouldn't I be? I'll see you later." Her voice was cheery but it sounded off, like hitting a wrong note on a piano.

Darcy scanned Natalie's face but it gave nothing away. "Okay, I'll be here a few minutes before the car comes. Text me if you need anything."

Back in her own room, Darcy pulled out the suit they'd given her to wear. She hung it on the outside of the closet door and flopped onto the bed.

The look in Natalie's eyes played on a loop in her head. It was a combination of shyness and something else. But Natalie wasn't usually shy. Maybe nervousness? It would be normal for her to be a little nervous about meeting all the corporate bigwigs at the game.

The game.

Darcy had been so focused on what this party might mean for her next career step that she hadn't considered how much it would suck for Natalie to be stuck in the box watching her team play. Not to mention that Darcy had been too busy looking for the next thing she could say to tease Natalie that she missed the very real thing going on right in front of her eyes.

She rolled over and grabbed her phone, ready to text Natalie. But to say what, exactly? Sorry this sucks? Hey, we never talked about that kiss and now we have to go to this work thing? She flipped her phone over. No need to text something that might make all of this worse.

They *should* talk about the kiss, though.

If she had to, Darcy could play it off like she got caught up in the moment. They'd been pretending to be together, they'd been flirty for the cameras, and she'd gotten carried away. That wasn't true. But Natalie didn't need to know that if she thought the whole thing was a giant mistake. If she still hated Darcy as much as she did at the end of college, Darcy would play it off like it had been an extension of their flirting in front of the camera. Another bit of theater for the lesbian hashtag crew.

You weren't on camera when you kissed.

Ugh. She'd have to figure out how to explain why kissing Natalie with no one around was part of their social media gig.

In reality, she'd kissed her because she'd been wanting to kiss Natalie for a long time. She was irritating and needled her constantly, but Darcy had never gotten over her. She'd never gotten over the betrayed look on her face when Darcy had made the mistake of pretending Natalie meant nothing to her.

It haunted her. She didn't regret anything in her life as much as she regretted hurting Natalie. Darcy had proved every one of her fears right. She was nothing but a famous last name, not actually worthy of the attention she received. When it came down to it, she'd blown it.

She wasn't going to make the same mistake twice. If Natalie wanted to act like the kiss was fake and part of their ruse, she'd do it. It was a lie, but if that's what Natalie wanted, she'd do it. She was never going to hurt Natalie like that again. She couldn't bear the thought of disappointing her, seeing that look of hurt and betrayal on her face. It would be too much for her.

Shc'd follow Natalie's lead. That was the only logical choice.

Chapter Forty-One

Natalie got out of the shower and stared at the suit hanging in her closet. How the wardrobe department had something so perfect for her she didn't know. But thank god they did because she wasn't going to show up to watch her former team looking like a loser in a *Wake Up, USA* polo shirt.

By some miracle, the pants fit perfectly over her hockey thighs and ass. She ran her hand over the satin stripe down the side of the pants. She loved tuxedo pants but never had a reason to buy them. Until now.

She might not have picked it out for herself, but the deep blue tank top they gave her was perfect. Without the suit jacket, it showed off her shoulder muscles and complemented her eyes. It made her feel hot and powerful. What would Darcy say when she saw her?

She left the suit jacket on the hanger. She didn't need to get her nervous sweat on her clothes before she even left the room. Having to watch her former team filled her stomach with something closer to bees than butterflies. It wasn't like she thought she could go the entire Olympics without seeing them but she didn't expect to have it sprung on her like this. Watching the game was one thing, she loved watching hockey, but having to be there to talk to a bunch of old dudes wasn't her idea of a good time.

At least Darcy would be there with her.

Darcy. Who she kissed that morning. What on earth had she been thinking? They were coworkers now, that's it. Regardless of all the foolish flirting for the people at home, Darcy was still the same woman who broke her stupid heart in college.

Natalie couldn't give Darcy another chance to wreck her like that. It had taken a long time for Natalie to get over it the first time. Though, if she was honest with herself, she wasn't over it.

But it was just a kiss. She'd been caught up in the moment and the feel of Darcy pressed against her. It wasn't a big deal. It was nice. And hot. And she would gladly do it, and more, again if Darcy was up for something without strings. They were in a foreign country, doing a completely ridiculous job, why not add a few benefits to this rekindled friendship? It wasn't permanent. Like this job, it was something to do until she figured out how she wanted to spend the rest of her post-hockey life.

She should really figure out what she wanted to do next but in the meantime she wouldn't mind spending the rest of the trip making out with Darcy.

With that thought in her head, she walked into the bathroom to check her appearance. She wanted Darcy to lose her mind when she saw her. Even wearing the world's most perfect tank top, she wasn't sure she had that effect on Darcy anymore.

Natalie was still fiddling with her hair when Darcy knocked on the door. She gave it one last look in the mirror before opening the door. She stepped backward to let Darcy come in.

"Give me two seconds to put on my shoes," Natalie said before stopping to stare at Darcy. Her hair was down, in soft waves around her shoulders. They'd given her a suit as well, but instead of a tank top, she had on a button-down, open at the neck to reveal her collarbones.

Holy shit.

"You look hot," Natalie said, her mouth running way ahead of her brain.

Darcy smiled. "Thanks, you do, too."

Natalie blushed. "I mean. You look nice. Sorry. I didn't mean to be all gross."

Darcy shook her head and laughed. "By all means objectify me. It's been a while since anyone has."

Natalie stepped into her shoes. "Bullshit. People have been thinking you're hot, even if they haven't told you about it."

Darcy rolled her eyes, but her smile stayed. "You trying to get in my pants, Carpenter?"

Natalie straightened up and found Darcy's eyes. "What if I was?"

Darcy's mouth dropped open and Natalie raised one eyebrow. When Darcy didn't say anything, Natalie reached past her to get her jacket off the hanger. "It's no big deal. I thought that kiss earlier was pretty hot and figured we might be able to have some fun together while we're here. No strings or whatever. Think about it." She opened the door. "Shall we?"

Darcy looked dazed as she walked out the door ahead of Natalie. Natalie smiled to herself. Whatever happened tonight, she felt triumphant at short-circuiting Darcy's brain.

Natalie made sure the door was closed before following Darcy down the hallway. It gave her an excuse to check out Darcy's ass in her perfectly tailored suit pants.

At the elevator, she allowed herself another look at Darcy's face, which was a little flushed. "Do we need to talk about the kiss?" Darcy asked, her voice low.

Natalie shrugged. "I liked it, if you're wondering what I'm thinking."

Darcy's hands dug deeper into the pockets in her suit, which forced her shoulders to roll forward.

Natalie took a step closer. "I'm not trying to make you un-comfortable. I can stop," she said, her eyes soft.

Darcy smiled. "It's okay. I'm surprised, that's all. A couple weeks ago you hated me and wanted to punish me for...everything that happened." She took a shaky breath. "And now..." She shook her head, unable to finish the thought.

"I was mad," Natalie explained. "But we spend all day flirting for the cameras, why not have a little fun, too?" She shrugged. "Only if you want to, of course."

Darcy took a deep breath, her eyes traveling over Natalie's face before breaking into a shy smile. "You really do look amazing."

"Is that a yes?" Natalie asked. The elevator door dinged and popped open, revealing a family inside.

Darcy raised an eyebrow and gestured toward the elevator. "Let's see where the night takes us."

Chapter Forty-Two

During the ride down in the elevator, Darcy could think of nothing else but Natalie's proposed friends-with-benefits scenario. It sounded good. Too good. If there was nothing behind it, like there was nothing behind their flirting for the cameras, no one could end up hurt, right? She couldn't hurt Natalie again, she couldn't be that same massive disappointment she'd been in college. She couldn't disappoint Natalie the way she had disappointed her last girlfriend by choosing work over her.

Once they got in the car, Darcy glanced at Natalie, who was scrolling through her phone. Darcy let her eyes sweep over Natalie's legs, noting the way the muscles of her thighs pressed against the fabric. Her brain flashed a picture of Natalie's bare legs, an image that had been there for more than a decade. She'd had a whole year to sneak glances at Natalie in the locker room and it allowed her to imagine exactly what Natalie looked like under that suit.

She closed her eyes. If Natalie saw her, she'd assume Darcy was feeling gross in the car, not trying to tamp down her overwhelming desire to find out what was under Natalie's suit. Natalie's collarbones were on full display, her tank top modest enough not to show too much cleavage but with a deep enough

V that Darcy could have looked down if she craned her neck a little higher.

Cut it out, you perv.

Darcy swallowed. Yes, Natalie suggested that they could hook up, but that wasn't an invitation to leer at her in the back of the car that was taking them to a work function.

The driver didn't seem to be paying attention to them, but she didn't want to risk it, so she took out her phone.

How would this work?

Darcy sent the text and waited for it to pop up on Natalie's phone. When it did, Natalie swiped her thumb across it and then looked over at Darcy, her mouth twisted in a confused smile.

How would what work? Us having a little fun?

Darcy nodded at Natalie when she read the reply. Natalie went back to typing.

I think we can handle no-strings. Unless you're afraid you're going to fall in love with me.

Darcy looked at Natalie, who waggled her eyebrows. Darcy suppressed a laugh.

The car pulled up to the curb outside the venue. The driver looked at them in the rearview. "I'll be parked at the arena. You can text me when you want to leave." He handed them a card with his number on it.

Darcy took it and thanked the driver. She slid out onto the sidewalk and held the door open for Natalie to slide out after her. She held out her hand and Natalie took it with a smile.

"I'm not exactly a damsel in distress," Natalie said, wryly.

Darcy gave her hand a squeeze before dropping it. "Maybe I just wanted an excuse to hold your hand," she said before striding toward the entrance.

They held out their credentials and the guards pointed them in the direction of the studio's VIP box. All the flirting in the car had distracted Darcy from her nerves. But once they reached the area outside the box, they came flooding back. Inside, they would meet a bunch of people who could make or break her career and she'd spent the last hour thinking about how much she wanted to get Natalie out of her clothes.

Get it together, LaCroix.

Her internal pep talk did nothing to calm her nerves. She took a deep breath and pulled the door open, holding it for Natalie. Natalie stepped toward her. All sense of her earlier playfulness was gone. Instead, she looked gray.

"Are you okay?" Darcy asked, laying her hand on Natalie's arm.

Natalie nodded. "I'll be fine." She walked into the room, her eyes on the people milling around holding cocktails and small plates of food.

Darcy noted that Natalie's gaze flicked to the ice below but quickly flitted back to the people. Darcy's own nerves disappeared once she realized what a hard time Natalie was having being here. She tugged on the elbow of Natalie's jacket, gently pulling her toward the bar. Once there, she ordered a glass of wine for herself and then looked at Natalie.

"I'll have the same," Natalie managed to say.

Darcy took the glasses from the bartender and handed one to Natalie. "Since when do you drink white wine? Didn't you say that's a drink for bored housewives?"

The laugh that came out of Natalie's mouth surprised them both. "How on earth did you remember me saying that?"

Darcy shrugged. "I remember pretty much everything you ever said to me." She looked at the floor, wishing she could forget the harsh things.

Natalie watched her over the rim of her glass. She gulped a generous sip. "You ready to mingle?"

Darcy led them toward a group of well-dressed men and women standing toward the front of the box. None of them were paying attention to the teams warming up below. Natalie glanced down, her eyes tracking the familiar choreography of her former team's warm-ups.

Raquel stepped out of the group to welcome Natalie and Darcy. "I'd like to introduce you all to Darcy LaCroix and Natalie Carpenter, our newest hosts for the Olympics on *Wake Up, USA*."

Darcy and Natalie took turns shaking hands with everyone in the group. Darcy smiled. "Nice to meet all of you. How are you enjoying your time here?"

One of the women, a middle-aged woman in an expensive suit, grinned. "I got here yesterday but I love it already." She gestured to the panel of glass overlooking the ice. "I can't wait to watch the game." She looked slightly sheepish. "Is it deeply uncool to admit I am a giant fan of both of you?"

Natalie looked at Darcy. "Nope. Nothing uncool about liking women's hockey!"

"I was a big fan of your father's. Wonderful player." The man smiled. "You should get him to come on your show," he said to Darcy before making sure Raquel heard him. "Having an actual Hall of Famer would be a real ratings coup." The man took a sip of scotch, looking very pleased with his suggestion.

Darcy clenched her jaw. She would not fire back at this man. She was here to play nice, make the network happy, not get into a fight with some rich old guy. But the suggestion, no matter how absurd, stung. She'd gotten this job on her own merit and the network liked it, not because she was Marty LaCroix's daughter but because they liked her. She was good at this. No matter what this asshole said, she didn't need her dad to help her do her job.

Chapter Forty-Three

Natalie glanced at Raquel, who was pointedly not looking at Darcy. If neither of them was going to say anything, she would. "I'm so glad you could be here to offer suggestions on our show. We're always looking for ways to improve. Darcy, didn't your dad have to get his knee replaced? I'm not sure how he'd do trying out all the sports with us." Natalie hoped her smile was big enough to cover the way her brain was repeating "fuck you" in her head.

Darcy gave Natalie a relieved smile that seemed to break whatever freeze she was in. "That's right. I'm sure he'd be flattered that you thought of him, but his doctor would probably kill him if he tried half the stuff Raquel has us doing." Her smile for the group was wide but lacking any real warmth.

Natalie knew that smile. It meant she was ready to kill someone. If she gave you that look before practice you were toast, and if you saw it before a game you were glad to be on her team. Natalie excused them and led Darcy toward the buffet table.

"You okay?"

Darcy smiled for anyone who might be watching them but Natalie knew it was fake. "Of course, why wouldn't I be?"

Natalie handed her a small plate so it wouldn't look like they disappeared to gossip. "That guy was out of line. No one wishes your dad was doing the show instead of you." She leaned closer. "I certainly don't. I like your dad but can you imagine if they asked me to flirt with him? Ew."

Darcy laughed so hard it surprised both of them. After a moment, Darcy wiped her eyes with the corner of her napkin. "Thank you for that back there. You didn't have to stick up for me."

"Sure I did. You're my teammate. And besides, that guy's a dumbass."

Darcy selected some food from the table and then waited for Natalie to do the same. "I know people think of my dad when they hear my last name. I get it. But..."

"It sucks," Natalie said.

"My dad's career will always be bigger than mine, you know?"

Natalie nodded. "That guy may think of your dad but those women were excited to see you. Neither of them gave a shit that your dad played in the NHL. They're *your* fans."

Darcy gave a weak smile and looked back at the group they'd just left. "Thanks. Although the brunette seemed particularly enamored with you."

Natalie looked over at the group and caught the eye of one of the women. She turned back to Darcy with a wicked smile. "Can't help it. I'm too irresistible for my own good. Straight middle-aged ladies fucking love me."

"Is that who you've been dating since college, a bunch of middle-aged straight ladies?" Her tone was playful but Natalie could hear the hint of concern underneath it.

She took a sip of her wine. "Nah. Haven't dated anyone seriously in a long time."

Since you broke my heart.

"I like to keep my options open." She sounded like an asshole. But that was fine. Darcy didn't need to know the entire truth. Natalie could feed her enough to sound sincere without revealing that she'd avoided letting anyone get close to her since college. One broken heart was plenty. She had no desire to risk that much hurt again.

Better to have Darcy think she was a player than pathetic.

Natalie heard the announcer's voice booming through the arena. They walked toward the glass at the front of the box to watch the player introductions. Natalie focused on covering up her feelings. She expected this hurt but it was worse than she imagined.

The starting lineups skated to the blue lines, followed by the rest of the teams. She could feel Darcy staring at her but forced herself to keep her eyes on the ice. She was supposed to be down there, standing at center ice, not up in the rafters with a bunch of rich assholes who bought their way in.

"It gets easier," Darcy whispered.

"Easy for you to say, you decided when to quit." Natalie's words came out sounding more sad than bitter.

Darcy shrugged. "True, but everyone assumed I got my spot because of my dad in the first place."

Natalie turned to face her and cracked up. "No one ever really thought that." She shook her head. "You really think anyone who knows anything about hockey actually thinks you didn't earn your way onto the team?"

Darcy looked surprised. "How many times have you called me a princess?"

Natalie laughed. "Oh, a thousand times. And you one hundred percent deserved it! But once I met you, there was no way I ever thought you didn't deserve to be on the ice." She watched Darcy's face soften. "But that wasn't going to stop me from giving you shit."

Darcy hid her smile behind her glass and took a sip. "God, you're a pain." Her words may have been teasing but her tone told a different story.

Natalie finished her drink. "Come on, I'll buy you another and you can tell me about your sad-sack love life."

Darcy followed her to the bar. "Who says my love life is sad?"

Natalie pointed to the wine bottle and gave the bartender their glasses. "Okay, fine. Wow me with the serious girlfriend you have and tell me tales of all your adventures."

Darcy took the now full glass. "You are such an asshole."

"I'm not and that's why you like me so much." She clinked her glass against Darcy's. "To two sad-sack retired hockey players."

"Cheers," Darcy said, her eyes locked on Natalie's.

Maybe the wine was working too much, but Natalie was overwhelmed with the desire to kiss Darcy. Not in this room full of people, obviously. But her entire body warmed at the thought. Before her thoughts could get any more interesting, Raquel appeared with another man, this one a bit younger and fitter than the last group.

"Natalie, Darcy, I'd like you to meet Todd Johnson. Todd works for All Sports Network."

Natalie and Darcy shook his hand in turn. "Nice to meet you, Todd."

Todd smiled, his teeth aggressively white. "Likewise. You two have quite a thing going on *Wake Up, USA*." His tone was friendly, but Natalie caught a hint of something else. "You girls sure look like you're having fun, together, on-screen."

There it was. He was practically leering at them over the thought that they were more than colleagues. What was it with dudes and lesbians? Natalie tried to keep her face neutral, but by the way Darcy jumped in, she must have been failing.

Darcy tucked her arm into Natalie's. "We've known each other for a long time and we always have a good time together."

His eyes lingered on Darcy's arm and the spot where their hips touched. "I'll bet you do." The look on his face made Natalie's skin crawl.

She opened her mouth but closed it when she felt Darcy's fingers press into her forearm like a warning. "So nice to meet you, Todd. Excuse us, we're going to try to catch a little of the game." Darcy practically ripped Nat's shoulder out of the socket dragging her away from Todd and his disgusting smirk.

"Oh my god, what a fucking creep," Natalie said into her glass when they were far enough away not to be overheard.

"I was pretty worried you might throw him through the window."

Natalie considered it. "Not the worst idea you've ever had. But it would probably cost us our jobs. Thanks for keeping me from getting us both fired." The action on the ice continued without her really seeing it. She turned to Darcy and found her staring back at her.

Natalie's eyes followed the line of Darcy's shirt collar down to the deepest spot of its V. There was the slightest hint of cleavage but it was enough for Natalie's heartbeat to accelerate. Darcy caught her looking and quirked an eyebrow. As if it were connected to the corner of her mouth with an invisible string, her mouth followed in a similar arch at the corner. Natalie wondered what those lips would taste like and was overcome with desire to get the hell out of the suite and back to the hotel.

"How long do you think we have to stay here?" Darcy asked, her voice raspy.

Natalie looked around the room for Raquel. She found her talking to yet another group of bigwigs. "We've only been here for like an hour. I think she'll kill us if we leave now."

Darcy huffed out a breath. "Fine. But I want to be out of here by the end of the second period." She fixed her eyes on Natalie. "We have to be up early tomorrow."

Natalie shrugged. "If we leave then, we'll be in bed before eleven. It will be rough but not too..." Darcy's eyes moved to Natalie's lips and Natalie understood what Darcy wasn't saying. "Oh." She swallowed but it did nothing to stop the wave of devastating desire flooding through her veins. "Right. You're right. We need to be sure we don't stay out too late. We gotta be fresh for the morning."

Oh fuck. Staying here, talking to all these people, was going to be impossible. All she could think about was stripping off every piece of impeccably tailored clothing Darcy had on and running her tongue over every square inch of her body. Instead, she drained the last sip of her wine.

"Thirsty?" Darcy said, biting her lower lip.

"You have no idea."

Chapter Forty-Four

The second the Zamboni hit the ice at the end of the second period, Darcy and Natalie told Raquel they were leaving. She looked jealous but assured them she wouldn't be staying much longer, either.

Darcy texted their driver and hoped he'd be at the curb by the time they wound their way through the arena to the exit. She walked next to Natalie, glancing at her any time she thought she could without being noticed. Natalie's cheeks were pink. Whether it was from the wine, the walk, or what Darcy hoped they were about to be doing, she didn't know. And she couldn't ask so she checked every few steps for clues.

At the door, Natalie put her winter coat on and pressed her face against the glass. "Not here yet." Her voice betrayed impatience.

"You got somewhere to be, Carpenter?" Darcy asked with a wicked grin. She was enjoying seeing Natalie just as flustered as she felt. She wanted to be back at the hotel, behind a locked door. Now. But she enjoyed watching Natalie's building impatience.

Natalie shoved the door open the instant a car rolled up to the curb. She paused to hold it open for Darcy, who considered grabbing Natalie's hand on her way by. Instead, she thanked Natalie and hurried ahead to open the car door for her. She thought about taking the front seat. Her stomach would feel better if she sat up front, but she had no interest in sitting with the driver when she could sit with Natalie.

She couldn't bear to keep her hands to herself for much longer, so she slid next to Natalie and let her shoulder bounce off Natalie.

"Sorry," she whispered, not meaning it.

Natalie looked at her, the arena lights allowing Darcy to see half of her face. Natalie's eyes were intense and anticipation shot through Darcy. She pressed her hand against the seat between them, using it to hold herself up but leaving it in hopes Natalie would reach toward her.

For a few agonizing seconds, Darcy stared at the space between them waiting, hoping. She was about to move her hand to her lap when Natalie reached out and wrapped her fingers around Darcy's.

It should have been a reassuring gesture, proof that Darcy hadn't imagined the electricity between them. Instead, the feel of Natalie's skin against hers—even the ridiculously PG skin of their pinkies—was enough to make the drive back to the hotel unbearable.

She didn't want chaste touches like they were a couple of schoolgirls holding hands on the bus after a game. She wanted to shove Natalie against the wall and trail kisses down her body until Natalie's legs were shaking and she was calling Darcy's name, her fingers digging into Darcy's scalp.

Darcy ventured a look across to Natalie and found her staring back. The streetlights allowed glimpses of Natalie's face and Darcy's mouth dropped open at the undisguised want in Natalie's eyes.

Darcy checked the traffic. Considering it was the Olympics

and the place was swarming with tourists, the traffic wasn't too bad. But no matter how long it took to get back to their rooms, it was too long.

The last time she got to touch Natalie, run her tongue along her abs and lick her nipples, was over a decade ago. She shook off the memory. It was too mixed up in the way things ended. She could hardly think of the way Natalie tasted, the way her tongue felt sliding along Darcy's lower lip, without remembering how she'd fucked it all up afterward.

No. She was not going to think about that. She was older and smarter and there was no way she was going to make the same mistake again.

Natalie slid her phone out of her pocket and nodded to Darcy. Then she started texting.

Are we there yet?

Darcy checked her phone and smiled. What are you, 5?

Natalie shot her a look and then sent another text. I don't think our driver would be very happy if I did what I want to do to you in here.

Darcy swallowed, her fingers shook slightly. She should shut this down. They were in public. In a work car.

What might that be? She shouldn't be egging Natalie on, but she really wanted to know what she had in mind.

Natalie's thumbs typed out her response. She paused, then deleted it. Her face, lit by the glow of her phone, contorted as though she were having an argument with herself. She started typing again. I want to find out what you're wearing under that ridiculously hot suit.

Darcy shifted in her seat but it did nothing to address the delicious ache overwhelming her. She checked where they were. Thank god, she could see the hotel. She flashed Natalie a smile and typed one last text. I hope you like them but I don't plan to be wearing them for long.

Natalie placed her hand on Darcy's leg, her fingers rubbing tiny circles along her inner thigh. She looked at Darcy, her eyes pure fire. Darcy's heart pounded with anticipation.

The car came to a stop. "Here you go, ladies." The driver's voice cut through the silent car. Natalie jerked her hand away like she'd been caught.

Darcy unbuckled her seat belt and swallowed, hoping she could force her voice to sound normal. "Thank you so much. Have a good rest of your night," she said, pushing the door open and sliding out onto the sidewalk. She didn't wait for his response. She didn't give a fuck about it. All she cared about was getting up to her room where she could kiss Natalie.

They hurried through the lobby to the elevators and waited what felt like an eternity for the doors to open. Once inside, Natalie jammed her finger against the button for their floor before hitting the door close button. She wasn't fast enough because two men got on after them. Darcy offered a polite smile that she hoped didn't invite conversation. She faced the front and forced herself not to look at Natalie. She didn't need these two dudes seeing how turned on she was and the way she couldn't stop imagining what was going to happen in a few minutes.

When the men stepped off the elevator a few floors before Natalie and Darcy, they both turned to look at each other. Even in the harsh, fluorescent lights of the elevator, Darcy could see the way Natalie's eyes blazed. She took half a step closer to Natalie and jabbed at the door close button.

"Impatient to get to bed?" Natalie asked, her voice low and husky.

Jesus.

The doors pinged open and Natalie led the way down the

hallway to her room. She paused at the door to her room. When Darcy stopped next to her, she grinned and held the door open.

Darcy took a deep breath and stepped into the room, barely able to resist the urge to pull Natalie in by the lapels of her incredibly hot suit.

Chapter Forty-Five

Natalie watched Darcy slowly walk into her room, and gave silent thanks that, for once, she hadn't left her belongings all over the floor. The wardrobe people had tailored Darcy's suit perfectly and dear lord her ass was killing Natalie.

Darcy turned and Natalie didn't waste a second. She took two steps forward and kissed Darcy, letting her fingers slide into her gorgeous hair. Darcy's hands found Natalie's waist before shoving higher to push Natalie's suit jacket off her shoulders.

Darcy pulled back. "Finally, I've been trying to get a look at you in this shirt all night." She ran her hands up Natalie's arms, which produced a wave of goose bumps. "Cold?"

"Fuck no," Natalie said, leaning in for another kiss. Darcy's mouth was hot and soft and it destroyed any remaining trace of restraint she had. She took a step forward, pushing Darcy against the wall.

Darcy gasped when her back hit the wall, and she nipped at Natalie's lower lip. Natalie's fingers found the buttons on Darcy's shirt and paused, waiting for Darcy to give her the go-ahead.

"What the fuck are you waiting for?" Darcy said, letting her own hands come to rest on Natalie's ass.

Natalie's hands fumbled the first button when Darcy pressed her hips into Natalie's. But instead of hurrying, she slowed down. She leaned back, without breaking any of the delicious pressure between their hips.

She looked Darcy in the eyes and slowly, so impossibly slowly, unbuttoned Darcy's shirt all the way to her pants. She untucked it in one smooth motion and then let her hands roam all over Darcy's skin, her hands coming to a rest under her bra to swipe her thumbs across Darcy's already hardened nipples.

Darcy's head fell back against the wall and she let fly with a string of expletives that made Natalie laugh. "And here I thought working in TV had turned you all boring."

"Shut up," Darcy said, gasping for air when Natalie pulled down the cup of her bra and licked her nipple. Darcy's hips leaped forward into Natalie's before she pushed herself off the wall and reached behind her back to unhook her bra. She struggled for a second before flinging it off along with her jacket and shirt.

"Holy fuck," Natalie said, not even pretending not to stare. She had a thing for athletes. Part of that was the muscles and coordination and some of it was the swagger that came from being so good at something physically demanding. She loved the way women's muscles looked and felt and Darcy was no exception.

Darcy had transformed from a hockey player's body to something more akin to a runner. She was smaller than she'd been in college, but no less hot. Natalie ran her hands down the front of Darcy's body, her fingers tracing the lines of her ab muscles, her eyes watching them ripple under her touch.

Darcy grabbed the hem of Natalie's shirt and tugged it up over her head. Darcy took her time drinking in every bit of Natalie's newly exposed skin. There was a time when Natalie would have felt shy about it, but not anymore. It had been a long time since Darcy had seen her without her clothes on, but

Natalie had grown more confident since then. She might have been crap at keeping a girlfriend but no one ever complained about her body. Perks of being a professional athlete.

Retired athlete.

Darcy traced a finger over the Olympic rings tattooed on Natalie's ribs. "I wondered about these." She let her finger trail lower.

She reached for Natalie's waistband and pulled her along as she walked backward into the room. With each step she gave a deliciously firm tug, coaxing Natalie along with her as she moved deeper into the room. She kept her eyes locked on Natalie's as she backed Natalie up to the edge of the bed. "This okay?"

Natalie nodded before capturing Darcy's mouth with hers. Darcy's fingers worked at the button on Nat's pants only to have Darcy let out a frustrated sigh when she couldn't get them undone.

Natalie smiled against Darcy's lips and unbuttoned her own damn pants before kicking them off across the room. Finding them was tomorrow's problem. She let Darcy shove her back until her legs buckled and she found herself seated on the bed, her face level with Darcy's stomach. She snaked her hands behind Darcy's back while she pressed hot kisses against Darcy's exposed skin. She felt Darcy's muscles ripple when her tongue tickled her.

Darcy grabbed the sides of her head when Natalie started to trail kisses lower. "Me first," Darcy said, her voice low and rough.

With one hand on Natalie's shoulder, she pushed her back onto the bed. Natalie scooted her entire body up toward the headboard and watched Darcy climb onto the bed and hover over her. Darcy cocked her head to one side. "Any requests?" She bit her lower lip and waited for Natalie's response.

"Stop talking and fuck me already," Natalie replied, hoping

she sounded less nervous than she felt. She reached behind her to rip off her bra, but Darcy grabbed her wrist.

"Let me, please." She breathed the last word, like she was afraid Natalie might say no. All those years of being a pain in the ass had colored the way she saw her and Natalie wasn't sure that was a good thing.

Natalie held up her hands in surrender and let Darcy take her time unhooking her bra and then sweeping her mouth across each of her nipples in turn. Natalie's hips lifted off the bed, trying to make contact as Darcy's tongue flicked back and forth across Natalie's nipple. Fucking hell, she was going to explode.

"Darce," she said between gasps.

Darcy lifted her head from Natalie's chest and fixed her with a wicked smile. "Something wrong?" She swept her tongue across the other nipple and smirked as Natalie's entire body shook.

Natalie hooked one leg around Darcy and rocked forward. Darcy laughed and let her fingers trail down to Natalie's bare thighs. She followed with the rest of her body, finally leaving a line of kisses up Natalie's thigh toward her completely soaked underwear.

"Mind if I get rid of these?" Darcy said. Confidence edging on cockiness somehow managed to turn Natalie on even more.

Natalie shoved the underwear off and threw them to the floor.

Darcy raised one eyebrow and trailed another round of kisses excruciatingly slowly across Natalie's thigh. One half second before Natalie was about to scream from impatience, Darcy lowered her tongue and licked the crease where Natalie's thigh met her hip. Darcy's tongue ran all the way up to Natalie's hip bone, where she sucked so hard Natalie was sure she'd have a mark in the morning. The thought of Darcy leaving a mark, a secret proof of this moment, had her gasping.

"Darcy, please."

Darcy's mouth rumbled with a low chuckle. She cocked her head to the side to look up at Natalie. "You sure?"

Natalie nodded. "Jesus Christ, Darcy. I'm dying here."

Darcy ran her tongue along Natalie's thigh, higher, deliciously higher, until she finally stopped torturing Natalie and let her tongue slide the length of her until she found her throbbing clitoris. Slowly at first. Excruciatingly slowly.

Patience was never Natalie's strong suit and Darcy was using it against her. Natalie would have been livid if Darcy's mouth didn't feel so good. Darcy reached up, her thumb finding the stiff peak of Natalie's nipple. It nearly sent Natalie spiraling over the edge.

Natalie lifted her head off the pillow and caught a glimpse of Darcy staring at her from between her thighs. Her eyes blazed, the green nearly invisible, her pupils were blown so wide with want.

It was too much. Natalie was going to actually die from too much incredible sensation at once. Her hips rocked against Darcy's face. She wanted more, more of Darcy, more of her mouth and her fingers, and every tiny bit of skin she could find. She wanted all of Darcy.

Natalie kept her eyes locked with Darcy's.

"Darcy, please," Natalie panted. "I want you inside me."

Darcy quirked an eyebrow, and grinned. When she slid two fingers into Natalie, Natalie came with a series of expletives that would have had her coaching staff either laughing their asses off or sending her to skate until her legs gave out.

"Holy fuck, Darcy," Natalie gasped when she could manage to pull in enough air to speak.

Darcy left a trail of gentle kisses on Natalie's stomach, chest, and finally across Natalie's collarbones as she pulled herself up on the bed. She draped an arm lazily across Natalie's stomach, tracing light circles on her side.

Chapter Forty-Six

"Hey," Darcy whispered. Natalie's skin was hot under the palm of her hand.

Natalie shifted onto her side to face Darcy. "Hey yourself. That was…" She swallowed.

Darcy studied her face in the dim light of the room. Was she upset? Oh shit. "Hey, I'm sorry, did I do something wrong?"

Natalie shook her head, a laugh bubbling up and escaping her mouth. "No. That was perfect. I'm sorry. I didn't think I would feel…"

Darcy kissed Natalie's shoulder. "It's okay."

Natalie's expression shifted. Gone was the emotion, replaced by her cocky grin. As sexy as that smile was, Darcy wished Natalie hadn't buried her emotions so quickly. But this thing between them, whatever it was, felt too fragile to say something. Even if she promised not to hurt her again, Darcy wasn't sure Natalie would believe her.

The problem was the past hung all around them. Darcy understood why Natalie closed herself off but it didn't stop her from wanting that sweet, gentle woman she knew was under the cocky smile and the sarcasm.

Natalie propped herself on one elbow and placed a feather-light kiss on Darcy's cheek. She shifted to place another on her shoulder. Another below her hair on her neck and then again between her shoulder blades. Each kiss no more than the touch of a butterfly landing on her skin. Darcy smiled, her skin tingling with anticipation as she waited to discover where Natalie would kiss her next. Her spine, the dip of her waist, the dimples at the base of her back. Each time her skin felt aflame for an instant, the anticipation of each touch making her heart pound.

Natalie's breath tickled and she pressed kiss and after kiss on Darcy's back. "I've always had a thing for your back."

Darcy lifted her head and tried to twist to look at Natalie. "What?"

Natalie smiled shyly. "When we were in college, it was the only part of you I could look at without you catching me." She blushed. "I spent an embarrassing amount of time mapping your muscles in my mind." She dipped her head and trailed kisses along Darcy's side, coming tantalizingly close to her nipples.

Darcy turned onto her side. "Really?"

Natalie gave her a crooked smile. "I didn't want to get caught staring at you." She shrugged, her bashfulness reaching right into Darcy's chest and squeezing her heart.

There was the person Darcy fell in love with. Natalie's sweetness wasn't gone, Darcy hadn't destroyed it.

Natalie bent to kiss Darcy and let her teeth scrape along Darcy's lower lip.

"Fuck," Darcy exhaled.

Natalie took her raspy curse as an invitation to kiss her harder. Darcy moaned at the feel of Natalie's tongue along her lower lip.

She threaded her fingers into Natalie's hair, not wanting Natalie to stop kissing her. Or she *thought* she wanted the kisses to go on forever until Natalie dragged her tongue across Darcy's nipple.

"Oh my god, Natalie," Darcy gasped as Natalie's tongue

swirled around her nipple, each lick making Darcy arch her back higher.

Darcy opened her eyes and saw Natalie staring at her, her mouth open, pink tongue drawing delicious circles on her skin. Natalie's eyes were full of mischief.

After a few minutes, Darcy thought she was going to come without Natalie taking off her underwear.

"Nat, holy shit. Your mouth!"

Natalie lifted her head, letting the tip of her tongue draw lazy circles around the stiff peak of Darcy's nipple. "You like that?"

God, she was sexy when she was like this. Fuck.

"Don't stop," Darcy begged. Natalie dragged her fingers across Darcy's stomach, stopping at the band of her underwear.

Darcy's hips lifted off the bed. "Carpenter, would you fucking touch me already?"

Natalie's tongue never left Darcy's chest, even as her fingers tugged her underwear off and flung them across the room. She paused until she caught Darcy's eye. Darcy nodded her consent.

Natalie's fingers slid up Darcy's thigh until they reached her soaking-wet center. "Jesus, Darce." Natalie ran her fingers the length of Darcy's slit so gently that Darcy considered committing murder. The teasing was actually going to kill her. Either that or the combination of Natalie's fingers sliding over her clit and her mouth on her nipple. But if she died, this would be the way to go.

Natalie was very precise with her fingers so when Darcy gasped "Right there, don't stop," Natalie did exactly as she was told until Darcy screamed her name so loudly she slapped a hand over her own mouth in embarrassment.

Natalie lifted her head and bit down on her lip. "Everything okay, LaCroix?"

Darcy laughed, unable to banter. Unable to do anything but laugh and lie on the bed feeling like her bones were jelly.

"Fuck, you're good at that."

Natalie grinned, the slightest hint of a blush creeping up her cheeks. She looked so proud of herself. The cute, confident smile was back and Darcy knew she was in trouble.

"Did it kill you to compliment me?"

Darcy shook her head. "I will compliment you as much as you want if you do that thing with your tongue again."

Natalie grinned and bent her head down but Darcy placed her hands on Natalie's cheeks to stop her. "Not now. I cannot take any more right now. Unless you want me to die from sex, I need a break from that incredible tongue of yours."

Natalie grinned and kissed Darcy, soft and slow. "Okay, but just so you know, I'm happy to do this all night." Her eyes glinted in the dim light.

Fuck. Darcy didn't know what it was about this woman that gave her the power to utterly wreck her, but she sure as hell wanted to find out.

Chapter Forty-Seven

The alarm on Darcy's phone blared at 4:00 AM.

"Make it stop," Natalie muttered.

Oh god. Darcy spent the night in Natalie's room. Did they talk about this? Did they both pass out after...? Holy shit. Darcy blinked and looked over at Natalie, who was still completely naked.

Natalie rolled toward her and opened her eyes. From the look on her face, she was having the same panic Darcy was having.

"Good morning," Darcy said, trying to give the appearance of being cool and calm.

Natalie sat up, yanking the blanket up over half of her torso. "Oh my god, did I pass out?"

Darcy smiled sleepily up at her. "It's okay. I take it as a compliment that I wore you out so thoroughly. Although, I would have thought you had a bit more stamina, Carpenter. Is this why you never back-checked in college?"

Natalie blushed. "I'm sorry. I'll make it up to you."

Darcy smiled, warmed by the sleepy look on Natalie's face. She was so cute. There was none of her usual bluster, only her hair falling softly around her face, the crease from the pillow across one cheek, and that deepening blush on her skin. Darcy checked the clock. "I'll hold you to that, but not now or we'll be late and Raquel will kill us."

Natalie leaned forward, letting the sheet fall off her chest. She smiled before kissing Darcy gently. "Not to sound clingy or weird, but this is kind of nice."

Darcy pressed her lips against Natalie's before getting up. "It is, but if I don't get out of here and into some work clothes soon, we're going to be late." She looked around the room, trying to decipher which of the various items on the floor, desk, and chair were hers and which were Natalie's.

Darcy picked up her bra and looked around for her pants. From the bed, she heard a muffled laugh. She turned and found Natalie staring at her back. "If you are laughing at my ass I *will* kill you."

Natalie shook her head. "Your ass is incredible. I'm laughing because you cannot leave this room in the clothes you wore to the event last night. I don't care if your room is only a few doors down, you can't get caught doing that particular walk of shame."

Darcy put her hand on her hip before feeling self-conscious about being naked. "I do not feel any shame about what happened last night. I'm not the one who fell asleep in the middle of round two."

Natalie stared at her, mouth agape. She threw off the covers and vaulted herself out of the bed with impressive skill. "Let's go, right now." Her hands rested on the sides of Darcy's waist.

Darcy laughed. "'Let's go, right now?' You really know how to talk to a girl, don't you?" She kissed the end of Natalie's nose. "We don't have time to do anything before work other than get our asses out the door. Unless you would prefer to get fired?"

Natalie scowled. "Fine. But you can't leave the room in those clothes." She rifled around in her bag for a minute before extracting a pair of shorts and a T-shirt. "Put these on. If anyone sees you in the hall they'll think you were at the gym."

Darcy looked around the room and found her shoes by the door. "Oh yes, gym shorts and heels. That will fool literally no one."

Natalie rolled her eyes and muttered, "Such a princess." She walked to her closet and pulled out a pair of sneakers. "You can wear these, Your Highness."

Darcy took the shoes, checked the size, and laughed. "I wore this size in like sixth grade."

Natalie's mouth hardened into a thin line. "Fine. Go out there in your bra. I hope you run into Raquel or the camera crew. In fact, I'll open the door so I can hear how you try to explain to them why you're wearing your clothes from last night and walking out of *my* room. It'll be just like college."

Mentioning college was like sucking all the air out of the room. Both women froze, eyes locked on each other. Darcy felt like she'd been punched in the gut. She'd messed up all those years ago, in a hotel room not so different from this one. She'd made the biggest mistake of her entire life and here Natalie was, reminding her of it the first chance she got.

The worst part, even worse than hearing Natalie bring it up, was knowing that she deserved it.

"Natalie, I'm sorry." Darcy's voice came out in a strangled whisper, her voice vibrating with emotion.

Natalie shook her head. "I didn't mean it like that, I swear. I was making a joke about the time we found you sneaking out of Hinch's room after working on the team skit."

Darcy's heart stopped hammering her chest. Natalie was teasing. A sweet, gentle tease. She wasn't throwing Darcy's worst moment in her face, she was just reminiscing about college. Darcy wrapped her arms around Natalie and hugged her. Natalie's skin was freezing.

"You need to put some clothes on," Darcy scolded, pressing a kiss to Natalie's cheek. "I meant what I said. I'm sorry for what I did. I've regretted it since the second it happened."

"It's okay. But you need to put this on and get back to your room for real." She handed Darcy her shirt, holding the end until Darcy tugged it out of her hand.

"Your shoes will never fit."

Natalie shrugged. "You only have to make it to your room, not run a marathon, Princess."

Darcy grinned. As much as it used to infuriate her, she now loved the way it sounded when Natalie called her princess. She slipped the shirt over her head and stepped into the shorts and sneakers.

"I'll bring my garment bag when I come by to get you for the car, okay? No one needs to know its contents are on your floor." She gave a shy smile.

Natalie walked her to the door. "See you in a few minutes."

Darcy kissed her before opening the door to leave. "Can't wait."

Chapter Forty-Eight

Natalie showered and dressed for work as fast as she could. She bustled around the room, collecting the pieces of her suit to take back to the office with her. The flurry of activity didn't distract her as much as she had hoped it would. She and Darcy had gone way beyond flirting for the cameras and now she didn't know what to make of it.

Was she the only one feeling like it was more than just something fun to do while they were here? Because last night didn't feel like nothing but a little fun. But that wasn't the plan. She'd told Grace she had this under control. She wasn't going to get hurt because she wasn't going to get involved. But then last night happened and she couldn't shake the feeling that this was the exact kind of thing that would end up with her heart getting smashed. Again.

She was tying her shoes when Darcy knocked on her door. She looked amazing with her wet hair loose around her shoulders. "Hi," Natalie said, stepping back to let Darcy in.

Darcy stood awkwardly for a moment before handing a pile of folded clothes to Natalie. "Thanks for the outfit," she said, her cheeks reddening. "Not that I ran into anyone." She hung her suit in her garment bag and then fiddled with the zipper.

"This is awkward, right?" Natalie asked.

Darcy nodded. "Yeah. I feel like I don't know the rules. Like when I walked in, I should have kissed you, right? But I didn't know how you felt about that so…"

Natalie smiled. There was something so sweet and soft about flustered Darcy. A complete change from her in-control work persona. She stepped forward and placed a light kiss at the corner of Darcy's mouth. "If you want to kiss me, you probably should." She lingered, hoping Darcy would return the kiss while knowing they did not have nearly enough time for what she really wanted to do, which was to bury her fingers inside Darcy and hear her scream her name.

Darcy turned her head and caught Natalie's lips with hers. Natalie pressed her against the wall, her hands quickly finding their way to Darcy's hips. There wasn't time for this, but no matter how many times her brain reminded her that they needed to go, she couldn't bring herself to stop kissing Darcy. Not when Darcy's tongue slid over her bottom lip.

Darcy pulled her head back. "Later?" she said, so close Natalie could smell the fresh mint of her toothpaste.

All Natalie could do was nod and try to ignore the persistent ache between her thighs. Goddamn Darcy for being so hot.

Darcy looked over her shoulder before opening the door. "You ready?"

Natalie hurried to grab her garment bag, messenger bag, and hotel key. "Yeah, I guess so." She didn't even try to keep the pout out of her voice and Darcy rewarded her with a laugh.

Darcy let Natalie walk ahead of her. When Natalie looked back, she caught Darcy obviously staring at her ass and exaggerated her hips' sway. Darcy blushed but didn't look away.

They waited, looking out the lobby windows for the car to show up. Every time the hotel doors opened, a fresh wave of freezing air blasted them.

Natalie stepped away from the doors. "Fuck, it's freezing."

"Weird, considering it's the Winter Games."

Natalie shook her head. "Thank god. I was worried having sex with you might change things between us. But no, you're still a sarcastic asshole."

Darcy laughed, her shoulders shaking in her puffy coat. She looked at Natalie, her eyes catching the light from a passing car's headlights. "Do you want things to change?"

Natalie looked out the glass doors. "Our car's here."

She couldn't dodge the question forever. But she could stall long enough to try to figure out what she wanted from whatever this was. She didn't want to get her heart broken again. But she didn't know if she could really keep her feelings in check. Or if she even wanted to.

The car was blissfully warm when Natalie slid into the back seat. It took mere minutes for them to pull up to the speed skating venue. Natalie hopped out and hurried inside with Darcy right next to her.

Darcy shivered when they stepped into the arena. "Fuck, it's freezing."

Natalie giggled. "I'm sorry, but someone told me this is to be expected for the Winter Games."

Darcy stuck her tongue out at Natalie before cracking up. "It might make sense but it doesn't make it any more pleasant to be freezing at the ass crack of dawn." She bounced up and down a few times.

Natalie reached toward her and rubbed her hands up and down Darcy's arms in an attempt to warm her up. Darcy stopped bouncing and stared at Natalie. "What?"

Darcy looked over Natalie's shoulder. "Nothing, you're just being very nice." She flicked her eyes to Natalie's. "But here comes our producer so don't do anything too nice." She winked so quickly Natalie wasn't sure if she'd imagined it.

Raquel walked up to them and gave them each a bag. "Wanted to give you these myself." Raquel laughed. "Today is going to be so fun. I trust you're not too hungover from last night?"

Natalie shook her head. "Bright-eyed and bushy-tailed."

Raquel narrowed her eyes but didn't comment on their appearances. "So, are you ready to learn how to speed skate?"

Chapter Forty-Nine

Darcy pulled out the contents of the bag. *You have got to be kidding me.* "More spandex? Why do you hate us?"

Natalie made a face at the stretchy suit in her hands. "Come on."

Raquel fixed them with a stare that said, *I'm your fucking boss, deal with it.* "I assumed you two would know the proper attire for speed skating. I'm a little disappointed you're surprised."

She was enjoying this way too much for Darcy's liking.

"Once you've gotten into your outfits," Raquel said, with a smile tugging at the corners of her mouth, "go that way and find the bench area. We have skates for both of you to try on before the segment."

Darcy pulled the suit all the way out of the bag. Hers was red and white and Natalie's looked like an American flag. "We're going to look so stupid."

Raquel laughed. "It's going to be great TV." She answered her phone and walked away, leaving them in the dimly lit underside of the stadium.

Natalie pulled at the suit, testing out its stretch. "I'm going to look like a knock-off Captain America."

Darcy showed her suit. "I'll look like a cross between Waldo and a candy cane." She stepped closer to Natalie's suit. "But think how it's going to look on your ass."

Natalie looked up at her. "Oh god, my ass in spandex on national TV. Remind me why they make us wear the outfits for each sport? It's not like we couldn't try this in a nice comfy pair of sweats."

Darcy looked around. "No idea. Do you see the dressing rooms? I don't really want to strip down right here."

Natalie shrugged. "Could be fun."

Darcy rolled her eyes and walked off in search of someplace with a door where she could squeeze herself into this ridiculous outfit without the entire crew watching. Natalie hurried to catch up.

Darcy stopped in front of a gender-neutral bathroom. "This might be as good as it gets." She opened the door. At least it was clean.

Natalie grinned. "You need any help? I'm very handy."

Darcy lowered her voice to a harsh whisper. "You have to stop. We are at work. You cannot be doing whatever this is where there are people!"

Natalie put her hands up. "Okay. There's no one here, I thought it was safe to joke around with you." She stepped back. "But clearly I was wrong." She held the door open. "Your dressing room awaits."

Darcy suppressed the grin threatening to give away how amused she was. She stepped into the bathroom and flicked the lock. Stripping out of her clothes was no problem, but it was only afterward that she realized how hard it was to get into the tight spandex of her skating suit. Ugh. She did not want to have to ask for help. Natalie would never let her forget it. She tugged on the legs but they refused to budge enough to get the shoulders of the suit on, too.

Fuck.

She sighed and stared at herself in the bathroom mirror. Her suit was up over her thighs but then it stuck, leaving the top of her with only a sports bra and one arm halfway into the sleeve. She looked like a complete dipshit.

"Natalie?"

There was a soft knock on the door. "You okay in there?"

Darcy shook her head. This was not how she wanted the day to go. Especially not the morning after they had sex. "Can you come help me?"

She unlocked the door and slowly swung it open enough for Natalie to slip inside. "Couldn't resist my offer, could you?" Natalie joked before seeing Darcy. "Oh my god. Are you stuck?"

Darcy met Natalie's eyes in the mirror and nodded sadly. "I fear this is going to kill you ever thinking of having sex with me again." She hadn't meant to say that out loud.

Natalie smiled and placed a gentle kiss on Darcy's cheek. "Don't be stupid. We were teammates for a year. I've seen you look way stupider than this." She looked at the suit. "Is it okay for me to help you?" Darcy gave her an impatient look. "I just mean, I kind of have to put my hands on you for that and I wanted to be sure you were okay with it…"

Darcy turned around and grabbed Natalie's face in her hands. "You're really hot when you ask for consent."

Natalie gave a half smile. "I never, ever want to do something you don't want." Her face hardened for an instant before she smiled again, leaving Darcy to wonder what thought interrupted Natalie's smile. "Where are you stuck?"

Darcy looked down. "It feels like it's not sliding over my thighs."

"That's not what she said."

Darcy sighed but couldn't fight the laugh rising in her chest. "Oh my god, I am trapped in a spandex outfit in a public bathroom and you're making stupid sex jokes!"

Natalie spun Darcy around to face her. "You're freaking out.

We can fix this and honestly you're cute like this, so whatever you're worrying about, don't." She grabbed the fabric that was clinging to Darcy's legs and tugged until it released.

"Thanks," Darcy said in a low voice, embarrassed by her freak-out. No longer held hostage by the suit, she tugged the fabric up her arms and over her shoulders. She reached for the zipper but Natalie stopped her.

"May I?" she asked, her eyes burning into Darcy's.

The warmth of Natalie's hand on her stomach was more than she could handle. She leaned into the feeling of her warm palm on her bare skin and kissed Natalie hard. Natalie smiled, her lips curling against Darcy's.

"As much as I would love to have sex with you right now, I would rather wait until we are not in a public bathroom."

Darcy smacked Natalie playfully on the arm. "I'll hold you to that. I can turn around if you want while you get into your suit."

Natalie laughed. "I think we're way past you needing to turn around. Unless, of course, you won't be able to control yourself at the sight of me in spandex."

Darcy laughed. "You. Are. Ridiculous."

Natalie shot her a wicked grin and pulled her shirt over her head, revealing a Team USA sports bra and the delicious abs that Darcy enjoyed licking the night before. Jesus Christ, she was cocky but with good reason. Darcy swallowed and reminded herself that they were at work and there was no way she was going to lose her job and her reputation by fucking Natalie in a public bathroom. No matter how much she wanted to.

Natalie stripped out of her pants and smiled up at Darcy. She was going to die. Standing there, seeing Natalie's muscular thighs on full display and not being able to do anything but let images of the night before run through her mind, was actually going to kill her.

"Fuck, Carpenter. Why do you have to be so hot?"

Natalie shrugged, which only exaggerated the muscles in her arms and shoulders. "Maybe we can do more research on how both of us are so hot later?" She pulled her suit on with so much ease that Darcy felt like a complete loser for needing help.

Natalie leaned forward and kissed her, slow but with hints of the kind of heat that made Darcy want to quit her job and run back to the hotel room.

Chapter Fifty

Natalie lifted one foot to inspect the giant blade on her skate. "How the hell do you move in these things?" she asked the skaters who had come to give them a lesson during the segment. The blade jutted several inches past her toes and heel. It was like they attached a boot to a machete.

Carrie, a short white woman with a strawberry blonde ponytail, laughed. "You get used to it. They're not meant for quick turns, that's for sure."

Peter, a Black man who was about the same height as Darcy, pointed at Natalie's foot. "Yeah, there's no rocker so don't try to spin or make a quick turn like you guys would in your skates. If you do, you'll end up on your ass."

During the segment, Carrie and Peter talked them through how they trained, things Natalie and Darcy needed to know about the skates and the turns, and how they felt about the spandex suits.

"Have either of you ever gotten stuck in your suits?" Natalie asked, a twinkle in her eye.

Carrie laughed. "Not stuck but it takes a little practice to get used to putting it on."

Peter nodded. "They have to be tight to do their jobs so it's not like putting on a pair of sweats. Why, did you have trouble?"

Darcy shot Natalie a fierce look before smiling for the camera. "Let's just say it was a learning experience for all of us this morning."

They cut for commercial and got in position for the part of the segment where they had to skate. Natalie slowly glided to the starting line, terrified she was going to fall on her face. The skates were heavy and impossible to turn. It was like skating for the first time, and not in a good way. Instead of being a toddler close to the surface of the ice if she fell, it was a long, publicly embarrassing way down if she ate it on camera.

Darcy came to a shaky stop next to her. "You ready for me to kick your ass?"

Natalie looked down to the ice where Darcy was trying to get her skates arranged to start the way Carrie and Peter had shown them. "Please. No one is going to win except Raquel, and the blooper reel she's making to watch every time she gets annoyed with us. I'll settle for making it around the track without falling."

The camera operator signaled for them to get ready. "Welcome back, everyone. We're coming to you live from the speed skating oval and are just about ready to give you all what you tuned in to see!"

Natalie chuckled. "Yes, we are aware that a large portion of our viewers tune in with the hope that we will fail spectacularly." She turned to look at Darcy. "Ready to race, Canada?"

"Bring it on, Captain America."

Carrie and Peter covered their laughter and tried to look serious as they counted down to the start of the race. Carrie dropped one arm and Natalie and Darcy took off. Well, "took off" implied that they had any speed whatsoever. It took them half of the straightaway to get up any speed and they both looked panic-stricken when they had to make the wide turn.

Natalie grew slightly more comfortable as she crossed her

skates over around the turn. She picked up speed and confidence as she sped past Darcy.

Darcy was not going to lose without a fight and started pushing harder down the backstretch. They swapped lanes halfway and were neck and neck around the final turn. Once they hit the final piece of the oval, they both pushed hard. Natalie's lungs burned and she tried to suck in as much air as possible. At the line she lunged forward, beating Darcy but losing her balance. She tried to recover, arms outstretched, muscles struggling to keep her upright. But just as she looked like she would recover, she neared the turn again and overcorrected. She caught an edge and found herself sliding on her ass across the ice and into the padded board. When she bounced off the side, she kept her wits about her enough to look for the camera and smile. Darcy slowed to a stop next to her.

"Well, there you have it, folks, Natalie beat me but at what cost, really?" She cracked up. "We hope you will all come back tomorrow to see what other sport we can ruin."

She held out a hand and pulled Natalie up. They both thought the camera had cut away but it caught the way Natalie's hand lingered on her arm and the way their hips pressed together before gently moving apart.

"You okay?" Darcy asked in a low voice.

Natalie nodded. "I'm going to have a hell of a bruise on my ass, though."

Darcy raised one eyebrow. "Maybe I should take a look at it for you."

Natalie grabbed for the mic clipped to Darcy's chest and shook her head. "Maybe we can have this conversation later?" *When we're not being recorded.*

"Oh shit," Darcy said in a low voice. She glided over to the camera crew and unclipped her mic and handed it to them. "Hopefully Natalie didn't break hers when she hit the ice," she said with a teasing tone.

Natalie arrived at the boards and took off her mic, too. "I landed squarely on my ass, the mic pack is fine."

The camera operator chuckled. "I caught the whole thing. Sorry, but I think by the time you get changed you're going to be a GIF."

Natalie rolled her eyes. "Great. And the Twitter lesbians are probably losing their minds because you helped me off the ice." Despite her growly tone, she didn't mind. Not that she'd admit it to anyone. She liked it when other people confirmed the fact that Darcy freaking LaCroix liked her and it wasn't only in her head.

She liked knowing that other people could tell that Darcy was flirting with her, letting her hand linger for a few seconds too long when she helped her up. She liked the feeling of being wanted. And after last night, she liked the idea that it wasn't just something they were doing for ratings or because Raquel wanted to keep the audience watching for hockey player subtext. Whatever was going on was more than for the cameras.

That was exciting. That was terrifying. Because the last time she let Darcy in close enough for something real to happen, she broke her stupid teenage heart.

Chapter Fifty-One

Darcy was glued to her phone the entire ride back to the offices. Natalie kept trying to catch her eye, Darcy could feel it, but she couldn't stop scrolling through Twitter and Instagram. As the camera guy predicted, there were GIFs of Natalie's fall. They were hilarious but the thing keeping Darcy scrolling was the GIFs and comments and sheer number of tweets talking about the two of them. The way they stood, the way they held hands for half a second after Darcy hauled Natalie up off the ice. Someone had even zoomed in on the way their hips bumped. Good grief, these people needed a better hobby. One that didn't involve Darcy and her love life.

She finally looked at Natalie. Could she call it a love life yet? Was it that? Or was it just a one-night thing?

"You all right? You look like you're freaking out." Natalie gave Darcy a sweet smile.

Darcy nodded. "Yeah, I'm fine." She flipped her phone to face Natalie. "This is..."

"Overwhelming?" Natalie chuckled. "I'm sorry to tell you but as someone who has a long history of fans talking about her on the internet—"

"What?" Darcy cut in.

Natalie laughed. "I'm kidding. The only time people GIF'd me before was when I was on the show after the Olympics and clearly still tipsy from the night before. My mom was horrified but it seems like that performance got me here so it wasn't all bad."

When they reached the offices, Darcy was silent until they got to the conference room they'd taken over as their own. "Before it was funny, you know? But now it feels..."

"Uncomfortable?" Natalie said.

Darcy shook her head. "It was kind of a game before, you know? Seeing people thinking we were flirting with each other all this time. It was fun."

"I *was* flirting with you, for the record."

Darcy smiled and reached out to squeeze Natalie's hand. "This feels more exposed or something and I don't really know what's going on with us or whatever and oh my god, I'm being such a weirdo. Sorry. It's fine. I'm totally cool and not at all freaking out."

Natalie's smile softened. "You can just say you like me."

Darcy laughed. Leave it to Natalie to be both adorable and obnoxious at the same time. She hadn't changed a bit since they first met and Darcy still found her irresistible.

Not that she was ready to tell Natalie that. Instead of saying any of that, she looked at the table covered with their mess from the day before.

When she looked up, Natalie was studying her. An awkward moment passed with neither of them saying anything before Natalie stepped toward the door. "Are you hungry? I'm starving. Why don't I go see if there's any food around. I'll bring you something."

She was gone before Darcy had a chance to speak. Darcy collected the random papers they'd left behind into a pile and set it in the center of the table. She was embarrassed that they left it so messy that other people probably felt like they couldn't use the room.

She sank into one of the chairs just as Chip walked by the room. *Please don't stop, please don't stop.*

He stopped and spun on the heel of his stupid shiny shoes. "Darcy, haven't seen you around for a bit." He gave her a smile that displayed far too many of his shockingly white teeth. "I guess you've been *busy* with your little friend." He raised his eyebrows like one of the creepy frat boys she'd dealt with in college.

Ugh. Why must he be so gross? Darcy took a deep breath and gave him a smile she hoped he knew was fake. "Natalie and I have been busy. You know, meeting the top brass, recording our segments…"

He held up his phone. "Oh, don't pretend like you aren't having a bit of fun, too. The internet is ablaze with your *relationship.*"

Ew. How could a person merely saying a word make it sound dirty? Darcy bristled. "You of all people should know better than to believe everything you read online." It was a vague shot across the bow. She hoped he'd take it as a warning. She knew the rumors about him and even more, she knew how he made every woman on staff feel. The guy was a creep.

The toothy smile returned. "I don't begrudge you enjoying a little fun with your costar. Who among us hasn't dabbled in a little fun at work?"

If they'd been on the ice, this is the point where Darcy would earn herself a suspension by throwing the first punch. Instead, she clenched her fists and jaw as tightly as she could to stop herself from ripping this guy's head off. There was nothing similar about his creepy harassment and whatever she had going on with Natalie. In a few words, he'd catapulted her back to college. She listed the reasons in her head. First of all, they were equals, coworkers. She wasn't Natalie's boss and she didn't cross any lines without consent. And second, fuck this guy forever for thinking he knew anything about her based on a few internet rumors. "Chip, you clearly have no idea what you're talking about." Darcy paused to collect herself, to find the words that would make him fuck off but wouldn't get her fired. "Natalie and I go way back. We were college teammates and we've been *friends* for a long time. That's it."

Chip shrugged. "Call it whatever you like." He waved his phone in the air. "But we both know what's going on here." He swept away, revealing Natalie standing behind him, holding two cups of coffee, each with a plate of food balanced on top.

Darcy met her eyes and saw a wave of hurt before Natalie clamped down and stuck one hand out toward Darcy. "Here's your food, *friend*."

Darcy took the plate and cup feeling like she'd broken something priceless. "Nat, that's not what I meant and you know it."

Natalie stopped but kept one of the chairs between them.

Darcy put her food on the table and stepped toward Natalie. "Please let me explain."

Natalie crossed her arms over her chest, saying "fuck you" with her entire body. But she didn't walk away.

Darcy didn't waste her chance. "Chip came in here waving Twitter in my face and claiming that he and I are the same because, according to the internet, you and I are a thing." She paused to calm her nerves and steady her voice. "I am *nothing* like Chip. He's a scummy, skeevy, serial sexual harasser. And I am…" She trailed off. She couldn't tell Natalie that. Not yet. "So no, I didn't tell him that you and I slept together last night. I didn't tell him that I might really, really like you. I didn't tell him that you are the most beautiful, most infuriating, most incredible person I know because he doesn't deserve to know anything about me. He doesn't get to know how I feel about this sandwich let alone how I feel about you." She took a deep breath.

No matter what Natalie said next, at least she'd said everything she wanted to say. Well, not everything, but how on earth could she tell Natalie she loved her after one night together, especially if she was going to fly off the handle because Darcy didn't tell Chip they were together? *Were* they even together? Wait, was this a time-limited thing? Did Natalie just want a little bit of fun while they were working together?

Darcy told herself she had to be okay with whatever Natalie wanted. Natalie didn't owe her more after she'd been clear with her yesterday. But sitting there in that fishbowl of a conference room, Darcy already knew she wanted more.

Chapter Fifty-Two

Natalie stood there, her arms uncrossing and falling to her sides without her noticing. She didn't try to stop the smile from slowly spreading across her face.

"How do you feel about me?" Natalie asked, not sure she was prepared for the answer and positive she wouldn't be able to answer the same question if Darcy asked.

Darcy shrugged. "I like you. I've always liked you. But I don't know if you think this is just a little fun while we're thousands of miles from home or…"

Natalie stepped closer, all too aware that the conference room walls were glass and there was no privacy. "I don't know what I'm doing, either, if that makes you feel any better." She looked down at the foot of carpet between their feet. Twelve inches she would not cross in public, where anyone could walk by and confirm whatever suspicions were already flying around.

Darcy tilted her head to one side. "Well, there goes my hope that one of us had a clue." She gave a wry smile. "I don't know what's happening or where it's going to go, but me not sharing that or anything else with Chip doesn't mean I don't care about you." She swallowed. "I know I have a history of fucking up when it comes to you but that's not what this is. I swear."

Natalie pulled out a chair and slumped into it, hiding behind her hunger as she tore off a hunk of her cinnamon roll.
"Right. Okay. But you get why…" She couldn't bring herself
to say it. She couldn't form the words. That wasn't true. She
didn't want to invite them in, like a monster that would devour
their relationship before it had a chance to go anywhere. She
didn't even want to think that this was like college. She would
not end up heartbroken. Maybe if she didn't put her hurt into
words it couldn't catch her this time.

Darcy sat next to her. "Nat, I don't know how I can make
up for what I did. I was stupid. I was twenty-two and scared
of my feelings for you and terrified that I was graduating and
we wouldn't survive that. And in one stupid sentence I broke
everything. I won't do it again. I hope you know that. And I
hope you know that me not telling Chip that we had sex last
night is not anything like what happened in college."

Then why does it feel so much like college?

Natalie knew Darcy was right even if it still felt shitty. But
she wasn't going to start an argument in the office, not about
this. For once she would hold her tongue and think for more
than half a second before flying off the handle. Or before flying off the handle a second time.

"Nat." Darcy's voice was more breath than words and it sent
a shiver across Natalie's skin as it curled its way to her ears.
"That was a long time ago and I'm not the same scared kid I
was. I'm not going to hurt you."

Natalie peeled another strand of cinnamon roll away from
the rest but couldn't bring herself to eat it. Instead, it dangled
between her fingers, waiting for her to decide whether to take
a bite. "Okay."

"Okay?" Darcy asked, sounding completely baffled.

Natalie took a bite, the cinnamon and sugar delicious in her
mouth and buying her a few more seconds to figure out what
to say. She was being ridiculous. Chip *was* gross. She knew that.

She wouldn't have told him that she and Darcy had slept together, either, but it still hurt. No matter how far she'd buried that wound under years of telling herself she didn't give a shit, that she was better off with a string of women, none of them getting close enough to wound her, the cut was still there. No amount of scar tissue could stop her from feeling it.

"Yeah, it's fine. I must've gotten hangry or something. It's not like you needed to tell Chip anything about us and besides, we haven't even talked about what's going on here…" She trailed off, her smile plastered across her face. She didn't feel fine but she'd get there. Her brain told her that this was fine, she didn't need to freak out. Not yet, anyway.

Darcy reached over and put her hand on Natalie's. "Maybe we should talk about that now?" Her eyes, warm and gentle, searched Natalie's. "Are you just having fun with me or…"

Natalie swallowed. Admitting her feelings was the right thing to do but it was scary. Inside, she was clamping down, the wall dropping to keep Darcy away from those old wounds. If she kept her away, she couldn't get hurt.

"I mean, last night was fun, right? I know I passed out in the middle there, but hopefully I'll get a chance to rectify that? Tonight, maybe?" She didn't answer the question and hoped Darcy would let her get away with it.

Darcy smiled. "I'd like that." She squeezed Natalie's hand. "But you ducked the question. Are you planning to ditch me at the end of this? Or is there a chance you'll go out with me when we're back in the U.S.?"

Natalie grinned. "I thought you might want to sample the merchandise more than once before you decided on whether you want to keep me or not."

"You're such a gross frat boy!" Darcy cackled and then slapped a hand over her mouth, her cheeks turning a deep crimson.

Natalie giggled. "I'm not gross, just being realistic."

Darcy took a deep breath, her laughter subsiding. "I want to take you on a date, Carpenter." Her eyes sparkled. "I want to take you out, go to a movie or dinner, and then walk around together talking about everything and nothing." Her tongue ran along her lower lip. "And then I want to take you back to my place." She sat back. "That's what I want."

"Okay," Natalie said. "I'm in. Can we start with dinner tonight?" She flicked her hair off her forehead. "Give me a chance to redeem myself."

Darcy grinned. "You're on, Carpenter."

Chapter Fifty-Three

The restaurant was full. People sitting around circular tables, their heads bowed toward each other, occasionally thrown back with laughter. Darcy walked behind Natalie as their server weaved between tables to the small table at the back. Darcy's eyes looked at the faces of the people at the other tables and recognized a few, TV personalities, Olympic officials, and a few other people who she couldn't place but who looked familiar.

They sat and opened their menus.

"Hi," Darcy said, her eyes catching Natalie's over the tops of their menus.

Natalie returned the smile. "Hi. This is nice." Her voice was wary, guarded.

Darcy flicked her eyes over the menu, her mind spinning. "Can I confess something?"

Natalie set her menu flat on the table. "Oh my god, if you're going to tell me you're married, I will kill you."

Darcy laughed. "No. Definitely not married. My sister called me this afternoon to yell at me."

Natalie froze. "What did you do?"

Darcy chuckled. "You."

"Your sister called you from Canada to yell at you because of me? Are there no hobbies in the Great White North?"

Darcy smiled. "Yelling at me is Kit's favorite hobby. Always has been. She's convinced that I'm going to fuck this up and you're going to break my heart." *Again.* She didn't say the word. She swallowed it down. She resisted the urge to fiddle with her silverware. Instead, she unfolded her napkin and concentrated way too hard on spreading it over her lap.

When she finally looked up, Natalie was staring at her. "I think you're not remembering what happened very well. I remember you breaking my heart, not the other way around."

Darcy turned her knife over, then back again. When she took a breath and spoke, her voice came out low, somewhere between a whisper and a prayer. "I remember everything." She looked up, her eyes finding Natalie's. "I remember every mistake I made, the stupid things I said. I remember the way you looked. Trust me, I broke both of our hearts." Darcy's throat thickened and a sharp pain bloomed at the top of her nose. She was not going to cry before they ordered. Jesus. She forced herself to make eye contact with Natalie.

Natalie looked stunned. "Then why did you do it? Why did you tell everyone nothing happened like I was some pathetic little freshman chasing after you?" Emotion filled her voice. It rushed across the table like a rogue wave, crushing everything in its way.

The waiter appeared at that moment, right as Darcy was trying to find the words to explain. They ordered drinks and food; Darcy hoped it would give them a few uninterrupted minutes.

"I didn't really plan to start our date this way but fuck it." She looked at Natalie, her nerves jangling. "In college, I screwed everything up. I got scared. When Sammy found us, I panicked. She called me a hypocrite for giving her a hard time for dating that freshman on the men's team. She made me feel like I was taking advantage of you."

Natalie tried to interrupt but Darcy waved her hand.

"I didn't say I was smart. I said I panicked. I was afraid of what people would think and what they'd say. I liked you so much that I didn't know how to deal with it and instead of saying that I pretended like I didn't care about you at all." She grabbed for her water glass, her hand visibly shaking. She'd tried to forget everything that happened back then, tried to make it go away by sheer force of will, but it didn't work. Of course it didn't work. The strength of her feelings for Natalie couldn't be shoved aside that easily.

The cold water, the ice cube bumping gently against her lips, brought her back to the present. "I'm sorry. I should have told you that then."

"You did," Natalie said, finally able to break through Darcy's speech.

"Not like I should've. I should have explained. I told you about the team, but there was more I didn't say. I was afraid about what our future would look like after I graduated and we were on different teams, in different countries. But instead of sharing those fears with you, I was a coward and it cost me everything." Darcy's voice sounded thick with emotion. Ugh, why couldn't she talk without getting choked up?

Natalie leaned forward, her hands hovering above the table-cloth for a second before she reached across the table and put her hands on top of Darcy's. "If it makes you feel any better, Grace spent like half an hour yelling at me this afternoon, too. It seems like the people who care about us don't trust us not to screw this up." She smiled and it made the stinging in Darcy's eyes worse for a second. "College sucked. And obviously, I wasn't your biggest fan for a while there. But who knows how any of it would have turned out. Maybe we would have been able to work through your fears, but maybe not. Maybe it would have been perfect, but maybe it would have turned out even worse. There's no way to know. Who knows, maybe I would have fucked everything up." Darcy laughed and squeezed Natalie's hands. "But that was a long time ago, right? We're grown-ups now. We don't have to make the same stupid mistakes again. Like, maybe acting like a baby because you didn't tell Chip about us wasn't my best move. But…"

The waiter interrupted them with a tray of drinks. She set them on the table and disappeared without a word.

Darcy sighed. "I'm sorry. It must have felt like I was pulling the same shit all over again."

Natalie shrugged, took a sip of her beer. "Sure, but I'm not nineteen anymore, I know better than to act like a complete jackass."

"Do you, though?" Darcy said, her tongue peeking out from between her teeth.

Natalie laughed and took another sip of beer. "God, have you always been this fucking insufferable?" She shook her head. "Don't answer that. Of course you have. But you've always been devastatingly hot, too."

Darcy spread her hands over the table. "What can I say? I'm irresistible."

Natalie relaxed, her jaw unclenched, her hands found their way to her lap. "You really are."

Darcy's breath caught. The way Natalie stared at her—like she was the best thing she'd ever seen—stopped her from making the flippant comment that had been at the tip of her tongue. Natalie had dropped her sarcasm, her goofiness, and gone back to the look she gave Darcy in college, the one that said she was serious about this, about them. Maybe this wasn't a fling. Maybe this meant as much to Natalie as it did to her.

Darcy picked up her glass and held it in front of her mouth. "When this is done, do you think you want to stick with TV?"

Natalie cocked her head to the side. "Are you asking me to be your cohost on a permanent basis?"

Darcy shook her head to buy time while she swallowed her water. She hadn't meant it like that. "You're annoyingly good at this but I'm more wondering if you've fallen in love with being on TV or if there's something else you want to try when all this is over."

Natalie inhaled deeply. "This is going to sound stupid… Coming here, I wasn't sure what it would be like." She looked across the dining room, her eyes focusing on some faraway spot. "But it reminded me how much I love being on the ice and being a part of a team." She fiddled with her silverware. "I think I want to coach. Then I get to be on the ice every day and I can be part of something, even if it's not the way I'm used to. I think I'd like that." She dipped her head like she was embarrassed.

Darcy's heart squeezed like Natalie had put it in a vise. "You'd be a great coach. Anyone would be lucky to learn from you."

Natalie looked up, her eyes searching Darcy's. "You think?"

Darcy smiled. "I think it sounds perfect for you." She considered her words carefully. "Not to sound like my dad, but if there's anything I can do to help I hope you'll let me. I have some friends who are coaching…" Darcy couldn't promise they would have a job for Natalie, but she knew they'd talk to her and help any way they could. "Not that you need any help. Anyone would be lucky to work with you." She looked down. "I know I have been."

Deep pink flooded Natalie's cheeks and her smile was radiant. Darcy loved seeing her this happy, she loved *making* her this happy. She could see her chasing this exact feeling forever. She swallowed. It was too early for words like "forever." But when Natalie smiled like that, she couldn't help it.

"Natalie?"

Darcy followed Natalie's gaze, startled to see John Huntington standing next to their table.

"Coach?" Natalie said before her face shifted, hardened. Her eyes flicked to Darcy's before returning to the man standing over their table. "John. What are you doing here?"

"I'm having dinner with Todd and Jim." He gestured toward

a table filled with white men holding glasses of whiskey. "But I wanted to say hello. I'm happy to hear you found something to do so quickly after…"

Natalie's face contorted into an awful attempt at a smile. "After you cut me?" She nodded across the table. "You remember Darcy LaCroix."

He turned and offered his hand. "Sure. Big fan of your dad."

Darcy put on the smile she perfected for every person who ignored her achievements to praise her father's. "Thank you, I'll be sure to tell him."

"He was my favorite player," John said, unable to help himself from gushing. He swallowed when neither woman said more. "Well, good to see you, Natalie. The team's looking great."

After he left, Darcy drained her glass of wine. "What the fuck was that? Are you okay?"

Natalie bit her lip, her face stunned but otherwise unreadable. "Yeah, of course. Why wouldn't I be?" She picked up her beer, took two large swallows, and then put it back down. "I mean, it's not like he came over here just to tell me how well the team's doing since he cut me, right?"

Darcy took her hand, trying to fend off the emotion she could hear overwhelming Natalie's voice. "He's an asshole. 'Tell your dad I say hi!' Yeah, go fuck yourself, John."

Natalie laughed and her shoulders descended from somewhere up around her ears back to where they belonged. "You gotta give him credit for insulting both of us in less than two minutes." She finished her drink. "Fuck, I hate that guy."

The waiter arrived to deliver their dinners. Darcy waited for her to leave before speaking. "That guy sucks but he can't take away the fact that you are a three-time Olympian. I know you're pissed that you're not competing this time, but it doesn't change the fact that you're one of the best players the U.S. has ever had."

Natalie's eyes filled with tears, but she blinked them away.

"Did you just tell me I was good? I didn't think Canadians were *allowed* to compliment us. I thought they'd come swooping in and take away your Timbits." Her tone was playful, but Darcy didn't miss how much hurt there was in her eyes and in the tension in her body.

"You can deflect all you want, but that asshole can't take away any of the things you did in your career." Darcy let her foot touch Natalie's under the table, simply to let her know she was there.

Natalie stared at her plate, her fork hovering above her salmon. "I didn't want it to end like this. I wanted one more chance to pull on that jersey, you know?"

Darcy nodded. "I understand. On the plus side, it makes Team Canada's chances of winning gold a lot higher."

Natalie laughed. "Oh shut up. There's no way some has-been like me would make any damn difference. They weren't even going to let me play fourth line out there." Natalie forced a light tone, but it didn't fool Darcy for a second.

"I'm going to tell you something that I will deny ever saying if you tell anyone." Natalie looked up from her plate. "Except when we were teammates, you were always the player I worried the most about on the ice. In college, I knew that if something needed to be done on a shift, you'd make sure it happened. You were already the best player on the ice."

"Bullshit. You were."

Darcy shook her head. "Don't interrupt. When Canada played the U.S., I knew that there was only one player who had the ability to take over the game. Not me, you. So, whatever they said to you when they cut you, they were wrong. I don't care if there are younger, faster players. If I'm team captain and we're picking sides, you're the first person I'm picking. Every time."

The way Natalie looked at her made Darcy's heart clench. Natalie's smile peeked out from behind her sadness like the first glimmer of sun on a dreary day. And then Natalie forced a grin. "You're only saying that because we had sex."

Darcy rolled her eyes. "If you think that then you're an absolute dumbass."

Natalie's real smile emerged. "Thank you. I don't care why you said it. It means a lot to me. I've been trying to impress you since I was a teenager. Good to know I finally managed it."

Darcy took a bite of her pasta. "Don't be silly. I've been impressed with you since the first time I stepped on the ice with you. I never said anything because your ego was already out of control."

"It's not bragging if you can back it up," Natalie said, her eyes telling Darcy she wasn't just talking about hockey.

Chapter Fifty-Four

This time, Natalie had left her room pristine. She wasn't going to risk throwing off her game by having Darcy walk into her usual mess. But in the end it didn't matter because Darcy led them to her room.

When Darcy opened the door and flicked on the light, Natalie noticed her hands were shaking.

Darcy let the door close behind her and as the lock caught, Natalie took her hand. "Do I make you nervous?"

"Of course."

Natalie ran her thumb across the back of Darcy's hand before bringing Darcy's hand to her lips. She placed a series of butterfly-light kisses across her knuckles, her eyes never leaving Darcy's.

"How long did it take to lose the calluses?" Natalie asked, holding her hand open to show Darcy.

Darcy ran a finger down the length of Natalie's fingers, tracing the rough spots caused by decades of playing. She displayed her own hands for Natalie to inspect, tingling when Natalie let her fingertip ghost over her skin. "I think I'll have them forever."

Natalie traced a scar on Darcy's forearm, a jagged line across the back of her wrist. "What this one's story?"

"Slash. One of your teammates, actually."

Natalie winced as though she could feel the stick striking her own arm. "You broke your arm?"

Darcy shook her head. "Nope. Skin split open, though. The doctors had a hell of a time putting me back together."

Natalie looked up at her. "Who did this to you? I'll kill them."

Darcy laughed and tugged Natalie toward the bed. "Okay, tough guy." Darcy ran her hand up the back of Natalie's neck before threading her fingers into her hair. As their kisses became more urgent, her fingers tightened and pulled Natalie's hair. Not enough to hurt, but plenty hard enough to get Natalie's attention.

"Fuck," Natalie growled.

Darcy pulled her head back so she could see Natalie's face. "Oh yeah?"

Natalie nodded, her tongue finding Darcy's and her hips pressing forward when Darcy gave her hair another tug.

"Fuck, Darcy." Natalie pressed forward, crashing them both onto the bed.

Darcy let out a surprised laugh until Natalie's hands found her breasts. Natalie's thumb circled Darcy's nipple, first teasing and then increasing pressure until Darcy was arching off the bed.

"Nat." She reached down and grabbed a fistful of Natalie's hair. "Get me out of these clothes."

Darcy reached for her zipper but Natalie stopped her. "Let me." She looked up at Darcy. "Please."

Darcy put her hands over her head in surrender while she watched Natalie take her time unbuttoning her pants and sliding them down over her hips. Darcy grew impatient but when she reached for the hem of her shirt, Natalie grabbed her hands and pulled them back over her head.

Natalie held her there, hovering over Darcy's body. "Let me

take your clothes off." She dipped her head and captured Darcy's lip between her teeth and gave it a gentle tug.

"Fucking hurry, then. Any slower and I'd think you were a goalie."

Natalie laughed. "Fighting words, LaCroix." She sat on Darcy's thigh so she could use both hands to undo the buttons on Darcy's shirt. She moved excruciatingly slowly, pausing to tease Darcy's nipples through her bra before finally, finally removing the rest of her clothes.

Darcy huffed. "There are glaciers that move faster than you."

"But they don't make you come as hard," Natalie said, wrapping her lips around Darcy's nipple. For all her shit-talking and cocky banter, Natalie wanted to savor this. She wanted to explore every inch of Darcy's body slowly, thoroughly, and until she was begging Natalie for release.

All her intentions went out the window when Darcy tugged on her hair again. She didn't even know that was a thing she liked but holy fuck, it was making her lose her ability to take things slowly.

Darcy grabbed for her when Natalie had one nipple in her mouth and teased the other with the pads of her fingers. The feeling of Darcy tugging her hair—not rough, but possessive—made Natalie moan.

"If you do that, I'm not going to be able to concentrate on what I'm doing."

Darcy's nails dragged across Natalie's scalp and her fingers tightened in her hair. "Is that so?"

Natalie, chin resting on Darcy's chest, stared up at her. "You are a menace."

"You have no idea," Darcy said with a deep, throaty laugh. She lifted her head off the mattress to kiss Natalie, and sucked Natalie's lower lip until Natalie's hips pressed into hers.

She let her head fall against the pillow. "I want you inside me. Now."

Natalie licked a line across Darcy's collarbone while her hand found its way between them. "Are you sure?"

"Carpenter, if you don't fuck me right now I'm going to do it myself."

"Whatever you say, Cap."

Darcy arched against Natalie's fingers as they slid through her soaking pussy. Natalie moaned knowing she made Darcy want her that much. As her fingers circled Darcy's clit and her breaths grew more desperate, Natalie lowered her mouth to Darcy's chest and resumed sucking and licking until Darcy screamed her name.

Natalie hummed against the soft, sensitive skin of Darcy's chest. She let her head rest against Darcy's sternum so she could look up at her. "Good?"

Instead of responding, laughter bubbled in Darcy's chest in waves. It was the best sound Natalie had ever heard. She'd heard Darcy laugh before, but this was different. It was soft, intimate. She was laughing again and again with the happiest sighs Natalie had ever heard.

She loved it. She never wanted to stop hearing it. *Shit.* She swallowed. She could not be falling for Darcy LaCroix. Not her laugh or her smile or the amazing way she felt when she moved against Natalie's hands.

No. She couldn't feel like this.

Shit. She already did.

Chapter Fifty-Five

The smell of coffee persuaded Darcy to open her eyes. Her reward was Natalie sitting in her robe at the tiny table in her room, clutching a mug between her hands.

"Good morning," she whispered over the lip of the cup.

Darcy sat up, clutching the sheet to her chest and swiping her hair out of her face. "How long have you been awake?" She squinted into the sunlight streaming in the window behind Natalie. It lit her hair like a halo and cast a shadow across her face.

"A little while. Are you hungry? I ordered breakfast." Natalie grinned. "I figured I was safe charging it to your room, superstar." She gestured to the spread of coffee, fruit, and pancakes.

Darcy grabbed an extra pillow and propped herself against the headboard. "I'd kill for some coffee."

Natalie poured a cup, added half a spoon of sugar and half-and-half until it turned the perfect shade of light brown.

"How do you know how I like my coffee?" Darcy asked, leaning forward to take it in both hands.

"I told you. When it comes to you, I notice everything." Natalie smiled, soft and shy. She joined Darcy in the bed when Darcy patted the space next to her.

Darcy kissed her on the cheek. "All this time you've been trying to get everyone to think you're this swaggering, mouthy, pain in the ass when really you're a complete marshmallow."

"Lies," Natalie said, dipping her head. "Lies and I will deny it if you ever tell anyone." She reached for a plate of pancakes and held them in front of Darcy. "I got you chocolate chip."

"Oh my god, I lo—" She stopped talking. Her eyes widened in surprise. She gulped coffee and then coughed when it burned her mouth. Oh god, she was making a complete mess of this.

Natalie handed her a napkin. "It's just breakfast, Darce." Her tone was teasing but her face was kind, her eyes searching Darcy's.

Darcy leaned forward and pressed a kiss at the corner of Natalie's mouth. "It's not just pancakes and you know it." She picked up a pancake, folded it in half, and took a giant bite.

Natalie shrugged. "How do you know I don't do this for everyone?"

Darcy laughed. "Because you hate everyone."

Natalie settled her back against the headboard and sipped her coffee. "Maybe if you tell your sister I don't suck she'll stop warning you about me."

"She's protective, that's all. Same as Grace."

Natalie sighed. "It's so nice of them both to think we're incapable of having a love life without their help."

"We *did* royally fuck it up last time," Darcy said. "But I told my sister we are older and smarter now."

Natalie let her head rest on Darcy's shoulder. "I'd like to think we've matured in a decade and a half. At least in some ways."

Darcy kissed the top of Natalie's head, breathing in the scent of her shampoo. The weight of Natalie resting against her made this feel solid, like together they had heft, weight. She liked it. She imagined more mornings like this, more nights together and easy mornings drinking coffee in bed together.

"I had an idea," Natalie said, her voice vibrating against Darcy's collarbone. "There's this place I think we should go. Together." She added the last word like maybe Darcy wouldn't understand that Natalie was making a plan for the two of them.

It was adorable. "Where do you want to take me?"

Natalie shifted so she could look at Darcy. "There's this restaurant on the top of a mountain and the restaurant spins while you eat."

"That sounds like a recipe for motion sickness," Darcy said.

Natalie shook her head. "No, it goes so slowly that you don't even feel it but over the course of your meal it rotates three hundred sixty degrees so you get to see the entire view from the top of the mountain." Natalie's cheeks pinked under Darcy's gaze. "I would like to take you to the rotating restaurant on top of the mountain."

Darcy kissed Natalie gently on her smiling lips. "I'd love that."

A serious expression passed over Natalie's face. "To get to the top you take a series of gondolas. I know you don't like heights but do you think you can handle it? If not, I can plan something else…"

Darcy took her hand. "I can handle your high-flying adventure date. I'd love to eat delicious food with you at the top of a mountain and watch the view change. Though, it might not be worth it because I might not be able to take my eyes off you."

Natalie smiled. "Your charm is appreciated but if it's halfway as impressive as the pictures you'll have no trouble tearing your eyes off my boring old face. This place looks incredible."

Natalie pulled up the photos on her phone and handed it to Darcy. "We're done with all our segments soon, and I thought we could go away afterward. Just the two of us having an adventure before we have to fly back to the real world." Natalie's tone was light, but Darcy heard the hint of trepidation.

"This looks amazing. And you know, flying home doesn't make this any less real."

Natalie kissed her slowly, her mouth still warm from her coffee. "I've been trying not to think about what comes next. It hasn't been too hard with Raquel running us all over the place. But I..." She paused, licked her lips nervously, and looked up at Darcy. "This isn't some fling to me."

Darcy wrapped her arms around Natalie and pulled her into a tight hug, placing another kiss on the top of Natalie's head. "It isn't for me, either," Darcy said softly. Natalie relaxed against her side, their bodies tangled together. This was nice. Darcy would be happy to stay here all day if they could.

After another week of segments where they had a great time making fools out of themselves, laughing over the hysterical fan tweets, nights spent falling asleep in each other's arms, and the two of them planning their trip to the mountaintop restaurant, they woke to Darcy's phone buzzing aggressively on the nightstand.

Darcy reached for it. "Raquel," she said to Natalie.

"Good morning, Raquel."

"I need you to come in right away."

Natalie got up from the bed and poured herself another cup of coffee.

"Is everything all right?" Darcy looked over at Natalie, unsure of whether she should turn up the volume so she could listen in.

Raquel sighed. "Nothing's on fire, but I need you to come in."

Darcy's stomach dropped. "Did I do something wrong? I thought our last segment went well." Darcy caught Natalie's eye. She had no idea what was going on but if they did something wrong, she wanted Natalie to be prepared.

"No, nothing like that. You two have been great. I have an opportunity I want to talk to you about."

"Oh, okay." Natalie raised her eyebrows and Darcy shrugged. "I'll get Natalie and we'll hop in a car right away."

Natalie set her coffee down and gathered her clothes.

Darcy caught her eye. "Give us an hour and we'll see you in the office." She hung up and flipped her phone onto the bed.

As Darcy ended the call, she missed Raquel saying, "Natalie doesn't need to come."

"What's going on?"

Darcy climbed out of the bed, realized she was completely naked, and reached for a robe. "I don't know. Raquel says it's nothing to worry about but since when does she call us to come in on short notice?"

"You've worked with her for a while. What do you think she wants?"

Darcy shook her head. "No idea. But I told her we could be there in an hour so we better get showered and out the door."

Natalie stepped closer. "Are you implying I smell bad?"

Darcy laughed. "I'm implying that we both smell like sex. Really good sex, but I don't want to show up to work smelling like we spent the night fucking. Do you?"

Natalie's tongue slowly slid along her bottom lip. "You have a point." Her hand snaked around Darcy's back. "It would confirm what half the internet is already saying."

Darcy smacked her on the ass. "The internet does not need to know what I smell like, thank you very much."

Natalie kissed her, her tongue doing the same lazy slide across Darcy's lip it had just done on her own.

"We don't have time for this," Darcy sighed, regretting telling Raquel how quickly they'd arrive.

Natalie let her head fall back in disappointment. "Fine, but I'm going to spend the whole day thinking about how you looked when—"

"Oh my god, Carpenter. We cannot do this right now." She stepped back and smacked Natalie on the ass again. "Go. Get cleaned up before we're late."

Natalie pouted as she backed toward the door. "Fine. But let the record show I wanted a morning skate and you declined."

Darcy laughed and reached for the handle. Before she opened the door, she kissed Natalie again. "One of us has to be the grown-up."

Darcy closed the door and rushed around grabbing clothes and getting the shower warming up. By the time she hopped in, the water was hot, and she'd had time for curiosity to set in.

What on earth did Raquel want with them that she couldn't tell her over the phone or wait until later? Things had been going well with the segments, the audience—or a subset of it at least—was invested in the two of them together, and the ratings had been good. So, what on earth did Raquel want to say?

By the time Darcy was dressed and walking out the door she was convinced that they were either about to get fired because they were actually dating and it was against some obscure policy or they were getting hired full-time to be a team on camera. The first option seemed unlikely considering Raquel asked them to pretend to date and it would be distinct asshole behavior to then fire them for doing what she asked. The second option seemed both more likely and like a complete dream.

Would she want to work with Natalie full-time? Part of the beauty of this job was that it was limited. That had seemed especially important at the start when they were fighting constantly. But now, she worried that the relationship brewing between them—had she really almost told Natalie she loved her over pancakes this morning?—might be too fragile for them to work together full-time. Not to mention the fact that Natalie wanted to coach, not be on *Wake Up, USA.*

Darcy snatched her bag, credentials, and phone before walking out the door. Whatever it was, they'd find out soon enough. Well, not soon enough for Darcy's anxiety.

Chapter Fifty-Six

They walked into the offices together just under an hour later. Raquel texted Darcy to meet her in the conference room as soon as she got in. When they arrived, Raquel was talking to a man in a dark suit.

Natalie knocked on the glass door and opened it when Raquel gestured for them to enter.

"Natalie, what a surprise. Good morning. Darcy, thanks for coming in on such short notice." Raquel gestured to the man in the suit. "This is Hank Dunlop, our head of programming for the live sports division."

Darcy shook his hand. "Of course, nice to meet you."

Natalie followed suit.

Hank squinted at Natalie like he was trying to place her. "Carpenter, you just missed making the team for the Olympics, right? Lucky for you they needed someone to spar with Darcy."

Natalie couldn't keep from making a "what the fuck" face. She looked at Raquel. Was it possible she was invited to a meeting to get insulted?

"Why don't we sit down," Raquel said before Natalie had a chance to respond. Natalie took the seat farthest from Hank and Darcy sat next to her.

Hank leaned back in his chair, seemingly unaware that he'd insulted her. Unaware or unconcerned with her feelings. "Girls, we've been really impressed with the ratings for your little segments."

Natalie ground her teeth together. Could this fucking guy be more patronizing?

Raquel cleared her throat. "The ratings have been better than we had hoped and the engagement has been off the charts." Raquel's mouth twitched at the corner, leaving Natalie to wonder if she could see that she and Darcy were no longer pretending for the cameras.

"Exactly," Hank said. "And we want to take some of that to our hockey broadcasts."

Natalie sat up in her chair. Darcy looked stunned.

Hank grinned. "Well, I see I have your attention. We'd like you, Darcy, to join our pregame studio for the Canada game. We think it would really appeal to our hockey fans who might not be as familiar with the women's game."

Darcy blinked. "Excuse me?"

"Of course, we all know your playing career speaks for itself, but we think having you in the studio might bring some of our men's hockey fans to the broadcast. If we can't have the man himself, we think they'll be interested in seeing Marty LaCroix's daughter."

Darcy looked like a deer in the headlights. Natalie bumped her under the table with her knee.

Raquel cut in. "What Hank's trying to say is you're a huge name in women's hockey and would be an asset in the studio for the Canada game. Who better to talk about the Canadian's women's team than one of its biggest stars?"

"Who are they playing?" Natalie asked. She was sure she knew the answer.

Hank smiled. "The next game is the marquee matchup with the U.S. team. Your old team."

She knew how she would handle this kind of fuckery on the ice. She'd start with the butt end of her stick to his stomach, a quick chop of the stick on the top of his foot, and if all of that didn't work, she'd find a way to deck him behind the ref's back. Too bad the ref, Raquel, was sitting right there, staring at her.

She swallowed. "So, you want us in the studio together, talking about our old teams?"

Hank looked at Raquel, who shuffled the papers in front of her.

"Actually, Natalie, Hank is only looking for Darcy to join the team they already have." She gave a tight smile. At least she knew this sucked.

"Right," Hank jumped in. "LaCroix is a household name, even in the United States. We'd be stupid to pass up the chance to have her join the team." He smiled at her like she was five years old.

Natalie's face flamed with embarrassment. They didn't want her. They took a look at what she and Darcy did as a team and decided she was expendable. Her ears started ringing. Hank's mouth was still moving but she couldn't hear anything he was saying. It was like shame at being left off the team, again, had blocked all sound from reaching her ears.

Darcy's hand found Natalie's leg under the table. She squeezed. "I don't understand. You said you liked our segments, which we do together, but you only want me for the studio?"

Hank nodded. "You two are funny and your little segments are cute, but that's not our style in-studio. We offer a more serious look for our fans. They want to know what to expect, the players to watch, that kind of thing. We want you to provide commentary before the game, not make the audience laugh by falling on your asses."

Natalie pushed her chair back from the table, but Darcy clamped her fingers around her thigh.

Hank narrowed his eyes at Natalie. "No offense, Natalie.

We just don't think you bring what we need to the table. I'm sure you understand."

Unbelievable. She looked at Darcy, hoping to see anger in her eyes. Instead, Darcy was looking at Raquel and Hank.

Natalie stood up, aware that she was rapidly losing her shit and wanting to leave before she screamed at someone with the power to fire her ass. "I understand that despite saying you think *our* segments have been such a success you want to hire her because of her last name." She crossed her arms over her chest.

"She's right. We're a team. Whatever it was you saw on the screen that you liked so much, and the engagement Raquel mentioned, that's because we're a team."

Raquel ran a hand through her hair. "Darcy, you've been begging me for three years to get you on the hockey broadcast. This is your shot."

Darcy looked up at Natalie, her eyes pleading. For what? For Natalie to give her blessing to do this thing without her? To toss her aside for her own opportunity? Jesus Christ.

Natalie took a step toward the door. "Well, it doesn't seem like you need me here for this."

"Natalie," Darcy said, her voice low and pleading.

Natalie turned, a grim smile on her face masking the seething shame-injected anger burning in her chest. "It's fine, Darcy. It's your dream. Good luck." She yanked the door open and strode off down the hallway, refusing to let her anger turn into tears. Not in front of that jackass, Hank, or even Raquel.

As she walked toward the bathroom, she kept hoping to hear footsteps behind her. But when she reached the bathroom, she ventured a glance back toward the conference room. Darcy was still seated, talking to Hank and Raquel. She hadn't followed her. From the looks of it, she hadn't even paused a moment before diving into planning for her big debut.

Not good enough for another team. Not important enough for Darcy to fight for. Natalie leaned against the sink and stared into the mirror. What the fuck was she doing here? This job? Darcy?

Of course, it stung that they didn't want her for the job and that they insulted Darcy by picking her because of her last name, her famous father. But worse than those insults was the fact that Darcy hardly fought for her at all. She got what she wanted and set Natalie aside.

Natalie blinked and tears fell into the sink. What was it about her that made her so easy to discard? Were her expectations too high? No. This was why she kept people away. So they couldn't hurt her, disappoint her.

The door to the bathroom creaked open. Natalie cupped her hands under the water and splashed her face quickly.

She didn't have control over much, but they weren't going to see her cry.

Chapter Fifty-Seven

Darcy's eyes tracked Natalie walking down the hall away from the conference room. Only when she disappeared into the bathroom did Darcy realize Hank was talking to her.

Darcy blinked. "I'm sorry, can we go back a second? You really want me to do this without Natalie? You do realize that she could give you incredible insight into the U.S. team, right?"

Raquel shot her a warning look. But Darcy realized she didn't care about being warned. This was a stupid decision even if it was good for her. Yes, she wanted this job. A lot. But she knew she'd be better at it with Natalie there, too.

Hank gave her a patronizing smile. "I applaud you for standing up for your coworker, but I assure you we have the Team USA angle covered. What we need is you with your star power and knowledge of the Canadian team, of course."

Darcy's stomach dropped. They wanted her last name. That was the only reason they were offering her a job she'd been working toward for years. When it came down to it, it wasn't her hard work, her knowledge of the sport, or how good she was on camera. All this guy cared about was that she was Marty LaCroix's daughter.

It didn't matter that she turned down the Canadian network who wanted her because her dad called in a favor. It didn't matter that she came to New York to work for a network full of people who knew nothing about hockey. It didn't matter that she'd done everything she could think of to avoid this exact situation. She was getting the chance she'd always wanted but only because her dad was such a big name that even people in the United States knew who he was.

"You and Natalie only have two more segments to film before the end of the Games. We're hoping you can film one today and one tomorrow and then you'll be free to concentrate on getting up to speed for the hockey game. How does that sound?" Raquel asked.

Darcy nodded slowly. How did they have so few segments left to do together? It didn't feel like they'd been there long enough to be done. At the same time, it felt like a year since this started. "Right. We have biathlon today." She forced herself to smile at Hank. "Giving us guns seemed like a good idea at the time."

Raquel nodded. "And then we'll have you finish up with hockey, which will segue nicely into your debut in the studio for that game."

"Raquel and I talked about you having a chance to talk to some Team USA players in your final segment and you could get some information from them to bring to the game broadcast. I think it will work out quite nicely."

Darcy cringed internally. It might work out nicely for him. But how would Natalie feel about doing the goofy segment with her and then knowing that Darcy was going to continue on without her? What a fucking mess.

Darcy leaned forward, her elbows resting on the cool tabletop. "I'm thrilled with this opportunity. And I'm very appreciative, but I think you're making a mistake not considering Natalie for the show, too."

"Darcy," Raquel said, her tone a warning.

Darcy held her hands up. "I know. It's not my place."

Hank crossed his arms over his chest. "Are you saying you

won't do it without Natalie? Raquel assured me this was your dream job. Are you sure you want to pass up a chance to make your dream a reality? If Natalie is truly your *friend*, surely she'd want you to seize the chance."

Darcy caught the emphasis on "friend" and didn't like the look on his face when he said it. But she'd pushed as hard as she dared. When it came down to it, she wanted the job. This *was* her dream and she'd worked too hard to make it happen to let it pass her by.

She only hoped Natalie would understand that, too.

"The game's only a few days away. Why don't you fill me in on everything I need to know to be prepared."

After the meeting ended, Darcy went looking for Natalie. She weaved her way through the cubicles, checked the bathroom, and finally found Natalie sitting in the makeshift kitchen.

"Hey," Darcy said, immediately realizing how stupid that sounded.

"Hey?" Natalie said, spinning around. "That's it?"

"Are you okay?" Darcy really meant *are we okay*, but she couldn't bring herself to ask that. What if the answer was no?

"I'm great," Natalie said, her voice filled with sarcasm. "I love it when my, Jesus, I don't even know. Are you my girlfriend? I thought you were but it doesn't matter. I love it when I get casually tossed aside. It's truly my favorite thing." She pushed past Darcy and headed back toward the cubicles.

Darcy trailed behind her, stunned but growing increasingly pissed off. Her sister was right, Natalie didn't give her a chance to explain anything before storming off. Dammit, she hated when Kit was right.

They reached the cubicles they'd been assigned but never used. Darcy looked at the conference room. Raquel was still in there, talking on her cell phone.

She rested her forearms on the partition between the cubicles and looked down at Natalie. "Are you going to ignore me all day?"

Natalie looked up. "Seriously?"

Darcy stepped closer, her eyes darting to the other folks in the area. "Can we go talk somewhere?"

Natalie shoved her chair back, sending it spinning across the floor. "Sure, LaCroix. We can talk all about how you dropped me as soon as they offered you something better. I guess some things don't change."

Darcy took a step back when Natalie pushed past her. "Have you lost your mind?" Everyone looked at Darcy. She grabbed her coat off her chair and rushed to catch up with Natalie.

Natalie made it to the front door of the offices before Darcy caught her.

"Were we in the same meeting? I asked them if we could do the segment together. After you stormed out of there, I told them they were making a mistake not having you do it, too. What the hell else do you expect me to do?"

Natalie crossed her arms over her chest. "So, you're fine taking a job even if you're only getting it because of your last name? What happened to you always telling me no one cared who your dad is?"

It felt like the air had been sucked out of Darcy's lungs or forced out with a stick to the gut. She blinked at Natalie. How fucking dare she? "Do you think I *like* being told they're giving me a chance because I'm Marty LaCroix's daughter? Do you think that makes me feel good about the *years* of work I've put in? Yeah. I came to the U.S. to work my ass off for an opportunity only to have people like Hank tell me the only reason they will even consider me isn't my work, it's my name? Yeah. That's super. And imagine how I feel when my *girlfriend* throws it in my face?" Darcy gulped air as she rapidly unraveled in front of Natalie.

"Now I'm your girlfriend? Convenient since back in the meeting you couldn't be bothered to stand up for me."

"Fuck you, Carpenter. I fought for you in there."

"Not hard enough," Natalie grumbled like a petulant teen-ager.

"Jesus Christ. All this time you've been giving me shit for getting stuff I didn't deserve because of my dad's name but now you're pissed that I didn't push hard enough to get you an opportunity based on *my* hard work? You're the worst kind of hypocrite. God forbid I get a chance at something I've worked for years for if you can't just waltz right in and have it too with-out doing a fraction of the work. You haven't changed a bit since college."

Natalie's mouth twisted, and her face was frighteningly red.

"Ladies!"

Natalie and Darcy turned and found Raquel striding toward them, looking nearly as angry as they were.

"Do I have to remind you that other people work here, too? If you want to have a fight, go outside. But may I remind you that you have to be up at the biathlon training center in an hour. So, whatever your problem is, fix it now because no one will be on any segments or doing any commentary if you can't put on a happy face and do your current jobs."

Darcy and Natalie looked at each other like they were fight-ing for a gold medal all over again.

"Fine," Natalie said, sounding like a petulant fifteen-year-old. She stormed back toward her desk.

"Understood," Darcy said, putting her coat on and heading out the door. If Natalie cost her a chance at doing the hockey broadcast, she would never, ever forgive her. She walked out to the waiting van and climbed in the front seat. She didn't so much as glance back when Natalie got in and slammed the door.

This segment was going to be so much fun.

Chapter Fifty-Eight

After a trip to the venue during which no one spoke, Natalie jumped out of the van the second it stopped moving. She didn't want to spend another second seething at the back of Darcy's head.

Natalie was livid with Darcy but if she was honest with herself—which she absolutely was not at the moment—she was more hurt by finding out, again, that there was no space for her on the team. They didn't need her any more than the U.S. team needed her. She was an afterthought, unnecessary on the ice, in the commentary studio, or even in that fucking meeting.

She and Darcy had gone from happily planning a trip together to fighting in the matter of a few short hours. She couldn't help but feel a sense of déjà vu.

She shoved her hands deep into the pockets of her coat and tromped through the snow to the location for their biathlon lesson. When she first heard about the segment, she wasn't sure she wanted to shoot anything. She hated guns but now that her day had turned into a complete nightmare, she didn't mind the idea of shooting something. It might help with the seething anger she felt toward everyone from Hank and Raquel to Darcy.

Why did they bring her into that meeting if all they were going to do was make her feel like shit? They could've had the meeting with Darcy by herself if they weren't going to offer her the job with Darcy. Why bring her in at all?

A chill slipped down her spine. Oh fuck. *Did* they invite her to the meeting? Or did she assume she was supposed to go with Darcy because they thought of themselves as a package deal?

The setup for the day was near the shooting range at the biathlon event. Natalie met two of the athletes, Jesse and Kira, when she arrived.

"Wasn't enough for you to do one sport?"

Kira smiled. "Too slow to beat the folks who do the straight skiing. But I'm a good shot so that helps me here."

Jesse adjusted his knit hat. "I grew up shooting targets with my mom when I was a kid and I had so much energy she made me get outside and burn it off. Biathlon seemed like the perfect thing."

Darcy arrived with one of the producers to explain what they were doing for the segment. "We don't think people want to see us try to ski again so we are going to have you teach us how to hit the targets."

"Or not look too stupid when we miss badly," Natalie added with a smile to Jesse and Kira.

The producer, a short, square woman named Iris, interrupted them. "Raquel doesn't want them to show you how to do anything before we start filming."

Natalie shook her head. "Great. She wants to get every second of us looking terrible on film. With any luck she'll make a whole blooper reel."

Jesse and Kira shared a nervous look.

Darcy reassured them. "Don't worry, she would never make you two look silly. That's our whole entire job."

The athletes laughed and took Iris's direction about the segment. A few minutes later, the camera operator signaled she was ready for them to start.

They explained the sport and asked the athletes to show them how to shoot at the targets. Jesse showed them how to shoot lying on the ground and Kira showed them the standing approach.

They each nailed all their targets with no problem.

"Well, that looks fairly straightforward," Natalie said. "Which clearly means we'll make a mess of it."

Darcy took one of the rifles and lined up the targets. "Those things are tiny. I can hardly see them!"

Natalie laughed. "So was your point total in college," she said.

Darcy scowled. "Know what score is easy to remember? Three to one in gold medals."

Natalie forced herself to smile for the camera but inwardly she seethed. She lined up her shot and pulled the trigger. And ended up hitting one of Darcy's targets.

Darcy gestured for the camera to get a close-up. "I'm so good I don't even have to try to score!"

Jesse and Kira smiled and gave them each another lesson in shooting. Once they'd unloaded their first round, they paused.

"Okay, now I want you to get a sense of what it's like to shoot under the conditions we deal with. So, why don't you run to that pole over there and sprint back."

"You're kidding," Natalie said.

Kira shook her head. "Nope, one of the hardest parts is trying to keep steady after you've been skiing hard. Your producer asked how we could mimic that without putting you both back on skis. We came up with this idea. Run over there and sprint back and then when you get here we may have you do a few other things to get your heart rate up."

Iris gave them a look that told them not to argue. The camera operator held up her hand and then signaled for them to go. They took off at a dead sprint, Darcy in the lead until Natalie used her superior conditioning to pull ahead of Darcy's longer strides. They looped around a pole and came rushing back, practically elbowing each other out of the way as they did.

When they returned to the shooting station, Jesse had his hand over his mouth, covering a smile. "Now, ten burpees should get you both really breathing hard."

Darcy and Natalie glared at the camera but dropped and started doing burpees as fast as they could. At seven, Darcy swore under her breath and Natalie cracked up.

"God, I hope you got that on camera."

By the time they both finished, they were breathing hard, and Darcy looked homicidal.

"Now you know what it feels like when we make it into a shooting station." He handed them each a rifle. "Why don't you try the prone position for this since it will be easier to hold steady."

Natalie and Darcy rushed to drop to the ground. Holy shit it was hard to breath and line up the gun on the tiny little targets.

"This sport is completely wild," Natalie said, panting. "Who on earth thought it was a good idea?"

Kira laughed. "It was a military thing at first and the shooting just stuck."

Both Darcy and Natalie tried for the targets and failed spectacularly.

"Last shot," Natalie said, turning to look at Darcy. "It all comes down to this, LaCroix. Kind of like my last-minute goal in the gold medal game, eh?"

Darcy rolled her eyes. "Look, glory days, why don't you concentrate on how I'm about to kick your ass today." She paused and took her final shot. She hit the target, placing the pressure squarely on Natalie to match her skill.

Natalie took a deep breath and steadied herself. The last thing she needed on this disaster of a day was to lose to Darcy on camera. She found the final target, squeezed the trigger, and waited.

Kira thrust her hands toward the sky. "Nailed it!"

Natalie jumped up, leaving her rifle on the ground. She was happy to be done with it and even happier not to have lost to Darcy. "Looks like we'll have to call it a tie, LaCroix. Thank you to our excellent tutors. Good luck in your races, we'll be pulling for you."

Darcy smiled for the camera. "And we'll see you again for our final segment of the Olympics. We have something special in store for all of you, so we hope you'll tune in."

They said goodbye to Jesse and Kira and did a few more shots without them to make sure their segment had everything they needed. By the time they were done, they both trudged back to the van, exhausted.

Natalie had almost forgotten about the disastrous meeting earlier in the day. Her anger had cooled a bit after so much running around and goofing off in the segment.

But when they got back to the van there was a message waiting for them.

Darcy rubbed a hand over her cold cheeks and showed Natalie her messages. "Raquel asked me to come back to the office for the afternoon."

Natalie's heart sank. "Of course. You have to be ready for your big break." She sneered. "Don't worry about me, I'll be fine in the hotel all afternoon. I won't get in your way."

"Nat, you know that's not what I was saying."

Natalie climbed into the van and slammed the door. Sure, she was being childish but she was pissed. Left off the team, again. Expendable. Not worth fighting for. All these thoughts swirled into a dangerous tornado in her head.

She put her earbuds in and stared out the window all the way back to the offices. When Darcy hopped out, Natalie found a shuttle to take her back to the hotel without bothering to stop at her desk.

She didn't want to be anywhere she wasn't welcome.

Chapter Fifty-Nine

Raquel called them into yet another meeting on the morning of their last segment. Natalie refused to even look at Darcy.

"I want to thank you for all the hard work the two of you have put into these segments. The ratings and viewer engagement has been better than we expected. Viewers love the two of you together. That means all of our viewers and not just the ones on the #PuckingHotties hashtag." She chuckled. "When I hired you, I didn't think you'd set the internet on fire but I'm glad you did.

"Which reminds me." She paused to give each of them a stern look. "I don't know what the hell is going on with the two of you, but I need you to make it through one more segment without the public knowing you're ready to scream at each other behind the scenes, okay?"

Natalie rolled her eyes. The last thing she wanted to do was flirt with Darcy today.

"Got it," Darcy said without looking at Natalie.

"Good. Because your segment today will lead into the big USA-Canada game. We want people to see you two on the ice together and feel like they *have* to tune into the game."

Natalie scowled. "Got it. We're all here to make sure the princess succeeds."

Hurt, Darcy glared at Natalie to cover up her emotions. "Who are we meeting at the rink?" Even if Natalie was going to act like a toddler, she could be professional.

Raquel glanced at her computer. "You're meeting Lassiter and Cox."

Natalie's face crumpled. She recovered quickly, but Darcy saw it. Natalie forced a smile. "Aw, that's great. Coxie is a good kid and Lassie will be good on camera." Her leg bounced and seeing it made Darcy feel like her nerves were jangling, too.

"Anything else we need to know before we head out?" Darcy asked, hoping to god the meeting was over. Natalie looked ready to make a run for it.

Raquel waved a hand. "No. Go ahead. Have fun with your last segment."

Natalie was out the door before Darcy could get out of her chair. Darcy chased her down the hall, walking as fast as she could without drawing the attention of the rest of the staff. She caught Natalie outside the bathroom.

"Natalie," Darcy said gently.

Natalie shoved her hands in her pockets. For a second it looked like she was gearing up to fight, but instead her shoulders slumped, and she leaned against the wall.

"What are you doing here? You were pretty clear yesterday about what you think of me."

Darcy suppressed the urge to roll her eyes. "Cox took your spot, didn't she?"

Natalie sighed. "Yeah. I know it was inevitable. We all get old, right? But I really thought I had one more in me and then she showed up and..." Natalie took a deep, shuddering breath but no tears fell. "She's good, Darce." She looked up, her eyes shining with tears. "She deserved the spot." She swallowed. "But that doesn't make any of this easier."

Darcy wrapped her arms around Natalie. Natalie stiffened before melting into Darcy's arms. "Look, I know a thing or two about newbies showing up and being better than they have any right to be."

Natalie laughed. "Is this you giving me a compliment?"

Darcy shook her head. "Who says I'm talking about you?" She let Natalie go. Things were still weird between them and in the office people didn't know they were together. The internet's theories about them were well-known, but they were still rumors at best.

Natalie wiped her face. "Come on, let's do this thing. I plan to kick your ass all over the ice."

Darcy smiled. "Good to know that even if you're not speaking to me, that hasn't changed."

Natalie frowned. "You're the one who claimed I didn't deserve to be here."

"That's not what I said."

Natalie shoved herself off the wall. "Forget it. We better not be late for our segment. Gotta make sure everyone tunes in for your big debut, LaCroix."

Natalie walked away, leaving Darcy stunned. What the fuck was happening between them? One second things were great and the next Natalie was biting her head off. It wasn't her fault that the network asked her to fill in for the hockey broadcast. Beyond that, this was her dream and if Natalie couldn't support her then what were they doing together?

Darcy grabbed her coat on the way through the office, growing increasingly pissed off with each step.

Chapter Sixty

Natalie saw her former teammates as soon as she walked into the rink. They were standing against the boards in their team warm-ups laughing at a shared joke. She stopped, feeling as awkward as she did the first time she walked into the cafeteria at the training center.

She wasn't one of them. Not anymore. Sure, she'd "always be part of the team" or whatever bullshit they said about the program. But this year, this tournament, she wasn't one of them. She was on the outside, a fan staring through the glass around the rink.

And she fucking hated it.

Darcy walked past her and was shaking hands with both players before Natalie realized what was happening.

She hurried over. "Coxie, Lass! How's it going? How'd you end up with this gig?" The players gave her hugs and fist bumps. "I thought for sure Roberts would be all over this."

"We could ask you the same thing. Who the hell thought it was a good idea to put your ass on TV?" Lassiter asked. "Did they not see your ugly mug before offering the job?"

Natalie laughed and relaxed. She missed her teammates as much as she missed her team. She should have kept in better touch.

"You two ready for your game tomorrow?" Natalie asked, grasping for a topic that wouldn't make her hate her life.

"Can't wait to beat those fucking Canucks." Coxie tapped her stick on the floor for emphasis.

"Hey, some of us *are* those fucking Canucks!" Darcy said before cracking up.

Lassiter shoved Cox and the two of them laughed so hard they made Natalie's abs feel like they were on fire.

Natalie gestured to Darcy like she was on a game show and Darcy was what was behind door number two. "I'm sure you know the legendary Darcy LaCroix. Superstar princess of Canada."

Darcy sighed. "Carpenter, why are you like this?" She turned and led them down the hallway. "You three ready to find out what the producers have in store for us today?"

Natalie caught the way Cox and Lassiter shared a look. "Wait, did they tell you what we're doing?"

Both players nodded. "This is going to be epic, dude."

Oh god, what had Raquel planned for their last segment?

When they turned the corner of the rink and got to the benches, they saw two piles of equipment waiting for them.

Goalie equipment.

"You have to be shitting me," Natalie said under her breath.

Darcy got to the gear first and stood in front of it. "Did you know they were doing this?" she asked Natalie.

"Since when do they tell me anything you don't already know?" She couldn't keep the bitterness out of her voice.

"Have either of you played in goal before?" Lassiter asked.

Natalie sighed. "When I was eight. It was a disaster."

Darcy shook her head. "I took a turn just like everyone else when I was a kid. Hated it."

"I can show you how to put everything on," Lassiter said.

"And I can show you how to take it off," Cox said with a laugh. She and Lassiter bumped fists.

Darcy looked lost and Natalie took pity on her.

"Coxie has a thing for goalies. It's super weird. She's dated like three of them. I don't know at what point it becomes a fetish."

Cox shrugged, unbothered by the teasing. "It's the intensity. It's hot."

Iris leaned over the glass behind the benches. "You'll introduce your guests and then I want to get some video of the two of you putting all that gear on."

"You realize it's going to take us longer than the segment to put this stuff on, right?"

Iris smiled. "Oh yeah. We'll play it at two or three times its regular speed. It's going to be great."

Darcy sat down next to the gear. "Do you get the sense Raquel is hazing us in our last segment?"

It's not your last segment. Natalie shrugged, trying to hide her annoyance.

While the camera crew set up to capture them putting the gear on, Natalie and Darcy talked with the players about the upcoming game.

"LaCroix is doing commentary between periods, so she's pumping you for tidbits she can use." Natalie couldn't keep an edge out of her voice but her former teammates seemed oblivious.

"In that case, you can tell the folks at home that the U.S. players are ready to kick the ever-living crap out of Canada."

Darcy laughed. "I think I can safely assume the Canadians feel the same way. Cox, it's your first Olympics, right? How are you feeling?"

Cox grinned. "So excited." She glanced at Natalie and then looked away. "We all have really big shoes to fill and none of us want to let anyone down."

Cox caught Natalie's eye for a moment before they both looked away. Seeing this kid nervous about letting her down deflated the anger Natalie had about doing this segment with her former teammates. Yes, it still sucked to be reminded that she wasn't on the team, and it sucked even harder to find out she wasn't going to be picked for the hockey broadcast team. But seeing her teammates again and realizing how much they cared about winning and making her proud soothed most of the sting.

Chapter Sixty-One

Iris reappeared with a clipboard. "Okay, so first I want you to introduce the players and do the basic intro for the segment."

Darcy looked over at Cox and Lassiter. "Natalie, do you want to introduce them?"

Natalie shrugged. "Sure." She looked at the camera and waited for the signal. But as soon as the camera operator gave her the signal she froze.

Darcy laughed. "Oh my god, you don't know their names."

Cox and Lassiter looked horrified for a second before laughing so hard they had to wipe their eyes.

"Carpenter, we were teammates for years!"

Natalie blushed scarlet. "I know your names! I just can't think of them right now." She buried her face in her hands, but the tips of her ears were getting redder by the second. "In my defense, when was the last time I called either of you by your first names?"

Darcy had to take deep breaths to compose herself. She held out her hand. "I'm Darcy LaCroix, it's nice to meet you."

Cox shook her hand first. "JT Cox."

"Melissa Lassiter."

"Melissa! Oh my god, I knew it was an M word."

Darcy shook her head. "Unbelievable, Carpenter. You were teammates! How did you not know their names?" She looked at the camera. "Please tell me you got all that on tape."

Natalie waved her hands frantically. "You can't use that! Oh my god! No!"

The camera operator's shoulders shook beneath the equipment blocking her face. "Don't worry. I wasn't recording."

JT and Melissa were laughing so hard they each had to grip the rink boards to hold themselves up. "Carpenter, we've been teammates for years and you didn't know my name? Un-fucking-believable."

Natalie hung her head. "I forgot. I'm sorry. You two are going to aim for my head, aren't you?"

The players smirked but didn't answer. After they filmed the introductions, Natalie and Darcy sat on the bench to put on their gear. Darcy had only vague memories of the order she needed to put everything on and quickly realized that she had to put her skates and leg pads on before her chest protector.

Looking to her left, Natalie's legs looked impossibly skinny underneath her hockey pants. Without shin guards they looked like toothpicks.

Lassiter had to step in and tell Natalie she had her leg pads on the wrong legs, but only after Natalie had put them both on.

"Come on! You could have told me that five minutes ago!"

Coxie laughed. "And miss this high-quality TV? No way."

"They could have waited until you got on the ice," Darcy said with a snort. She was rather smug about getting everything on without incident until she tried to put her jersey on and got herself stuck. Her arms wedged themselves into the jersey sleeves and she was trapped. She tried to shimmy out of it and only made it worse. She turned her head to see what was stuck in the back but couldn't turn far enough to figure it out.

Natalie caught her eye and pointed to the camera. "You better be getting every second of this. Canada's princess isn't looking too royal right now."

Lassiter took pity on her and tugged the back of her jersey free and helped her get everything untwisted.

"Keep talking shit, Carpenter, but you don't even have both pads on. Not surprising considering how slow your ass is on the ice." Darcy pulled her mask over her ponytail and glided out onto the ice. She made it a few feet before falling flat on her face.

She rolled over and stared at the ceiling. If the ice could swallow her now, that would be great. She could hear Natalie and the other players laughing their asses off at her. Dear god, she would never live this down as long as she lived.

Cox came into view over her. "Hold on, let me see if there's something on your skate." She bent down and checked the runners of Darcy's skate and held up a small piece of tape.

"Found the culprit." She put her hand out and pulled Darcy to her feet. She held Darcy's arm while she got her feet set.

Cox's face was only a few inches from Darcy's, making it easy for Darcy to see the deep brown of her eyes and the smattering of freckles across the bridge of her nose.

"Thanks," Darcy said.

Lassiter banged her stick against the boards to get their attention. "Coxie! For Christ's sake, she's not actually a goalie! Quit flirting with the Canuck."

Cox shrugged.

Natalie barreled onto the ice with the grace of a drunk rhino and bumped Cox on her way by.

Darcy blinked. What was happening? One second, she's flat on her back after the world's most embarrassing fall and the next Natalie is pitching a fit because she thinks her teammate was making eyes at her? She'd had less drama in middle school.

Iris called them back over to the bench to explain what they were doing. "Each of you gets a turn in the net. The players are going to shoot the same number of shots at both of you. We were going to do a shootout, but the studio was afraid you might get hurt."

Natalie glowered at Cox. Darcy fought the urge to laugh. There was no way Natalie could possibly be jealous from something as small as getting helped off her ass. It was absurd. But everything between them had felt absurd since Raquel offered her the job doing commentary. She sighed, grateful her mask made it impossible for anyone to look too closely at her.

She carefully skated over to the net. Goalie skates were almost as bad as the figure skates they'd had to wear. Never had she felt so uncomfortable playing hockey. Raquel really was an evil genius.

Natalie went first. She blocked the first two shots but then fell trying to move in front of the third. She struggled to get up, falling three times as she tried to get her feet under her.

Cox and Lassiter put their hands over their mouths to hide their laughter for the cameras, but it was no use. Finally, Cox glided in to help Natalie get up, but Natalie wouldn't take her hand.

"You're being a baby," Darcy said under her breath. She would've helped Natalie but she didn't want the two of them to end up tangled on the ice in a heap.

Finally, Natalie got to her feet for the next shot. Lassiter waited to be sure she was ready before taking a slap shot that pinged off Natalie's helmet.

Natalie, stunned, stood still for a few seconds before dropping both gloves and skating after Lassiter with the speed of a penguin on dry land. Lassiter easily evaded her while yelling apologies over her shoulder.

"I didn't mean to bean you, Carpenter, I swear!"

Darcy looked at the camera operator. "You're getting this, right?"

The operator gave her a thumbs-up as she turned to follow

the former teammates around the rink until Natalie gave up and leaned against the boards.

Darcy's turn in the net was much less eventful, though she found the entire process baffling. How did goalies do this without finding themselves on their asses after every shot? She finished the segment with a newfound respect for her former teammates and was thankful she'd never had to try to do it in a high-pressure game.

Natalie and Darcy pulled their masks up to sign off. "We want to thank JT Cox and Melissa Lassiter for joining us today."

"I do not want to thank Lassie for hitting me in the head, though," Natalie said on the first take, and they had to reshoot it.

"Thanks for having us and be sure to tune in for our game."

Darcy grinned, thrilled to know she was going to be a part of it. "Yes, please tune in. I'll see you from the studio. Otherwise, that's it for Natalie and me. We've had a great time showing you how impressive all these athletes are."

Natalie did a terrible job hiding her emotions. "Yes, thanks for tuning in to watch us make fools out of ourselves every day. It's been more fun than I ever could have imagined." She looked at Darcy and gave her a smile tinged with so much sadness.

"So long from the ice palace." They waved at the camera with their massive goalie gloves.

While the crew cleaned up, Darcy and Natalie thanked the players and wished them luck.

"But not too much luck," Darcy said, her eyes sparkling.

Natalie rolled her eyes. "Crush 'em." She tapped gloves with Cox and Lassiter before shuffling toward the bench to get out of her gear.

Lassiter hopped up on the boards next to her.

Darcy reached for her stick but found Cox already had it. She held it out to Darcy.

"Thanks."

Cox smiled and tapped her stick on the ice. "I was wondering what you were doing after this?"

Was this kid for real? "Excuse me?"

Cox took off one glove and ran her hand through her long brown hair. "Maybe we could get some lunch or something?"

Darcy cocked her head to the side, unable to believe that this kid was hitting on her when her...whatever Natalie was to her was like ten feet away. She pasted on a smile. "That's really nice of you, but things are really busy right now. I have to get ready for your game." She paused. "And I'm sure you do, too."

Cox looked over her shoulder. "Oh shit, are the rumors real? Are you and Carpenter a thing? Jesus, she's going to kill me, isn't she?"

Darcy smiled the way she would at an upset toddler. "It's fine. Thanks for coming and I look forward to the game tomorrow."

Coxie skated off the ice. "You coming, Lass?"

Lassiter hopped off the boards. "Good to see you, Carpenter."

"Good luck tomorrow night," Darcy said, flinging one of her leg pads toward the end of the bench.

Chapter Sixty-Two

Darcy dropped to the bench and peeled out of her jersey. Natalie focused on untying her skates. She didn't need to start a fight here. Not now.

"Coxie seems like a good kid," Darcy said.

Natalie straightened. "Oh really? Is that why you were flirting with her or is that why you failed to mention you and I are together?"

"What?"

"I heard her ask you out and you didn't say 'Oh, I have a girlfriend.' Or anything other than you're busy. Good to know where I stand." Natalie kicked off her skates and let them slide across the floor in front of her.

"You have *got* to be kidding me. You haven't said more than five words to me since yesterday and now you're flipping out because I didn't tell your former teammate we're together? Maybe I didn't know based on you giving me the silent treatment like a spoiled teenager."

Natalie stood up and took off the rest of her equipment, leaving it in a pile at her feet. "It's déjà vu with you. Anytime someone asks you if we're together it's like you stop being able to speak. But you had no problem using my connections with them to get information for the game. You're welcome by the way."

"I'm sorry, are you now taking credit for me doing my job? You're unbelievable."

"More unbelievable than you completely casting me aside? I don't think so. You haven't even mentioned once the fact that you taking this job means canceling the trip I planned for us."

Darcy's eyes widened.

"I'm sorry, did you forget? Am I so insignificant that you forgot you made plans with me?" Natalie stomped her feet into her boots. "You know what's unbelievable? I thought you had changed. But no. I hope you and my younger, faster, better replacement are very happy together."

She stepped over Darcy's feet and disappeared down the hallway. She didn't make it to the bathroom before the tears overwhelmed her. She shouldered her way into a stall and slammed the door shut before anyone could see her.

Fucking Darcy LaCroix.

It was only ever going to end up like this. Everything between them was a disaster. She'd hoped this time would be different, that they were different. But it turned out that they were just older versions of the same chickenshit kids they'd been in college. And Natalie couldn't take it anymore.

She couldn't be the person Darcy didn't admit to loving. She couldn't be the one left off the team, again. Especially when that team was supposed to be the two of them.

She'd been so stupid to give Darcy another chance to break her heart. Grace had warned her that this exact thing would happen.

Fuck.

At least this was her last segment. She didn't have anything to stick around for now.

She took out her phone and sent a message to Raquel. She didn't want to be here a second longer than she had to be.

Chapter Sixty-Three

Darcy snuck glances at Natalie in the mirror as they rode back to the office together. Natalie's red-rimmed eyes were a dead giveaway that she'd been crying. Darcy wanted to say something, but nothing that came to mind would help. Because she was pissed.

She'd done nothing wrong in talking to the Team USA players. She'd been doing her job, both the job they had together and preparing for her first shot in the booth the next day. She'd been given an opportunity to make her dream come true and Natalie *should* be happy for her. She should be supportive, not sitting in the back of the van sulking.

They walked into Raquel's office together, but not side by side. Natalie slumped in her chair, refusing to look at Darcy. Fine, if that's who she wanted to be, Darcy would ignore her.

Raquel set her phone down after finishing a text. "I want to thank you both for all your hard work and your willingness to take risks on camera. Your segments have been a bright spot for the network and it's because the two of you clearly were having so much fun out there and were so willing to do whatever we asked." She leaned forward, resting her forearms on her desk.

"I know I asked a lot of you when I encouraged you to play

up your natural chemistry. I hope you don't regret it. Fan engagement was through the roof and all your flirty banter helped give them something to root for every day."

Natalie sighed. "That's it for me, then?"

Raquel nodded slowly, her eyes narrowing at Natalie before turning to look at Darcy. Darcy gave her a tiny shrug.

"Yes, your final segment is done so you are free to enjoy the remainder of the Games. If you want tickets to any events—"

"Great. Who do I talk to about changing my flight?"

Darcy stared. "There's still a few more days," she said in a low voice.

Natalie refused to look at her. "I can't see a reason to stick around."

Raquel nodded. "If that's what you want, send my assistant an email letting him know when you want to leave and he'll work on getting your flight switched."

Natalie stood up and stuck out her hand. "Thanks for the opportunity." She shook Raquel's hand and left without looking at Darcy.

Darcy blinked at her lap. What the fuck was that? Anger rose in her chest, her face heated.

"Do you need to go after her?" Raquel asked quietly.

Darcy shook her head. "There's no point. She's mad you picked me to do the hockey broadcast. Nothing I say will change that."

Raquel stared at her; her face relaxed. "Is that really what you think?"

Darcy frowned. "She's jealous that I've been working my ass off for three years and got a job I earned, and she didn't get to waltz in here and get the same."

Raquel sighed. "Having the two of you let the internet rumors fly was risky. But I didn't imagine it would blow up this badly." Her eyes bored into Darcy's. "I'm not as clueless as you think. I have eyes."

"That's not—" Darcy slumped. "Like you said, the Games are almost over. This was inevitable."

"Was it?" Raquel shook her head. "If that's what you have to tell yourself to get through the hockey broadcast, fine. But don't lie to yourself forever." She glanced at her computer. "You have a meeting with the broadcast team. Go on, don't be late. I'll be rooting for you." She looked out the door. "If you hurry you might catch her before your meeting."

Darcy hustled her ass down the hall, stopping at the desks they used sporadically, checking the conference room they regularly took over, and finally ran for the exit. She found Natalie staring at her phone at the curb.

"Nat!"

Natalie turned around. "I didn't steal any of your shit out of the office. Promise."

"Don't leave like this," Darcy said, panting slightly from her rush outside.

"It's over, Darcy. The Games are ending, so I might as well go now." She shoved her hands deep into her coat pockets.

Darcy wrapped her arms around herself. In her rush she hadn't grabbed a coat. "What about us?"

"Us? Half an hour ago you couldn't be bothered to tell Cox, the woman who took my spot on the team, that you had a girlfriend when she was asking you out! Now you want to talk about us? You jumped at the broadcasting job even though it meant we wouldn't be able to travel together like we talked about, what, an hour before you got the offer? Did you even consider, for a second, asking me if I minded if you blew off the trip I planned?" Natalie blew out a long breath and blinked away her tears.

"Nat, we can still go away," Darcy said, her voice breaking. She hated herself for not thinking of the trip. She was too focused on the job. She'd chosen work so quickly she didn't think to talk to Natalie about changing their plans.

Natalie made a pathetic attempt at a smile. "Let's admit this was just a fling. That's all you've ever wanted from me. The Games are over, the hashtag fans will move on to some other couple, and you'll go off and be a hockey broadcasting superstar without me weighing you down." Natalie turned away but Darcy saw the tears falling down her cheeks.

A car pulled up to the curb.

Darcy wiped at her face, tears falling faster than she could wipe them away. "If you thought this was just something I did for the show—Jesus Christ, Nat—if you think that then... I guess you're right. Have a safe flight."

Natalie walked toward the car. Darcy waited for her to look back. If they could see each other maybe this would be okay, but Natalie kept her eyes on the car, never wavering until she shut the door and the car left Darcy standing in the freezing cold.

Darcy wiped her face, took three deep breaths of the icy air before marching back into the offices. She'd worked too hard for too long to ruin this chance. Not even for a shattered heart.

Chapter Sixty-Four

Natalie left early for the airport the next day. There was no reason to hang around the hotel, nothing left for her in the office, and she really, really didn't want to run into Darcy. Yesterday had taken every last bit of fight out of her. The last thing she wanted was to bump into Darcy and have to see how happy she was while Natalie fell apart.

At least she would be safe from Darcy at the airport. Nothing in the world would keep her from making it to the broadcast booth. Despite her anger and the aching in her chest, Natalie was proud of Darcy. Instead of accepting the job with the Canadian broadcast, she'd earned her spot in the booth with years of hard work. No amount of pride at Darcy's accomplishments took away the pain of Darcy choosing the job over Natalie.

She shouldered her backpack and kicked her suitcase toward check-in. She got her boarding pass in exchange for her suitcase and made her way to the gate.

No first class this time. She didn't care. Not really. But it drove home the point for how much this sucked that she arrived in a comfortable seat and was flying home probably crammed into a middle row. She'd asked Jamal to get her on the first flight he could, and her legs would regret her impulsive request.

Several long hours later, Natalie boarded her flight. She found herself crammed between two passengers, one who recognized her immediately.

"You're from *Wake Up, USA*! Oh my god. I love your segments!"

Natalie smiled as graciously as she could under the circumstances. "Thanks, that's very nice of you." Natalie shoved her backpack under the seat in front of her and buckled her seat belt.

"You and your girlfriend are so cute and funny. I just love watching you two clown around."

Natalie frowned. "She's not…" Fuck, she really didn't want to be having this conversation. Especially not with a complete stranger. On an airplane where she would be stuck next to this person for nearly eight hours.

Natalie swallowed the lump threatening to block her throat. "We had a good time." She reached for her earbuds, hoping this woman would get the message. Natalie attempted to find a comfortable position. The trip would be more bearable if she could manage to sleep through most of it.

A while later the woman next to Natalie nudged her with her elbow. "Aren't you going to watch the game?"

Natalie pulled out an earbud. "What?"

She pointed at the tiny screen. "The USA–Canada game starts in half an hour. Aren't you going to watch?"

Natalie couldn't hear the sound on the other woman's screen, but she could see Darcy sitting in the studio, wearing the suit they gave her for the hockey party. Dammit, she looked amazing. If Natalie had been hoping for evidence that Darcy felt as horrible as she did, she wasn't going to find it here.

"Thanks," Natalie said, turning her TV to the right channel.

"Joining us to give us some perspective on the women's tournament is Darcy LaCroix. Darcy is the daughter of Canadian hockey legend Marty LaCroix. I'm sure all our viewers are familiar with Marty's Hall of Fame career." The host, a guy with salt-and-pepper hair and an unnatural tan, said before turning to Darcy.

Natalie knew the smile on Darcy's face was the one she pasted on right before she destroyed someone on the ice.

"Oh shit," Natalie whispered.

"Thanks for that introduction, Brent. I'm sure my father appreciates it. But I think I'm here to talk about the women's game. My credentials have nothing to do with my dad. Perhaps you've forgotten that I captained the NCAA national champions, played in four Olympics, and won three golds and one silver medal." Darcy smiled into the camera before turning to Brent.

Natalie punched the air. Pride filled her chest at Darcy telling off that asshole and every other person who thought of her dad first and her second.

The host swallowed, looking deeply uncomfortable before clearing his throat. "Of course, Darcy. Your résumé speaks for itself." He glanced at his notes.

Those can't save you now, asshole.

"In your expert opinion, do you think the U.S. team lacks leadership from more seasoned veterans? Your cohost on *Wake Up, USA*, three-time Olympian Natalie Carpenter, was left off the roster in favor of a younger player. It seems like the coaching staff didn't think she could hack it anymore."

If Natalie had any thought that she was over being cut from the team, this guy's question put those thoughts to rest. This fucking sucked. She felt the woman next to her staring. She forced herself to keep her composure even if she clenched her jaw so tight she risked cracking a tooth.

Darcy took a deep breath. Natalie thought she saw red creeping up her neck, but maybe it was the light. Darcy looked directly into the camera, like she was talking directly to her.

"Natalie Carpenter has a hockey résumé that puts her with the greatest players of all time. She won two NCAA titles, three Olympic medals, including a gold. She was the captain of the team that won international tournaments. Frankly, she was the player I least wanted to go against on the big stage. Whether she's on the team for this Olympics or not changes none of that.

"As for the younger players, we won't know if the coaching staff bet on the right roster or not until they play this game. The games leading to this one haven't been especially close. What happens when they play Canada? Can the young players on their roster hang in there? We'll find out soon."

Natalie stared at the screen, not seeing any of the images. Darcy didn't have to stick up for her like that.

The woman tapped her gently on the arm. "Your girlfriend sure thinks a lot of you," she said with a warm smile.

Natalie couldn't bring herself to correct her this time. Darcy wasn't her girlfriend anymore, but it didn't stop her from telling that guy to shove his stupid question. She stood up for her, on national television. It made Natalie want to cry.

She'd been so stupid. She'd screamed at Darcy, accused her of flirting with her teammate, told her she hadn't done enough to advocate for her. But here she was, after their breakup, telling the whole world how much she admired Natalie.

Natalie waved to the flight attendant as he walked by. She needed a drink.

She pulled out her phone and did something she'd been avoiding for days; she went on Twitter. She scrolled through their hashtag and found people wondering why they looked so off in their last few segments. Some people thought they were fighting, others thought for sure they'd broken up, a small group defended them against every bit of well-earned gossip.

But as she scrolled to the present, the tweets changed. In front of her eyes, they flooded the feed. People had tuned in to watch Darcy and were now sharing clips of her defending Natalie.

When your GF loves you enough to read your CV on-screen #PuckingHotties #RelationshipGoals.

Natalie smiled to herself. The more she read, the more people seemed to be cheering for them, speculating that maybe they had been fighting but everything was better now.

If only they knew that Natalie was on her way halfway across the world to get away from Darcy.

Fuck.

Natalie had made a huge mistake. Again. She'd broken her own stupid heart. Again.

And she had seven more hours on a plane to figure out how to fix it.

Chapter Sixty-Five

If a person can be exhausted and exhilarated at the same time, that was how Darcy felt. She rode the high of her first time in the broadcast booth—and telling Brent off—all the way back to the hotel, but as soon as she stepped into the elevator, her adrenaline fell away and left her completely drained.

Walking down the hall to her room, she looked at Natalie's door before remembering that it wasn't Natalie's anymore. Someone else had that room now. Natalie was gone.

The weariness mixed with sadness and threatened to drag her down. Her phone rang.

"Hi, Kit." She pushed into her room, threw her jacket on a chair, and set the phone to speaker. Not to piss off her sister this time, she needed to get out of these clothes and into some sweats.

"First of all, you fucking rocked tonight. I've been waiting for you to tell someone off like that for *years*. It was even better than I imagined."

"You watched?"

Kit scoffed. "You think any of us were going to miss your big debut? Mom spent half the afternoon figuring out how we could stream it in Canada and the other half figuring out how to show it on the living room TV."

Darcy slumped onto her bed, the corners of her eyes pricking with tears. "Wow, thank you. It felt really good."

"Second, what the hell happened between you and Natalie?"

"What?" Darcy moved up the bed until she could lean against the headboard.

"Anyone with eyes, which includes half of Twitter, can tell you guys fucked everything up. Tell me what happened."

Darcy relayed the last few days.

"You took the job, ditched the date she had planned—which sounds awesome, by the way. I want to go to a rotating restaurant on the top of a mountain! And then you didn't say anything to her teammate when she asked you out in front of Natalie. Jesus, Darce, I thought you were smarter than that."

Darcy's head thudded against the headboard. "Wow, thanks for being such a supportive sister. I'm so glad you called to yell at me."

"Stop being dramatic. I'm not saying Natalie is blameless. Her main thing seems to be bailing the second she gets even a little bit hurt. But you keep doing the same shit over and over to hurt her. After Sabrina, I thought you'd be smarter about picking work over your relationship."

"You think I should apologize for getting the job I've been working three years to get?"

Kit scoffed. "Of course not. But why do you pick work every time a relationship gets real?"

"I don't!"

Kit sighed. "Did I imagine Sabrina breaking up with you for choosing work?"

"No," Darcy admitted.

"And Natalie? You're telling me you really wanted to be with her so much that you had a long, adult conversation about how much you wanted to go on your date but that this was a once-in-a-lifetime opportunity for you. That's what happened?"

Darcy groaned. "God, you're a pain in the ass when you're right."

"Darcy, call me a pain in the ass all you want but I want you to be happy and for some reason you keep screwing that up." Kit's voice was gentle and full of concern. "Do you even know why you do that?"

Darcy nodded. "Yeah," she said, her voice scratchy with emotion. "Yeah, I think I do. I think whenever it gets too real, I freak out." She paused, trying to collect her thoughts. "I've always known she could destroy me and I hated being that vulnerable."

"And you like this better?"

"No, this is awful." Darcy laughed.

"Then I think you know what you have to do."

Darcy stood. "Well, this has been super fun."

"Don't you dare hang up. Mom and Dad want to know when you're getting in for their party."

Darcy groaned. "Seriously?"

"You didn't forget, did you?"

"Of course not. But I have had a few other things going on. I'll send you all the information as soon as I have it."

Kit made a sound between a grunt and growl. "Fine. But don't forget or I will tell Dad that you want him to help you with a job in Canada."

"You wouldn't!"

Kit cackled. "Sort your shit out. Fix everything you broke with Natalie. I don't want you moping around the anniversary party. Got it?"

Darcy sighed. "I love you, Kit."

"I know. I love you, too, even if you are a giant dumbass when it comes to your love life. Thank god you have me to help you fix it."

She hung up before Darcy could yell at her. Instead, she sighed and slid under her covers. She had too many things to think about and the very last of her adrenaline was gone, leaving her wrung out and shattered.

Maybe it would seem better in the morning.

Chapter Sixty-Six

Natalie had texted her parents with her flight itinerary but told them she'd take a cab from the airport. It was going to be late, and she didn't want to have to explain to them why she was home and looking like shit.

She dragged her suitcase behind her and adjusted her backpack on her shoulder as she walked toward the doors.

"Natalie!"

She stopped and looked around, her eyes not capturing anyone familiar. Maybe she was hallucinating. It was late and she'd been traveling for what felt like forever.

"Natalie, wait up!"

Natalie turned toward the voice. "Grace?"

Grace barreled into her, nearly knocking her over and sending her suitcase flopping onto its back like a turtle. "You didn't think we would actually let you take a taxi home, did you?"

Natalie sighed against Grace's shoulder. A wave of gratitude hit her hard. "How did you even know?"

"Your parents called me. They told me you were rushing home and I figured it was because you fucked everything up with Darcy again and you could probably use a friend."

Natalie followed Grace toward the exit. She was too exhausted to argue. "You're right, I did."

Natalie spent the drive home explaining everything that happened. "It was so great. I was so happy, we were so happy." She paused. "I really thought this was our chance. But then she got offered that job without me and it felt like getting cut all over again. And then when Coxie was flirting with her, Darcy didn't tell her we were dating. All of it felt like I was reliving college all over again."

"So you ran away, is that right?" Grace's voice was gentler than her words.

Natalie watched the city lights roll by out her window. "You're the one who told me not to trust her. You're the one who said she was going to break my heart all over again."

In the light of the passing cars, Natalie could see Grace's hand tighten on the wheel.

"I know it's my fault. She got her dream job and I made it about missing out on a trip I'd planned for us. It would have been great if she'd talked to me about it first, but I wasn't going to tell her to pass up her dream job to go away with me. We would have found a way to do something else. But..." Natalie searched for the right words. "But I wanted her to think of me, you know? Instead she accepted the job like I didn't exist, like I hadn't fallen in love with her all over again. I did freak out."

Natalie's head rested against the seat. She stared into the dark. "When Coxie flirted with her and Darcy didn't say she and I were together, it felt final, like she'd decided we were done." She sighed, the excitement of seeing Grace fading away, leaving her weary from her long, emotional trip. "I couldn't be the only one fighting for us, you know?"

Grace steered her car into the driveway. A streetlight illuminated half her face. "You're my best friend. If you honestly tell me that Darcy LaCroix is an asshole bitch who ripped your heart out, I will curse her name and swear to hate her until my dying day."

Natalie laughed, high and slightly hysterical.

"But from everything you said, I don't think that's what happened. I think you love her, and it scares you so much you ran away because breaking your own heart has always been easier for you than letting anyone get close."

"Shit," Natalie said, her voice a low growl.

Grace patted her arm. "That's what I thought. Come on, let's get you inside. You have to sleep so tomorrow we can figure out how you're going to win her back."

Chapter Sixty-Seven

Darcy had one meeting left before she could fly home. She walked into Raquel's office, feeling no more confident she knew what Raquel wanted than she did the day Raquel offered this job. Raquel waved to the chair in front of her desk.

"How are you doing?"

Darcy shrugged. "Fine. A little tired but fine. Grateful."

Raquel leaned forward, her elbows resting on her desk. "Don't give me that 'grateful' bullshit. How are you *actually* doing?"

"Terrible." Darcy froze. Raquel didn't need to hear about her emotional state. She was her boss, not her friend. She should not be having this meeting when she was this exhausted. "Forget I said that. I'm fine, just tired."

"Can you forget that I'm your boss for two minutes?" Raquel looked over her glasses at Darcy. "You're not fine. Ever since Natalie left you've been walking around like someone stole your puppy."

"I'm not sure Natalie would like being compared to a puppy," Darcy said. She sighed. "The truth? Off the boss-employee record?"

Raquel nodded.

Darcy hoped she wouldn't regret sharing this with Raquel. "The short version is I screwed up."

Raquel made a "go on" gesture with her hands.

"We had a thing in college, it ended badly. That was also my fault." Darcy rubbed her face with both hands. "This time, Natalie flew off the handle, which is what Natalie does. But I screwed up by choosing work over her. She left and I haven't heard from her since."

"Not even after you basically wrote her a love note on live TV?" Raquel asked, the corner of her mouth twitching.

Darcy shook her head. "My last serious relationship ended because I chose work over time with her."

"And you think Natalie bailed because you got the shot at doing commentary?" Raquel shook her head. "I have to say, if she couldn't be happy for you, maybe she isn't worth your time."

Darcy shook her head slowly. "I don't think it's that simple. We had plans and I jumped at the chance to work the game without talking to her about it. And then it got worse from there." Darcy leaned forward to rest her elbows on her thighs. "I don't regret taking the job I earned, but I handled all of it so badly. She had every right to be hurt and angry with me and I minimized her feelings so I wouldn't have to feel so bad."

Raquel's face softened. "And how's that working out for you?"

Darcy laughed. "Super. I'm spilling my guts in my boss's office so really nothing could be more perfect."

"Do you want my advice?"

Darcy looked at her boss and weighed how to answer.

"You don't have to take it just because I'm your boss. Obviously, I don't know everything that happened, but from what I could see in your segments, at that party, and around the office, there's something real and worth trying to save between you and Natalie. I think you should fly home, fix whatever you broke, and convince Natalie to take a vacation with you.

A long vacation. You worked really hard here, and you need to take some time to rest and recharge." She leaned back in her chair and returned to her full-boss mode. "I need you ready to work when you come back." She smiled like she had a secret. "Go, get away from work for a while. You're long overdue for some time off. I hope you'll use it wisely."

Darcy walked wearily to the door.

"Jamal can help you make any changes you want to your travel arrangements," Raquel said without taking her eyes off her computer screen.

"Thanks," Darcy said, leaving the office and calling for a car to take her back to the hotel. That was the weirdest meeting she'd ever had with Raquel. She had been cryptic about her next job and weird about her changing her flights. She'd already had to change her flight when she found out she was staying a few more days to do commentary. That was all taken care of.

"Oh," she said to herself when it all came into focus. She pulled her phone out of her pocket and dialed Jamal.

"I need to change my flight and I need a favor."

"I don't think asking me to do my job counts as a favor. Tell me what you need."

Darcy explained the changes she needed him to make.

"You want me to make the layover in Boston longer? You know my job is to make everyone's life easier, not saddle you with a bunch of time to kill in an airport. Do you want me to book you a hotel?"

"No, thank you. That's okay." She waited for the confirmation email before hanging up. The car waited at the curb to take her back to the hotel. She opened the back door before realizing, without Natalie, she had no reason not to sit in the front.

She got in, said hello to the driver, and forwarded the flight itinerary to her sister. She closed her eyes, trying to ward off the queasy feeling she got from staring at her phone in the car. Her phone buzzed several times, the vibrations traveling through her fingers up her arm. She ignored the incoming messages until she reached the hotel. Being this tired made her more susceptible to motion sickness.

Once she hopped out of the car at the hotel, she checked the texts from her sister. As she read the first two, three more came in. Darcy sighed and scrolled.

You better not miss mom and dad's party

Seriously, do not leave me there alone

Darcy?

Darcy sent back a series of texts reassuring her sister that she would make it in plenty of time to get to the party.

Don't forget to pick me up

Kit sent the eye roll emoji along with a shot of her giving Darcy the middle finger.

Darcy laughed while she waited for the elevator.

The typing bubbles appeared and disappeared twice before the next message came through.

I'm proud of you. Tell me how it goes. Xo

Darcy wasn't sure if it was creepy or reassuring that Kit understood what she was planning without Darcy actually telling her. Probably a mixture of both. When she passed Natalie's old room, her heart gave a lurch and she knew she was doing the right thing.

She had no idea if it would work, but she wasn't giving up without a fight.

Everything in her room reminded her of Natalie. She remembered the time she and Natalie spent lounging in the bed, having breakfast, having sex. Laughing. She swallowed her emotions. She wanted to hear that laugh again. She wanted that light, bubbly feeling of being so happy that everything made you laugh. She wanted the feeling of Natalie looking at her over her cup of coffee, of her weight pressed against her side, her hair tickling Darcy's nose. She wanted that adorable scowl on Natalie's face when Darcy beat her at any of the stupid sports they had to try. She wanted Natalie to leap off a box and trust Darcy to catch her, even if it didn't go as either of them planned. She wanted every single silly thing that went awry to end with them laughing and kissing. She wanted it all.

She wanted Natalie.

Chapter Sixty-Eight

The smell of coffee woke Natalie up. She groaned. She would have happily slept for another eight thousand hours.

"What time is it?" she asked into her pillow.

"Almost ten."

Natalie rolled over, squinting at the light coming through her curtains. "Why are you waking me up?"

Grace folded her arms across her chest. "You have shit to do and if you sleep any longer the jet lag is never going to get any better." She swatted Natalie's foot through the covers.

Natalie groaned again. If she got out of bed then she had to deal with everything. If she went back to sleep she could pretend she hadn't fucked everything up with Darcy. She could pretend she hadn't left the Olympics in a fit of embarrassment and anger.

Grace hadn't moved. "I can see you freaking out. Get your ass out of bed and into the shower. There's no food in your apartment so I'm going to get bagels. I expect you to be clean, dressed, and way less grumpy when I get back."

Natalie pulled the covers over her head but being awake meant all her problems came flooding back in. Dammit.

She showered and dressed in her comfiest sweats.

Grace walked through the front door as Natalie drank her second cup of coffee. Grace handed her the bag of bagels. "You look like a dirtbag college student, but at least you showered."

Natalie laughed. "You always know what to say to cheer me up."

"Have you figured out your plan yet?"

Natalie covered her everything bagel with cream cheese, avoiding Grace's eyes. "I've been up for like thirty minutes." She sighed. "Did it ever occur to you that she might not want anything to do with me after the way I acted?"

"Of course it did. You were a complete dipshit."

Natalie winced. "Hey!"

"Let me finish. But I saw the way she talked about you during the game. She wasn't defending your honor as a player out of some sense of fairness. She did it because she loves you." Natalie opened her mouth, but Grace held up her hand. "She might think you're a colossal jackass, but she still loves you."

Natalie stared into her coffee. She wanted Grace to be right so badly. She wanted Darcy to miss her. She wanted to know she wasn't the only one suffering. But she kept circling back to the way she left things. Flipping out over Darcy getting the job, acting like a brat, and then leaving without even saying goodbye. If the roles were reversed, would she forgive Darcy?

"Fuuuuuck."

"Yup, even I'm impressed by how badly you fucked this up."

Natalie took another bagel and her coffee into the living room and slumped on the couch. "Okay, so what am I supposed to do?"

Grace shrugged. "Well, first you should apologize to your best friend who warned you this would happen and who you told you had it under control and she was overreacting." She grinned.

Natalie gave a sheepish smile. "I did not have it under control. Not even close."

Grace gave her a smug look. "And I should never again doubt the wisdom of Grace."

Natalie glowered. "No. I'm not saying that."

"Fine." Grace dropped onto the couch next to Natalie and turned the TV on. "Did you watch all of your segments?"

"Ew, no. Who watches themself on TV? I'm not a narcissist."

Natalie rolled her eyes. "Maybe you should. It might remind you how good you and Darcy were together." She held up her hand. "I know I said you two shouldn't be together. I was wrong."

Natalie made a smug face.

"She's the only person I have ever seen make you so happy."

Natalie hugged a pillow as if it could protect her from the truth. "Even if that's true, it's not like she's going to want to see me after I was a complete jerk."

Grace fiddled with the remote. "You need a grand gesture."

"No."

Grace smacked the pillow. "Don't say no to me. The only way you are going to win her back is by doing something big."

Natalie scowled. "Even if I didn't think grand gestures were bullshit—which I do—she's halfway across the world."

"She isn't going to be in another country forever. Find out when she gets back and meet her at her apartment. Meet her at the airport! Oh, that's good! Think of all the airport scenes in movies. Damn, I'm good." Grace gave Natalie a very satisfied smile.

Natalie shook her head. "That sounds creepy as hell."

"Okay, then what's your idea of how you're going to win her back?"

Natalie pulled the pillow over her face. "A series of 'I've made a very serious mistake' memes?"

"She's the ice hockey princess of Canada and you want to try to woo her with a couple of memes and what else? A case of Natty Ice? Jesus, Carpenter. When did you turn into a frat boy?"

"I was joking," Natalie said from under the pillow.

Grace ripped the pillow away. "No. This is your whole problem. You're fucking miserable and instead of doing something about it you make jokes, hide behind a pillow, and pretend like it's no big deal. It's a fucking big deal. You love this woman and you're acting like that hardly matters, like finding love happens every day."

"That's not—"

"Oh, I'm not done. You have been fucking up your love life since you were nineteen and I figured it was because you were so broken by losing Darcy that you didn't want to or couldn't try with anyone else. But now you have a second, precious chance with her and you've fucked that up, too! If you're going to get a third chance, a final fucking chance, it's going to take a whole lot more than some half-ass thing.

"You can't half-ass your love life. I know you think that not giving a shit is how you keep from being hurt. But it's not. That's how you keep yourself from being happy. It's how you maintain this pathetic little shell around your heart. That shell isn't protecting you; it's ruining your chance at love."

Grace stood up. "You have a chance at the real thing and you're making memes? Don't be a coward, Nat. Put yourself out there. Take a fucking big risk."

Grace stomped to the door.

"Where are you going?" asked Natalie, stunned.

"For a walk. If I look at you right now, I'm going to keep yelling. Figure your shit out while I'm gone."

The slamming of the door shook the walls. Natalie sat forward, her elbows on her thighs, and wished she could go back to bed and start the day over. Maybe then, Grace wouldn't have yelled at her. As much as she didn't want to admit it, Grace was right. Darcy deserved more than some lukewarm gesture. Even if she'd called Darcy the ice princess in the past as a joke, there was a kernel of truth there. She didn't deserve better because her dad was famous and everyone in Canada worshipped her.

She deserved better because she was the best person on the planet. Natalie had to make her understand that out of almost eight billion people, Darcy was the best one. She was funny and smart, sweet and sexy, and she made Natalie feel so safe and loved.

"Fuck."

She dialed the number for the *Wake Up, USA* offices. A familiar voice picked up. "Jamal, I need a favor."

Chapter Sixty-Nine

Darcy was bleary-eyed from the flight. She texted her sister to let her know she had arrived. Now came the hard part. She walked through the airport wishing she hadn't fallen asleep on the plane. Wishing she had a better plan than this half-baked, probably pointless one.

Don't you dare leave the airport without getting me something from the Black Dog.

Darcy stared at her phone. Was she hallucinating? Her sister was asking her to run an errand? Now?

No

Her phone rang in her hand. "I swear to god, Darcy. Get your ass to the Black Dog store by gate..." She paused. "It's in Terminal C. I want you to get me one of their sweatshirts."

Darcy protested.

"It's the least you can do for making me do all the party planning with Mom." She hung up and Darcy stared at her phone.

She needed more sleep. She trudged through the airport until she hit Terminal C. At least it was near where she had to go for her next flight. Not that she needed to be here, the whole point was that she had time to leave and come back.

Fucking Kit.

She stared at the sweatshirt display. They came in a million colors and with or without hoods. She touched a few of them, like that was going to help her decide what Kit wanted. She typed out a furious text.

As she typed, she heard someone talking outside the store.

"Grace, why did you make me get here so early? My flight isn't for hours."

Darcy's thumb hovered over the send button. She knew that voice.

"What do you mean you got the time wrong?"

Darcy tucked her phone in her pocket and wandered out into the terminal. Now she *had* to be hallucinating.

"Natalie?" Darcy stepped forward.

Natalie spun at the sound of her name. "Darcy?" Natalie stared at her for a minute before realizing her phone was screaming at her. "Sorry, Grace. I gotta go."

Darcy took another step closer, still not believing her eyes. "What are you doing here?"

A family of five bustled between them, the parents shepherding their children through the crowd and dragging suitcases behind them. Natalie and Darcy had to take a step back to avoid being kneecapped by a rogue rolling bag.

Natalie fiddled with the straps to her bag. "I have a flight." She looked at her watch. "In four hours." She smiled. "Grace insisted on dropping me off a hundred hours early. What are you doing here? I thought you were back home?"

Darcy shifted her weight. "Can we step over there?" Natalie followed her to an empty seating area by a closed gate. She should have prepared something to say, written something down, even a few notes. She was going to fuck this up. She looked at Natalie and set her backpack down on the seat next to her.

"Did you stop at Logan just so you could shop at the Black Dog? I would have sent you a T-shirt if that's what you wanted," Natalie said with a hint of a smile playing at the corner of her mouth.

Darcy shook her head. "I came for you." She looked at the floor, trying to gather her thoughts into something coherent. "My plan was to go to your house between my flights. But then my sister asked me to get her some stupid sweatshirt and you walked by and now... Now none of the things I wanted to say sound right."

A smile spread across Natalie's face. "You were coming to find me? How did you even know where I live?"

"Grace."

Natalie shook her head. "That explains why she brought me here forty-seven hours early."

"Would have been helpful if she told me you'd be here." Darcy sighed. "Nat, I screwed up. I was so overwhelmed by getting my dream job I didn't even talk to you about it or how it would change our plans before accepting." Darcy searched Natalie's face. "I'm so sorry. It was stupid and selfish and it cost me the most important thing. You.

"I was focused on all the wrong things. I wanted to prove to everyone, including me, that I deserved the job. I thought I had to do everything perfectly so no one would ever think I got a spot on a team or got a job because of my last name."

"Darcy, no one seriously thinks that."

Darcy laughed. "You know that's not true. You were there with those guys who wished my dad would make our show worth watching or that I would talk more about how great he is. I wanted to prove I was great, too."

Darcy's throat felt full of gravel. She paused to take a breath, her emotions threatening to overwhelm her. "What I didn't understand was that no amount of hard work, preparation, or perfection would stop them from saying that. No job, not even the job I've been dreaming about since I was a kid, could make me feel worthy.

"But you did." Darcy looked at Natalie and blinked away the tears she couldn't stop coming. "You made me feel everything I thought my dream job would. Being with you has always been the best thing in my life and I've done a fucking terrible job of showing you that. I got scared that without the job, I'd never feel like enough. But in chasing that I lost sight of the fact that you have always made me feel like I was enough. Not because of my last name, not because I could score goals or win games, but because you saw who I am and wanted to be with me anyway. You're thoughtful and sweet and such a massive pain in my ass and I cannot imagine living the rest of my life without you."

Natalie took her hand. Darcy smiled, not caring that people had stopped to stare at them. She was sure she was a sight with tears streaming down her face. She gave Natalie a watery smile.

"I love you and I'm so sorry I screwed this up, again. That's why I'm here. That's why I called Grace to find out how I could have one last chance to talk to you." Darcy looked down at their interlaced fingers. "I don't know how you feel but I hope you'll give me another chance. Because I love you and I would like a chance to work as hard at being worthy of your love as I've worked at everything else in my life."

Natalie wrapped her in a tight hug. "That was some speech, LaCroix." When she blinked, Darcy could feel her eyelashes against her cheek. "Do you know how long I've waited for you to say you love me?"

Darcy sniffled and kissed Natalie on the cheek. "Does that mean you forgive me?"

Natalie grinned.

"Wait, you never said what you're doing at the airport. Where are you going?"

Natalie rubbed the back of her neck, her cheeks showing the first signs of the red creeping up her neck. She shoved her boarding pass toward Darcy. "I was flying to see you."

"What?" Darcy scanned the ticket. "I was coming to see you and you were planning to fly to Toronto to see me?"

Natalie laughed. "I had to slide into your sister's DMs to find out when you were coming home."

Darcy covered her mouth with her hand. "Oh my god. She knew you were going to be here and instead of telling me she tried to get me to buy her a sweatshirt? I'm going to kill Kit."

Natalie laughed. "I guess I can thank Grace for not making me buy her airport swag."

Darcy cocked her head to one side. "You were flying to meet me? And then what?"

"I had a speech prepared." Natalie rubbed her thumb across the back of Darcy's hand.

"I want to hear it."

Natalie shook her head. "What? You already asked me to take you back, I think my speech is unnecessary."

"Well, I don't know. I might need some convincing." Darcy squeezed Natalie's hand before dropping it. "Woo me, Carpenter."

Natalie sighed and rubbed her palms against her jeans.

Darcy wondered if Natalie knew how impossibly cute she was when she was nervous.

Natalie tucked her hands in her pockets, her shoulders rolling forward. God, she was adorable. "Do you remember Kelly?"

Darcy nodded, a flicker of confusion crossing her face.

"Kelly was a fucking showboat. Her crowning college achievement was the goal she scored when we played Team USA. She spent the next two weeks crowing about it. But the only reason she scored was because she was hanging out at center ice while the rest of us dug the puck out of the corner. The only reason she ended up on goddamned breakaway is because McD sent a perfect pass across half the ice. We lost the game but she walked around like she was god's gift to hockey because she scored that goal."

Darcy couldn't keep the confusion off her face. Nothing about this speech seemed designed to win her heart.

"Don't look at me like that. You wanted the speech, just listen without being all judgy."

Darcy nodded solemnly and suppressed the urge to kiss Natalie.

Natalie huffed out a breath. "This may sound stupid coming from the woman who was planning to fly to Toronto to talk to you, but grand gestures are showboating. They're hanging out at center ice while the other person does the hard fucking work of digging in the corners, killing penalties, blocking shots. Grand gestures get all the credit.

"I love you and I want you for-fucking-ever. But there's more. I planned to fly to Canada to get your attention, to talk to you. To tell you I want to be with you in the corners, scrapping for everything, stepping in front of the shots when they come, picking you up when you need it. I want you to trust that when we're together I'm not floating around looking for a way to make a splash. I want you to *know* that whether I'm having a good shift or a shitty one, I'm going to go after the next one just as hard.

"That's what I want. I know I'm going to fuck up. Because you will, too. I know it because we always fuck up. But when that happens, I want you to know that I'm not going to storm off the ice or break my stick or have whatever fucking tantrum. I want you to know I'm going to hop over the boards and pour my heart into doing it better the next time. I know how much you worry about being perfect. I don't need you to be perfect,

I need you to be the scrappy, hardworking, play-to-the-last-whistle woman I fell in love with.

"So, yes, I planned to fly to Toronto to make this big speech, but this isn't about a grand gesture. I need a teammate who will pick me up when I have a bad day or a bad week or when things are just really terrible. I need someone willing to do the work. I promise you, I'm willing to be that for you. I'm willing to do *all the work* and not swan around looking for the breakaway to cover up for the fact that I haven't been doing the work." Natalie paused, her chest heaving from emotion as she caught her breath. "I fucked up. I got scared and I ran away. But I promise you, in the middle of the airport like the end of some cheesy movie, I'm in this with you. I want you and I can't imagine doing this with anyone else. You've been the one for me since I was eighteen. And I know I fucked this up at least seventeen different ways, but..." She took a deep breath. "I love you. I've always loved you. And if you can forgive me for being scared and running away, twice, I want to spend the rest of my life with you as my teammate." She swallowed, terrified that Darcy wasn't saying anything. "If you'll have me."

Darcy looked around, people were staring at them. One person had their phone out, taking a picture or maybe a video. She took a deep breath. People might recognize them here. People knew who her dad was and who she was and for the first time, she didn't give a shit.

She kissed Natalie right there in the middle of the gate. Her heart was beating too hard, her entire body vibrated with the feeling that kissing Natalie Carpenter was the only thing that mattered to her.

She pulled back. "That was a good speech. I'm glad I asked to hear it."

"Brave of you to ask for it knowing mine was obviously going to be better." Natalie laughed.

Darcy rolled her eyes. "I love you. You are the most frustrating, amazing, sexy, infuriating woman I have ever known, and I love you so much I can't think straight."

Natalie half sighed, half laughed. She took Darcy's hand. "I can live with that. I'm a pain in the ass, but I'm your pain in the ass."

"Kiss her again!" someone yelled from behind them.

Darcy turned to find a two-mom family waving to them. One of their kids was wearing a Team Canada jersey.

Natalie grinned. "We better give them what they want, eh, Princess?"

"Shut up," Darcy said before pressing her smiling lips against Natalie's. "I can't believe you're coming home with me. You do know that there's a big, stupid party at my parents' house, right?"

Natalie smiled. "Yeah. I heard you weren't too thrilled about having to go alone. I was hoping you'd let me be your date."

Darcy kissed Natalie again. "I fucking love you."

"I know," Natalie said with a satisfied grin.

Chapter Seventy

Even with Natalie urging Darcy to take a nap, the flight was too short, and they were too excited to sleep. They held hands all the way to baggage claim.

Darcy swung their hands while they waited. "So, don't be mad, but I called a friend who might have a job for you."

Natalie stopped their hands mid-swing. "You did? Why?"

Darcy looked at the floor. "You said you wanted to get into coaching. I'm not nearly as big of a name as my dad, but I do know a few people in hockey. I figured it couldn't hurt to see if any of them needed a brilliant hockey mind on their bench. So if you get a call from Yale, answer it."

Natalie's smile was all the thanks Darcy could have hoped for. "Yale's not very far from New York is it?"

Darcy shook her head. "Okay, maybe I hoped that if any of my plan worked out that maybe you'd be working close to the City."

Natalie bumped her shoulder against Darcy's. "Pretty sure of yourself, huh?"

Darcy shook her head. "Not at all. But I wanted to help you even if you never spoke to me again."

Darcy's phone buzzed in her pocket. "Kit's here."

Natalie squeezed her hand. "You okay?" She looked up at Darcy.

Darcy pressed a kiss to Natalie's forehead. "This isn't a dream, is it?"

Natalie shook her head. "No but we should buy Kit and Grace something good as a thank-you."

"Grace would look good in a Mountie hat."

Natalie snorted. The conveyor belt whirred to life and a bag tumbled down the chute. "I'm sure Kit would love a Team Carpenter jersey. I can get one for you, too."

Darcy laughed so loudly she scared the man standing next to her. "Sorry, sir." Darcy grabbed her bag and walked next to Natalie toward the exit. "I will not wear a Team USA jersey but I will consider Team Carpenter as long as it isn't red, white, and blue."

"Fine." Natalie shivered against the blast of frigid air that hit her as soon as they stepped outside. "Fuck Canada."

"Watch your mouth or you'll get deported." Kit's voice found them amid the beeping, police whistling at drivers, and the bustle of families being picked up.

Kit popped the trunk and hurried back to the driver's seat. "Let's go, it's freezing!"

Natalie opened the passenger door for Darcy, but she shook her head.

"I want to sit with my girlfriend." She bent down to look through the window at Kit. "Thanks for the ride."

"You're welcome but I swear to god if you puke in my car because you chose to sit in the back, I *will* kill you."

"Deal." Darcy slid into the car, letting her thigh press into Natalie's. "Home, Jeeves."

Kit glared at Darcy in the rearview mirror, but her eyes softened when she saw Darcy lean her head against Natalie's shoulder.

Natalie pressed a kiss to Darcy's forehead and wrapped her

arm around her. Darcy relaxed against her, wishing for the first time in her life for her sister to take the long way home.

As soon as they arrived at the LaCroixs' house, Kit hopped out of the car. "Mom and Dad are probably going to sprint out to see you as soon as they realize you're home."

Darcy looked up at Natalie. "You sure you're ready for this?"

Natalie smiled. "I've met them before, remember?"

"But not as my girlfriend." Darcy placed a soft kiss at the corner of Natalie's mouth.

Natalie grabbed her phone. "I have to tell Grace I made it, okay?"

Darcy nodded and fiddled with her phone while she waited. She opened Twitter and found her account flooded with mentions. What the hell?

"Holy shit, Nat." She scrolled through hundreds of tweets on the #PuckingHotties hashtag. There were three different videos of them from the airports. She recognized pictures and videos from Boston and even a few of them walking through the Toronto airport. They'd only been in the car for forty-five minutes and the internet had lost its collective mind.

She turned her phone to show Natalie. "I think we may have to say something."

Natalie smiled. "Look at this." She showed a text from Grace with a link to an article: "Marty LaCroix's daughter comes out with epic airport PDA-fest."

Darcy scowled. "I don't know what's worse, that they call me his daughter like I don't have a name of my own, or that they think *that* was epic PDA."

Natalie kissed her gently. "You okay?"

Darcy nodded. Something red caught her eye. "What the hell?"

Natalie looked out the windshield. Darcy's dad, a tall, fit man with graying hair, was striding toward the car in a Team Canada jersey.

Darcy and Natalie climbed out of the back seat. "Hi, Dad. What's with the outfit?"

He grinned and gave her a bear hug. "I need your mom to take a picture of me. It's for social media."

Darcy looked at her mom and sister. "What?"

He smiled and held his arms open for Natalie. "So good to see you again, Natalie." She allowed him to hug her.

"Hi, Mr. LaCroix. Thanks for letting me crash your party."

"Marty. No one calls me Mr. LaCroix unless they want something from me. By the looks of it you've already got what you want." He smiled at the two of them, looking less like a famous NHL player and more like a proud papa.

"Now, time to take this picture." He stood with his back to his wife and pointed to the name on the jersey.

Darcy's mom, Joanna, handed him the phone and a pair of reading glasses. He fiddled with the phone before handing it to his daughter. "You okay with this?"

Darcy took the phone. Natalie stared over her shoulder. He'd drafted a tweet with him wearing his daughter's jersey responding to the crappy headline. "You spelled NCAA champion, four-time Olympian, three-time gold medalist wrong." He added, "Proud to be Darcy LaCroix's dad."

Darcy smiled, the corners of her eyes prickling. "Dad." She hugged him and kissed his scratchy cheek.

She stepped back. "Mom, Dad, if it's okay with you, my girlfriend is going to be staying with us this weekend."

Joanna screeched. "Finally! Natalie, I'm so glad you're here and that my daughter stopped being a dumbass long enough to convince you to be her girlfriend."

Natalie looked at Darcy and they both cracked up. "Thank you for having me."

Chapter Seventy-One

"Okay, are you ready?" Natalie asked.

"Definitely." Darcy's voice shook.

Natalie punched a series of buttons on her Instagram.

"Hi, everyone. We just wanted to take a minute to thank you for all the love you've sent our way."

Darcy grinned. "A special thank-you to all of you on the #PuckingHotties hashtag. You've all been so funny and sweet to us. We thought you deserved to hear it from us."

Natalie kissed her cheek. "That's right, this isn't just good sportsmanship."

Darcy smiled at her like she was the only person on the planet. "I think you all knew it before we did. But I've been in love with Natalie Carpenter since I met her in college."

"Same. Maybe it took us a while to figure it all out. But you know, the best games go into overtime."

Chapter Seventy-Two

Eight months later

"You okay?" Natalie asked, taking her eyes off the road to check on Darcy in the passenger seat.

"Fine," Darcy said, her jaw tight.

Natalie squeezed her hand and pointed to the glove compartment. "There's snacks in there, crackers, a few candies."

"Thanks, I'm okay. Or I would be if you would just tell me what we're doing."

Natalie slowed the car and turned off the main road. The road curved up and around a bend. "You'll see in like three minutes." The road curved off to the left but they took a small dirt driveway to the right. It opened into a parking lot dotted with cars.

Families with little kids walked toward the small tent set up near an old barn.

"Apples?" Darcy said with a grin. "The big secret was apples?"

Natalie leaned across the center of the car to kiss Darcy. "Try not to sound so disappointed." She pulled back only to stop when Darcy grabbed a fistful of her T-shirt and pulled her back for another kiss.

"You know how I feel about apples."

Natalie laughed. "Yes, I do."

Darcy grabbed Natalie's hand, threading their fingers together. "I appreciate the gesture but I can't believe Clarky gave you the weekend off during the season to go apple picking."

Natalie smiled to herself. "I told her it was important for us to get away before our seasons start. It's not like you are going to have tons of free time once the NHL season starts for real. Besides, our first game isn't for a month." She kissed the back of Darcy's hand. "I can be very persuasive, when I need to be."

They walked to the tent where Natalie paid for a bag while Darcy grabbed a map of the orchard.

"They have Honeycrisp!" she squealed.

Natalie laughed. "I know. I called ahead."

Darcy tugged Natalie through the grassy spaces between the rows in search of the red-and-white ribbon marking her favorite variety. Natalie let Darcy lead the way, smiling at Darcy's giddy excitement. She checked her jacket pocket for what must have been the hundredth time since they left their apartment.

"Catch!" Darcy plucked an apple from the tree, shined it on her jeans, and tossed it to Natalie. She bit into an apple the size of her fist and had to wipe the juice before it ran off her chin.

Natalie stopped next to the tree to take a picture of Darcy with the apple wedged between her teeth. She hadn't gotten a picture of Darcy from the day they met, but the wide smile, the apple juice dripping down her face, and the absolute joy in Darcy's eyes were identical. So was the way Natalie couldn't take her eyes off her.

Darcy cocked her head. "You brought me here and you're not even going to help me pick?"

Natalie held out the bag for Darcy. "Apologies. I took three seconds to admire you instead of getting right to work on the serious apple business."

"Smart-ass," Darcy said, shaking her head. She'd already eaten her first apple and was starting on her second.

Natalie tried to grab an apple out of her reach. Even on her toes she couldn't grab it. Darcy stepped closer and twisted the apple free, while staring down at Natalie.

"Did you really want that one, or was this a ploy to get me to come over here?" The corner of her mouth lifted.

Natalie licked her lips. Darcy stood deliciously close, holding the apple between them. Natalie's left hand snaked behind Darcy's back. "What do you think?" She kissed Darcy, her lips soft and gentle.

"I think you're entirely too smooth for your own good."

Natalie laughed. "You love it."

Darcy dropped another apple into the bag, careful not to let it bruise. "I do. You may still be a cocky little shit, but you're mine."

Natalie took a deep breath. This had to be the moment. "Do you remember the first time we met?" she asked, cursing the way her voice shook.

"Oh yes. When you walked up to me and told me maybe *I* should consider moving to the wing?" She wrapped her arms around Natalie's waist. "There has never been and will never be a cockier freshman in the history of women's hockey."

Natalie laughed. "Well, that seems unlikely. If you remember, you told me that we would be good together. You took one look at me in that orchard and decided that we would be a good pair."

"I've always been very smart," Darcy said, placing a kiss on the end of Natalie's nose and leaving a trace of apple juice behind.

Natalie put her hand in her pocket. "I had no idea how right you were. I *did* know, as soon as I saw you sitting on the bench with an apple hanging out of your mouth, that I was in deep trouble." She stepped out of Darcy's embrace and dropped to one knee.

"What?" Darcy gasped and brought her hands to her mouth.

"Darcy LaCroix, will you make good on your prediction and be my teammate forever?" She popped open the ring box, only to have the ring fall out of the box and disappear into the deep grass by her feet. "Shit," Natalie muttered.

Darcy dropped to the ground next to her and the two of them combed through the grass until they found it.

Natalie looked up. "So? Will you marry me?"

Darcy laughed, her eyes damp with tears. "Of course! Yes!"

Natalie slipped the ring onto Darcy's finger. Darcy admired the way the ring looked before reaching for Natalie's hand. "Now your hand looks a little plain, don't you think?"

Natalie shrugged.

Darcy's hand disappeared into her jacket pocket and pulled out a box. She handed it to Natalie. "Think you can open it without the ring falling out?"

Natalie blinked. "What?"

Darcy opened the box slowly, revealing a ring. "I've been carrying this around for a week, trying to find the right moment. I can't believe you beat me to it." She plucked the ring from the box and held it out for Natalie.

Natalie laughed; her chest filled with more joy than she thought it could hold. "God, of course we'd propose at the same time. Our friends are going to have a field day with this."

Darcy slid the ring onto Natalie's finger and kissed her, letting her lips linger until they were interrupted by a wet nose.

Natalie opened her eyes to a black Lab wagging her tail and licking her face. "Hi, puppy!" Natalie rubbed the dog's ears.

"Puffin! Puffin, leave them alone!"

Darcy stood up, leaving Natalie crouched down patting the dog.

"Oh my god, I'm so sorry. Puffin, come here!"

Natalie laughed. "Don't apologize."

Darcy smiled down at them. "My girlfriend loves dogs."

Natalie looked up at her with a wicked grin. "Girlfriend? I'm your fiancée now, LaCroix."

Darcy blushed. "Excuse me. My *fiancée* loves dogs."

The dog's owner squealed. "Did Puffin just interrupt your proposal? Oh my god, I'm so sorry." She reached for the dog's collar.

Natalie shook her head. "No, she waited until we were done. Such a polite girl."

Puffin wagged so hard her butt swayed from side to side. Puffin's owner finally got the dog's attention and was able to steer her away. "Congratulations."

Natalie stood up and looped her arm through Darcy's. "I think it's a sign we need to get a dog." She tugged Darcy toward the end of the row where they could watch Puffin tromping through the long grass, tail wagging the whole time.

Darcy laughed and kissed Natalie's cheek. "God, you're a pain in the ass."

"And now you're stuck with me forever."

★ ★ ★ ★ ★

Acknowledgments

Natalie and Darcy know how crucial good teammates are, both on and off the ice. So here are the folks who I'm lucky to have on my team.

First, thank you to my incredible agent, Paige Terlip, who not only believed in this book when she signed me but, more importantly, believed in me. My path to being a published author has not been exactly speedy, but your unwavering belief in this book and in me has made all the difference. Cheers to many more books together!

Next, I want to thank my editor, Errin Toma, for loving this book and for all your thoughtful, caring, and encouraging edits. Like a great coach, you've helped this book live up to its potential. Working with you has been a dream.

Thank you to Carina's Stephanie Doig, Katixa Espinoza, Shana Mongroo, Sara Marinac, Amy Wetton, and the entire Harlequin team.

It's taken me a long time to realize this dream and there are so many friends, fellow writers, and kind folks who have helped me along the way. Thank you to Courtney Kae, Ruby Barrett, Rosie Danan, Charish Reid, Denise Williams, and Keena Roberts for your kind and helpful feedback along the way.

To my writing cheerleaders: Carrie Allen, Brooke Innis, Anita Kelly, Malinda Lo, and my Lambda Literary cohort, and all the writers who have taken the time to buck me up over the last thirteen years when the road seemed too long. I wouldn't have made it here without you all.

Thank you to my siblings, George, Nell, and Charlie, and my parents, Eleanor and Doug, for their support. Thanks especially, Mom and Dad, for driving me to every rink in New England. I wouldn't have been a hockey player without you.

A special thanks to Jen St. Jude and Isla Lassiter, who read so many drafts of this (and other) books. You two have kept me going when writing and querying and being on submission felt hopeless. I love you both and can't thank you enough.

Finally, thank you to my wife and children.

Augusta and Beatrix, thank you for tolerating me stealing time to write and for your patience when I was distracted by some plot hole or other. You are the smartest, funniest, most daring and wonderful people and you inspire me every single day to make you both proud. Being your mom is the best adventure. I love you more than words can express.

Jennifer, you were there at the start in the days when I wrote out of desperation to have one single thing that was mine while we were knee-deep in the exhaustion (and joy) of babies and toddlers. You supported me when my writing meant I would steal time from vacations, from mornings and nights, all for the infinitesimal hope that, one day, I would get to write these acknowledgments in a real book. Thank you for believing in me even when I didn't and for the bottomless well of patience it takes to be married to me. You're the best teammate in life I could have ever dreamed up. I may never get there, but I promise to keep trying to write a love story worthy of you.

And to Bear. You've only been here for some of this journey, but if I didn't thank you the girls would riot. You are a ridiculous, perfect dog who I love endlessly.